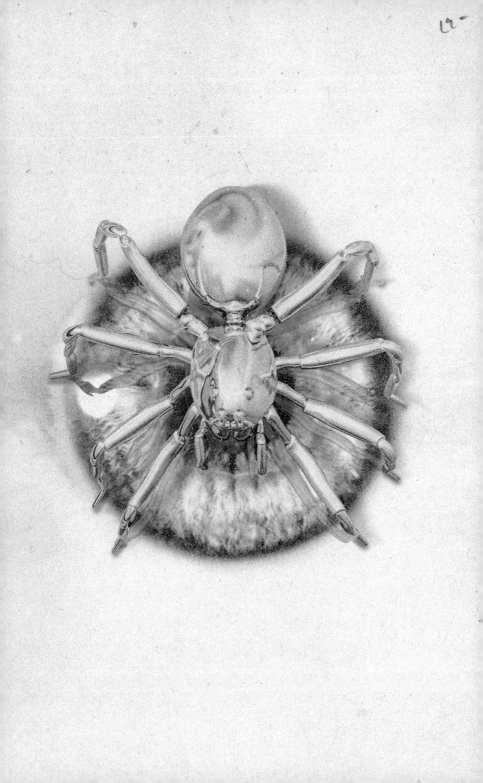

BEHOLDER

RYAN LA SALA

Library of Congress Cataloging-in-Publication Data available

ISBN 978-1-338-74534-4

10 9 8 7 6 5 4 3 2 1   23 24 25 26 27

First edition, October 2023

Printed in the U.S.A. 37

Book design by Maeve Norton

THIS BOOK ISN'T DEDICATED TO YOU, SUSAN, BUT I KNOW YOU'LL READ IT ONE DAY. SO I JUST WANTED TO LET YOU KNOW YOU STILL OWE ME THE REST OF MY SECURITY DEPOSIT. HOPE THOSE BOOKS OF YOURS ARE GOING WELL!

Beholder is a contemporary supernatural horror story that includes elements of suicide ideation. Reader discretion is advised. If you or a loved one is struggling with thoughts of suicide, please call or text the Suicide & Crisis Lifeline at 988.

There are things in that paper that nobody knows but me,
or ever will.

—Charlotte Perkins Gilman,
"The Yellow Wallpaper"

The Sunday night of the party, a few hours before everyone dies, a girl with bleached bangs is telling you all about her future.

She is, of course, very wrong about what comes next. Her hand spiders up your leg (she thinks you're older than you are; everyone does). You are uncomfortable (with her, but also in general; the outfit you shoplifted for tonight is way too tight, and you're sitting on the arm of a sofa that's probably worth a year of your rent).

You aren't sure why you're still here, in this exquisite penthouse apartment. Uhler brought you but, old as he is, he probably left hours ago. And your yiayia, even older, is probably still awake at home, praying over her mirror, begging God to deliver you back to her safely.

You, you, *you.*

You are Athanasios Bakirtzis. Reckless, charming, self-destructive Athanasios. Athan to your friends, if you kept any, but that last part—the self-destructive part—usually scares them off. Which you like. It means the next time you burn your life to the ground, no one else gets caught in the blaze.

The girl with bleached bangs squeezes your thigh, and you turn back to her. For a moment, you were just staring off at the wall. Specifically at the wall*paper.* It's a sickly yellow color, infested with a sprawling, golden design that seems to shift every time you blink. It looks like neurons—rotting neurons that flicker with poisonous thoughts. And just for a moment, while your eyes sought some logical escape from the pattern—a break or seam or anything that would disrupt that unending, wretched design—it felt like *your* brain was slowly filling with poison, too.

What's in your future? the girl asks, her hand squeezing again. *What's fate got in store for you?*

Your fate, your future. Two things you refuse to think about, thanks to years of your grandmother's superstitions. You glance at the wallpaper again, and it's like being wrapped in your yiayia's claustrophobic beliefs. Is tonight the night you finally cut your way free?

My future . . . you say, trying out the words.

The girl squeezes, and her eyes focus on you for what feels like the first time in almost an hour of one-sided conversation. She really wants to know.

You make an excuse to go to the bathroom. Alone.

This is the excuse that saves your life.

CHAPTER ONE

I close the bathroom door, shutting out the party.

The room smells like the perfume of the trio of girls who were just in here. It's a tiny, beautiful space. The dark green wallpaper rustles with monstera leaves, and a golden faucet gleams in the candlelight.

It's serene. Safe.

I wish I could match it. I often feel this harsh contrast between me and the artful rooms I pass through, working for a designer like Uhler. Someone arranged this space with love and intention. I wish someone would peer into the chaos of my interior and pull me into peaceful composition. It's no wonder the rich enjoy life; they get to live it in such beautiful spaces. Like this penthouse. It's softly lit and artfully decorated and way, way too big for the bachelor who Uhler introduced as the host when we arrived. It's hard to believe anyone lives in so much gorgeous emptiness.

I'm not threatened by the casual grandeur, though. I've faked my way through dozens of these parties before. It's easy. The guests are always the same: brand-new New Yorkers trying out being fascinating, looking for someone to listen to them prove it. As Uhler's personal party date, that person is usually me.

I'm a good listener, they always tell me, which is true. But the actual truth is that I know if I ask people about themselves, they're less likely to ask about me. By the night's end, I know everything about them.

For instance, Hannah Chloe Kaplan, the girl with bleached bangs, thinks she's an empath because she can read "vibes," and for the record mine are immaculate, and she doesn't believe in New Year's resolutions because they're for weak people who don't believe in spontaneous evolution, whatever that is, and she's upset with her boyfriend because he doesn't flush the toilet all the time, which I agreed sounded like weaponized helplessness of the first degree. All this I learned just by letting her talk, and I don't think she even knows my name.

Athan.

I'm still not ready to head back out there. I flush the toilet with gusto and take my time washing my hands.

Athanasios.

My name means "immortal" in Greek, but it might as well mean "survivor's guilt." In my head, I hear the whole thing spoken in Yiayia's pleading voice. *Athanaaaasios.* I should go home—this is far too long to be away from an old woman who depends on me—but lately I can't be around her for more than a few minutes a day. Her rituals, her superstitions, her wards against some all-seeing evil eye that's searching, searching, *searching* for what's left of our family. She's gotten so much worse in the past few months.

Look, just look, my mind whispers as I wash my hands, but I keep my eyes off the mirror. Not yet.

How long can I hide in here? I don't want to go back out to the party until that girl has found another person to talk at. There was a cute boy watching me over by the window, but his eyes were shooting daggers. Probably someone I ghosted. Oh well. I *should* look for Uhler, but he never stays at these things long. And besides, I can't keep running to him every time I start to feel lost. His charity won't last forever. I'm not even sure it *is* charity. All these party invitations, all the checks slipped to me so that Yiayia and I can keep up with our monthly rent—it's got to add up to something, right? I'm not eager to find out what.

Look. Just a peek, I urge myself.

It's embarrassing, but I'm building up the courage to look at myself in the mirror. Most people look at themselves without a second thought, but not me. Of all Yiayia's superstitions, avoiding mirrors is the most important.

Yiayia doesn't want me to end up like her, I think.

Morning to evening, my grandmother clutches a scratched-up hand mirror and prays. Sometimes it's a frantic song, and sometimes it's a quiet mumble I hear through the thin walls of our apartment. For a while we could still go on walks, me leading her with one hand while she used the other to hold the mirror up so she never had to look away. Not anymore. Now she won't leave our apartment. The praying has gone from a few minutes each hour to a constant babble. She even falls asleep with the mirror buried on her chest, clutching it with hands that have gone clammy and stiff since they used to tuck me in. The few times I've tried to slip it away, her grip seizes like a nightmare is blowing through her dreams.

That mirror has her trapped, and I don't need to wonder why. She tells me, in her rare moments of lucidity. *Athanasios!* she'll cry out suddenly, her voice rising like a siren wailing over the din of the city. *Our eyes cast curses!* On and on, her warnings reel with the momentum of a far-off catastrophe rushing toward us. *What we can see, can see us!*

Ever since the fire that took our home and family, she's filled my head with cautions against the evil eye and all the doom its focus brings. *Never let it find you, Athanasios. Promise me you will never look for it.* Greek superstitions, as ancient as the Acropolis. Myths that have turned into a madness I'm afraid I'll inherit.

Dr. Wei says the resentment I sometimes feel toward Yiayia is okay. That it doesn't mean I don't love her, or miss her, or want the old her back. Dr. Wei says that sometimes we self-mythologize to make ourselves big in our own minds, and Yiayia believes her praying is an act of heroic sacrifice. It's called a compulsion. He says that I probably have a predisposition, but I still have the chance to prove to myself that mirrors can't trap or hurt me. Gently, Dr. Wei has asked if I really believe in evil eyes. In mirrors and their magic.

I said I don't believe in any of it.

But I'm lying.

Because it's not all myths. I've known that since the first time I broke Yiayia's rule, found a mirror at the very back of our family's frame shop, and saw what our eyes could truly do. I'm not sure if the Sight is a superpower. It feels more like a curse I can't control. It happens automatically in any mirror—in anything reflective—when my reflection's gaze meets my own. It makes living in a place like New York City, an entire world gilded in reflective glass and chrome, a hazard. But I've gotten good at dodging myself.

I've experimented here and there when I'm feeling brave, mostly just to prove to myself that I'm not suffering from some contagious delusion. I'm not. The power, or blessing, or curse, is real. But that's all the more reason to fear it. Dr. Wei says my fear enables the mythology, but Dr. Wei can't see what we can see.

I dry my hands on expensive towels, the kind with tassels. I'm done. Nothing else to do now but face my fears.

Look. Just for a moment. Just for a blink.

I look at myself in the bathroom mirror.

For the briefest moment before it happens, I'm able to see my reflection. It's like looking at a stranger. Someone else's eyebrows in an unsure furrow, someone else's chestnut curls, someone else's fear clenched in an unfamiliar jaw. Then I look into my own eyes, and the Sight activates.

Time reverses in the mirror, showing me everything it has seen this night. I watch my reflection look away, then reach for the towels. I watch me un-dry my hands, then un-wash them; watch the water flow up into the faucet; watch myself back out of the bathroom and the girls from before cram inside; watch a cloud of perfume hang in the air over them before sucking back into their little spritzing bottles.

Now that I've finally looked, I'm captivated. The girls gaze at one another in the mirror as they touch up their makeup, but it feels like they're gazing at me. They smile and laugh. They look so close. I put a hand on the glass and tap, like they're in an aquarium.

Something slams into the bathroom door and I jump. The reflection in the mirror lurches with my shock, jumping into the previous day, showing a man on the toilet, scrolling on his phone. I cover my eyes, blushing.

The slam turns into knocking. "Just a minute!" I shout.

I rush to reset the mirror. My mind scrambles, and so do the images in the glass. The edges glow white-hot.

"Stop," I beg the mirror. "Stop. *Please.*"

I shouldn't have looked for so long. I tap my fingertips over my eyebrows, like Yiayia used to do when I was a little kid and had even less control over our family power. If she'd only let me practice, if she'd just told me how . . .

The slam comes again.

Tap tap tap. Stop stop stop.

A scream squeezes through the gap as the door is pushed open. I only just catch it with my foot. The lock must be broken. I peek, and the mirror is back to normal. This time, I avoid my reflection as I swipe my phone from the counter, put on a smile, and swing the door all the way open.

"Sorry—" I start, but no one is there.

The hallway is empty. The party has gone silent. I turn toward the living room, expecting to find it suddenly vacated, but everyone is still there. Just standing still, like statues. Is it a game? Or a prank? A surprise, maybe? But they aren't huddled in gleeful anticipation, waiting for a person to walk through so they can explode with *Surprise! Happy birthday!* They look scared. Everyone is facing the walls. Hannah Chloe Kaplan, the girl who said she was an empath, notices me standing in the doorway. Tears are gushing from her unblinking eyes, dragging dark stripes of mascara to her chin.

"Help me," she whispers. Her eyes rise to the wall behind me.

I turn, but before I can see what she's looking at, a shadow cuts through the crowd and rams into me, knocking my phone from my hand. It's a person. They grab me around the waist, driving me backward until I stumble back into the bathroom.

I land on my ass, swearing.

"Hey, what the f—"

The person—the boy I saw earlier, the one watching me from the window—cuts me off. "Don't open this door. If you don't open it, they won't see it. I'll come back for you when it's safe."

He slams the door in my face, and I'm left with just the flash of an impression. I recognize him now as one of Uhler's many interns. I remember him because he always wears that bandanna knotted around his neck. Orange, black, and white, like a monarch butterfly's wings. I caught those colors now. I'm sure it was the same guy.

But . . . what the fuck?

I race to open the door, but hesitate. What did he mean? *I'll come back for you when it's safe.*

It's the tiniest pause, but in that time something *unleashes* beyond the bathroom door. It shakes on its hinges as screams flood the penthouse. High, keening cries. Voices pushed to their limits, cracking, breaking, wrenching out of bodies thrown into violent motion.

It's the other party guests, but how could people sound like that? It sounds evil. Rotten. I back away from the door, expecting something foul to gush from under it.

The screams go on.

And on.

And on.

For minutes.

For an hour.

I press to the back wall and stare at the door, imagining myself opening it and running, imagining my phone somewhere on the floor where I dropped it. Could I grab it? Dial 911? Call Uhler, or even Yiayia? Pointless visions. I'm too much of a coward to go for it. Whatever evil Yiayia warned me against, it's found me. I looked into the mirror for too long, and it looked back. I don't know what's happening, only that I deserve it. I ball myself up next to the toilet and stifle my sobs, afraid they'll hear me.

The screaming finally resolves into words. Pleading words. The people scream *Can anyone hear us?* They start to bicker, and it turns into an argument. But at least they sound human now. I nearly work up the courage to swing open the door and try to help, but that's when the fighting breaks out.

Crashing. Breaking. Agonizing moans. I don't know how long this goes on for. An hour? Hours? Time frays and unravels as the sounds of violence shred through the thin walls hiding me.

Then someone knocks.

A very polite knock.

So polite, I nearly shout "Occupied!" Like I would in the single-person bathroom of a crowded restaurant. But the memory of the boy with the butterfly bandanna stops me.

He said they couldn't see the door.

I stay quiet. The knocking moves around, like someone is trying to find the hollow space behind a wall. I creep to the door and just barely make out whispering. It's Hannah! The empath. Was the boy right? Can she not see the bathroom's entrance?

She knocks and knocks, whispering, *"Please God please God please God don't let me die in here."*

She's not looking for a way into the bathroom. She's looking for a way *out* of wherever she is.

I'm scared. I'm tired. But hearing her plead like that . . . it awakens something in me. I turn off the lights so I can see her walking through the glowing band at the door's bottom edge. The next time her knocking takes her toward me, I give a gentle knock back, just for her to hear.

She goes quiet. I can see her shuffling back and forth.

I knock again. If I can draw her close, I can open the door just enough to squeeze her in, then shut it again. Then she'll be safe, too. She'll have a phone. We can call for help.

Her knocks are soft. Questioning. She's close now. I can hear her breathing.

I knock back one more time.

She shouts, right behind the door, "HERE! HE'S IN HERE!"

All at once the bathroom vibrates as an entire crowd stampedes down the hall, ramming against the walls with terrifying speed. People crawl over one another to get at the door. I fling myself against it, holding it shut, but they don't even turn the knob. They just pound their fists, desperate and furious. Their cries layer into a messy chant.

Come out, come out, little Athanasios!

The lights flicker. The mirror flickers, too, like it's responding to the thing in the hall. Not the people, but the *thing* that's taken hold of them. The thing that is searching for me.

Then it all goes wrong for Hannah Chloe Kaplan. Within the chaos, I hear her screaming, *Back off! Hey! Stop! You're hurting me!* Her voice slides down to the bottom of the door as the crowd begins to crush her. Her cries turn strangled and then I hear a crack. Then another. Meaty snaps of bones. Bloody, bent fingers thrust beneath the door— the only visual evidence I get. They twitch as the chaos outside pulverizes her.

Then it all goes still.

It's still for minutes. Maybe an hour. I can't look away from the fingers, and the blood drying on shattered nails. Then, with a *schwoop*, the hand pulls away. Gone. I blink, realizing that the light from the hall has turned from gold to white.

It's morning.

I get up slowly.

I crawl to the door, bending as close to the bloody gap at the bottom as I dare. I listen. I can hear the far-off sound of a siren. Traffic. New York, reappearing on the other side of whatever hell the penthouse vanished into for the past five hours.

It's quiet. It's so quiet now. Is it finally over? Has the eye finally turned elsewhere?

I close my eyes as I stand, afraid to even glance in the mirror. My hand finds the doorknob, shaking as it twists.

I open the door and my eyes at the same time.

You should know better, Athanasios. We cannot run from what reflects us. The farther you run from a mirror, the deeper your reflection vanishes into it.

CHAPTER TWO

I step into a burning brightness. Morning pours into the hallway.

The hall is empty except for a dark smear of red where something was dragged off into the living room. I forget my rule of not looking and follow the smear, but clap my hands back over my eyes immediately. I saw my phone, but I also saw something else. On the floor, peeking around the doorframe, I saw one of them. A person. Just the top of their head was visible, but their eyes were wide open. Dull, dead, and staring back at me.

"Fuck," I say, too loud. I lower my voice to a whisper and repeat: "Fuck, fuck, like seriously: Fuck." I chant this as I tiptoe around the smear, hovering a hand out to snatch up my phone, afraid the person will spring to life and grab me. They don't. My phone is sticky and, when I flip it in my hand, badly cracked. I shove it into my pocket and rush backward, down the hall and to the front door. Home.

Oddly, the rest of the penthouse is totally untouched by the violence. The kitchen is a mess of poured-out wine bottles, the trash can overflowing with killed cans of seltzer. The picked-over remnants of cheese, olives, and crackers look like a still-life painting atop a wooden cutting board.

Whatever happened in the living room, it never made it past the hallway. But there aren't any doors. Nothing that could have stopped those people from escaping. So why didn't they run? What held them in that room against their will? A person? One another? I hold my breath as I creep to the exit, afraid that at any moment one of them will lunge from the penthouse's tasteful decor and drag me backward, along that bloody smear.

A sound from the outside hallway stops me right before I open the front door. Chattering walkie-talkies. People talking. Careful not to touch it, I look through the peephole.

There are men outside. They exchange hushed orders. One pushes to the front and gives the doorbell a jab. I recoil at the loud buzz and my hip catches the narrow console table, toppling a thin-necked vase of tulips. I lunge for it.

I miss.

The silence shatters.

"Open up!" a voice booms through the door. "Police!" They knock three times, each a demand.

I'm frozen in place.

OPEN UP. POLICE.

I'm a good person, a good boy. I reach for the latch but stop. I'm once again facing down a door that both traps me and saves me. What did the boy with the butterfly bandanna say?

I'll come back for you when it's safe.

He never came back. Maybe, I realize, because it's not safe.

The knocking turns brutal, shaking the photographs hung in the entryway. I step away from the door. They're going to think I did this. *Did* I do this? My power, the mirrors, the evil eye—ancient superstitions whisper inside my head. Did I cause all this? I don't even know what *this* is, but it doesn't matter. I'll be blamed, and they'll take me away, and Yiayia will be alone, and—

Yiayia. I need to get home to Yiayia.

"We're coming in. Step away from the door. Do not attempt to run," the police instruct. Something scrapes against the lock. A key. Of course they have a key.

I need to open the door. I need to hide. I need to run. I need to confess. I can still make this choice. My future is still in my hands. But if I don't act now, that lock will tumble apart and fate will decide it for me.

Fate versus me.

I decide.

I watch the doorknob turn.

I decide.

I twist the dead bolt and slap on the door chain, then run backward into the apartment. I pass the kitchen. My tiny bathroom. I tear down the hallway, careful of the blood, and plunge into the sun-drenched living room. I'm running to the windows—the fire escape—but then the banging stops. Or my hearing fails as my eyes fill with the sight before me.

This is nothing like the room I sat in just hours ago. That room was laid out in a low lounge style, with a wide couch covered in fuzzy pillows of velvet and bouclé. I remember the carpets, thin and tufted, layered over one another like overlapping lily pads so that the floor shifted beneath you as you stepped around low tables of perfectly clear, tempered glass. There were abstract lamps on heavy marble bases, and bookshelves with no books, and chairs of polished chrome, and little framed mirrors speckling the walls, like unblinking eyes peering out from the wallpaper.

It's all in ruins now. All the furniture has been overturned and smashed and bent into a mountain at the room's center. It reaches upward, toward the only overhead lighting: a chandelier with all the bulbs smashed out. It's like whoever built it was desperate to turn off the lights but couldn't find the switch.

Second, I notice the walls. They've been stripped of their wallpaper, about as high as a person could reach. Small smears of blood edge the barren patches, like someone's nails split while doing it.

15

And finally, I see the people.

Bare backs, spines flexed under flesh. Legs and arms and faces frozen in shock.

The people are in piles. I only see them now as I circle the mountain of furniture. They're crammed into the back corner of the room, in the mountain's shadow, as though hiding from . . .

The sunlight. It hardens everything into cruel, inescapable details. Makes the dead flesh look like stiff rubber. The sight burns away my ability to think, and a single word blinks in the emptiness of my shock. *Sculpture*. The way the bodies have tangled over themselves . . . it doesn't look like the chaos I overheard. No, there is something verging on artful about the arrangement. Someone did this. A person knotted these limbs together before the stiffness of death set in. My mind is on the verge of making sense of the shape—the limbs all aimed outward, a knot of necks and heads in the middle, but then my footsteps crunch on something.

Broken glass. I look down into a shattered mirror, my lifetime of avoidance saving me from making eye contact with myself. Instead, I gaze past my reflection at the ceiling and see something there. All above me, hovering in the sun-soaked air, are glimmering threads.

I reach up to pluck at one, but jerk away when I hear the front door bang open and the hall fill with footsteps. The police have made it inside. I give the horrific sculpture one more glance before running out of the room, into the master suite. The inside is untouched, jackets tossed onto the bed. I lock the door and rush to the far side of the room—a wall entirely made of windows that overlook the city. If my memory is right, there's a door here and—yes!—a balcony. I rush outside.

New York is a welcome assault on my senses. It's cold and windy and *loud*. Buildings rise all around me. The city shifts below, cars sluggishly braiding around a hundred faceless pedestrians. The air is frigid. Clear. It's another overcast November day, like any other.

I accidentally catch my reflection in the window of an office building across from me—I look terrified, wild, guilty—but a second later the reflection wobbles backward through time, the pane darkening to a square of night. It answers the question blaring in my thoughts: What happened?

The reflection rewinds through an outside view of the penthouse, hours before. Bodies fly at one another in time-lapsed violence. A fight, too fast to make sense of.

Stop, I urge them. Urge myself. I have to go. *Now*. I tear my eyes away and look down the seven-story drop. Several cruisers wait below. I whip back and climb upward instead, to the roof. It's easy with the steep metal stairs of the fire escape. The roof of the building is a dead garden. I bound past raised beds of withered plants and grimy patio furniture, onto the next roof. I scramble over the buildings, turning the block's corner, then find another fire escape hidden from the police. I race down it, reaching the emergency ladder suspended above the sidewalk. I drop the last ten feet and roll to a stop, right in the path of a baby stroller.

"Oh," says the lady pushing it.

My charm kicks in. I stand and pretend to dust myself off as I step aside with overacted chivalry. Friendly, a little embarrassed, like *Yikes, you wouldn't believe the night I just had*. Her face eases into a knowing smile, like *Yeah, I've been there, too*, and she passes by.

I force myself to walk now, but quickly, like I've got somewhere to go. Sirens are getting closer. By now the police have probably called in the crime scene. Did they see me as I escaped, or did I really get away? My adrenaline mixes with a sudden wave of sickness, like I'm being flung high in the air on a roller coaster. I hug the buildings, just in case I let loose the mouthful of acid I keep swallowing back.

Those people. Arranged like that. What the fuck?

An ambulance lurches to a halt right in front of me and paramedics spill out. I'm wide open in what's about to be a hive of police. I pull off the sidewalk and into a storefront at the building's base, which just happens to be a coffee shop. I park myself at the counter, my back to the street, and sink my head into my hands.

"Can I help you?"

The barista eyes me with undecided suspicion. I throw on a smile, and the barista's face softens. My smile is useful like that. It's the dimples.

"Depends," I say. "Your espresso machine working?"

"You bet she is," the barista says, slapping a hand on a big chrome piece of equipment right in front of me. In the reflection, I can see out the café window behind me. It's perfect for keeping a lookout.

"Long night?" the barista prompts.

"The longest."

I get a cappuccino and pay with cash, even though the price is painful. The barista gives the espresso machine another pat when he hands me the drink, saying, "Let me know how I did." He winks.

I grin, forcing myself to hold eye contact as I take a sip. I'm surprised how easily charm comes to my defense, but I shouldn't be. I've hidden behind charisma for years.

"Good," I say, licking foam from my lips.

"Darn. Usually I do great," he pouts. There's a double meaning there.

"I'll look forward to great next time, then." I smile. He heads off to help the next customer.

I drop the act right away, my face back in my hands. But then I make myself sit up. *Don't look suspicious, Athan. Look at your phone, even though it's dead.* I hold it up but look past it, at the reflection swimming in the chrome body of the espresso machine. By accident I look into my own eyes, and my reflection instantly retreats. Backward, out of the coffee shop, into a busy street that quickly empties as the sun un-rises.

Stop it, I demand. *Not now. Not here.*

I'm about to close my eyes so I can tap on my temples again, but then I see something in the reverse world of the reflection. I see *him*.

The boy with the butterfly bandanna.

I jump up, drawing the barista's attention. I pretend like I'm just getting up to leave, but my eyes are watching the reflection. I missed the moment, but maybe I can get it back. I lean in, slow my breathing, and do what I haven't done since I was little. I consciously direct the reflection toward a particular moment in time. It's easy; mirrors have always been eager to show me what I want to see, if it means I keep looking. Cars and people blur until I snag that familiar combo of orange-black-white.

There. There he is! The boy with the monarch bandanna, who shoved me into the bathroom. He's right there on the street, framed perfectly by the coffee shop's front window, just standing there with his phone out. I wish this was an actual mirror, not polished metal. The image is warped by the machine's shape. Something is off about the boy, but I can't quite make out what.

I slide the image of him walking back and forth, like moving through frames of a video. The reflections don't like to be controlled this specifically. The metal face of the espresso machine begins to heat up. The air shimmers and warmth prickles the skin of my face, but I lean closer. I need to see more. In the reflection a car passes behind the boy, the taillight streaking him in bloody red, and I see it: Silvery threads trail his body, coiled around his neck, just like I saw in the sun-lit penthouse. They pulse and heave, like something out of frame pulls upon them. I get the strange sense that even though this scene happened last night, whatever pulls upon the strings is with me right now, in the present. It's watching me back, through the mirror.

Hello, Athanasios, it whispers.

I clap my hands over my face, severing the connection.

"You good?"

I jerk upright. The barista is looking at me with a smirk.

"I'm good," I assure him.

"Like what you see?"

He means my own reflection. I must have looked entranced with myself just now. I swallow, fighting the shiver that's sweeping over my skin. I find my smile and say, "You got me there."

"That makes two of us," the barista says. "Look, I never do this, but are you around this Friday? I've got a catering gig downtown, but then I'm free. I'd love to take you out for a drink."

My mind goes blank. He's asking me out—I know how to handle this—but I'm too twisted up from what I just experienced.

"You can think about it," he adds quickly, and he hands me a napkin with his number scrawled on it. "I'm Sam."

"Athan," I say automatically. "Like Nathan without the *N*."

"Nice," Sam says. "Unique. I'll remember that."

Shit. I shouldn't have given my name. I mask my wince with a stiff smile.

"I'll text you," I lie, pocketing the napkin. Coy, easy. But I'm sweating bullets as I leave the shop. I beeline through the crowd thickening around the flashing police cruisers. The ambulance remains parked, engine idling and its back doors open, but no one exits the building. They haven't found any survivors yet.

I rush down into the nearest subway entrance. If I was fucked before, I'm super fucked now. That barista has my name. Those cops saw me.

Then, when I pass a shattered monitor in the subway, something flashes in my reflection. I back up. On my shoulder gleams a trailing thread, shining like a filament of starlight. I brush at it, feeling its ghostly touch, but when I look at my actual shoulder, it's barely visible. I try to use my reflection to pick it off, but no matter what I do, it won't go away. In fact, it just tugs tighter.

But toward what?

I think of the silvery threads wrapped around that boy's reflection like a tangled marionette, the same threads that hung in the air at the penthouse. Though it seems absurd, I can't shake the sense of being led—dragged to the café by . . . something. Fate or a force with less kind intentions. Had it spoken to me? No, that's nuts. I'm shaken and sleep-deprived. But I can almost feel the words still creeping around my head.

Hello, Athanasios.

I mash the heels of my hands against my eyes, crushing my thoughts—and whatever else might be nesting within them. This isn't just a debate between superstition and psychology anymore. People died last night, and even Dr. Wei would struggle to explain how.

I find an uptown train and get on. I need to get home to Yiayia.

It will break her heart, but I'll tell her what I've done. I looked, and something looked back.

The first lie New York City ever told you was on a placard bolted to an emergency exit door in the subway.

ALARM WILL SOUND.

As a child, you were told that following the rules would keep you safe, even rules that didn't make sense. Like going through the scary subway turnstiles instead of just pushing a door open. That door was for emergencies only, like fires or floods or fights. But then an older kid shouldered through it, and everyone followed—everyone—and no alarm sounded.

The sign is a lie. New Yorkers know alarms never sound. In fact, they count on it. In a city this big, it's often that what's meant to go right goes terribly wrong. Rules are broken, civility fails, but alarms never sound. The people of the city rush onward, indifferent, and the broken promise is ground to dust beneath so many lives trying to be lived.

You always wondered why this trivial thing bothered you. But sitting on the uptown A train, watching the signs flash by in every station, it all comes together.

In your life, the alarms have always stayed quiet. They didn't sound the day the fire burned up your parents. That's why it took the trucks so long to get there. Your life was ashes by then.

And then when you and Yiayia had to keep moving and the insurance money never arrived, no alarms sounded. You had to live with Uhler. Yiayia had to sell him the family framing business your grandfather started almost a hundred years ago. And it was years before you realized the sinister nature of that exchange, because Yiayia kept quiet about it. Just like she stayed quiet during the fire. Maybe in shock, or maybe she was afraid to approach the firefighters with her broken English to tell them her daughter and son-in-law were still inside.

In the smothering silence of Greek pride, no alarms are ever allowed to sound. And that fire has never really gone out, has it? Yiayia's mind burned next, dementia smoldering through her fortitude, leaving just enough behind to refuse to see doctors. No alarms there, either.

You stopped showing up for school so that you could take shifts at the frame shop, doing the one thing you couldn't mess up: picking things up, moving them, and putting them down. You weren't even sixteen years old, the required age to drop out, but you were a big kid. No one thought twice about bringing the former owner's son on. And no one from the school called, or if they did, they called Yiayia. By then her phone was forgotten and she only spoke in those long, rambling prayers that dipped through English, Greek, and the incomprehensible language of her superstitions.

It never occurred to you to add everything up like this, but it does now. Something horrible has happened. Something evil. But here the city is, just grinding past it, the people around you skillfully avoiding your tear-streaked face as you all sway together on the A train.

No alarm. Nothing ringing. Nothing wrong, if no one looks.

But you looked, and you know.

I whisper, *You did this, Athanasios.* And despite all of Dr. Wei's carefully placed precautions against such delusions, you begin to believe me.

You look down into your hands and try to unthink what you've just thought. How could you have killed all those people yet walked away with hands so clean? It wasn't you. It was a brawl. A riot. Bad drugs. A gas leak. You can think of a hundred excuses that exempt you from responsibility. Just like the people all around you on the A train can easily ignore your suffering. Just like everyone in this city ignores everyone else.

But you can't ignore this terrible knowing, just as the people who died at the party couldn't ignore the deadly design that has stalked you all your life.

You did this, Athanasios. And if no alarm sounds, you might just be able to get away with it.

CHAPTER THREE

Our front door is open.

We have a tiny one-bedroom apartment on the basement level of an old brownstone in Harlem. Our door is tucked beneath the building's stoop. No one would know it was unlocked, or even there, but I'm not worried about who could have gotten in.

I'm worried about who got out.

"Yiayia?" I call, stepping into the dark apartment. There are windows, but they only get light when the sun is at its highest and pours directly into the cracks of the city, like this crack we live in. It's a close, low-ceilinged apartment, full of too much furniture. Too many chairs and never any guests to sit in them.

I snap on the kitchen lights. In the living room, my bed (the couch) is made up. Yiayia even draped my blanket over the back. A guilt trip in the shape of my unused bed. There's just one bedroom—Yiayia's— and the door is closed.

"Yiayia?" I call again. No answer.

I want to believe she's still asleep, but I know better. Sometimes I wake up on the couch and hear her already up in her room, babbling to herself. With the thin walls between us, it sounds like a constant, low static from an ancient radio.

Right now, I hear nothing. I wonder if I'm about to find yet another room full of death.

I open the door and it collides with something soft on the floor. In the dark room, a woman screams.

"Excuse me, haven't you heard of knocking?"

It's not Yiayia. I instantly relax. I know who this intruder is. I wipe the fear from my face as the door swings open and reveals a squat white lady with messy hair and a perpetually sweaty upper lip.

"Good morning, Linda," I say.

Linda, our landlady these past two years, has a strange relationship with boundaries—as in she neglects them completely. Technically this is all her house, but I read online that landlords have to ask to come into tenant spaces, and Linda has never done that. She just pops in whenever she wants. Maybe it's because the basement apartment is still crammed with all her stuff. When we moved in, she made a big show about how the apartment was furnished, like she was doing us this huge favor even though we had our own furniture. Really, she just has nowhere to put her junk, so we live among it as though we're ghosts in her storage unit. She treats us like ghosts, too, always startled when we show up in our own house.

Yiayia hates how chatty she is. After dealing with Linda's visits for only one week, Yiayia promptly forgot how to speak any English whatsoever. Now I get to deal with Linda alone.

"Good morning, dear," Linda says, shuffling into our kitchen. She opens drawers and cabinets, moving aside our things. "I know I left it around here somewhere . . ."

I sigh.

"Not here, not here," she murmurs. "Hard to find anything in here. All this stuff . . ."

Finally I give in. "Can I help you find something, Linda?"

"Oh, dear, why yes. How funny you should ask. I *am* looking for something!"

Linda is not slick. Linda does not know she's not slick. But I need to get her out of here so I can resume freaking out about my missing grandmother. I wait for Linda to tell me what she needs, but she just knots her hands together like a little girl.

"What do you need, Linda?" I ask.

"Oh, such a dear." She beams. "I don't suppose you've seen a small set of paint rollers, have you? I'm doing some remodeling. I usually keep them down here in the closet, on the floor, but someone must have moved them."

She says it like *isn't that the strangest thing?* As if she can't figure out why someone—such as the people who live here—might have put their own stuff in the closet in the past two years.

"On top of the fridge."

The cabinets above the fridge are where I've hidden away some of Linda's things. All sorts of garbage she left behind, like a stove-top espresso maker (rusty as fuck) and a vegetable spiralizer (broken; also, gross). I find the paint supplies quickly but pause to take down a bunch of other items, too.

"Do you want to just take it all?" I ask.

"Ah, no, no, thank you, dear." Linda pats my arm. "Hold on to it. Some great stuff in there."

It's literally garbage, but okay.

Linda sits on the couch—my bed—and starts chattering about neighborhood gossip. I keep glancing at Yiayia's bedroom door. If she's not here, where is she? Taking a walk? The last walk we took, I had to guide her so that she could watch herself in her mirror. We only made it to the end of the block before she nearly fell. There's no way she's out there alone and still upright. Yet I'm in here, trapped with Linda as she divulges that she thinks a pigeon she keeps seeing is the reincarnation of her great-grandmother.

"Linda," I cut her off. "Speaking of grandmothers, did you happen to see *my* grandmother at all this morning?"

I try to ask casually, as if I myself just stepped out this morning, but Linda isn't as out of it as she pretends to be.

"You don't know where your grandmother is?" she asks. "You know, dear, I wondered where you were this morning. It's Monday—shouldn't you be on your way to school?"

"Exam week," I say.

Linda smiles. Her eyes take in my wrinkled clothes and messy hair. I probably smell like alcohol and sweat. She knows I'm lying. As oblivious as she pretends to be, it's only so that she can use her status as an old white lady to get away with shit like sneaking and snooping.

"Don't worry." Linda winks, surprising me. "Your secret is safe with me."

I smile gratefully, but the truth is I don't care about that.

"But Yiayia?" I prompt.

"Oh yes, dear, as I was saying . . ." She sighs at my manners, as if she was just on the verge of telling but my impatience interrupted her. "I hope she's okay. I worry about her when you're not here. Is she really safe to be by herself?"

"She's fine," I snap, but then I hear what she's saying. "Wait, you hope she's okay? What happened?"

Linda opens her eyes wide. "You don't know?"

I want to grab the sides of her face and shout at her to tell me, but that won't work. I have to just play along. Linda, I remember, is a failed playwright. Her words, not mine. I've long suspected her antics are her revenge on a world that took one look at her dramas and asked her to keep them to herself.

"I don't know," I confess to her through gritted teeth.

"Ah, youth. Such is the privilege for the young to absent themselves from the gravity of death." She grins in a way that lets me know she's quoting herself. Then she gathers the paint supplies and finds her way to the stairs. Foot on the first step, she finally gets to the point.

"It's not my business, dear, but I'd hope that if *I* were to have a fall, my family would be there to help me back up." A long sigh. "But really, it's not my business. Really, it's not. I just happened to be looking out the window when the ambulance showed up. They knocked on my door but it was past visiting hours for this ole gal. Imagine my surprise when they broke open the downstairs door. Someone will have to fix that, you know. I hate to be the bearer of bad news, but that will come out of your security deposit. That's just the way it goes. Legally."

"An ambulance?" I say, shocked. "My grandmother got taken away in an ambulance?"

Linda shrugs. "It's not my business."

She starts up the steps and I nearly chase after.

"I'm sure she's fine," Linda says as she rises up the steps. "A tough woman, your yiayia. Immigrants always are. I'd love to talk to her for a play I'm writing, you know."

"Do you know where they took her?" I'm almost begging.

Linda stops, like a thought just occurred to her. She looks down the stairs at me.

"Can you do me a favor, dear? When you see your yiayia, tell her no more of that incense. I believe I've told you both a few times that I'm very sensitive. I get just the worst migraines. My doctors say it's all the impurities people put in candles and stuff. It's bad for the body's energy. Can you tell your yiayia that when you see her?"

"I will," I say through clenched teeth. The urge to physically throw her up the stairs flickers in my muscles, but then she starts to rise up the steps again. Of course, she stops a second later.

"Oh! But essential oils are okay," she says. "I have some great ones if your yiayia wants to try them out. Stuff that's actually good for you.

Cutting-edge medicine, really. I've been reading all about it online. Have you seen the news about 5G poisoning yet? It's in your cell phones and the Wi-Fi. Causes headaches! Go figure. A friend told me about it, but she's got a great doctor treating her with this blend of oils and mantras. Ancient, cutting-edge stuff. Not like what you could find in Rite Aid. Want me to get you some?"

"It's okay—"

"Please, I insist. It's expensive, but you can't put a price on peace of mind. I'm sure you know that." She smiles, feigning tender pity. "Your yiayia. Oh, it must be hard. Death by a thousand cuts. I hope she makes it, dear. But you'll tell her about the incense? That's a no-no. You'll let her know?"

I'm not often too stunned to speak, but this one gets me. I don't even know what to respond to. Linda mistakes my confusion as gratitude.

"You worry about Yiayia," she assures me. "And leave the Wi-Fi poisoning to me. Can't be good, having the entire summation of human knowledge flowing through our heads at all times, can it? The mind is a vulnerable thing, right, dear?"

By now I'm sure Yiayia is flatlining in an ER somewhere. Another body to add to my trail of destruction, all because I'm trapped here being polite. "Right," I rasp.

Linda waits for me to say more. I realize she's waiting to be thanked. "Thanks, Linda."

"Oh, it's nothing," she says, patting her thigh. Finally she heads all the way up the stairs, and out of the basement.

The second she's gone, I dig my charger out from behind the couch. My phone is so dead that it takes a few minutes to wake up, so I take the chance to douse my hair under the spitting, freezing showerhead in our tiny bathroom. No time to shower and change, though. Still dripping, I pounce on my awoken phone. Instead of the barrage of messages that I expect, there's an error. No service. And the Wi-Fi isn't working. I unplug and move to the window and when my phone starts up again, I text Linda.

ATHAN: Hi Linda, can you check the router?

She responds right away.

LINDA: Hi dear. I unplugged it. Didn't you hear what I said? Not good for you without some protection. Safety first until we know more. - Linda.

I am practically glowing with rage, but I make my fingers tap out something kinder than how I feel.

ATHAN: Would you feel safer if we moved the router down here?
LINDA: No. - Linda.

And that's the end of that. I don't have time to argue with her. I continue leaning over the bureau, waiting for my trickle of phone service to deliver the night's notifications.

A few emails show up. Mostly coupons and promotions. I posted a few pics of my outfit on some of my social platforms, and a slew of lewd comments from random guys on the internet flash by. My dating apps are cluttered with notifications, too, but I keep those silenced.

Finally, a few texts roll in. Nothing from Uhler. No new voice mails, either, not that my inbox can take any more. I keep it full on purpose.

My phone finally goes still. All caught up. Somehow, none of my notifications show any signs of what happened last night. I search headlines for anything about the crime scene. I'm stunned. I feel like I dreamt it. All of it.

I push my still-wet hair out of my face. How do I find Yiayia?

I call Uhler, out of habit.

His phone actually rings, which is a shock. In my mind he goes from dead to dying, maybe still in that room of corpses, his phone lighting up in his pocket as they zip him into a body bag.

But then he picks up.

"Athan. Thank goodness. Where have you been? I've been trying you for hours."

Uhler's voice is usually smooth and pleasant, but right now it's stricken. I'm shocked to hear him at all. How did he escape the party?

"You *are* okay, aren't you?" he asks when I don't say anything.

"I'm okay. But Yiayia . . ."

"She's with me," Uhler cuts in. "Your grandmother is going to be all right. She had a little fall last night and called me, no doubt out of desperation. I tried your cell phone but you weren't picking up, so I called her an ambulance and met her at the hospital. She was released this morning, and I brought her back to my apartment. She shouldn't be alone. Where are you?"

"Home." I sound guilty and clueless.

"Well, come here."

He says it like I'm not already racing around trying to find my shoes.

"I'm on my way," I say. "But she's really okay?"

Uhler chuckles at my panic, but kindly, as though to put me at ease. "She'll be fine. But you know your yiayia. Doom and disaster. She'll be glad to hear you're alive. I swear, she's been saying the most outrageous things all morning. Something about you being trapped in a jungle. Just absurd."

I think of the small bathroom I spent the night in, and the wall-paper of lush monstera leaves.

"I'm fine," I say. "But the party . . ."

"See you soon," Uhler says, then hangs up.

I yank my charger from the wall and rush back out the door.

You know the way to Uhler's apartment on the Upper West Side. It's carved into you by the blade of panic. Somehow you're always running from something, and that means that somehow, you're always running back to him.

Uhler is a peculiar person to all, but he's always shown kindness to you and Yiayia. Always. You remember him being around a lot when you were little. At first he was just another person your parents worked with at the frame shop, constantly sweeping in and out of your life like a large, rumbling storm cloud. You knew him by his silver hair, and the fact that he always wore funny, dark glasses, even inside. He had no idea how to talk to a child, which meant he talked to you like you were an adult, which you loved. Uhler scared you, but he also saw you, and you were instantly friends.

Then, after the fire, he was around a lot more, though you could tell it was not at all what he wanted. For a time, you and Yiayia even lived with him, in the very apartment you race to now. You were sad when you left to move into Linda's basement unit, but by then you were old enough to understand Yiayia's strange pride, and the way it controlled what kind of help you could and could not accept.

For instance, you weren't allowed to accept Uhler's money for rent, though you often did behind her back. Similarly, you couldn't let Yiayia know that Uhler found you a weekly therapist—Dr. Wei—after you refused to go to school because you were afraid the school building would burn down, too, and all your friends would die, and it would be your fault again.

You told Yiayia about none of that, but she noticed you growing apart from her in other ways. You stopped praying with her, for one. And you stopped responding to her in Greek, even though you understood every word. Her eyes grew scolding. Cold. But she never asked where the rent money came from, or where you went every Thursday.

Yiayia accepted other help, though, like when she lost the storage unit and had to empty it out into the already crowded basement apartment. The handlers from the frame shop (no longer Yiayia's on paper, but still forever hers in spirit) got together to help with a box truck and manpower, saving what they could and leaving the rest on the curb. It was hard for Yiayia to part with anything that had survived the fire—except, of course, the mirror that used to hang in your old bedroom, with the sea glass mosaic frame. That, Yiayia didn't even allow into the new house, her eyes frenzied with what would be the earliest signs of her coming decline. You were devastated by the decision. You'd wanted to explore the mirror for the history it contained of your parents. But before you could retrieve it later that night, it was gone. Taken by a passerby—and all your childhood memories taken with it.

You still look for it sometimes, at dusk in your Harlem neighborhood, when the light is just right and you can see into the lit windows of your neighbors' apartments.

As you run to Uhler's apartment on the Upper West Side, your eyes search for any sign that the world knows what's wrong. Your power, or your paranoia, causes your eyes to flash over the reflections sliding past you. The many subtle mirrors of the city rewind, taunting you with fragments of your history.

You pass by the playground you used to frequent, and in the ancient metal fun-house orbs you catch sight of you and Uhler kneeling on the ground, building something. Yiayia hovers behind in the shade, so much younger it's like staring at an old photo. She watches with subdued resentment as this man fascinates you with a small house made of twigs and flowers. Her hand mirror is nowhere to be seen, but you recognize the bag she hugs to her chest, and you know why she hugs it so fiercely. The mirror is waiting inside. She hasn't yet begun to stare into it in public.

In a dry cleaner's front window (now abandoned) you see a memory from when you were twelve and Yiayia was only just starting to lose it. The window's reflection perfectly frames a bus stop where you and Yiayia would sit for hours, your paper bags of groceries getting hot on the pavement as bus after bus passed by without you ever getting on.

Yiayia just stared through the buses, her mirror rising and lowering in some incomprehensible ritual, leaving twelve-year-old you to stare at the opposite building. You could draw the entire facade from memory—the corner store, the bike shop, the impossibly narrow nail salon, the gap of wall overtaken by graffiti of flowers and butterflies and bees.

You'd even draw in the door hidden under the graffiti, so unremarkable you'd never have noticed it if you weren't bored out of your mind. In the vision, a car pulls up, and Uhler gets out. Yiayia looks betrayed when she realizes you called him on the cell phone he'd bought for you.

"For emergencies," he'd said. And didn't this count?

You still don't understand her reaction. Didn't she know she needed help? Didn't she see the wasps that had found the groceries? But she just scowls and refuses to enter the car as Uhler ushers you in, taking you to safety, leaving her behind to stare—stare on—into nothing.

Yiayia never acknowledged Uhler's help. Even now you're not sure why. She said it was okay that the frame shop had given you a job, and that the handlers showed up with food from time to time. That, Yiayia said, was what family was for. But for some reason, even though it was probably Uhler who commanded all those things, *he* never made it into the word *family*. He was there all the same, persistent in a brooding way, like a dark cloud bringing much-needed rain to the increasingly brittle, crumbling world of you and Yiayia.

And if you're honest with yourself—which you have to be now—you are relieved that she's with him. Yiayia was dead wrong about accepting charity. She was wrong about what you needed as a child growing up with dead parents.

She was right about only one thing: Disaster would come back for the rest of your family someday.

It has.

It's here.

Now you truly do need Uhler's help. And even though you feel ashamed of the thought, you're glad Yiayia must finally accept it.

CHAPTER FOUR

Uhler's building has always scared me. Just a little. It faces north, into the side of a taller condo complex so that its entrance is always cast in shade. There are doormen. Multiple. Not the cheery kind you always see opening cabs for the rich in old movies, but the stone-faced kind who never smile for visitors.

Like all things surrounding Uhler, the building is expensive and intimidating. The lobby is made up of black tile buffed to a high shine, and couches of blushing velvet huddle together as if they're scared of the massive neon chandelier above. Even the doormen are fashionable, in matching turtlenecks and blazers. I nod at them as I wind through the couches. They take down my name like they don't recognize me from the years I lived here, then call Uhler to confirm I'm allowed up.

"Second elevator," the doorman tells me. Only one of the three goes all the way up to Uhler's floor, and it opens directly into his apartment. Without a key or a command from the front desk, it won't budge.

I get into the elevator and, right before it closes, I see a police cruiser pull to a stop in front of the building. My first thought is that they're here for me, but I know I'm being paranoid. Even if by some horrible miracle they already questioned Sam the barista and got my nickname, there's no way the cops from this morning could have figured out who I am and where I was headed.

The doors close. I stare at my shoes because the elevators are walled-in mirrors. I've had enough of the past for today. What do I tell Uhler about last night? When I talk to Yiayia, will she be lucid? Or will I lose her in another one of her trancelike prayers? I need her now, more than ever. I need her to take back a lifetime of wild superstitions and over-wrought warnings. I need her to hold my face and smile—and tell me this isn't my fault.

Guilt coats the inside of my throat, thick as paint. It betrays me from the inside out, letting me know what my body really believes. The rushing upward momentum of the elevator flips my stomach. I shove down the dark thoughts. Yiayia's thoughts, not mine. I need to be strong now if I'm going to find a way forward. Uhler will help us.

I know I've arrived at his apartment by the sound of far-off piano music. There's a ding. The doors swoosh open, the music rushing over me. Suddenly I'm facing not just Uhler's living room, but Uhler himself.

"Oh—"

Uhler interrupts my surprise with a clipped greeting.

"Athan. Finally. Come in."

Dressed in his usual black ensemble, Uhler is a pop of darkness against his apartment of restrained pastels and frosty ivory. What sur-prised me, however, is the fact that he's not wearing his glasses. I stare into watery blue eyes that shine like he's tired, or he just got done cry-ing, or both.

Then he hugs me. He's never hugged me before. No one has hugged me in a really long time, actually.

"She's okay," he assures me. When we break apart he's dabbing his eyes, laughing a little, like his emotions have surprised him. "My apol-ogies. I was just thinking how strange the circumstances are that have brought us all together again, back beneath my roof. Would you think less of me if I admitted a part of me is pleased?"

Do I hear love in Uhler's voice? Toward me? Toward *Yiayia*? I've often wondered about Yiayia's feelings toward Uhler, but never how he felt about her. Uhler doesn't have any other family. Only us. Maybe, in all the years we've been kept away by Yiayia's pride, he's missed having us home.

"She's in her old room," he says as he sweeps the low coffee table clear of design boards and wallpaper samples. "She calmed down the moment I told her you were okay, and she's resting now. We should let her sleep. She was up all night. Here, sit. You look like you've had quite the night as well. Would you like coffee? I ordered breakfast. Do you still like strawberry pancakes?"

I sit, frozen, as Uhler unpacks a delivery bag with—yes—strawberry pancakes in a Styrofoam container. Not knowing what else to do, I take a few bites, but it tastes too sweet. My stomach still churns with guilt. Uhler doesn't know what happened at the penthouse. If he saw what I saw, there's no way he'd be chitchatting over pancakes. I push the food away.

"Where were you last night?" I ask.

Uhler floats around the living room, tidying up like he's expecting company. "With you at the party, of course."

"That's not true."

I've never pushed back on Uhler like this, and instantly I regret it. In a flash, he's pulled his dark glasses from his pocket. Back on, they douse his emotions and the storm cloud re-forms. The smile he gives me is impossible to decipher, but it feels as sickeningly sweet as the pancakes.

"You're upset that I left early? Well, it's a good thing I did. Yiayia called us both, but *you* didn't pick up. Too involved with yet another silly girl, I saw. Or was it a boy this time?"

"The party," I bite out. "Don't you know? Don't you . . . know what happened?"

Uhler cocks his head. His smile grows. "I'm guessing it turned into quite the rager, considering you look like you've had the night from hell."

Quite the rager. Night from hell. He has no idea how right he is.

"S-something happened," I stammer. "Something bad."

Uhler's teasing tone falls away instantly. "Did someone hurt you, Athan?"

"No."

"Did someone else get hurt?"

"Yes."

"Did . . . did you hurt someone?" Uhler asks this without judgment, like he's asking what train I took to get here.

No, I try to answer, but I can't. My body is too tired to lie.

Uhler takes my hesitance as a confession, which I suppose it is. He sits beside me, placing his hand on mine. I can feel the iciness of his many silver rings. I look at their dark gemstones instead of looking at him.

"We'll figure this out," he assures me, lowering his voice like he already knows I'm guilty. "I spoke with Artemis this morning. Just briefly. He's hungover as hell but said it all wrapped up nicely, except a few stragglers that he had to raise from the dead this morning."

Off my confused look, Uhler adds, "Artemis Levy? The host? The bald man I introduced you to? He did a series of illustrated papers for Orion House two years ago. It was his party, Athan. And if he woke up to anything out of the ordinary, I'm sure he would have told me. We've known each other since before you were born."

I'm stunned. There was a survivor? No, wait—

I take a slow breath as I reexamine everything. Every gruesome moment. With almost gleeful relief, I see just how cartoonishly grotesque it all was—how obviously nightmarish. All along I was looking for a cause outside myself, never once considering the cause was within.

I imagined it. It was all in my head. Maybe the magic of the mirror finally crawled through my eyes and into my brain, filling my mind with home-brewed catastrophe.

Maybe I'm just like Yiayia, after all.

I feel like I've tipped over a cliff, until Uhler pats my knee. "I haven't heard a thing today, I swear. Not from anyone. Whatever you did, we can still get in front of it."

Shame bubbles up through my stomach. Elation, too. I feel myself begin to cry, but then Uhler's phone rings. He answers automatically.

"Hello, this is Stefan Uhler." A pause, then: "Yes, I'm still home. Why?" Someone garbles something that makes Uhler stand up and step away from me. He says, "Oh, I wasn't expecting—no, it's fine—no, don't send them up. I've got someone . . ." He looks down at me, placing a hand on my head to smooth out my hair. "I've got a project up here. I'll come down." He holds the phone to his sweater and mouths for me to *stay put*, then heads to the waiting elevator. He's still talking when the doors close.

I nearly collapse on the couch among his strewn papers and designs, but then I remember Yiayia is here. I rush down the halls, stopping in front of the closed door to her old bedroom. I shouldn't bother her, but I know there's no way I can relax unless I see that she's okay. Selfishly, I ease open the door.

Yiayia isn't inside.

I'm looking into a room that's clearly been lived in recently—there are clothes strewn about and books piled on top of a bureau—but the bed is tidily made. I step inside, my toe clipping a stack of notebooks. They look like sketchbooks. I grab one and am surprised to find its pages are glued shut. In fact, all the sketchbooks have been glued shut.

How strange.

"Yiayia?" I call, backing out of the room. I hear only that soft piano music. I check Uhler's suite, a minor maze of sleek black furniture and bare concrete walls. It's empty. I check both bathrooms and the kitchen. Empty. I finally find myself before Uhler's office, where I used to sleep. The door is ajar.

"Yiayia?" I whisper, opening it. Piano music sweeps over me.

I'm looking into a darkness created by blackout curtains. The room pulses with the cold light of several computer monitors showing psychedelic screen savers. My old twin bed is gone. Boxes of files crowd the room's corners, and the walls are scaly with tacked-up papers. They rustle, like I've let something huge and invisible escape from the room.

There's no Yiayia.

I just stand there, utterly baffled. Did Uhler lie about her being here? Why? And if he lied about that, what else has he been lying about? With a cold prickle of dread, I realize that something has been off this whole time. About Uhler—about me being here.

Fresh guilt stabs at me for doubting the man who has always been my savior, but I parry. Something is definitely wrong. I have to figure out where Yiayia is. I rush to the desk, shaking the mouse, but encounter a lock screen. I rifle through the papers next to the keyboard, hoping Uhler wrote down the name of a hospital, or a phone number, or anything I could use.

I pause. The papers are scans of ancient-looking books—pages crawling with some inscrutable alphabet. There are photos of vases showing figures kneeling below a massive eye. Another page is a diagram of the same oval shape, though more recently drawn. I recognize Uhler's brisk, impatient strokes. Except this version of the eye is webbed in cracks. Its fragments are labeled in Uhler's handwriting. I glance up and find a similar coding system on the papers hanging from the walls, only these are attached to photographs of people.

The computers shift back to their screen savers, drowning the room in Technicolor. It's enough light for me to see by and I finally find her: Yiayia, in a photo so old it's gone yellow, casting her then-young face in a ghoulish tint. A sticky note adorns her image. I peel it off to read: *O-654-A.*

The lights in the room snap on.

"You shouldn't be here."

I jump, ready to apologize to Uhler, but it's not Uhler. It takes me a beat to realize who caught me. When I do, my heart stops. In the doorway stands the boy with the butterfly bandanna.

"You need to go," he says.

"You're . . . real?" I blurt.

"That's right," he says, like it's his great misfortune. "We need to go. Now. The police will be up here any second."

I've never had a conversation with this boy, but I've spent hours with him in my head. He was all I had while I hid in that bathroom. Seeing him again feels like being confronted by an imaginary friend. He brings with him the reality of the night, which I was so ready to deny. It happened, and he's the proof. All I can do is stare at him. I can't even remember what he just said. I simply wait for him to vanish like last time.

"Athan. Please. We don't have time for this."

"How do you know my name?"

The boy grabs my hand and pulls me from the office. He's almost a foot shorter than me, but I just bob after him like a balloon on a string. Is he strong, or am I weak? He talks fast, in a hush that makes it feel like we're hiding.

"You shouldn't have come here. Uhler is setting you up."

"For what?" I ask. "Who are you?"

"You're searching for your grandmother, right? She's not here."

"Uhler said—"

"Uhler *lied.* Can't you see that?"

We reach the elevator, which is miraculously open and waiting. It keeps trying to descend, but a slouchy leather bag stops it from closing.

"I'm not leaving," I say, backing into the living room. "Uhler is going to help me."

Waiting for me in the elevator, the boy is surrounded by mirrors—and in them I can see those strange, phantom threads still clinging to his clothes.

He was there, last night. He's here now. It's as though the invisible pattern of my life has woven into a person, sent to personally escort me to the next waiting horror.

"You know better," the boy says.

"Who are you?" I demand.

Though it clearly pains him, the boy steps toward me with his hands up in surrender. "I'll tell you, but right now you just need to trust me, Athan. You're not safe here. Look outside. See for yourself."

I follow his gaze out the windows. Far below, police cruisers line the streets. Uniformed officers stand in clumps, gesturing up at the building.

I race to the intercom next to the elevator and slap the button that lights up the tiny screen. It shows the lobby. I can just make out Uhler talking with two cops. I even recognize the motion of his arms. It's the gesture he makes when he's giving instructions that must be followed precisely.

The boy is right.

I'm trapped.

It's all real.

Fuck. Fuck. Fuck. But where can I run? I sink to my knees. This is the end. The relief of failure—the urge to just succumb—is almost too great to resist. I am tired and alone, and this is too much.

The boy kneels beside me. He doesn't try to drag me away or shake me. He doesn't touch me. He gets on my level and waits for me to look him in the eye. Then he asks, "Athan, do you believe in destiny?"

I take a shaky breath. "What?"

"Do you believe we can change our fate?"

He has an earnest face, and a stare so dark and steady that it gives me something to hold on to.

"No," I whisper.

"You chose to hide last night," the boy says. "And you survived. And then you chose to run, and you survived. And now I'm asking you to choose again. Stay in the trap or come with me. And survive. It's not over. So long as you have choices, you're not done."

I swallow down my rising emotions. I'm confused and scared. The boy takes my hand and says, "And the truth is, I need your help."

I feel my heart kick back to life. The way he pleads, I get the sense he's not the sort of person who asks for help easily. For some reason, *this* is why I believe him. Hope spreads through me like a wildfire. I nod and we stand together.

"I'm Dom," he says.

"Athan," I say automatically, even though he clearly already knows who I am.

Dom pulls me into the elevator, snatching up his bag and jamming the *L* button, for lobby, then the *G* button, for garage. He speaks in crisp orders. "I'll get off at the lobby and pretend I was just on my way out. To distract them so you can descend to the garage. Walk straight out of the elevator, turn left, then left again, and find the staircase to the emergency exit. It goes to the street. I'll meet you at the exit and knock when it's clear."

I want to ask Dom why he knows any of this; how he magically appeared in this apartment. The last question is answered when he pulls a key from the lock inside the elevator.

He lives in the building, then? Is that how he knows Uhler? A million questions buzz in my head as we sink. The tiny space still smells of Uhler's cologne, reminding me of the moment he stepped into the elevator just a few minutes ago, still talking on the phone.

Was he talking to the police? What did he tell them? The mirror pulses in my periphery, tempting me to use the Sight. *See for yourself,* my mind whispers. I turn from Dom, take a deep breath, and catch my own gaze in the nearest reflection. It flips backward to a few rides before, as Uhler steps into the elevator holding his phone. He keeps his voice low even though there's no one to overhear him.

Are you there? Show me what to do . . .

His tone is so submissive. So unlike him. I try to hear the response but sounds are always warped in the mirror's sight.

The witch is contained, Uhler whispers. His breath fogs on the glass. His hand drops to his side, his phone dark. *And I possess the offspring. I'm fulfilling my end of the deal. Please, be patient. The gala is only days away. We nearly have all the pieces in place.*

He shudders and lets out a low, pained sob. It's a sound I've never heard him make. Then he's gone, the vision aborted as the elevator clangs to a stop in real life.

"What's happening?" My voice is loud but flat in the stillness. The elevator dial indicates we're halted somewhere between floors five and six.

"It does this sometimes," Dom says. "It'll go in a second." When it doesn't, he tries his key again and jams the button with his thumb.

Something is wrong. I can feel it. I turn, like I'll find a way out in the infinite maze of reflections created by the mirrors. Pairs of me and Dom repeat forever, all of us trapped in the same gilded elevator. Except . . .

I squint into the infinity. I raise my hand and wave. A dozen Athans wave back in sync.

Except for one.

Far, far away—so far that the slight warps in the mirrors have disfigured the reflection—something moves out of sync.

Something massive. Something strange.

The lights in the elevator flicker and I lose sight of it. Beside me, Dom huffs, like this is all an inconvenience to him. I'm afraid the lights will go out fully, but they just come back on even brighter. Dom taps his foot and pushes the L button again. He can't see the thing shifting around out there, in the infinity mirror.

Can I? Even though I'm looking right at it, I can't seem to catch its actual shape. It's like looking through a blister forming upon my own eye. There is something so clearly there, something alien and *wrong*, yet I only register a knotted translucence. And it's not just big, it's fast. The shape darts sideways, circling us, stopping in a version of the elevator a dozen deep. Our reflections warp as it slides over them, shivering every few seconds. The hairs on the back of my neck stand straight up.

"We have to get out of here," I whisper at Dom.

"Athan?" Dom asks. "What are you looking at?"

"Nothing," I say, trying to blink it away. It won't leave. Dread takes hold of me, but then the elevator finally lurches into motion. Dom pushes me into a corner just before the door slides open, hiding me from anyone waiting in the elevator bank.

"Garage. Straight out," he says under the sound of walkie-talkie chatter and boots stomping across tiled floors. "Emergency exit. Wait for my knock. See you soon." Dom slaps the door close button as he leaves, dismissing the elevator and me inside it. Now I'm alone.

Except I'm not. The feeling of being watched crawls over my skin as I stare into the mirrors. The elevator drops, but slowly, an inch at a time. It's like the whole world is holding still, trying not to catch the attention of the thing in the reflections. I need to look away. Maybe if I pretend I can't see it, then it can't see me. Maybe if I just close my eyes, like Yiayia used to do, it will vanish—

Suddenly, the thing bursts forward, caving in the far-off reflection with a muffled crash. That shouldn't be possible. The barrier it broke through isn't *real*. I'm staring into reflections of reflections, into an optical illusion of depth created by light and mirrors.

And yet, the translucent shape scuttles through the breach, toward me. I press into the corner, but I can't look away from it. The details never form an image. It has legs, too many legs. It uses them to draw up its strange, bulbous body and *slam* against the next reflection. Once, twice, it throws its immense body against the wobbling barrier. And just like last time—no, easier—the barrier breaks, causing the thing to tumble one dimension closer to me.

This isn't real. Dr. Wei would tell me this is a projection, a manifestation of trauma. Yet the elevator is physically shaking around me as the thing crashes forward. I can hear the mirrors actually shattering. And I can *feel* it getting closer, like a vise squeezing my skull. I'm cracking, like the glass. Terror webs through me, but when I try to scream, nothing comes out.

It's going to get me.

It's only a few reflections away now. The lights flicker and the flickering makes it easier to see. My eyes gorge themselves on the confused horror of it. Its body shimmers like oil on water. In the iridescent slickness of its coat I make out a great many eyes. Somehow, without meaning to, I've moved to stand right before the mirror, my arms raised up in prayer or protest or resignation.

It's going to get me.

At full speed, it rams the mirror. The real mirror. The one I stand before. I'm looking into a dozen eyes all at once, each the size of my head. In these wet, reflective orbs, I see the elevator door slide open behind me, the garage's dark escape ready for me to run. But I don't move. I can't look away from all these eyes. I can't even blink. My will has been dissolved, and I sense myself being eaten from the inside out.

A thought that is not my own pins me down: *Doesn't it feel so lovely to finally stop running, Athanasios?*

Then, from the dark, Dom jumps into the elevator and claps his hands over my eyes. I snap out of the hypnosis, my terror finally unleashing into my limbs. I grab his hand and keep my head down as we run. The concrete of the garage races below me. We push through a series of doors marked EMERGENCY, but no alarms sound. My feet slap against the pavement until we finally cross a street and I'm met with the rolling cobblestone that borders Central Park.

I see the world rushing by, but at the same time, I see nothing but the memory of that thing burned into the backs of my eyes. The thing that tore through a dozen dimensions to get to me. It was fast, and elegant, and incomprehensible. Its pieces fly together in my imagination, almost against my will, fusing into a monstrous, familiar shape that spreads its legs across the insides of my eyelids.

A spider.

I spy, with my little eyes, the Little Prince.

That's your nickname at the frame shop, isn't it?

It's never quite fit. You've never been little, first of all. At ten you were as tall as Aunt Bernie. She's not really your aunt—you understood that even as a child. She's just someone your parents treated like family because she'd been working at the frame shop since your grandpa ran it. Probably it was she who started the nickname, and she meant it as a badge of honor. After the fire, you felt like you needed to find a reason to hang around the shop, so you made yourself useful and helped the handlers load up their trucks. Seeing a little kid work like that, and with such a serious scowl? It was precious, but it was sad. There was no turning you away, so Bernie let you stay, and she even added your new name to the schedule.

Little Prince. A tribute to who you were when your parents ran the shop, before your yiayia had to sell the business to Uhler. It fit the myth that one day you would be old enough to take it back, and a little prince would become a little king.

You believed that. You took your job so seriously. On the days you worked, you arrived first, warming the truck even before the sunrise. You helped load in the freshly framed artwork, helped navigate to the addresses on the day's delivery route, helped unload the priceless pieces into their new homes, and even hung them up when the clients asked.

You were very, very careful. Always. You never so much as scratched the glass atop a priceless painting, until the day you saw me.

You probably don't remember. You were in a gallery somewhere in Chelsea, helping carry a large painting that had just been sold and needed to be wrapped up. You grasped one side while someone else—not Bernie, it was too heavy for her—held the other. You were looking down into the glass as you carried it, and you passed beneath a mirrored ceiling. The light above shone just right, bouncing up into your eyes at the perfect angle, and you saw it. Something massive in the reflection above, hurtling toward you with a wide and hungry embrace.

You dropped the painting, and the glass webbed in cracks. The painting was fine, but the frame job wasn't. When the men told Bernie, she brushed it off, saying it wasn't a big deal and pointing out they shouldn't be too diligent about reporting it to Uhler, since you were underage and shouldn't have been helping at all. Someone else took the fall, and after a hundred apologies from you, the others finally told you to get over it. Shit happens, they said. Shit happens to everyone, all the time. You ain't special. Toughen up and do it right the next time.

But after that, *Little Prince* was said with a sneer.

And isn't that when you finally started believing Yiayia about the thing inside the mirrors?

CHAPTER FIVE

We stop running somewhere deep in the north woods of Central Park. Surrounded by trees, I feel the sickening captivation from the elevator detach, and not in a subtle way. It's a distinct feeling of being released, like something had curled around my mind until now, where it was forced to let go in this dense forest.

Maybe Dom feels it, too. He stands near me, panting for breath, saying nothing. His eyes never leave the direction we ran from.

"They're not chasing us," he says through deep gasps.

I'm panting so hard, my lungs burn. "Who?"

"The police. Who else?"

Dom thought we were escaping from the police, but I was running from that thing in the mirror. Was it really there, or some trick of my Sight? If I had stood in the elevator a moment longer, would it have really broken into our world? Or might it have broken into *me*? There was a psychic . . . pressure to it that I felt boring into my mind. The longer I looked, the less I could look away.

Just like Yiayia and her hand mirror.

My mind races with all Yiayia's warnings about what might look back at me if I stared into a mirror too long. For Yiayia, a curse wasn't some mystical abstraction. It was conscious. Aware. Real enough to reach out and touch you, if you let it. It's why she purged our apartment of mirrors, even tossing out our television when she caught me trying to rewind its reflective black face.

Is this what we've been hiding from? What's captivated my grandmother for all these years, eating away her mind bit by bit?

"What the fuck happened back there?"

Dom's voice knocks me out of my spiral. I stop pacing and glance at him. He's holding his bag to his chest, studying me. He must have seen the way I was transfixed in the elevator, but he couldn't see by what. In a way, I'm relieved. Yiayia always says that curses can be contagious. That certain things can never be unseen.

I think of the people at the party the night before. I still don't know what happened, but clearly *something* sinister had spread between them. This boy, Dom, was there, too. Twice now, he's warned me of danger just before it hits. So what does he know?

Determined not to answer Dom's question until I'm sure I can trust him, I shrug.

"When you didn't meet me at the exit, I thought maybe the elevator got stuck again," he says slowly. "But then I found you downstairs, just standing there. You're lucky I found you before those cops did."

"I'm sorry," I say, shrugging again.

Dom shakes his head. "You were staring into that mirror pretty hard. Why?"

"It was nothing," I say, my throat dry and my voice cracking. If I don't sound the alarm, there's nothing to be alarmed about.

Dom leans back against a tree. The noises of the woods fill in our silence. I always forget Central Park has these pockets of forest that block out any sight of the city, like you're off in the middle of the Catskills or something. Then a siren wails down the West Side and the illusion breaks.

Dom's breathing steadies. He never looks away from me. I have a chance to finally study him now, too. He is short and sharp and poised, like a drawing of a fairy. He has rich brown skin and pretty black eyelashes—each perfectly spaced, like the delicate spikes of a Venus fly-trap. His eyes are such a dark brown they're nearly onyx, absorbing the light around us and pulling me into a stare that never falters, never wavers from me, never even blinks. He reminds me of someone.

He reminds me of Uhler.

"Who are you?" I ask. Again.

No response. Dom just stares at me. I can feel the gravity of that stare lifting me up and weighing me against whatever mysterious considerations are going on behind his eyes. Is he deciding how much to tell me? Or how much I can handle?

Well, even if on the inside I'm scared, I know my outsides look tough. I rise to my full height, towering over him.

"You know . . ." I growl. "I've had a *really* rough morning, on exactly no sleep. And I'm finding myself short on patience. I'm not going to ask again, so line up your answers and we'll knock out the small talk all at once, okay?" I count on my fingers, leaning a little closer with each question. "Who are you? What were you doing at the party last night? And *where* is my motherfucking grandmother?"

I'm inches from Dom's face yet he doesn't budge. Like, at all. I end up being the one to flinch back. I cross my arms and try to look tough, but Dom just pushes off the tree and walks around me, completely unintimidated.

"Fine," he says, glancing around warily, "but not here."

Dom leads me through the woods and down a trail. He hides us under a stone bridge arching over a sluggish stream, then turns back to me with a sigh.

"I'm a survivor, just like you," he says. "Last night, at the party, when everything went . . . wrong? That's not the first time something like that has happened in this city."

Dom fusses with his bandanna while he talks. A nervous tic. He whispers so low it's hard to hear him over the echoing water, and all this tells me he's just as scared to open up as I am.

"For months I've been looking into similar outbreaks of violence," he continues, "trying to figure out the cause. And I think I'm close."

I'm breathing fast again. Every word he says scares me, but I need more.

"What do you know?" I press.

"There's a pattern to the outbreaks. The types of places, the types of people, the timing. I've been tracking it all for . . . for a while." He holds his bag tighter. "The police cover up the scenes. Paperwork on the victims gets buried. The news doesn't report on it, and anyone who talks too much winds up hurt. It's not safe to look into the attacks, so I have to be careful. Still, I've managed to put together a theory, which was proven correct last night. I predicted something would happen at that party. I was right."

"If you knew it was going to happen, why didn't you try to stop it?"

"I *did*," Dom says bitterly. "Why do you think I was there? But it's not that easy. Something . . . overcomes the victims. That's why I hid you. I meant to come back, but the police beat me there. I wasn't even sure you'd survived. I just hope others—"

"No one else survived," I say. "Only me."

Dom goes quiet. We listen to the stream for a moment. I expect him to defend his decision to run away, but he doesn't. When he speaks again, there's an edge to his whisper.

"That's not true. Uhler was at the party. He escaped, too."

I shiver. Uhler, who insisted I attend the party in the first place. And who was ready to give me up to the cops. Who *tricked* me by telling me he had Yiayia safe and sound, and he was just happy to have us all under his roof again. But all he had was that room full of weird notes and photos, and that ancient photo of Yiayia—the only sign he might know where she actually is.

Uhler lied, Dom said.

Is Dom suggesting Uhler had something to do with all those people dying? How is that even possible? If there's a pattern here, I can't find it among the grisly pieces. It's too much, too fast.

"I've been watching him for years," Dom pushes on. "As an intern, at Orion House, his company. I've infiltrated his work and his home. I've read his notes and studied his schedule, and it's all led me to this. Nothing is what it seems." Dom takes a deep breath. "Not this city. Not Uhler. Not even you and me. Everything we know is held up by hidden strings, and there's a group of people pulling those strings."

"Like a secret society?" I say skeptically.

"I don't know."

"A cult?"

Dom glances up at the mossy underside of the bridge. The whites of his eyes shine. "They don't have a public name, at least not one I could find. It's taken me years to even figure out they're real and not some wild conspiracy theory."

"No offense, but yeah, this kinda sounds like a conspiracy theory. Let me guess—your secret society is unfathomably influential?"

He narrows his eyes. "And very dangerous. And they kill anyone who sees too much."

"Like . . ." I try to keep my voice doubtful, but it cracks. "Like the people who died at the party?"

Dom shrugs. "Maybe. I think the deaths are part of a ritual, or maybe an experiment or game. Like I said, there's a pattern to the deaths, but I still don't know the *why*."

I cross my arms. I'm skeptical, but the more Dom says, the deeper the chill gets beneath my skin. I try to shake it off. What would Dr. Wei say if he knew I was starting to buy this secret society bullshit?

"What do you know?" I ask. "The *facts*, please."

"Uhler is one of them," Dom blurts. "His company, Orion House, provides spaces for their meetings and activities. And handlers, for moving their most secure stuff—art and artifacts. They seem to collect things. Rare or dangerous things."

At the mention of handlers, that chill becomes full-fledged frostbite.

I think of my family's frame shop, and the countless boxes of priceless art I've moved in and out of anonymous swanky apartments. I've seen palatial interiors hidden within unremarkable buildings. I've seen modest doors with no addresses open into entire worlds of excess, completely incongruous with the grime of the city, like hidden dimensions. Is this the world Dom speaks of? And if so, have I been a part of it all along?

Suddenly, Dom's reason for rescuing me begins to make sense. If I can access this alleged secret society, then I'm useful to him.

"You believe me," Dom says, reading the understanding on my face.

"I'm just listening." I shake my head. There's a frenzied look to Dom now, something that tells me to be careful. Dr. Wei would say that we mustn't light our way with the flame of fear. It'll make the shadows of even small things into impossible monsters. This, I decide, is Dom's impossible monster.

"Orion House absorbed a framing and handling company years ago," Dom says. "That belonged to your family, didn't it? You're the 'Little Prince'?"

The mention of my nickname betrays just how much Dom actually knows about me. So far, he's given me only the bare minimum, baiting me out of my shell. And as cute and fascinating as this boy is, his fixation with Uhler can't become mine. I have to find Yiayia before that thing in the mirror finds me.

Refocused, I step back. "Listen, all I know for sure is that my grandmother is missing and I need to find her. She could still be in a hospital somewhere." Dom tries to protest but I cut him off. "Yes, Uhler bought her company, but only because *she* couldn't manage it anymore. She got sick, so she sold it to him. But as soon as she's well again, we're buying it back for cheap. He promised."

Dom shakes his head. "You don't know."

I'm getting annoyed now. "Know what?"

Dom opens his bag and pulls out a sketchbook. It looks familiar, but I can't think where I'd have seen it before. In a sheaf at the back, he pulls out a pack of papers, photos, and clippings. He locates one and hands it to me, stating, "That's from seven years ago."

I'm looking at a scanned document. The top reads CERTIFICATE OF DEATH. I have to read the name a few times. Evangeline Bakirtzis. That's Yiayia's name, too.

I thrust the paper toward him. "What the fuck is this?"

"Your yiayia is dead," Dom states. "Legally. Until I met you, I thought she was another victim. But she's been alive all this time, hasn't she?"

"Of course she's alive," I croak.

"I know that now. But Athan, she didn't sell Uhler her company willingly. She lost everything when her death was filed almost a decade ago. Uhler took it all over. She didn't have a choice."

My hand is trembling as Dom gently takes back the paper, folds it, and hides it away.

"I don't understand," I whisper in a small voice. It's like I can feel my memories rotting in my head, peeling away to reveal an ugly truth I'm not ready to face.

Dom is gentle as he lines it all up. "The spontaneous outbreaks of violence. The cover-ups. Uhler and his connections. Your family's business. They're connected, and I'm close to figuring out how. But I'm missing something important."

"What?"

"You."

I swallow. Absurdly, I find myself standing straighter, wanting to look the part of the hero Dom's mistaken me for.

"What do you want from me?"

Dom steps toward me. Just two small, polite steps. There's a formality to his posture that alerts me to the serious nature of what he's about to propose.

"Uhler has property all over the city. Places without addresses, that aren't on any maps. But I've been trailing him for years. I'll help you find your grandmother, but in exchange, I need your help finding out what his group is up to. Then, once we do, I need you to promise you won't stop me."

"Stop you from what?"

Dom blinks, like it's the most obvious thing in the world.

"I'm going to kill him, Athan. I'm going to kill all of them."

Of all the things said to you at all the parties, of all the drunk pledges people breathed into your face, of all the brags and begs and boasts that have spilled from lips loosened by alcohol, or drugs, or the ever-more-potent rush of possibility, you believed approximately none of it.

None. Of. It.

Occasionally you even wanted to, but you know the future is never guaranteed. The only certainty is death—the quiet catastrophe that awaits everyone. But even that could be diverted if you were good enough, scared enough, or small enough to never get noticed.

But you're not at a party, and this doesn't sound like a drunken pledge. It's certainly not a boast.

It's a promise.

This boy, the one who has pulled you away from certain death each time he's met you, means to drag you into the death of another.

A great many others, if he has his way.

The question is, Little Prince, what scares you more? The chance that he's wrong about everything, or the chance that he's right?

CHAPTER SIX

I'm going to kill him, Athan. I'm going to kill all of them.

I blink at Dom.

"You're joking, right?"

"Try me," he says grimly. I blink again and he's gone—walking out onto the wooded path, his hands shoved into his jacket pockets. I chase after him.

"You're plotting a *murder*?" I rasp. I have to keep my voice down as two joggers lope toward us. "Based on what? Rumors?"

"Spare me the pearl clutching. You saw what happened to those people at the party, right? Imagine that times ten. Times twenty. Uhler's slaughters are getting grander every time. He's hosting a gala at the end of this week. What if that's his next target?"

"What if it's not? What if all this is in your head?"

Eyes straight ahead, Dom says, "If he's dead, it won't matter either way."

I shake my head, marveling at the irony here. He's got this all wrong. I can't say what Uhler is or isn't involved in, but I do know what I saw in that mirror. That thing was so much less comprehensible than some secret society of murderous art collectors, and so much worse. I almost laugh.

"But . . . *how*?" I ask.

Dom won't say more. I adjust to his quick pace and we hurry side by side, past a man walking three dogs at once. Pit bulls with huge, goofy grins. They pull the man along on leashes clipped to his belt. I feel like that with Dom—yanked forward by tethers I can't unclip. I'm speeding out of control, and I don't like it. So I do the only thing I can think of and turn on the charm.

"Look, I don't spook easily," I say, "but isn't this a bit much for a first meeting? Can't we start with coffee, and then maybe save murdering people for date two?"

"This isn't a date."

"What is it, then?"

"We're making a deal. Help for help."

"Do you even know which hospital my grandmother is actually in?"

"She's not in a hospital."

"Then where is she? The Times Square Olive Garden?"

Dom sighs. I'm not focusing on his grand revenge, which is clearly all-consuming. He offers no further response. I switch to an easier line of questions.

"How old are you?"

"Seventeen. Eighteen in March."

"A Pisces?"

He clenches his jaw. "I don't see why it matters."

I grin. "I'm a Scorpio myself. What's Dom short for?"

"Dominik."

Aha! Progress. "Well, you know, Dominik, you're very hard to nego-tiate with."

He stops and I nearly run into his back. He doesn't turn to face me, just gives me his profile. Honestly, that's enough to shut me up for a second. How can someone so small be so scary?

"Probably because this isn't a negotiation, Athanasios."

Damn, did he have to whip out the entire *Athanasios*? Our walk resumes. I try again. "You want something from me; I want something from you. Didn't anyone ever teach you how to work with others? Or were you one of those gifted kids who always got pulled out of playtime to go impress the adults? You've got that gifted look—"

"This usually works for you, doesn't it?" Dom spins around fully now, halting us both. "The charm, the flirtation?"

"Well, I assume you didn't rescue me twice in twenty-four hours because I'm *not* cute, right?"

"Quit it," Dom says. "I'm sure a lot of people fall for the clueless muscular guy, but you're not actually that clueless, are you? You're terrified. But if you can pretend hard enough, maybe you can be the kind of person that nothing bad ever happens to, right? Handsome, affable, no strings attached, no real vulnerabilities or chances to get hurt. Well, that's not going to work on me—just like it didn't work on Uhler. The only person you're fooling is yourself—and look what happened. You practically *invited* Uhler to manipulate you."

I step back. My instincts scream to make some sort of evasive joke to lighten the mood, but I know now that won't work. Dom's immune to my charms.

"I see you," Dom says, stepping toward me, finger thrust into my chest. "I see you, Athan, and I need you to be real with me, or we're both going to die very painful deaths."

The muscles of my face twitch in a nervous grin. The ground feels unsteady here, like Dom's pushed me to the edge of a cliff. "You've known me for ten minutes total," I say.

"I've got a good eye for fakes."

This, for some reason, is what cracks me.

"Fine," I grind out. "You want direct? Yes, I'm scared—of *you*. I'm halfway convinced you're more dangerous than Uhler at this point. I'm worried about my grandmother, and I don't have *any* fucking idea what just happened back there. Uhler's a longtime family friend. He invites me to parties! Yes, he can be distant and haughty—but *murderous*? I thought he was going to help me, and I saw—"

I cut myself off, remembering the conversation I witnessed in the elevator mirrors. Uhler said he had the *witch*, and something about offspring. Did he mean Yiayia and me?

I draw a quick breath. "That's all I've got for you," I finish, hoping Dom isn't nearly as observant as he believes.

"You saw something in the elevator," he says. "What?"

Fuck, I think. He's way too perceptive. But if Dom could actually read my mind, he'd run. He's not ready for what hides in my head.

I shrug.

"I don't blame you for being cagey," he says. "But have you considered the thing you're trying to hide might be the key to all this—including finding your grandmother?"

I've never told anyone about my Sight. Not even Dr. Wei. Curses and evil eyes hiding behind every reflection? Sure. But not that. I have so much fear surrounding the power that even just holding the thought long enough to explain it to someone is terrifying. And Dom is a stranger. Totally, utterly strange.

But unlike everyone I've ever met, he seems to see right through me. Into me. And for some unfathomable reason, I yearn to be the version of Athan he's looking for. Honest, for once. Free from all this shame.

"Mirrors show you things, don't they?" Dom presses.

If I never look into a mirror again, it'll still be too soon. But Dom faces me like a dark reflection, like *I'm* the mirror and there's no way he'll settle with just a glimpse. He wants to see it all.

"What if I said yes?" I ask. "Would you even believe me?"

"No," Dom says simply.

I nearly collapse. What the fuck is wrong with this boy?

"Seeing is believing," he says with a sly smile. "It's time for a test."

We end up at the Guggenheim.

Like, the big white beehive-looking museum on the east side of Central Park. I nearly dig my heels into the ground when Dom leads us through the glass doors. Places like this are for tourists and cost money, but Dom just rolls his eyes at me and pays for both our tickets.

All this feels off-limits. The inside of the museum is too vast, too nice, too white. It's more like a sculpture than a building. It's all hollow on the inside, with just a single ramp winding along the walls, circling up and up and up into a bright, hushed emptiness.

The very top of the museum is a huge sunroof. The way the bars between the windows spread out in a radial pattern, it looks like a huge, unblinking eye. Or the web of a spider. I think of the afterimage of whatever attacked me in the elevator, and just as quickly shove it all away.

"Athan."

Dom's hand wraps around my elbow, steadying me. I guess I was starting to lean, looking straight up instead of where I was going. Good thing Dom is keeping a close eye on me, or I'd have toppled into a low basin of water on the lobby floor.

"Why here?" I ask. We start up the ramp, to the first floor of art.

"It's public. And the whole museum is basically a single path. We can see anyone trailing us."

"You really think they'll come after us?"

"Not us. Barely anyone noticed me in the lobby. You. And no, I doubt they'd track us here, but it's better to be safe. Uhler prefers discretion, so the best place for us to hide is in plain sight."

I wrap my arms around myself. I'm shivering. My adrenaline is running out and what's left is a throbbing fatigue in my muscles. I want to just lie down; I want to keep running. I want answers. I want to forget all this. I want to go home and find Yiayia in our tiny kitchen, have her tell me to take a nap while she boils a pot of water for dinner.

Dom is studying me again. I throw him a sly smile to hide my stress. He's been in a better mood since I agreed to his little test. He might even be kind of cute, when he's not being so scary.

"Thanks for helping me," I say. "Last night and just now. I'm grateful."

"You shouldn't thank me," Dom says, breaking eye contact, like he's embarrassed by my gratitude. "I did it so I could use you." It's the first time I've seen him look any type of vulnerable since he told me he needed my help at Uhler's apartment.

"Ah, is the serial-killer-to-be feeling shy?" I can't help how much this amuses me. Finally, this boy has a crack in his guard. I must be delirious, because I decide to poke at it. "I'm alive and I thank you for it. You're my hero. Deal with it."

Dom blushes. He looks at the floor as we walk. I can't tell if he's thinking or if he's mad or if he's scared. He's unreadable to me. Probably on purpose.

He stops us halfway up the museum, near a section lit in warm lights the color of afternoon sunbeams. A group of schoolchildren clump before an intricate crisscross of spikes jutting from a low concrete dais. Skewered among the spikes is a massive, metallic amoeba. It drips into mirrored puddles on the dais. It looks like it's melting, but the whole thing is solid.

Dom sucks in a breath.

"Mirrors," he says finally. "They . . . respond to you."

I go still. So this is it?

Duh, Athan, I think. *What did you think this test would be?* Once I tell him about the Sight, there's no taking it back.

"You . . . see things in them. Visions. Things that happened in the past, right?"

Suddenly, it's like I'm alone with Dom. Just him and me in the vast white space. I feel trapped. I can run, sure, but it wouldn't do any good. The question has been asked. My family's most precious secret has been flung out like a lasso. It's around me now, a tether formed between us, and Dom is gradually pulling it tight.

He draws close. "I'm right. I can see it in your face. Listen, Athan. Listen to me. Maybe you thought it wasn't real, or that you were going insane. But I'm here to tell you it's none of those things. In Uhler's office, you saw all those photos on the wall, right? Uhler has been tracking down people like you for years. You and your yiayia are all over his notes. He knows she can do it, but he's unsure about you. It's less common in men. I'll admit I was skeptical myself, but just now in the elevator, you saw something, didn't you?"

I hate this.

I hate the conflicting fear and validation breaking over me, like waves of ice and fire.

Up until this moment, I still could have vanished into the deception that my power and the monster it showed me were nothing more than a nervous breakdown. And I could have dismissed Dom and his theories about Uhler as unfounded paranoia. Apart, we were just two broken boys transfixed by our own impossible monsters, like Dr. Wei warned me against. But now we're together, and with each word Dom is overlapping our monsters. He's layering them together like two incoherent patterns combined to create an optical illusion, shocking the eye with the sudden, uncanny depth.

It's all starting to feel horribly real. Right now, *Dr. Wei* feels like the abstraction.

"Yeah," I say finally. "I mean, yes. Mirrors show me things. And I know I'm not crazy."

Not yet, I think.

"And your . . . power. Does it work on anything reflective? Will it work on this?"

I don't say yes, but I don't say no.

"Show me. Please." Dom turns toward the sculpture. Kids are making faces into it.

"You won't be able to see what I see," I tell him.

"That's okay. I just need proof."

"How?"

Dom moves us closer as his answer. The second our reflections slide into view, I want to back up. Stepping forward feels like reaching into a darkness where something hungry lurks. What if that thing is waiting to strike again?

Dom reads my hesitation. "Try. And I'll be right here the whole time, standing guard."

I fake a smug smile and brush him off as I position myself before my waiting reflection. It hovers over me on the metallic surface like a ghost. When I'm ready, I look into its eyes and feel the connection go taut. I watch myself slide away, into the past; I watch the sculpture reflect hundreds of other faces peering at it from where I now stand. Then the reflection empties as the museum rewinds into early morning, then last night.

Yesterday begins to play backward on the surface, starting with a janitor mopping the floors in the late evening. As I watch, I scan the background for any distortions of the air, but the metal's surface stretches everything. If that thing is in there, I won't see it until it's too close.

"What am I looking for?" I ask.

"Do you always need to know what you're looking for?" Dom's voice asks from beside me.

"No, but it helps."

"You'll know it when you see it," Dom says. His voice is low and strained, like he's focusing very hard to see what I see. But he can't. I know he can't, because eventually he gives up and just studies me from my periphery.

I focus on the mirror, pushing it into the previous day. People slide by, stop, make silly faces, take photos, give peace signs. A father holds his baby up to it. The baby stares, all starry-eyed, and then smiles a big, goofy grin. I know it's smiling at its dad, not me, but I feel the warmth. I feel the inquisitive joy in all the faces that pass the globe. People look into mirrors with such unguarded curiosity, never thinking that someone else is looking back.

I wonder what that must be like—and as I lose focus, the visions fly by faster. The mirror's edge begins to glow and warm, like they always do if I push them too far. Dom gasps. He steps back, along with many of the museum visitors, as heat exhales from the sculpture.

My focus frays even more, and I nearly lose the reflection. But then something flashes in the vision. Orange, black, and white. I skim back to it, careful to catch it this time. I pause, and then smirk.

I release the reflection. Dom looks at me with dour scrutiny.

"You were here last week," I say. "You stood right in this spot, for a few minutes."

"What was I wearing?"

"Your bandanna."

"I always wear this. What else?"

I think back to the brief glimpse. I didn't think there would be a quiz.

"A . . . windbreaker?"

"Be more specific."

I roll my eyes. "Look, babe, I'm not that kind of gay. I'm pansexual. We don't know shit about jackets."

"That's reductive," Dom quips. "It's a bomber jacket, for your pansexual information."

"I'll let the other pansexuals know. Do you want me to guess the designer of your shoes, too? Or do you believe me now?"

Dom gives me what I suspect is a very, very rare smile. There's wonder in his voice now. "So it's true. The Sight is really real."

I shrug. "As really real as it gets, I guess."

"You don't seem excited about being the literal embodiment of proof that psychic powers are real?"

I shrug again. "It's not how I think of it. I'm not like *whoa, cool, I have powers* because powers are useful in movies and stuff. All I can do is see what mirrors have seen. And do you know what mirrors see? A lot of people staring at themselves, fixing their hair, and popping zits. Private stuff I don't want to watch. I'm not a perv."

Dom shakes his head. "You're wrong. It *is* useful."

I grin. "So *you're* the perv?"

I end up having to chase after Dom again as he stalks away, higher into the museum's coil. I'm laughing, but that smile has vanished when I catch up.

"I passed, right? I passed your little test."

"You did."

"So what, then? We're partners? Officially?"

"No."

I have never met someone less willing to give me anything to work with. Maybe I'm just loopy with exhaustion, but talking to this guy is kind of thrilling. He's like a little puzzle that I have no idea how to figure out. We pull off to the side of the ramp, overlooking the drop. Dom is quiet, like he's doing math in his head or something. I stare down toward the lobby below and feel a flicker of vertigo before pulling back. It reminds me of being on the roof this morning, running to escape the penthouse. I shove down the memory the moment I think of it, turning back to Dom. Someone's got to break the ice and it might as well be me.

"Okay, my turn, then. Secret for secret. Who are you? Like. Actually."

Dom answers right away. "I'm no one."

"No one is no one," I say.

"Exactly. I'm no one, who is no one. Ask something more specific."

"Were you always no one? Were you assigned *no one* at birth, or is this a recent transition into anonymity?"

Dom's lips twitch, like he might just smile again, but then he says, "Does it ever get tiring? Trying to be so pleasant."

"Harsh. But fair. And why yes, it does. I'm exhausted. I could fall asleep, right here." For effect I close my eyes and make like I'm going to tip over the railing, right into the drop, and I'm pleased to feel Dom rush to grab on to me. I crack an eye open.

"Gotcha." I grin.

He rolls his eyes. "You're *not* funny."

"And you're *kind of* a dick."

I feel bad the moment I say it, but Dom doesn't look offended. There's a flicker of surprise in his eyes, like he's never actually realized this about himself. I conclude he doesn't talk to other people a lot.

"You're right," he says. "I'm not nice. I'm not like you. I don't really know how to be . . . good. I don't even know how to try. I'm sorry."

"You don't need to be someone you're not," I say. I put on my Dr. Wei voice, even though Dom won't get the reference. "But why don't we start with who you actually are? Before this obsession with Uhler. Before secret societies and clandestine internships—who was Dom?"

Dom nods. He doesn't look sure, though. "That's exactly the issue," he says slowly. Then, after a deep breath, "I'm Uhler's son."

Oh.

Oh.

Oh, indeed.

You have a lot of questions.

A lot.

Uhler came to your birthdays and school plays and picnics. You lived with him for years. And in all that time he spent hovering over your life, a dark thunderhead that pressurized every space he entered, he never once indicated having a family outside of you and Yiayia.

But what about the guest room at his house, full of another person's things? There were sketchbooks there, just like the one you saw this boy leaf through under the bridge. And of course Dom had his own key to the elevator.

Most damning of all is the way the boy talks. So deliberate, with such conviction; a modest presence betraying an interior as vast and rich as any well-appointed penthouse. It's the same quiet pressure. The same storm in a jar.

He's not lying.

It's subtle, but you back away from him. Of course he notices, and he seems to accept the distance as inevitable.

I don't know if you believe in hell, he says, *but I do. I'll end up there one way or another. I've made peace with that. But you're not sure yet. So that's why I'm being specific in my wording. I'm not asking you to hurt anyone. I am asking that when the time comes, you won't stop me from doing what I need to do.*

You ask how you could possibly promise something like that. Dom shrugs and says, *That's between you and your gods. Think about it. If you're ready to learn more, meet me at the café that looks like a church one block up. If you don't want to, then don't. I understand. All I'll say to persuade you is that you've only just started to see what Uhler is capable of, and you know it's not pretty.*

The only way to stop what comes next is to see what came before, and that's something only you can do. Only you can look.

The vision of all those bodies piled up in the penthouse glows in the dark of your mind. You thought it was you and your predatory curse that did that to those people, but what if Dom's right? About Uhler? About the killings and the people behind them? Dom is telling you there's much more to uncover, so many ugly truths trapped in the gaze of mirrors that never looked away, never even blinked.

I'll see you in an hour, Dom says. *Or I won't.*

Dom leaves you in the museum and you're alone with your questions. They only seem to multiply the more you think about them. So do the bodies in your mind. A few becomes a dozen, and a dozen becomes a hundred. As many bodies as you have questions.

Eventually, none of these questions end up mattering, because the one answer you have glows brightest of all. Uhler tried to hurt you, and he will certainly hurt Yiayia unless you do something to stop him.

And then you see the strands again. Silvery threads slipping in the air, like you saw slashed through the gore of the penthouse party. You follow their glimmering lines until you see what they lead to. It's Dom, crossing the lobby. When he exits the museum, the strands follow, melting through the walls like liquid light.

A web has been spun. One that connects Dom and Uhler, you and Yiayia; that connects the slaughter you survived to the thing that rampaged up from the depths of infinity to find you. You're caught in it, that much is clear. But so is Dom.

The part of you that needs to be a hero blazes to life. You keep stoking that flame with your determination to save Yiayia, but hidden in the brightness is the spark of something you won't be aware of until it's much too late. A tricky bit of vanity that slyly whispers: *He needs you, Athan. More than he knows. More than he's asking. Only you can save him, not from Uhler, but from the darkness threading his words.*

That's what I tug upon, to move you past these doubts.

You hurry down the spiral of the Guggenheim. Down, down, down you go, the unblinking eye of the skylight glaring at your back the whole time.

CHAPTER SEVEN

I find the café. A hostess seats me inside, at a table tucked into a stone arch. The café really is inside a church, it feels like. I order a coffee just to have something to do while I wait.

Without Dom here staring at me, it's easier to think. And not for the first time today, I think of Dr. Wei.

He warns against the type of grandiose paranoia that places us as the focal points of some vast conspiracy. The way my life has been, and the way Yiayia is, it's easy to see how I might succumb to that kind of delusion. Now I'm not sure. I'm not sure of anything at all.

My coffee arrives. The smell reminds me of early mornings at the frame shop, and the simple happiness I felt watching the handlers joke around while we worked. But soon the memory darkens, like a photograph overdeveloping. Colors grow overbright, revealing patterns in their saturation. Designs, all around me. My doubt is reaching backward in time, infecting my memories.

No. *No.* I rub the sleepiness from my eyes and gulp down the scalding coffee. Dom is so sure of what he's seen, but delusions can be all-consuming like that. Am I really willing to let him kill, just to find out if he's right?

This question spins and spins in my head, finally wobbling to a stop and giving me my answer. But in the same moment, Dom enters. He looks at me, plainly excited, like he wasn't sure I'd be here. He joins me at the table and when the server swings by, he orders hot cocoa. Despite my misgivings, my heart softens. Mass murderers don't order hot cocoa, right?

I scoot my empty coffee cup around on its saucer. It's no wonder I'm so jumpy. All I've had today is caffeine, two bites of strawberry pancake, and a whole lot of pain. The diet of a real New Yorker.

"I know you think there's some kind of conspiracy going on," I whisper after the cocoa has been delivered. "I'm not saying shit isn't fucked up, but no matter what happens, I'm not hurting anyone. I'm in this to find my yiayia."

Dom purses his lips and I'm quick to say the rest.

"If Uhler is really as bad as you say he is, we'll figure out a way to stop him. But *no* murder."

"I'm not asking you to hurt anyone—"

"No," I cut him off. "I know what you're asking, and I'm telling you it doesn't matter whose hands do the hurting. We'll find another way, or you can find someone else to do your fancy forensic mirror magic."

Dom stares sullenly at his cocoa. It's kind of cute but, like, in a murdery way? Like a drenched cat.

"Fine," he says.

"Fine, what?"

"Fine, I will not hurt Uhler."

"Or any others."

"Or any others," Dom mutters.

"Including my yiayia."

Dom shoots me an exasperated glare.

I shrug. "Can't be too careful."

Dom shrugs back, like this is a reasonable conversation to be having in a coffee shop that looks like a church. I notice that he's dressed differently now. He wears the same bandanna around his neck, but now he's got on a simple black turtleneck, and he carries a bulging crossbody bag on one shoulder. He heaves it onto a nearby chair, rummages through it, and pulls out his large, leather-bound sketchbook.

"I went back to grab a few things," he explains. "No one was at the apartment. The police are gone, probably looking for you. Your phone is off, right?"

"Dead."

"Good. You can't go home. I have a plan, though, assuming you've decided to help me . . . stop Uhler."

I raise my nose primly, like I'm still deciding. Dom grips the sketchbook so tightly his knuckles change color. He doesn't see my smirk. I note the strange pride I feel at having gotten him to alter his plan. And I do want to help him. Like me, he's scared, and like me, he hides it so well.

It also doesn't hurt that he's very my type. I always fall for the artsy queers, dammit.

Behind our booth, there's a wall-mounted mirror. In the reflection, I scan the air above us for those silvery threads, but they're gone again. Still, it's not my imagination that Dom always seems to be pulling against an invisible tension. Even now, he's like a knot of stress.

"It's dangerous," he adds. "And probably not what you wanted. But I really think we have a chance at this if we team up. So, will you help me?"

He needs help. *My* help. I relent with a nod. He relaxes, but the moment doesn't feel grand enough. I reach across the table and extend the pinkie of my right hand.

"Let's make it official," I say.

Dom raises an eyebrow. "With a pinkie promise?"

"Did you want a contract?"

"No, but—"

"Do you see a notary in here?"

"No, but—"

"Pinkie, please."

Dom sighs, but he does it. We hook pinkies and in unison kiss the knuckles of our fists. A jolt pings down my spine. Dom's cheeks are flushed when he scoots back into his chair. We've touched before; he grabbed my hand to yank me out of the elevator. This feels different. This time, it was a little hard to let go.

We both sit there, embarrassed, and I have to prompt him to show me what he's got going on in that sketchbook. He opens it to the back page and pulls out, to no one's surprise, packets of papers and photos. It's like a minified version of Uhler's office.

"It's hard to know where to begin with this," he says. "I've never shared any of it."

"Start at the beginning?" I suggest.

"You know the basics already," he says. "Uhler is my dad, but just on paper. He took me in a few years ago, probably right after you moved out. I moved here from California, finished high school online early, and started working at Orion House doing mostly backroom stuff in their showroom. I was around a lot, and people tend to forget about me, and so I learned plenty just by listening and watching. That's when I met Dane Boucher. They were a young artist who Uhler was mentoring, so they were in the showroom all the time, too. Everyone knew them. We were kinda friendly. And then, just before their first big gallery show, they died."

"Died?" I stumble on the word. "Like, they went from alive to unalive?"

"Correct. The police reported it as an accident, but I . . . I thought there was more to it."

"How did they die?"

"They were impaled." Dom says this matter-of-factly, like stating that someone took a run to the corner store for ice cream.

"Impaled? Like, something stabbed them?"

"And came out the other side. Yes."

I put out my hand and Dom, unsure, gives me his pinkie again. I smooth out his fist so that I can cup his fingers in mine and give them a squeeze. "Do you think you could try a little harder to be a bit more detailed? Talking to you is like spooky twenty questions."

Dom pulls away his hand and opens his sketchbook. My eyes fill with drawings of what I first mistake for a sea urchin floating in the night sky. Then the rest of the sketch comes into focus and I see it's actually some sort of star hanging over a room full of people. It's done in colorful pencil, but it's soft and luminous. I whistle at Dom's talent.

"Dane's specialty was LED sculptures. Uhler was working with them on custom chandeliers. There was a show where the pieces were going to be revealed, but then Dane was found dead. One of the hanging sculptures fell while they were under it."

"But you don't think that it was an accident, do you?"

Dom points at his drawing. The urchin sculpture is held aloft by an elaborate web of cords.

"If one of these snapped, the sculpture would swing. But it fell straight down. For that to happen, all the cords would have to release at once, which they did."

"How is that possible?" I ask.

"Knots, I think," Dom says. "I only have this sketch I did a few days before, but the cords rigging the sculpture are knotted together. I read online that sometimes theaters use special knots to suspend things they want to drop straight down all at once, like a backdrop."

I'm not really understanding the relevance of this just yet. I ask, "You think Uhler dropped a chandelier on Dane, *Phantom of the Opera* style?"

"Uhler was nowhere near the gallery at the time. It was probably Dane who pulled the cord the wrong way while setting up for the show."

"But you said you thought it wasn't an accident."

Dom is getting flustered. "Let me finish."

I spread my hands out, showing Dom it's his show. He shuffles his papers and pulls out a few printed articles.

"Dane was the first I knew about, but there were others. People always seemed to be dying around Uhler—no one as close, but former associates and past clients and occasionally important people in the design world. At first I thought it was a coincidence, but then I found the pattern."

"What's the pattern?"

Dom shows me a few pages of texts and scanned photos. News articles and documents that look like redacted police reports from TV shows, except these are the real deal. Yiayia's death certificate is among them.

"Sometimes it's an accident that looks a little too tidy, and sometimes it's spontaneous violence among friends, like what you survived last night. But each time, there are three things in common."

Dom taps his drawing of the star that fell on Dane.

"Obviously, the first is death. People always die, but there's never a clear motive or outside weapon. Whatever kills the person is something in the room."

Dom taps the drawing again, this time indicating the people looking up at the star.

"Second, each incident is set up in a similar way. A person or a group of people are closed into a space. Communication with the outside world is cut off. Calls and texts go unanswered, sometimes just for a night, but sometimes for days. However long it takes, before . . ."

"Before what?"

"They give in."

"Give in to what? To the urge to drop a chandelier on themselves?"

Dom gathers up his papers. "You're not taking me seriously."

I rush to stop him. "No! I am. I'm sorry. Please, keep going. I'm just a little confused. This is a lot to take in."

"You said you wanted details."

"I did. I *do*. But I'm a big-picture person."

Dom looks unsure of himself now that I've derailed him. I give his hands another squeeze and sit back, doing my best to look very, very patient.

"Okay. Well." He points back at the drawing and I see a detail I hadn't noticed yet. All around the people, in the faintest brush of graphite on paper, is a barely visible pattern in the air. It hangs in sheets, the sprawling design repeating in clear panels that enclose the scene.

"The third thing is . . . strange. I haven't been able to verify it in all cases. I'm working off redacted police reports, old design magazines, and gossip. And records from Orion House, so not the best sources, I know. But now that you're here, we can prove it."

"Prove *what*?"

Dom takes a long breath. "Well, each time, the victims destroy the decor. Move it, break it. Use it to crush themselves. It varies. But they always destroy the walls, at least in the crime scenes I've been able to study. Dane, for instance, splashed white paint across the room before the light fixture fell. So I started looking into all the walls across all the crime scenes I identified, and they all had something in common."

I'm suddenly back in the penthouse this morning, walking into the ruined room and being confronted by walls that had been stripped bare. All the paintings and mirrors torn down, great gashes of blankness peeled from the room's perimeter. Bloody handprints where nails cracked but their hands kept picking. Tedious, obsessive destruction. Then violence. And then the sun rising, finding all the bodies piled against the back wall, like they were trying to escape the morning's light and all it revealed.

Dom must see the awful realization flicker within me. He stokes it.

"Uhler's company . . . Orion House. You know what their main business is, right? You know how they make their money?"

I know it. We say it together.

"Wallpaper."

You heard a saying once. *The devil is in the details*. That would make the devil a delicate predator indeed. And a beautiful one, too.

It's easy, then, to see why this boy is so transfixed by the details he's lovingly plucked from lost files and concealed crime scenes. You fall quiet as he comes alive, telling you story after story about death, pain, and wallpaper.

He begins with one about a family who'd called Orion House in a state of panic. Their son had come home from college for winter break, and after one night in his recently redecorated bedroom, he began to complain about an infestation of cockroaches. He swore he watched them crawl up the walls all night long, but an exterminator found nothing. Still, the son couldn't be convinced; he stayed up every night after that, watching for bugs, and one morning the family found that he had peeled the paper from the walls. It was Orion paper, sold to them by Uhler. A custom design Dom shows you a swatch of. To you, it just looks like a geometric pattern, but as Dom angles the swatch, you catch a darting movement to the design, a moment when it appears to crawl under the light.

The son tore down the paper, and Orion House was called to replace it. They were called back a few months later to help the landlord stage the apartment for sale. The family had moved out. That was the official story, but the landlord had the real details. Evidently, the son fumigated the apartment one night with a bath of homemade pesticides. Everyone was inside. Everyone died.

Dom has other stories, too. An old business partner of Uhler's died by suicide moments before a dinner party she was meant to host, in an apartment papered in a dove-white stippled print. A bachelor party erupted in sudden cannibalism on Fire Island, beneath the riotous embrace of a wall papered in an Orion-printed chinoiserie depicting the Garden of Eden.

Then he starts talking about the fires, and your skin prickles. An apartment where the warp in a southern-facing window caught a winter sunset just right, focusing the light onto a cloth wallpaper infused with flammable starch. A fire started by a self-immolating CEO, in a boardroom done in tasteful charcoal tones. A spark of psychosis here, a smoldering resentment there, a blackened interior at every end.

You half listen to all this, because out from Dom's files slips a photo. Just another bit of evidence to him, but in it you see something that stops your heart. You pick it up to confirm, then drop it just as quickly, like it's singed you.

Suddenly, you can't listen to any more of this. You can't be inside at all. You stand up, cutting off the boy and his monologue of death, and you run.

CHAPTER EIGHT

Dom finds me on a bench in Central Park, watching bikers zip by along the pedestrian-only path. The autumn trees, all gold and red, drift like fire above us. I keep my eyes down, on the gravel, and try to focus on the birds. The outside world.

"You said you'd help," Dom says, out of breath. He waves his pinkie at me. "You promised."

"I said I'd help if it meant finding Yiayia," I snap. "I never agreed to believe your crazy conspiracies."

"How can you say that?" Dom huffs. "After what just happened at the apartment, and what you saw last night, and what you saw in the mirror—"

"I don't *know* what I saw, and I don't *know* what happened last night. And *we* don't know that any of these things are connected."

"They are. It fits the pattern. It's real—"

"Stop." I stand suddenly, my voice cutting through the birdsong. "Just *stop*!"

My heel hits something and I stumble. Dom reaches for me and in the sudden clutch of gravity I knock the sketchbook from his hands. I hit the ground and down flutters a snow of papers and photos.

My ass hurts but I rush to scrape up the notes. The sketchbook itself landed open, facedown, and Dom snatches it up like a child, slapping it shut even though mud mars the pages. He picks up the rest delicately, and it makes me reconsider what I'm saying. Whatever this delusion is, it's precious to him.

Then I find the photo. The one that made me run from the café.

"Why do you have this?"

Dom tries to grab it from me but I pull away.

"It's a photo of one of the fires."

"Where did you get it, though?"

"I found it in Uhler's office but haven't placed it with a scene yet. I suspect it's part of an album. One I haven't been able to turn up. Why?"

I gaze into the secluded stretch of park I've brought us to. The earth tilts into a bowl here, and toward one edge a ridge of rocks pushes up through the soft mud to form a kind of wall. My hands tingle with the memory of scraping across these rocks. We came here every nice day in the summertime, which felt like every day, but I know it must have only been a few here and there. They were bright days, though. They mattered, and I've warmed myself with their glow for years.

And there at the bottom of the rocky ridge, where the treasure would be if the rocks were a point, is a golden tree.

"I'm not breaking my promise," I say. "I just needed you to see something."

Dom follows my gaze to the tree. It tilts to the side, as if its roots are pushing against the rocks under the earth. I always used to worry about the tree during storms and snow. I thought it would tip over, but it never has. Seeing it again, I feel bad that it's had to stand strong all these years alone, without me checking in.

"This is a tree," Dom says.

"This is a *ginkgo* tree," I say.

A breeze slips out of the city and wraps around the tree, causing a flurry of yellow leaves to spiral down. It's like flecks of gold falling through the air. I cup my hands to catch a few, like my mom used to do. I never could do it as a kid but now, big as I am, it's easy. I hold out the leaves to Dom to look at.

Dom clearly thinks I've lost it, but he takes the leaves. They're shaped like little fans, or fish tails, and are the bold yellow color of cartoon sunshine. Or fire. I hold up the photo and he sees it right away.

The photo shows the interior of an apartment that's been blackened by fire, except for a shock of bold yellow crawling up unburned sections of the walls. The yellow forms a pattern that looks like chains of ginkgo leaves falling upward, shimmering in the camera's flash like little tongues of flame.

"The wallpaper matches the leaves?" Dom guesses.

I nod. "You're sure this photo came from Uhler?"

Dom nods. "From his office. Tucked in a book. Some sort of trophy, maybe? I'm guessing the paper is by Orion, but I can't find evidence of it anywhere in the collections. There's a series of similar motifs about a decade back, but that's it. Why? You recognize it, don't you?"

I can't look at it anymore. Instead, I watch the ginkgo leaves twirl against the bright, overcast sky. It's a warm day, despite the clouds. I can smell smoke on the wind.

"It's a photo of my bedroom," I say. "My old bedroom, in my old apartment, when my parents were alive. And you can't find the paper anywhere because it's custom. Uhler made it just for them. Actually, he made it for me. Because we came here together a lot, and he saw how much I liked the leaves."

I force myself to glance at the photo. The sooty blackness of it throbs against the gold leaves carpeting the ground. My thoughts are in pieces, but they fit together slowly as I say something that would have been impossible just two days ago.

"My parents died in that fire. By your logic, Uhler killed them."

"Maybe. It's just another example of the pattern—"

"It's not *just* another example," I snap. Dom flinches. "It was my whole life that burned, and I've spent years trying to convince myself it was an accident. That I couldn't have done anything to stop it, because I was six, and sometimes shit happens to good people, and we just need to accept it and try to move on. And I *was* moving on, before all this started. I was ready to be someone else. But now you're telling me the fire might have been . . . what? A trap? Some sort of staged accident? Just another piece of evidence in your little investigation?"

Dom is withdrawn now, back to just staring at me. All the animation I saw when he talked through the deadly scenarios has evaporated. He goes so still he could be asleep, if not for his wide, dark stare. He looks like he's about to cry. I instantly lower my voice.

"Sorry," I say, handing him back the photo.

"I'm scared, too," Dom says, taking it.

My temper flares again. "I'm not scared anymore. I'm . . ."

What am I? I'm angry and confused and desperate for none of this to be real. Yiayia's warnings about doom and disaster have played on a loop in my head for years, and it's taken me all that time and therapy to realize what I'm hearing is an old woman trying to make sense of a cruel universe that gives and takes without any sort of logic. I know that. Or I knew it, until the moment I rewound the mirror at the party last night and felt that evil force finally notice me. We hid from it for so many years after we escaped those greedy flames, but now it's found us again, and it's wasting no time destroying what's left.

But Dom thinks it's a man. Uhler. A person. How could a person cause all this? How could wallpaper? And what if he's right? What if the malevolent force Yiayia prays against has been beside us all these years? What if it's not an evil, all-seeing eye, and it's just a man?

I catch a flash of hope in the spiral of my thoughts. A man is a real thing. A man can be fought. Stopped. Killed. I shake my head to dislodge the thought. It's like a burr of Dom's logic has stuck into the tender thoughts this photo exposed.

"Fires don't just start," Dom says. "Something always sparks them."

It's dangerous, giving voice to thoughts like this. Once you start seeing patterns in the mayhem of the world, it's harder to accept that anything is meaningless. In a strange way, it's a relief to think the universe has selected you—specifically you—to suffer. Soon, all you see are wicked designs. Sometimes they're real, but usually they're not. You won't know the difference, though, and you'll hide away from all of it just in case.

Yiayia and I have hidden for years. But maybe it's time to face this head-on. Maybe it's finally time to learn the truth.

"So what do we do?" I ask Dom.

The intensity of his stare falters, like he's surprised.

"You believe me?" he asks.

I'm not sure that I do. I keep thinking about the threads that trail behind him, and the phantom I saw crashing through the elevator mirrors. Whatever web Dom and I are caught in, it goes beyond just Uhler and his creepy wallpapers. There's more to this, and only someone with my eyes can see it.

"I believe I can help," I say. "So what's next?"

Dom smiles, and it's such a rare, delightful thing that I automatically smile, too.

"I'm so glad you asked," Dom says. "I've got a plan."

The sun sets earliest in the city, vanishing behind the buildings and darkening the streets before it's even midafternoon. It begins to rain, too. But in the dark, the city shines brightest.

You learned in science class once that all things shine. The color of something has to do with the kind of light it absorbs, and the kind it reflects. Red apples aren't red, they just reflect the red that you see. And so the sky isn't blue, and clouds aren't white, and the color of anything is actually the color it won't accept, because that's what it's giving to you.

You told Yiayia this, except when you said it, you said, *Yiayia, nothing is what it seems.* And she listened to what you learned, making you repeat it in Greek for her, and then she said: *Everything you see is an illusion. Everything is made of light. It bounces off the world and shines into you, where you make it make sense.*

You wonder what sense Dom makes of *you* as you walk together through the shining city. You have always been desperate to shine, and so you've always reflected a little too much, given a little too much away. You showed up to other people as every color, an unreal and impossible rainbow of a person. What people want to see, when they want to see it, then gone when the light of their attention goes out. That's not you, though.

With your guard dropped, you wonder what he'll see. What color, and how bright? Do you still shine at all if you're not always trying?

And you remember, deep in the vulnerable place this boy has put you in as he peels away all your glowing artifice, that though all things shine, some shine best in the dark.

CHAPTER NINE

Dom and I make a good pair, I decide, watching our reflections wobble across the store windows as we stroll down the East Side. I keep my eyes on him, and he keeps his eyes ahead, toward some unknown next step in his plan.

We end up sitting in the lobby of a hotel that is so fancy, it doesn't even advertise an address. Just a name on a modest brass placard out front. The Cordova. I'm uncomfortable in a massive leather chair, but Dom lounges on the sofa like a house cat. He has his sketchbook open and he doodles while I keep an eye on the door, daring anyone who passes through the lobby to stare at us too long. But no one looks. We're invisible here. I think it's because when we first sat down and a butler-looking man approached inquisitively, Dom didn't even wait to see what the man said before ordering a cappuccino. Dom didn't even look up from his phone.

The hotel worker, to my horror, obliged. Dom tipped him in cash, more than the drink itself cost, and not with a knowing wink. He did it like he had no idea how much a cup of coffee should cost.

"What?" he asked, pausing before his first sip.

I told him I was just surprised.

"Then you'll hate this," he said. He took a sip, winced, and pushed the cappuccino to the farthest edge of the coffee table between us. Somehow, this marked the small cluster of seats as ours, and no one has sat down since.

"I saw it in a movie," Dom confessed. "You decide what people see."

"What do you want people to see?"

"Nothing," he said. "In nice places like this, they know not to question the rich. If we look rich enough, we can be invisible."

With that, he opened his sketchbook and started drawing. He's still drawing now. He thinks I don't know he's drawing me, but I'm watching him in the faint reflection of the window beside us.

"Let me see," I eventually say.

Dom snaps the sketchbook closed.

I try to grab it, but he's quick. He shoves it between himself and the back of the couch. He's not smiling at all. I realize this isn't a game to him, so I let it go.

"Fine," I say. "Then at least tell me your plan for tonight."

"You'll see."

You'll see. You'll see. That's all I've gotten out of him since we left the park.

Going home is out of the question. Uhler knows where I live. Probably he's got someone parked on the street, waiting to see if I show up. Probably they've watched Linda enter and exit our apartment several times already, grabbing whatever she wants now that no one is there to shoo her away.

"Don't worry," Dom assures me. "I have a plan."

"Do you have a plan for all things?"

"I have anxiety about all things," Dom says. "So I come up with a lot of plans. I just . . . never thought I'd get to use so many."

"So why not tell me?"

Finally, a hint of mischief breaks into Dom's sour expression. "Because if I told you, you'd never come along."

We stay in the lobby for another few hours, until we're hungry. The rain has stopped by then, so we go to Shake Shack for an early dinner. I pay, making a big show of it, and Dom frowns the entire time. Over soggy fries, I prod him with questions about his life.

"So this bandanna. You wear it all the time?"

"Yes."

"Why?"

"So my head doesn't fall off."

I laugh. "No, really. You got a thing for monarch butterflies? They're pretty."

"They're poisonous."

I lift an eyebrow. "Are you?"

No answer. I try again.

"Where do you go to school?"

"Told you. I graduated early."

"What about college?"

"Deferred."

"Where?"

"Does it matter?"

I jab a fry at him. "You're very evasive."

"And you're very nosy."

"Most guys love my nose," I say, grinning. I show him my profile, glancing to make sure he's looking. He almost smiles. *Almost.*

"Oh, come on," I say. "Shouldn't we get to know each other? Doesn't your plan require us to work, like . . . together?"

Dom shrugs. "You can't work with a person if you don't know where they almost went to college? How elitist."

I roll my eyes and let out a groan, drawing the attention of a table nearby. Dom widens his eyes, a warning. I hunch over my food, playing up a defeated look and checking every few seconds to make sure Dom is watching. He is. He sighs, but I can see he's laughing behind that mask.

"Northeastern," he says. "For architecture. Happy?"

I beam. "Ecstatic. Boston, right? Beantown? Nice. You like beans?"

"Don't push it, Athan."

I continue to push it for another ten minutes until Dom announces that it's time to go. We walk down Park Avenue for what feels like miles, until we hit Fifty-Eighth Street. Dom guides us in a slow tour around a block, like he's looking for something. I just see a furniture store, a gym, and then suddenly something that makes me halt.

"This is the Orion House building," I realize aloud.

"It's the D&D Building," Dom says. "But it's closing in a few minutes. There's no way he's here this late."

"So why are *we*?"

Dom grabs my elbow, steering me across the street, toward the building.

"Just follow my lead," he says.

"Don't you need, like, an appointment to look at the showrooms?"

"You're not following my lead, Athan."

I shut up, adopting Dom's silence as we enter a beautiful hallway lined in displays of expensive furniture, drapes, carpets, and—right at the end—wallpapers. Names of brands and designers stack up on a massive directory. There are two men working at the desk, but they hardly pay attention to us as we stroll by to a bank of elevators that open just as easily. Dom jabs a button near the top and we slide upward. There are no mirrors to avoid, but even being back in an elevator makes my heart race. Dom is looking at me, though, like I'll reveal what happened before, so I keep it cool and just watch the doors.

Dom leads us through a maze of hallways on the top floor. It's carpeted and quiet, and all around us are glass walls leading into showrooms showing . . . everything. One is a small room full of hanging lamps. Another is a gallery of painted porcelain animals with jewels for eyes. The larger showrooms look like collapsed dollhouses, entire homes' worth of beautiful furniture jammed up into single rooms. And then there are the FOR LEASE showrooms. They are dark and mysterious, their expensive objects cleared out long ago, permitting us a glimpse through rare emptiness to the city outside.

Everything feels quiet. It reminds me of visiting the Museum of Natural History when I was little, wandering through the exhibits showing different environments from around the world. Here the safari, there the arctic. The rooms we pass now have the same complete, isolated quality, like little cubes cut out of other realities and dropped here to explore.

"Quiet," Dom says, which is pointless, because I haven't said a word. We enter a stairwell with a window that leads into an empty column at the building's heart, like an unused elevator shaft. Dom pulls me away from it, up the stairs, to an unmarked door. Through it, we are suddenly standing on the roof, seventeen stories above the street below.

I glance at the door we just went through, expecting to see ALARM WILL SOUND on it or something, but it's blank.

"The building is meant to be industry people only," Dom says, dropping his bag and unzipping it. "The security is pretty light."

"Isn't everything in those showrooms like a zillion dollars?"

"Who would steal a love seat?" Dom asks. "Or a curtain? There are antiques dealers, too, but you'd need to be pretty slick to get a chandelier out the door without someone stopping you. Anything worth any money would require the freight elevator to move, probably, and there's an attendant. Her name is Ingrid and she's a total bitch. We're friends."

By now Dom has pulled a blanket from his bag and unfolded it onto the roof. He sits on it and motions for me to join him. I stay standing, marveling at where we are.

"You work here?" I ask.

"Yeah. Orion House has an entire suite on the third floor, and their wall-covering showroom is on the fourth. I'm up and down the stairs all the time."

"What do you do again?"

"Keep track of the expensive shit rich people want to put in the rooms they never use."

"Do you ever want to design?"

Dom's hands are on his sketchbook when I ask, and he looks at me like I've caught him in a dirty secret.

"Design what?" he asks.

"I don't know. Expensive shit rich people want to put in the rooms they never use."

Dom looks actually horrified by this. "Never. My drawings are just for me."

The urge to join him on the blanket and ask to see his sketchbook comes and goes. He's about to bolt with me just looking at him. I dig my hands into my coat pockets and wander over to the edge. The city wraps around me, like I'm walking on thin air out among the buildings. Some reach way up, all the way into the low clouds. Other buildings seem to drag the eye down, toward the street. I lean a bit too far forward and feel the pull of the drop. For a second I'm about to lose my balance, but a hand on my waistband pulls me back.

Dom stands behind me, holding his own hand like he burned it pulling on me.

"I'm sorry," he says quickly. "I should have grabbed your collar but I can't reach it."

"So you grabbed my ass?"

"Your *belt*."

"I'm not wearing a belt," I point out, lifting up my shirt so he can see the little lines I like to show in my shirtless photos.

"Your belt loops." He's blushing.

I grin. "You grabbed my ass just now."

"To save your life," he shoots back.

My grin fades. "I wasn't going to fall. I was just looking."

We stand side by side and gaze over the drop together, daring each other to lean just a bit farther. I chicken out first and pull back, expecting Dom to follow, but there's an expression on his face as he stares down. He looks at peace, like a person staring into a cherished memory.

It's my turn to grab for him, but he leans back before I get the nerve to touch him.

Then he says, "*L'appel du vide.* The call of the void."

"The call of the what?"

"Void. Death. The beyond. Whatever's next."

"Yeah, about that call. I'm not picking it up," I say.

Dom shrugs. "You've never looked out over a great height and felt the sudden urge to jump? Not because you want to die or anything, but just because you have the morbid urge to see if you could actually do it?"

I guess I do know what he means. Maybe I heard the call just now, before he tugged me back.

"I looked it up once," Dom says. "It's called 'the high place phenomenon.' Lots of humans experience it but, for the most part, people don't actually want to die. It's a psychological paradox. People want to live, and the sudden flirtation with death makes them realize that. They step back from the edge and wonder: 'Did I want to die? No, I've scared myself. But now I know I want to live.' Or something like that."

"So it's like an intrusive thought, kinda?" I offer.

Dom glances at me sideways. "You get those, too?"

"Everyone does," I say.

"Not everyone," Dom replies, shutting down the conversation.

I glance at the city, like it might sympathize with me and this impossible boy I'm following around. I close my eyes and just listen, but all I get are wind and traffic. If the void calls, I can't hear it. Eventually, Dom marches off to his blanket and I follow a few minutes later. We spend an hour like that, on the blanket, until we're both shivering. Then an alarm on Dom's phone goes off and he announces: "It's time."

I ask *for what* and he says, "To go to bed."

We descend into the building, down the stairs forever, until we're on the third floor. The hallways are just as empty, just as dim, but now there are no people wandering through the showrooms. The place is abandoned.

Dom leads us past the entrance to Orion House, to an unmarked door. He unlocks it with a key card, and inside is a dark hallway that turns the corner into a small network of back rooms. Soon we're in a storage room. I realize this must be where Dom spends his time doing whatever Uhler makes his interns do.

And that's when I realize what his plan is.

"We're sleeping in . . . the bedding department?"

Dom shushes me as he cracks open a door and peers into the dark showroom. Once he's sure no one is inside, he motions for me to follow. He leads me through room after room, using only his cell phone for light. We reach a back corner, hidden from both the outside windows and the interior ones that make up the corridors of the D&D Building, and Dom kills his flashlight.

"We'll be safe here," he says. "For a night. Maybe two, if we reset everything just right. There are outlets, and I can grab water bottles from the offices. There's a bathroom for employees, but we should go together. I only have one of these."

He waves his key card at me.

"So Uhler must really trust you," I say.

Dom scoffs. "No, I stole this from one of his assistants."

"Won't they notice?"

"Uhler goes through assistants so often, I'd be surprised if half the city doesn't have a spare key card into Orion House. I don't think he's hiding anything here, though. I've already combed his office. He doesn't even lock it. He's only particular about his studio. Not even *I'm* allowed to see that. It's in Red Hook."

"I know," I say, which is a surprise to both Dom and me, actually. "We used to visit when I was little. The frame shop operates out of Red Hook, too."

"Go figure," Dom says.

"Go figure," I echo.

Dom gets busy moving half the pillows off the bed and onto a small love seat beside it. "We should both try to get some rest, because we'll need to be out of here early."

"What's happening tomorrow?"

Dom shakes his head. Locks up, like he did before.

"Fine," I huff.

Dom sits down on one of the staged couches in our corner. He takes off his shoes and unbuttons his shirt. I sit on the bed. Something about being in this dark labyrinth makes the silences between us feel so much fuller. All today we've been hiding right in the public eye. Now that we finally have some privacy, I feel suddenly exposed. I turn away as I peel off my own clothes.

"You can have the bed," Dom says.

"What? There are, like, twenty of them." I gesture at the other rooms, but Dom just shakes his head. "We have to keep it contained to this room. The rest show on the cameras, or you can see in from the outside."

I think there's literally zero chance anyone is going to glance in from across the street and see us, but I can sense Dom isn't going to budge on this.

"I'll take the couch," I say. "I'm used to it. I sleep on one at home."

"You do?"

"Every night."

"Why?"

I tilt my head at him, and he must realize why because he follows up with, "Oh, I'm sorry. I just figured because your family is in business with Uhler, you were . . ."

"Rich? Yeah, not anymore."

"I see. I'm sorry. I shouldn't have assumed."

"It's okay." I wave my hands. Even in the dark I can almost see him flushing. "Can we find that bathroom?"

"Of course," Dom says, rushing ahead, glad to lead us out of this awkward moment. We stick to a designated path through the showroom, finding the back rooms once again, and eventually a bathroom done in brass and brown marble. Dom's bag of tricks contains spare toiletries. While he waits outside, I clean myself up with a toothbrush, mouthwash, and deodorant, thank God. I even try to rub myself down with a damp face towel and soapy water in the sink, conscious of how close we're going to be for the next few hours. Then I wait outside until Dom is done. We head back together, and as we settle into our spot, I feel almost . . . safe. What a shock that is, to finally feel like I'm done running for the day.

I tear up, but catch myself. What? I'm exhausted. That's all. This bad day is finally over, and I'm relieved.

Dom gives me two pillows and peels off one of the many blankets piled onto the bed. Then he undresses. I'm amused when he just tosses his clothes on the floor. Oddly messy for such a tightly wound person, I think, as I fold my own grungy clothes.

Then we're both lying down, trying to ignore the other's breathing. Dom wins, falling asleep in no time at all, but I stare up at the ceiling.

I can barely hear the city this deep into the building, and the quiet prickles my ears. It brings me back to the silence of this morning, when I stepped out of that bathroom into a sun-drenched apartment.

I roll sideways, trying to block out the invasive thoughts. It's pointless, though. The second I try not to think of it, it blazes bright in my mind's eye. The pile of people, sculpted in a fleshy mass trying to hide from the sunrise. I can see it so clearly it's like if I reached out, my fingers would dance across the vertebrae of a spine arching under cold skin.

I bring my hands to my face and tap my fingertips over my brows. Like Yiayia does. Or did. *Tap tap tap*, on and on, trying to drum the thoughts away. I pretend she's with me, the Yiayia I remember from when I was really little. Warm, rough fingertips that smelled like flour and lemon juice, tapping with hardly any force at all. Like little bee kisses. That's what she called them, but in Greek. I always forget the phrase, but it's one of those things you never really try to memorize, because it's so fun to ask the person you love to begrudgingly repeat it.

Except now I can't ask Yiayia anything.

I sniff, letting my hands rest on my face. I swallow, but the lump in my throat won't go away. I'm so, so tired, yet my mind races with thoughts I can't control. I wish I wasn't here. I wish I was at home. Not the crammed apartment in Harlem, but the colorful, sunny walk-up in Brooklyn. The nights there were loud and close, like a hug at a party. But here it's so quiet in this fake house, and my crying is hard to hide.

"Athan."

I jerk up, but it's just Dom. He watches me from the bed, a shape in the dark.

"Sorry, I'll be quieter. I'm okay," I tell him, but my voice comes out crumbly.

"Do you . . . ?" Dom pushes back the covers and slides to make room in the bed. It takes me a second to realize it's an invitation.

"No, no," I say quickly. "I'm cool."

I lie back down. My heart is racing now. The last of the day's adrenaline twitches in my muscles, making every bump in this couch stand out. For something worth eighteen thousand dollars, it feels like shit.

I feel Dom watching me, though. It's dark enough that we're only outlines to each other, just a theory of a person in the dark. But the tension between us fills in the rest.

Finally, I push back my own covers and sit up.

"Okay," I whisper.

"Okay," Dom whispers.

I pull my blankets with me, like a kid racing through their dark house to find their parents after a bad dream. Dom scoots to the edge of the bed as I get in. It's warm. He's warm. I'm careful not to get too close, to not even hint at touching him. I turn away from him, but then his chest presses to my back. His arms pull around me. His knees fold up against the backs of my thighs.

He's holding me.

"Okay?" he asks.

"Okay," I answer.

I cry a little more after that. Dom just holds on.

You dream a familiar dream.

You are alone, in a featureless void. You are young, the Velcro on your shoes hastily slapped on.

You are holding a plate. On the plate is a slice of cake (pink icing) and in the slice of cake is a candle (green wax). Even in the dark you can see a curl of smoke winding away from it, like you just blew it out. But the smoke is flowing toward you, gathering around the candle until . . . *Aha!* The flame is alive again. Time is reversing, as though you stand on the other side of the mirror's glass.

By the candle's flame, you see pillars all around you. They are textured, abnormal columns that rise over your head and branch out. Trees, you think. Ginkgo trees. Why does seeing them rising over you fill you with dread?

You never remember in time.

The small flame of the candle brightens. Its orange light wobbles up into the trees. Their branches sway, like you've awoken them with the light. A few leaves fall. They twirl like fairies, twist like they're alive, making it a miracle when one lands right on the top of your toe. Like it chose you. Maybe it did. Dad says they're friendly.

The leaves on the ground flinch away from you before you can pick one up. They turn yellow, all at once, and the sound is like a sigh. All above you, the green canopy turns gold. The leaves rustle and whisper. And they fall, quickly now, in cascades that flicker like flame.

Then comes the part you always miss—a falling leaf slices over the candle you hold, igniting the sea of yellow below. Now curls of smoke slither into the sky.

Usually this is where you wake up, but not tonight. Tonight, you sense that you should hold on, and though the smoke pulls tears from your eyes, you look at what the smoldering landscape illuminates.

A pair of eyes hovering in the smoke. Huge, shiny eyes. Totally black and never blinking. They lower toward you, more eyes appearing beside them. Too many eyes, all fused together. Your reflection stares back at you in all of them, captured so precisely in their liquid surface that you can see every detail.

You are on fire.

CHAPTER TEN

I awaken in the dark, already sitting up. My hands plunge into the sheets around me—the bed is empty. I'm alone. Left behind. Then a hand reaches down to touch my shoulder.

"It's me."

Dom is already up and half-dressed.

"Sorry to startle you," he says. "It's time to go."

I take a few deep breaths and try to rub the dream I was having out of my eyes. I'm more tired than I was when I fell asleep.

"It's so early," I groan.

"Right," Dom says. "Get up."

We reset the space. Actually, Dom resets it, knowing the right way to place the pillows and how to fold down the blanket corners perfectly. It looks like we were never there, at least to my eye, but he fusses on and on until he's content.

We slip through the still-sleeping building, down the stairwell, and to a door marked EMERGENCY EXIT. Dom disregards the sign reading ALARM WILL SOUND, shouldering the door open. I flinch, but no alarm sounds, and I feel sheepish. No one ever seems to believe those signs but me.

"What do you want for breakfast?" he asks, like I'm his guest.

I shrug. I'm feeling a little more lost than before, a little less in control of myself. The small, intrusive thoughts skittering below the surface seem a little closer. I don't know why. The dread feels . . . stale, like it's carried on from whatever dream I was having.

Dom finds a café open early and gets us coffees and croissants.

People with suitcases swish in and out, ignoring us as we sit in the corner, sleepily chewing. Dom is on his phone, typing in a way that tells me not to disrupt his focus. When he puts it down for a sip of coffee, I take my chance.

"So. What are we doing?"

"Having breakfast."

"After that."

"Killing time before the shops open."

The food is helping me focus. I can play along with Dom's game if I have to. If he won't respond to questions, maybe he'll fall for teasing.

"That's your plan? To go shopping?"

Dom's eyes roam over me. His lips purse, like he's considering one of his sketches. "We have to look nice today. Rich."

I gesture at myself, because for all his looking, he clearly cannot see me.

"I'm wearing party clothes from two nights ago, and I'm badly in need of a shower. You've got bedhead. Like, *bad* bedhead."

Gingerly, Dom prods his mussed hair. He starts to respond, but stops himself. I can tell by the flush of his neck that I've flustered him.

"Listen," I say, scooting toward him. "You can trust me with the plan. I'm not gonna run. I promise. And besides, I have nowhere to even go. You know that."

After a bit, Dom nods.

"Okay. Fine. We're pretending to be two rich kids sent on an errand by their parents. It's . . . a meeting. We should look good, but not like we're trying too hard. I know where we can get clothes, but I hadn't really thought about the rest. You're right, though. Even with nice clothes, we look rough."

This isn't the whole plan, but it's something. I decide that I'm not just going to ask Dom to trust me, I'm going to show I can handle it.

"I've got an idea," I say. "Show me where we're shopping."

Dom hesitates, but then finally slides his phone to me. His map is full of symbols and pins, places he wants to go or remember. I swipe to the search and add a few stops to our route.

"What's your idea?" Dom asks.

"You'll see," I tell him, giving my most devilish smile. To Dom's credit, he smiles back.

———

Phase one of my plan has us naked in the park. Not entirely naked. Only briefly naked as we slip out of our old clothes and don fresh ones that I picked out and Dom paid for from his seemingly inexhaustible envelope of cash. Colorful shopping bags slump off to the side, watching us like little gossiping grandmas.

"For this to work," I say, "we need to be sweaty."

"I don't do that," Dom says.

"Everyone sweats," I tell him.

"Not on purpose." Dom is shivering in his little shorts. I fight the urge to pull him into a hug to warm him up. We'll both be warm soon enough.

I launch into jumping jacks.

"This will work?" Dom asks again. "You're sure?"

"I'm sure. I do this all the time."

By *this* I mean sneak into gyms. Fancy ones. It's an art form I've perfected, but I'm not sure Dom will be able to pull it off. Gyms are all about artfully ignoring other people. You never let anyone catch you looking, but Dom looks at everything. Stares, in fact. And he's not exactly the type that blends into a room full of guys grunting and sweating and pretending they are the only person who exists.

"Just try," I huff.

Dom copies me, but what he does can't rightfully be called jumping jacks. There's certainly jumping, and a lot of arm flailing, but he never manages to line it up. He gives up just as we hit twenty.

"All right, next up, high knees." I slip into my coaching voice. The one I used with the guys on the track team, before I dropped out. I wasn't the fastest, but I kept my teammates entertained. Dom groans, but follows me as I lead us in a prance around the small bit of grass I've chosen for our impromptu workout session.

"We need to look like we just went on a run," I tell him. "I've done it before. You jog into the gym, out of breath, and say you're just gonna go grab your stuff from the locker room. The people at the front desk assume you were already checked in."

"They won't recheck?"

"Not at the nice gyms. It's like you said yesterday. Rich people get to be invisible."

"I see," Dom says. He's completely out of breath. Good.

"Okay, butt kicks. Ready? Like this." I demonstrate, shifting into a trot and flicking my legs backward so that my heels kick my ass. Dom watches me with the most focus I have ever seen a person use to stare at my ass. I wait for a comment, but then he copies me. Or tries to. It's a rough start, but he figures it out.

"Most gyms get busy around midday, so we should be able to time it right. It's the bags we need to worry about. They're not really . . . sporty."

"I can handle that," Dom says. He doesn't say how, of course.

"Ready for the run?"

"The run?" Dom flinches. "You actually meant that?"

"We're not going far. Just a lap around the grass."

"But . . . the bags."

"Just gotta run fast."

Dom groans. Clearly I am making him regret every decision he's made since he decided to push me into that bathroom two days ago.

But after a second, he falls in line behind me. I feel a strange elation. Running, finding familiarity in the movement of my body, I feel real for the first time since the penthouse. Secure. With each step I burn my muscles into alertness, and gradually the burning thaws the chill that's been clinging to me this whole time.

"Athan. Slow down!"

I don't want to. Now that I'm running, I can't stop. I leave Dom panting behind me as I take off around the reservoir. He'll go back to our bags, probably. Good. I need this. Just one lap, I promise myself. And because it's just one, I take it in hungry strides that leave no room for relief. When I finally come upon Dom (sitting, dressed again in his normal clothes, head between his arms), I'm completely plastered in sweat.

"Sorry," I say, gulping in air. "You ready?"

Dom's eyes widen, trailing the trickles of sweat sliding down my neck, printing my excursion on the thin fabric of my shirt. I grin and flex. He rolls his eyes.

"Let's go," he says.

We pick an Equinox. Notoriously bougie. Ridiculously nice, but not so exclusive that they'd be able to recognize on-site that we're not members. Before we enter, Dom pulls me to the side, behind a large potted plant. He's looking for something.

"There, that one," he says, directing me at a massive mirror spanning the entryway. "Find me an older woman. Someone in the last twenty minutes."

I'm nervous to interact with my reflection again.

"I shouldn't look," I tell Dom.

"Why not?" he pries. "What did you see before?"

I sigh. "Fine." I focus on the mirror until it buzzes, focuses back on me. I shift it backward and the people of the gym zip by. I find a small lady, just bones and wispy hair.

"Found one," I say.

"Can you get her name?"

At the front desk, a man with a smile full of beautiful teeth greets her with practiced familiarity.

Mrs. Oglethorpe. How are ya today?

I relay this to Dom, along with a few other details. Her skin and hair color, her tights.

"Great," Dom says. "Okay. Go in. I'll meet you inside."

I wait until a couple is walking up to the front desk. Then I take a deep breath and step out from where we've hidden. I press my shirt over my abs, sopping up all the sweat I can, and breathe heavily. When I get to the front desk I give the guy a tired wave, a little sheepish as I gesture at my sweat-soaked outfit, like *No pain, no gain, man!* In a breathy, easy voice I say, "Just grabbing my stuff."

He waves me through as he checks the couple in. I duck around the corner, stopping right away, eager to see how Dom follows. Mirrors spanning the wall afford me a vantage point in real time.

Dom marches right up to the desk, bags clutched to him, and says, "Is she here?"

The couple slides away, spooked by Dom's sharp tone. The guy behind the desk assesses Dom. Whatever he sees must scare him, too, because his customer service smile flashes back on, and he just repeats Dom's question back to him.

"Is . . . she here?"

Dom rolls his eyes. "Mrs. Oglethorpe. She's here, right? She texted me. She needs her—" He interrupts himself to serve a withering glance at the couple, watching all of this with blatant interest. "Can I help you?"

They drift into the gym, giggling. Dom shifts his gaze back to the guy working the desk. He holds up the shopping bags.

"She made me run all the way from her office because she forgot some essentials. Is she here? She didn't say which Equinox. I've been all over the East Side. Please tell me she's here."

"I'm sorry. You're looking for . . . who?"

Another eye roll. "OGLETHORPE. Little white lady? Dyed blonde hair? Probably wearing pink tights?"

Recognition sparks in the worker's eyes. He starts to tap on his computer, and after a second he stutters, "Y-yes, she's . . ."

"Thank God." Dom thrusts the bags at him, but the man seems horrified by the idea of taking them.

Third eye roll from Dom. God, he's so good at that. Why do I love it when he does that?

"Fine," he says in a chipper, patronizing tone. "I'll do it myself."

And he walks right in. The worker doesn't even ask for Dom's name. He just turns to his coworker, that thousand-watt smile frozen to his face.

And that's it. We're in.

I trail after Dom as we head to the lockers.

"You've done that before?" I ask.

"Never," Dom says. His chin is high, chest puffed up like he's still in character. I get the hint and give him some space as we walk past a room of treadmills, down a staircase, and into the locker area. We find two empty lockers, and in goes the bag. Then Dom follows my lead as I snatch up a few towels and undress.

"This is wild," he whispers, kicking off his shorts.

"I know. I can't believe the towels are free."

"Not that," he says. "I've never been in a gym. Are they always this . . . clean?"

"Not always. We lucked out. Wait until you see the showers, though."

"They're bad?"

"No," I laugh. "They're the best part."

Dom trails after me toward the showers, but stops when a door at the end of the tiled hallway opens and out billows a cloud of eucalyptus-scented steam. Dom throws me a look, eyes wide and daring. I cock my head at the door, seeing if he'll go for it, and to my surprise he does.

We step into the steaming room. We're alone. When Dom talks, the humid air thickens his voice with resonance.

"You don't like mirrors," he says.

"I don't like my reflection," I correct him. "Or I guess it would be more accurate to say it doesn't like me."

"What do you mean?"

I sigh. "Looking at myself is what triggers the Sight. Looking at my own eyes, specifically."

"That must make it hard to brush your teeth. Or get dressed. Or—"

"The list goes on and on," I cut in. A pipe roars to life somewhere in the walls and steam billows into the room, hiding us from each other.

"So how do you see yourself?"

"Photos. I can still take a mean selfie."

"You know what I mean," Dom counters. "Be honest. Or else."

At any moment someone could enter, and we'll have to stop talking, which makes me want to say exactly what I want to say on the first try.

"You learn to see yourself in other things. People are the best mirrors of all. You watch them. See yourself in the way they react to you. All sorts of things are reflective if you know what to look for."

"But gyms are full of mirrors," Dom says.

"This entire city is," I say.

"And you avoid all of them?"

"You get good at looking away when . . ." I almost say *when it's life or death,* which I thought it was for a long time. I swallow. I say, "When you don't like what you see."

Dom can't ask what I mean because a few guys join us in the steam room, sliding onto the benches beside us. The pipe roars again, refilling the room, and we sit in a silent, awkward cloud. After a minute, one guy gets up to leave. The other leans back. His eyes skip over Dom and land on me. I make the mistake of looking back, and this triggers him to hook a thumb under the towel at his waist. It unfolds, not all the way, but just enough. I lock my eyes on the opposite wall, like I'm a statue.

The guy clears his throat, trying to get my attention back on him.

"How's Rebecca?"

I'm surprised that the person who asks this is Dom. He's pitched his voice down, to make himself sound older. The guy watching us doesn't answer, which means Dom is talking to me. He covers my lack of response with a quick follow-up: "Sam said she was talking about picking out rings. You two still thinking about getting engaged?"

Oh. I realize what Dom is doing. "Yeah," I say. "Rings all picked out. Just waiting for the right time, I guess."

The man is no longer watching us. After another few seconds, he gets up and leaves.

Now it's just me and Dom again.

"That happens to you often, doesn't it?"

"What does?"

"That. Just random guys flirting with you."

"I guess. I don't know. Was that flirting?"

Dom's tone flattens with sarcasm. "I guess hot people have problems, too."

I clear my throat, the air sticking to my insides as it goes down.

"I can't help what I look like," I say.

"You can't? Then what do you call that little workout routine you whipped out of nowhere? And I'm pretty sure those are abs."

"So I work out. So what?"

"So," Dom says, "you can't pretend you don't understand that the way you look changes the way people treat you. I think you're perfectly aware."

"Maybe."

"Sometimes I wonder what that's like," Dom says.

"To be flirted with by random old guys?"

"No," Dom says. "To be seen at all."

Another person enters the steam room. I want to ask Dom what he means, but he gets up and leaves. I follow a short while later, but he's already in a shower stall. I find an open one, duck inside, and all thoughts are forgotten as cool water washes over me.

All thoughts but one. The stall doors don't close all the way, affording me just enough of a gap to see a sliver of Dom in his own shower. I turn away even though my eyes are hungry to look. I tell myself it's just a studious curiosity that I'm battling. I already know the feeling of his body because of the way it curved around me last night; I just want to see it, to make sense of it, and to assign a shape to the pressure that has curved around my mind all day.

One look can't hurt, right?

I look.

Dom is already looking at me. We've caught each other.

"I see you," I whisper.

Perv, he mouths.

The slap of flip-flops alerts us to an adult entering the showers, and we both get back to the busy work of keeping ourselves clean.

You shouldn't look at what you can't have.

CHAPTER ELEVEN

We emerge from the gym brand-new.

Different people, basically.

I'm Windsor Buchanan, a child of the Upper East Side. Windsy, for short. I'm dressed in a camel sweater and fitted slacks. I think the sweater is too tight, but Dom says it's "European-fit," whatever that means.

And by Dom I mean Kenny Garfield.

"I'm not using that name," Dom cuts in as I explain our made-up personas to him.

"Garfield? Why not?"

"You named yourself after a character from *The Great Gatsby*, and me after a cat who likes lasagna."

"Fine. You can be Kenneth . . . I don't know . . . *Jenner*. Is that what you want?"

That earns me an eye roll. I'm starting to get a real collection of eye rolls from Dom. I'm detecting subtle differences in them, like a connoisseur. Sometimes they're quick and dismissive, other times exaggerated and grand. This one was humorous. Kinda coy, I think. My favorite yet.

I stop—literally stop—on the steps down into the subway and think to myself: *Has my flirting strategy turned into . . . actual flirting? Am I crushing on a guy? Now? Him?*

"I've got an alias picked out already," Dom says as I catch up on the platform. "I've been communicating with Realtors since last week as Ian McKenzie. You can be, I don't know, my stepbrother or something. Or my boyfriend, if you're up for it."

"Boyfriend," I say stiffly.

Now. Him, I conclude.

The conversation is cut off by the squeal of an oncoming train, and though we're nowhere near the edge, Dom backs away to the wall. He even puts a hand out to touch the subway tile, like he's afraid he'll be sucked in by the train's momentum. I note this. Lots of people fear the trains, and I've heard stories about folks getting pushed onto the tracks by accident. I saw it happen in a movie once. But that was a movie. Still, Dom feels somehow tenser beside me as we board the train. I wonder if this void calls to him, too.

I decide to not ask about it, and to get him back to talking about this plan of his.

"So? Fake boyfriends?" I put out my hand to see if he'll take it. "Who asked out who? Can we say we met somewhere fancy? But not too fancy. Like . . . Carmine's? No, wait! Summer camp in the Catskills? While fencing."

"If you don't shut up, you'll be an assistant by the time we get there."

But he takes my hand and holds it for the rest of the ride.

As it turns out, *there* is a cobblestone street in SoHo. From the scarce details I've picked out of Dom's very infrequent explanations, we're posing as potential home buyers. Dom finally confirms this in a rushed little catch-up as we stand outside an unassuming door.

"Just follow my lead. Look interested, but not too interested. We're pretending we've seen a bunch of properties like this because my parents are thinking of buying us a place in the city, so even though they put down the money, it's my decision. We're brats and we are used to this stuff and a little annoyed."

This sounds absolutely wild to me, but okay. I set my jaw and nod. Dom eases back, looking at me like I'm the crazy one.

"You're not scared?"

"Not scared," I confirm. "You thought I wouldn't be down? After everything else so far?"

A muscle jumps in Dom's jaw. It's like he's seeing me for the first time. Or re-seeing me.

"I wasn't counting on it," he said. "But you were right."

"About what."

"I can depend on you."

Then he smiles. *That's* when I get nervous.

The door buzzes, making me jump. Dom's smile turns playful as he leads us into a small parlor with checkered tiles. There's an elevator, but we take the stairs up to the third story, where a man waits in an open apartment doorway. The moment he sees us, I know this won't work—clearly he didn't expect us to be so young—but Dom thrusts out a hand in greeting.

"Bruno? Nice to meet you," he says. "I've heard great things."

The man—Bruno—takes Dom's hand and his eyes widen, probably shocked by the firm grip. I match this, and somehow we're through the hesitance, being invited into a beautiful apartment with no further scrutiny.

The first thing I register is the smell of paint. It wafts over us, and even though the day is chilly, the windows are all flung open. The apartment is massive, with only a few pieces of furniture left inside, all covered in plastic sheets. The walls, stretching two stories tall, are a fresh white. This seems to surprise Dom, and I realize why: He brought us here because he thought there'd be Orion paper on the walls. From the looks of it, it might be a recent change. Painter's tape still lines the molding and windows, like the walls were only just stripped and painted yesterday.

Bruno talks at us as we look around. His accent, like the rest of him, is sharp yet refined. Eastern European, I think, like some of the guys I work with.

"Duplex, renovated a few years ago, with lots of recent updates. Great southern exposure, as you can see. Don't mind the floors—the property managers are having them redone as soon as they get the rest of this stuff out of here. That's right, the boxes are not staying." It's a bad joke but we laugh. "Two full bedrooms and an office, which . . ." He looks us over. "Do you need an office?"

"Not yet," Dom says. "We could use a guest room, though. For when the king and queen visit." He says it with such sincerity that Bruno looks confused. Then Dom adds, "My parents. They usually stay in Times Square but we told them we're not venturing into that hellhole unless we've got tickets to a show. They're just going to have to slum it like the rest of us."

Slum it. When Dom says this, he gestures at the massive apartment. It's so subtle and so skilled, the way he totally vacates his tone of sarcasm at just the right time to indicate maximum out-of-touchness. His acting is superb. I have to wrestle a smile off my face in time for Bruno to look at me, as if asking, *He's serious?*

I just take out my phone, like I'm bored. It's off thanks to Dom's paranoia, but Bruno doesn't know that.

"Are there any offers?" Dom asks.

"Lots of interest, but the listing isn't even public yet. How did you know to mention it when you contacted my firm?"

Dom just outright ignores the question. "Any repairs needed?"

"None," Bruno says. "If—"

"The paint," Dom cuts in. "Did something happen?"

Here, the first hint of suspicion shows in Bruno's expression. "Just a courtesy," he says slowly. "You can update it, but the sellers wanted to give it a fresh start."

I know Dom is trying to get at something. And Bruno is talking around that something, too. They're dancing without moving.

"Is there a concern?" Bruno asks. Maybe Dom doesn't notice, but I see Bruno's hand drift to his pocket, like he's going to pull out his phone. To make a call? To look us up?

"We're paper people," I cut in. "His . . . mom is, I mean. She's never been able to stand a blank wall."

Bruno's expression softens into a smile. "Ah, you're looking at the right apartment, then. It's bright!" In that moment he turns, arms open to the windows, and Dom shoots me a sour look. I stick out my tongue. I can dance this dance, too.

"It can handle a lot of color. And actually . . ." Bruno drops his voice into just above a whisper, turning back to us like he's got a secret to share. "It wouldn't be the first time this apartment saw some bold design. It previously belonged to a famous artist."

Dom knew this. I know he knew this, because he lifts his eyebrows as though barely interested and goes, "Oh?" like he doesn't care. Bruno rushes to say more.

"Ellery Pike. The famous sculptor. She had shows in all the galleries down here, and then went into home goods. You'd know her stuff. Look her up, look her up. She lived here for years. It was featured in *Apartment Therapy*. She was famous for her dinner parties. Google her. She loved this place."

Dom looks skeptical. "So why is she selling? Don't tell me she's running off to Connecticut like everyone else. God, this city really is dying."

I hate that phrase, but Dom deploys it perfectly. Bruno splays his hands apologetically. I'm the one who answers, though. "She's dead."

I'm pretending to look at search results on my phone, but Bruno's baiting tells me more than any headline I might search on Google, so I just say it outright to see if he'll deny it.

Another sour glance from Dom. I realize too late this is part of his investigation.

"Yes. Quite unfortunate," Bruno says, and now he seems to regret bringing her up. It's instantly clear that this Ellery Pike died here. Dom must have known this, too, because with practiced ease he shifts the conversation back into banter.

"Too bad she didn't leave behind all her cool stuff. It would've made moving in a lot easier."

Bruno's pained expression clicks off, almost too fast. The tour resumes, lighthearted now as Dom and Bruno take turns imagining what artist paraphernalia went where in the bright, blank apartment. It's eerie to me, the way they paint Miss Ellery Pike back into the space.

I tune them out. Something has occurred to me. In Dom's files, he mentioned a business partner of Uhler's dying in her apartment right before a dinner party. I put out my hands like I can feel the ghostly memory of where the dining table used to go, maybe right here in the wide, low-ceilinged room we're chatting in. And then I notice something else. There are no mirrors anywhere in this apartment. Even the bathroom has just a blank, newly painted wall above the sink. It should put me at ease, but I'm beginning to suspect someone removed them all on purpose.

The tour winds back into the living room. Behind Bruno's back, Dom flicks my shoulder.

"Ow!" I whisper. He silences me with a wide-eyed glare, then tilts his head at something he wants me to see. It's a massive, low couch, one of the few things left in the apartment, and like everything else it's covered in plastic sheeting from the painters.

I shrug. What about it?

Bruno swings back around and we plaster on smiles. He turns again, still talking, and Dom flicks me again.

What? I mouth. I thought he wanted to do all the talking?

Without warning, he slaps my phone out of my hand. Bruno jumps at the sound, just as surprised as me, but Dom flips back into character. "Windsy," he scolds. "The way you're always on that thing, it's amazing how often you drop it." Then, to Bruno: "I keep telling him to get one of those cases but between us I think he likes buying a new one every few months." And then Dom points out some crown molding, taking Bruno's eyes upward.

What the hell?

I bend over to grab my phone and that's when I see it—what Dom was pointing at. I stand slowly, and when I catch Dom's next glance, we share a nod.

"Oh! I forgot to take photos of the primary bedroom!" Dom exclaims. "Can we circle back?"

"Of course! Next showing doesn't arrive for another few," Bruno says, following Dom out of the living room.

I'm alone. I get to work, dropping down onto my stomach, right on the floor. Before me is a leg of the couch, but it's not just any leg. It's a peg of polished steel. In fact, the entire sofa is shelled in steel. Providing a sleek and modern touch. It's not great, but it's just enough to see a watery reflection of the sunny room.

How long can Dom keep Bruno occupied in that room? I don't have time to wonder. I find my face in the badly warped reflection. I find my eyes.

God, I hope this works.

It does. Kind of. The reflection wobbles backward, showing our feet rushing backward as our tour reverses out of the living room. For a while I see many shoes walking through—anonymous, expensive shoes that I figure are other showings—and then the shoes transition into cruddy work boots. The kind of stuff I wore on my handling jobs. Everything is viewed through ripples in the metal. The sounds of the past ping off the steel, garbling the words of the workers as they paint.

It's hard to track anything for long, and then the reflection goes fuzzy when someone adjusts the plastic sheet on the couch.

Dammit!

In the present, I stand and rip away the rest of the plastic on the sofa, following the steel finishes to the other side, chasing any glimpse of the room in the past. I find a corner that's uncovered in the vision, and I squat back down to watch.

By now, I'm so far into the reflection's past that the apartment is a different color. The fresh white walls are a riot of frames. From my new vantage point, I can mostly see a colorful carpet. A tarp has been spread on the middle of it, hiding something dark. Suddenly, I'm looking at Bruno face-to-face. He's examining the carpet with the methodical eye of a detective.

I pause on him and play the vision forward. Focusing this hard on such a muddy reflection hurts in a place deep behind my eyes, but if I grit my teeth, I can bear it for just a second longer. It's enough time to hear his voice ring off the metal, and he says, *A beautiful specimen. Wrap it up with the rest and send the photos to our most funded collectors. Inform the Patrons once the job is complete.*

Pain shoots between my ears and I have to let go, let the vision continue rewinding. More boots stomp over the covered carpet. Again, I recognize something. There's a pallet, and upon it a wooden crate. People keep walking in front of it but I manage to halt the vision for just a moment to glimpse a sticker slapped onto the lower right corner. Even through the blur in the metal, I know exactly what I'm looking at.

The logo for Forum Fine Arts & Framing. My family's company. But I don't remember hearing about this job.

My heart races, causing the vision to slip backward and out of my control. I try to calm myself. What's so strange about this? Forum handles art for many clients in Manhattan. Just because I wasn't on this job doesn't mean it was illegal or something. The crate in the vision is moved, but for a long time the tarp on the carpet stays static. It's the one unchanging feature of the room.

I need to look away, or else—

The tarp tears away, and I see dark red. Before I can avert my eyes, the body is there before me. A woman on her stomach, head cocked so that she's staring back at me, her yawning mouth open. Her tongue presses into the blood-soaked carpet. Her red-stained hands clutch a phone.

Ellery Pike's corpse, right where it must have been found.

Time rushes backward. Her corpse goes from dull and desiccated to . . . fresh. To new. The phone in her hand suddenly regains its battery. It rings, and rings, and rings. In another moment, I'll watch her un-die, which means I'll see how it happened.

"Windsy?"

I jump back, reeling out of the vision and landing on my ass. I look up at Dom and Bruno, who look from me to the sofa that I've torn the plastic from.

"Dropped my phone again," I croak. I snatch it up.

There's a beat, and then Bruno gives a devilish smile. "It's nice, right?" He means the couch. "We haven't been able to figure out how to move it. It doesn't fit through any of the doors. It's almost like Ellery bought it as a love seat and then it just grew and grew, like a koi fish! We're hoping the next buyers will know what to do with it. Any thoughts?"

"It's a nice couch," I agree.

"Sofa," Dom corrects me.

My heart is still pounding. I just saw a dead woman. It doesn't matter that I saw many more bodies just a day ago—it was worse seeing her, frozen like that, like a crushed insect.

"She had some good taste," I say, because it's my turn to say something.

Dom is looking at me, no doubt detecting something is wrong. His silver tongue doesn't linger on my shock. He adopts a conspiratorial tone and, to Bruno, asks: "What became of the previous owner's things? Her *actual* things? It's common knowledge Ellery Pike was notorious for hoarding her own pieces."

"She was," Bruno agrees. "Her family claimed a few sentimental pieces, but I heard the rest is being shown . . ." Bruno lets the phrase drift unfinished.

"Shown where? Is there an address?" Dom asks. He's too quick with it. Bruno narrows his eyes.

"I'm afraid I don't know," the Realtor says, so apologetically that I know he's lying. Dom sets his jaw, defeated. I surprise myself by speaking up.

"What happened to the rug?"

Bruno raises an eyebrow. Just one.

"Who's asking?" he asks.

I think about the Forum crates I saw, and Dom's conspiracy theory about Uhler's society of shadowy art people. And I remember the way Bruno looked upon the ruined rug with appraisal. What do I call myself to indicate I know more than I do?

"A collector," I say, using the word he used in the vision.

For a moment he just looks at me, adjusting some assessment. I'm no stranger to watching my reflection shift in the eyes of another. Something about what I've asked has changed who I am to Bruno. I'm not sure it worked, though. As we wrap up, he's chilly. He goes through the courtesy of providing a card with his direct line if we'd like to put in an offer. Dom takes it, all sullen, and heads down the stairs. I go to follow, but Bruno clears his throat.

"You're serious?" he asks in a whisper. Does he mean about the apartment, or the rug? Something tells me Bruno knows Ellery died on that rug, and that he knows this is why I asked about it.

"Dead serious," I say.

"A collector . . ." Bruno lets the word hang between us. He tilts his head at the still-open door of Ellery's apartment. "I don't recognize you, though that's hardly a surprise. It's rare to have these kinds of conversations outside of Sub Rosa. Still, you seem new. And you're very young, aren't you?"

I give a small smile. The thing about smiles is that they show people whatever they want to see.

"Who referred you to me?" Bruno asks.

This is it. A glimpse through the surface of reality, into something huge and hidden beneath it. I feel like I'm bobbing in a vast ocean, searching for the horizon—for any sign of something to swim toward— and a massive shape has just brushed the tips of my toes. Is Dom right, after all? But what can I say that won't get me swallowed by the mystery I hunt? How do I hold on to the beast and ride it down into the dark depths?

Bruno waits for my answer.

Think, I urge myself, but this isn't a logic puzzle, it's an emotional one. Bruno isn't the beast; he's a barnacle stuck to it. He will help me if he thinks I'll help him.

Who referred you to me?

"A less funded collector," I say, with a wink.

Bruno's eyes light up, but before we can finish our exchange the buzzer inside the apartment goes off.

"Ah, my next showing," Bruno says, pressing a button to unlock the door downstairs. Footsteps hurry toward us. *Shit.* My time is up. What do I do?

I hesitate too long, and the moment ends as the couple reaches the landing. Bruno's face morphs into a bright, false smile for them. He takes out another of his cards and produces a cheap pen to jot something on the back, testing the ink with a small, deliberate squiggle, then hands it to me. "Try that place for lunch," he says jovially. "Dumplings to die for."

He closes the card into my hand with a little squeeze. I play along and thank him, then trot back down to ground level, where Dom awaits in an impatient cloud of gloom. He walks us two blocks away before allowing us to break character.

"That was a fucking bust," he says.

"No, it wasn't," I tell him, showing him the card.

The card *is* a fucking bust, actually.

At least that's what you're thinking right now, my Little Prince.

It's still a few hours before we meet, and you're trying to make sense of a clue you're quickly realizing might not have been a clue at all. You've checked and checked again. The address Bruno gave you really *is* a dumpling spot. It's tucked in a fancy food hall in the base of one of the many boring warehouses in the Meatpacking District. You should know. You're standing in front of it right now, with Dom at your side.

That's it? Dom asks you, for the tenth time.

You already told him about the vision of Ellery Pike. He didn't even flinch when you got to the part about her corpse, and the ringing phone clutched in her hand. You told him about your brief exchange with Bruno. You wonder about Bruno's side business of selling rugs stained by death. It doesn't seem too absurd that wherever that rug is, there may be other objects that surrounded Ellery as she died. But you're no closer to that place than you were before. You're at a stall in a food hall designed to look like an old-timey dumpling shop, paper lanterns and all.

That's it, you answer, disheartened. You feel like you've failed him. You don't know what to do, so while you circle the food hall, you coax him into telling you everything he knows about the legendary career of Ellery Pike. He starts slow, but quickly the topic brings him back to life. And the more he talks, the more Ellery herself comes to life as well. Her corpse sits up on the rug, alive, and she becomes a person again.

Dom begins with the *Apartment Therapy* article that the Realtor mentioned, showing you the pages collected in his files. You spend a long time looking at her. The *living* her. She has a kind of severe celebrity eccentricity about her—intense and icy eyes and a rigid, upright posture. In the photos accompanying the article, she sits in the apartment you just saw. Seeing it like this makes you feel as if you've just walked through the fossilized skeleton of a whale, all the flesh torn away by time. In Ellery's version, the walls are a warm white, and so is the furniture. It's an immaculate backdrop for everything else: dozens of sculptures spread all around her, some sticking up from the floor, some hanging from the ceiling, and some even dripping over the lips of tables, mantels, and windowsills.

Ellery, as it turns out, plumbed the depths of her artistic mind and sculpted her dreams out of mirrors.

Interesting, that part. Mirrors.

Not glass, and not flat, but amoebas of metal. Grouped together, they look like little families, like if you tried to separate them, they'd scream.

The last photo in the article is a shot of the vast living room you just stood in. Ellery glowers, arms crossed, gazing out the window. But the way she's positioned, it's almost as if she's looking at the strip of wall *between* the two windows. The wall. There's something about the wall that Dom wants you to see.

It's subtle, but it's there. The white isn't simply flat paint. No, as light floods the apartment and reflects off the polished floors, it digs into a texture upon the wall. A design of subtle luster.

Wallpaper.

You flip back through the other photos, and suddenly it's everywhere, reflected in all those metal objects. A pattern, clearer in reflection, wrapping around every bevel and curve.

What's clear is that Ellery Pike was surrounded by it, in life *and* through her art. What's unclear, Dom says, is how it killed her. And now it looks like you'll never know.

But failure is just a point of view. You should be so lucky to call it quits here.

CHAPTER TWELVE

Now I'm the one keeping my cool while Dom's slowly losing it. I pocket Bruno's card and chase after Dom as he storms from the food hall, out into the Meatpacking District.

"We have to find Ellery's personal collection," he's saying, skipping right over the *how* that's halted us in our tracks. "It's the only way to know for sure what happened to her."

"Maybe we're looking in the wrong direction," I call. "Backward—not forward at who might be next. And we still don't know where my grandmother—"

"Do you want to know who volunteered to move out her furniture?"

I know better than he does. I saw the logo in my vision of Ellery's apartment. Before I can answer, Dom barrels on.

"Uhler," he spits. "Uhler knew before anyone that something happened to Ellery Pike. He was in contact with the family well before the press reported her death. If there was evidence in that apartment, he got to it first. He got to *her* first."

I'm conscious of the kind of conversation we're having in public, so I guide us over to a tiny park, where we sit on the edge of a fountain. JACKSON SQUARE, a sign reads, ONE OF NEW YORK CITY'S OLDEST PARKS! The splatter of water masks our voices.

"Slow down," I urge him. "You're a little freaked out—so am I. But there's more to Ellery's death than you're telling me, isn't there?"

It must be hard for him, sharing this much at once. Dom's been on this hunt alone for years. But I'm not going anywhere. Not after seeing the photo of my family's burned home amid Uhler's trail of destruction.

"All right," he says finally.

I rub his back. He seems okay with this, so I keep going.

"Ellery's death was a shock to everyone," he says. "She was a big deal in the art world. The design industry, too. The *Times* wrote all about her impact. That's where I learned she and Uhler were more than just good friends. They were in business together, right at the start of Orion House. It was only a small note in the profile, but it was enough to start digging. They worked together for a few years before some sort of split. Officially, they stayed friends after, which is how I knew her."

Dom's shaking a little. His knuckles are white around his sketchbook.

"The relationship between her and Uhler seemed...strained, though. She'd come in sometimes and we could hear them yelling in his office. But when the door opened she always seemed so sweet. She was nice to me. She knew my name and always made sure to find me on her visits, ask how I was holding up. She was one of the few people who knew Uhler had adopted me. I think she knew he wasn't much of a dad, or a mom. She asked about my life, like you do. Sometimes she wanted me to show her my sketches. To me, she wasn't Ellery Pike. She was just Ellery, not the famous artist, not one of Uhler's eccentric, rich clients. Just a friend."

"I'm sorry, Dom," I say. "I didn't realize you actually knew her."

"I don't think I did," he says. "I only wish I did. It's hard to explain, but she felt so...alive. Vital. Like her life mattered so much to her, and to everyone around her. And I know I said I'm good at reading people, but with her, I never even saw, never even sensed..." He swallows and tries again. "I just don't understand how someone like that could...I just don't understand..."

Dom takes a big breath, and then blows it out. His composure resets, but barely.

"Her obituary didn't say how she died. I heard Uhler on the phone once, talking with lawyers, and soon everyone in the industry was whispering about it anyways. She killed herself, right in that apartment. No suicide note or anything. She did it only an hour before she was due to host a dinner party. Uhler had been invited but was running late. Another guest found her and called the ambulance."

"Dom, that's awful."

"There's more," he says. "You said in your vision, she had her phone, right?"

I nod.

"She was calling me," Dom says.

Chills rush down my back. Again and again, I see the light of a phone washing over Ellery Pike's wrenched jaw and bulging eyes.

"I didn't recognize the number, so I didn't answer," Dom says in a small voice. "When I called back, I got her voice mail. I guess it was too late."

There are no mirrors in sight, but in my mind I rewind my life just a few hours, to the moment Dom stepped into that apartment. He must have imagined the entrance countless times. What if he'd picked up that call? What if he'd shown up? Would he have found Ellery Pike dead, her body swimming in the shining faces of all her mirrors?

Would he have been able to save her?

But he didn't get the call, and he didn't show up. And all those what-ifs and could-have-beens must have been whirling within him as we walked into Ellery's apartment together—much, much too late.

Dom gazes at the middle distance. "Between her and Dane, I began to suspect something was connecting the deaths, something close to *me*. That's what accelerated my search." He looks down, into the dirty water of the fountain. "I know you want to find your grandmother, but it's personal for me, too."

I realize my hand has stopped its circles on Dom's back. I lift it off, surprised to even be touching him. This wakes him out of his reverie. He sits up straight. We both do. Dom flips back through his collected papers, to the picture of Ellery with her mirrored sculptures.

"They'd know what happened," he says wistfully.

Looking again at the pieces, I become sure of something that's been in the back of my mind since I first saw the sculptures.

"In the Guggenheim. The piece you had me look into. That was her work, wasn't it?"

No answer. I'm right, so I push on. "And that's why you were in the reflection. You visit the Guggenheim often. Like visiting a grave."

Dom looks unsure. Maybe a little nervous, like he hasn't quite decided how to react to my uncovering another piece of him. He nods, though, and again I'm watching the past through a new frame. We looked at the same piece of art and saw totally different things.

Reality, I realize, is only what our perspectives let us see.

I put out a hand to see if Dom will take it, and he does.

"I don't know where to go next," he admits.

"That's okay. I have a plan."

Dom stands, skeptical, and rightfully so. He probably thinks I'm going to restart our search, this time in the direction of Yiayia. But I surprise us both.

"I know a place that has dumplings to *die* for," I say, with gusto.

Dumplings and dead ends. What an intimate thing to share between friends.

The card sits faceup on the table, engaged in a staring contest with Dom to see who will reveal their secrets first. Your money is on Dom. Your eyes are on everywhere else. There's something off about this food hall. It's smaller on the inside than you'd think, and the configuration is confusing. Tourists crush together in knots that further crowd the space. You watch them, and that's how you see the lady.

She is restrained in her presentation, wearing sunglasses and an all-black coat as long as her legs. Though she looks nothing like him, the woman reminds you of Uhler, just like Dom reminds you of Uhler. It's the way she slides forward as smoothly as ink through water, even though she's walking in a crowd.

Watch, you tell Dom, and you chase her. Very slowly. She visits a few stands, orders some mochi to go, and floats off. But not toward the exit. She heads for the back of the food hall, stopping only to drop the fresh mochi into a garbage bin. She passes right by Dom, who looks from you to her, and back to you, with dawning realization. He's behind you a few steps later. Together, you watch the lady turn down the hallway with the bathrooms, where there's an elevator with a conciliatory OUT OF SERVICE sign.

She checks to see if she's alone. She is, because you've ducked into the bathrooms, which is why you miss what she does next. You only make it out in time to hear the elevator doors close. You try the elevator after her, but when you get in, it doesn't budge. It doesn't matter which floor you select, and there's no indicator you need a key, like at Uhler's.

The elevator really is out of service, but just for you. Not for her. Then it happens again. Another person with the same absurd, aloof aura floats in off the street, shops for twelve minutes, buys flowers, tosses them in the garbage, then vanishes into the elevator.

You leave Dom to keep watch while you go outside and circle the building. You expect to find another entrance or exit, but only see closed freight doors. You stare up at the blank windows, all of them made from reflective glass so that you can't see inside. What's a building this size doing with only a tiny food hall as a tenant? And the freight entrance is on the wrong side, too.

You know facades better than anyone. This is a front.

You run back to Dom, excited to tell him, but find him standing in front of the elevator, finger pointed out, like he's accusing it of something. He's holding up the card the real estate agent gave you, looking at the squiggle.

Which is more of a zigzag.

Which you remember Bruno drawing with such care.

Up, up, Dom whispers, *down, up, up, down, up, down.*

He presses the elevator buttons in that order, matching the directions to the peaks and valleys of the zigzag.

The elevator slides open, but it's different this time. The interior is cleaner, free of out-of-service signs. It's a different elevator entirely, which explains why the people who get into it end up in a different place entirely.

Dom enters right away, then stands there with his hand extended. He's smiling. He's excited. He's eager to get where you're going, to see what there is to be seen on the other side. Except he's not the one who will see it. That's for you, Athanasios.

Whatever it takes to watch something so gruesome, it'll be taken from you.

You take his hand and the elevator doors close. Even though the buttons indicate you're on the bottom floor, you begin to sink.

CHAPTER THIRTEEN

We go down.

"We found it," Dom whispers. He's ecstatic, practically vibrating next to me.

"Dom—"

"Kenneth," he corrects. A reminder that we have no idea what we're walking into, so we better walk in as someone else. There's a security camera in the corner, a red light winking at us. The farther we sink, the further Dom's convictions dig themselves. He squeezes my arm through my jacket as we finally slow. Is he nervous or giddy?

The doors rush open and Dom rushes out.

Giddy, I guess. I follow behind, adopting my familiar act of entitlement, trying my best to imitate Dom's cool demeanor from the duplex showing. I hope it's good enough for this, too. But something tells me this is much more dangerous than the open house.

We're in a hallway that reminds me of an old Broadway theater. Lush red carpets and softly lit walls. The hall is lined with small alcoves like ancient phone booths, all with beaded curtains that do a poor job of hiding the people tucked within. They speak in low, urgent voices into black phones. A woman approaches us with a knowing smile.

"Welcome, gentlemen, to the Sub Rosa Gallery. Will you be needing a line?"

"I don't do party drugs," I say. My automatic answer to that question.

The woman laughs at a joke I haven't made. "A *secure* line." She nods at the phone booths.

At our obvious confusion, she clarifies, "For making calls. Are you here on behalf of a client, or representing yourselves?"

"Ourselves," Dom answers. I smirk. He's lowered his voice to sound older. Still, the woman looks to me for confirmation, and I nod.

"Then you'll want to see the floor in person," she says, turning. "If you please." Similarly dressed attendants appear and take our coats and Dom's bag, but he holds on to his sketchbook. We follow the woman through a lobby, then up a staircase with the same crimson carpet, to a curtained door. Before we enter, she hands us two small silk pouches, like the kind nice sunglasses are sold in. And that's exactly what we find inside. Big, dark sunglasses. Just like Uhler's.

"Photos are allowed, but posting is not," the woman says. "Nor is naming Sub Rosa or any other negative spaces in the city. Per our policy, failure to be discreet will result in a dealer-wide blacklisting. You will not be provided a code for reentry. Enjoy, and happy bidding." Then she returns to the elevator to await the next arrival.

Dom and I exchange one more look. Our last, because once we put on the sunglasses, it's impossible to read each other. Shoulder to shoulder, we push through a heavy curtain.

We are standing in a box seat of an ancient theater, except the rows of seats have been ripped out. Below us, guests roam around a vast, sloping space leading down to the stage, where even more people stand around observing . . . stuff. That's the best I can do at a glance. There's just stuff everywhere, locked up in these glass boxes, with numbers scrawled on the sides in marker. A pianist sits at an upright grand where the pit should be, playing something melancholic. The atmosphere is reverent and somber, like a museum.

"Let's go," Dom whispers, leading us up into the mezzanine, which has also been cleared of seats. A bar has been built into the back of the theater. Others stand at the mezzanine's edge, arms draped over the railing, watching.

"Your order?"

A server has found us. I wouldn't normally even pause—the key to getting served liquor is to confidently order something kinda gross—but I'm speechless when I see her face. Or try to. She's been fitted with some sort of headpiece of leather and metal. All the servers have them on, even the bartender. A pit forms in my gut when I realize what they're all wearing: horse blinders.

"Boulevardier," Dom says, unfazed.

"Same," I choke.

The server leaves and Dom pulls me to the railing. "Get your jaw off the floor," he says.

"Easy for you to say," I shoot back. "Did you see what she was wearing? Blinders. Horses wear blinders. And what's with the sunglasses? And what the hell is a boulevard-whatever?"

"I don't know. I just heard someone order it once and it sounds fancy. And it'll make us look older."

"*You* need to look older. I look fine."

Dom snorts. "You look like you're gawking."

He has a point. "And you're not? How could something like this exist down here and no one knows about it?"

Dom nods thoughtfully. "Cow tunnels, probably."

"Cow tunnels?"

"Cow tunnels," he says. Definitively.

"Dom, you're making me play spooky twenty questions again."

"Sorry, sorry." He clears his throat, his tone turning academic. "In the nineteenth century, back when the Meatpacking District was actually, like, a district for packing . . . meat . . ." Dom pauses, no doubt because he can sense I'm about to make a joke, but instead I cross myself like the innocent little angel I am. He goes on, more animated. "Well, they would bring the cows over on barges, I guess from Jersey or something. But then there were more and more cows coming over, and this was before refrigeration so, like, it happened every single day. Eventually it started to cause these huge traffic jams, so they built a cow tunnel."

"A cow tunnel."

"Yes, Athan. A cow tunnel. A tunnel for cows."

I huff. "What does this have to do with a freaky theater beneath a food hall?"

"Simple," Dom says. "New York City is basically this infrastructural puzzle that has been complicating itself for centuries. Like, the city is four hundred years old, but it's never going to be *done*. It costs money to demolish the old and start fresh, though, so what's new is always just a thin layer built atop what's old. We build upward, not down. The result is that the city is riddled with these lost, forgotten spaces, like cow tunnels. Like this theater buried under a food hall. There are tons of speakeasies, too, left over from Prohibition. Half of them have been turned into gimmicky clubs. The other half were never found. They did what they were meant to do: keep everyone but the very wealthy, and very elite, outside."

Fair enough. I've heard of some of those clubs, like the one you get into through a phone booth in a hot dog store. But I also know about the other types of spaces, unmarked and unGoogleable, that never appear on blog lists or social media. I've moved art in and out of places I could have sworn vanished behind me when I left. Still, nothing on this scale.

"I guess I *am* a little surprised," Dom admits. "I just thought there would be . . ."

"Don't say cows—"

"Cows."

A beat of seriousness, and then Dom waves his fingers spookily. "Ghost cows, going *moooooo*!"

The huge glasses on Dom's face make this very bad joke actually funny. I stifle a laugh as the eerie spell of the theater breaks for a second. Dom does the same. I realize we're both feeling the elation of success—of making it this far into yet another place we clearly should not be—mixed with the fear of being found out. I'm nervous as hell, but this is the most fun I've had in ages.

The server materializes with our drinks, set upon a black velvet tray. She doesn't ask for payment, thank God. She waves away my attempt to tip her, too. Before she departs, she says, "Bidding closes in twenty minutes. You'll want to hurry. Good stuff is on the stage."

We nod like we have any idea what that means, then watch her tell another party the same. They move with purpose down a large staircase. We follow, ending up on the main floor of the theater among all the stuff we saw from above. Up close, it all begins to make a wicked sort of sense.

First, there are the portraits and paintings hung around the walls of the theater, each with a placard listing not just the artist but how they died. They're grouped into small collections based on cause of death. Homicide is the most popular, with subgenres. Death by a rival. A lover. Kin. And so on.

In the back of the theater, a spacious display of carpets has been hung up like I've seen at furniture stores. They look like the pages of an immense, upright book. Some have been taken down and spread out, and I instantly recognize the bold colors of Ellery's carpet. I even recognize the blackened stain of blood, just off-center. The rest of the carpets have been ruined by eerily similar marks. All of them, a small sign boasts, are guaranteed to have been died upon. When we pass, I notice an attendant eyeing me like she expects me to walk right up, but I turn us away to the next display.

This one is weapons. Guns, knives, and more creative instruments like fire pokers, a typewriter, and even an old iron sundial. Small cards tell who each item has killed. The guns are the least popular. "Too common," Dom remarks. I catch an old woman eyeing the sundial and telling a friend, "This! In the atrium, don't you think? I look for pieces that fit right in. It gives me a thrill when people ask me where they're from and I say I can't remember. Even better if they pick them up to get a closer look!" The two women titter.

We move on to—and then quickly rush past—a display of candy jars filled with teeth, but we just encounter more bones. Not just bones, but things made out of bones. Everything from a complete chess set to a rocking chair with bony arms for arms, the skeletal hands palm up, like you'd hold them when rocking yourself to sleep. And then the leather upholstery section begins, and that's when I feel the tickle of vomit at the back of my throat. Dom is flagging, too. We pull away, toward the only empty area, near the pianist.

My hands shake and I take a sip of the boulevard-whatever drink. I taste gasoline, but I welcome anything to take my focus off a lamp with veins.

"Are you good?" Dom asks, real concern in his whisper.

"Are *you*?"

"I just saw a love seat with nipples. I'm absolutely not good," he says.

"Well, me neither."

We sip our drinks, trading grimaces. I take the time to scan for Uhler, but everyone looks like Uhler in these big sunglasses. I keep jumping, thinking I see him, and have to talk myself out of losing my cool. If we break character, they catch us. And if they catch us, I'm pretty sure we'll be turned into kitschy decor for cannibals. Or silk-screened onto Oriental rugs using a steamroller. There seems to be no end to the potential tortures around us, so I stop looking at objects and keep my focus on the people. The *collectors*. Some gawk at the items, hiding their faces in the shoulders of friends, and some are so serious about their browsing that they don gloves to handle pieces up close.

"The people are interesting," I note. "Some are just like us. First-timers." I nod at a group of men taking photos with the bone rocking chair. No one stops them, like you'd expect in a museum.

Dom is frowning. "It's all so ostentatious, don't you think? Just another kind of tourism, but for sickos. I bet half this stuff isn't even legit."

"So let me get this straight," I butt in. "We manage to sneak our way into a secret subterranean treasure trove of morbid artifacts being sold to the über-wealthy, and it's not spooky enough for you?"

"It's an auction," Dom says. "A silent auction. How do they bid, though? There must be some kind of directory with a list of members."

"Got your eye on something?" That's my attempt at levity, but Dom's head has been on a swivel since we walked in. I know exactly what he thinks is hiding here, and there's one last place to look.

We turn toward the stage.

"Come on," Dom says, hooking his arm into mine. We step up the side stairs, joining a line of people who are notably reverent. It's the way they whisper as we snake through larger, more decadently lit displays, each on its own roped-off dais.

We pass by a hulking blitz of metal, so twisted it takes me a second to recognize it's a wrecked Corvette. I'm unsurprised when the next object is an ancient, upright sarcophagus, crude nails holding it shut. Maybe Dom is right—my New Yorker senses are starting to catch the whiff of tourism. But for who? Certainly this isn't an attraction for the flyover-state families that cram into Carmine's before their seven o'clock showtime for *Wicked*, right? So vampires? Serial killers? Or just people so wealthy they're bored by life, and so gentrify death?

We reach the end of the displays and there's no sign of Ellery's art. I turn to Dom to apologize, but in the reflection of his sunglasses I see a strand of light stretched through the air.

"Hold still," I order, and he does. I use him as a mirror to scan the room and, sure enough, the air is crisscrossed with silvery threads. Those threads cling to Dom, and to me, and presumably anyone who passed through them. And here, in this theater, they seem to lead to something. It takes me a few moments of strategically maneuvering Dom around, like we're tangoing, before I trace them to the very back of the stage.

We push through a crowd congregating in the wings, and all of a sudden, I'm looking upon a lustrous graveyard. People hang back from it, though the lines taped onto the floor indicate spectators are allowed much closer. Everyone seems to know better than to hover over them, though. It's the bizarre way they've been laid out; the amoeba-like objects of Ellery Pike's apartment have been interlocked into a solid form—that of a woman lying on the floor. I slowly realize that it's Ellery's body, in the pose of her death. The impression is so complete that as we draw near and the light slides over it, there's a moment when I'm sure it's about to sit up. Did a person do this to taunt her? Or did Ellery create her own pieces as a puzzle, and in the absence of her life they flew together with their own morbid magnetism?

And then we move, and the shape of the body dissolves. It's been intentionally set up as an optical illusion. I step back, and the illusion flashes into coherence again. If I rock back and forth, it dissolves, binds, dissolves. Like the silvery threads I keep seeing in reflections.

"What?" Dom asks. "What do you see, Athan?"

"I'm not sure," I tell him honestly. A wall of dread goes up within me. Just like I recognized Ellery's hand in the creation of the Guggenheim piece, I sense a familiar artistry in this arrangement, one that I first glimpsed in the bodies arranged at the penthouse. The same artist working in a different medium.

I don't want to look into these reflections. I'm scared of seeing Ellery alive, and I'm scared of seeing who killed her. But Dom keeps me rooted to the spot, his hand squeezing mine. That sense of gravity is back within my bones. I'm drawing near to something important. I am being pulled, or I am pulling myself closer, I'm not sure which.

Dom is breathing quickly, too. I can feel his heart racing in his hand. I give it a little squeeze and glance down at him.

"Just do it," he whispers, eyes locked on the display.

"Easy for you to say," I whisper back.

"Please, Athan."

"Athan? Who is Athan?"

There it is! An eye roll.

"Please, *Windsy*."

I wipe the smirk from my face and take a deep breath, trying to take my easy humor and turn it outside in.

I find myself in the textured reflections. At first it's hard to pick just one, but then my power picks for me, and I'm no longer looking at the many objects. I'm looking into the mirror-world within them. Dark to bright, bright to dark, and a hundred anonymous people in big, bug-eyed glasses—the last few days on display flicker by until suddenly the vision surges with radiance. The light of Ellery Pike's apartment is familiar after just seeing it myself a few hours ago. I squint, though I'm the only one who can see the brightness. I feel it, too—warm and embracing.

And there's a new sense added to my sight. A physical sense to being back there, back in the space, back in time. I gasp as the radiance goes red, like blood suddenly stains my eyes.

The visions that flash over the reflections make no sense. A hand, an eye, a sapphire-blue spray. Red again. An eye. More red. Bright lights. Hands, raised upward, as though praying. Crying.

Red.

Red.

Red.

It doesn't make sense. There's too much, in too many parts, and the arrangement of the pieces is all wrong. I can't get ahold of the vision across this many mirrors. Instead, they get ahold of me, and I slip further into their kaleidoscopic memory.

I lose sensation in my body. Dom's hand vanishes from mine because I vanish from the world. I become only a viewer, only eyes. And instead of Dom next to me, I feel a different presence in the mirror's realm. A heaviness wraps around my mind. There is something else *within* the reflection, watching all this, with many more eyes than mine. And suddenly I am watching through them.

You are Ellery Pike.

You stand in your home, and you wonder how it came to feel like such a prison. You've touched every surface, crafted every angle. What a horror, you think, to understand that all your toiling has built you a cage that you can't even see.

I blink, and briefly flicker back into my own perspective. I am Athan, I am with Dom. I am rewinding a complex series of mirrors, trying to piece together what happened to Ellery Pike. I was just looking at her, standing in her home, wondering how it came to feel like such a prison. I try to focus on that—the image of her standing, but once again

You are Ellery Pike.

You watch me as much as I watch you, but of course you do. You are an artist. Your entire body of work is a study in yourself. To you, I look like you. We have the same face. You blink, I blink. You move, I move. Sometimes a little after, if you're quick, but you can't seem to replicate that moment when your reflection smiled while you didn't.

There was a time when you tried constantly to surprise me, moving oddly, making faces in the reflections on cars and windows to see if I'd slip, but I only did that once.

Just once was enough, though.

Funny how all you needed was some tiny, terrible proof, and it's enough to make everything else just come apart.

I blink.

You run to the windows and pull the curtains closed, but it's too late. You've seen every spot you've missed, grime in every corner of your house, and in the heaving darkness you think you can hear it spreading.

I blink.

You stare at the droplet of red. Droplets, actually. One sits round and perfect on the tile. The other has already soaked into the grout.

You'll never get that out.

The party vanishes from your mind because you'll never get that out.

You could die trying, but you'll never—

I force my eyes shut, but I can't get that voice out of my head. I can't unsee Ellery, twisted within the terrible radiance of the silver strings pulling her in every direction. I clap my hands over my face and tap, tap, tap my forehead, but I'm not tapping. I'm hitting myself, over and over, until stronger hands force me to stop. They yank my arms to my sides and I nearly fall, but they can't make me open my eyes. I won't look. Not for a second longer. I won't look.

I won't look again.

Yes, you will.

CHAPTER FOURTEEN

Dom and I are back at the dumpling shop, somehow.

I remember hands. Hands, drawing me back into myself, holding me within my shivering body as I was dragged out of the theater, back to the elevator, and into the chaos of the food hall. A few concerned tourists hover nearby, worried about the boy shaking and crying for no clear reason. Security guards have appeared, but instead of chasing us away, they come bearing water bottles and our jackets from the Sub Rosa coat check.

Dom takes the water on my behalf, apologizes on my behalf. I can't make sense of the way we're being treated until I remember our clothes. Costumes. For a moment I can see how we look to everyone else, like every face staring at me is a mirror, the expression my reflection. I watch myself from others' eyes. I'm not an I; I'm a *you*.

I shiver, thinking of the presence that filled me within the fractured remembrance of Ellery Pike's mirrors. It wasn't me in there, and it wasn't Ellery. It was something *talking* to her. Whispering in a voice as thin as the breath of space between a mirror's surface and the reflection behind it. It knew about her, all about her.

And so did I, just for a minute. In glimpses through time and space, I saw what was. So much *more* than just my usual backward visions. The actual past. But only fragments of it. The way those mirrors were placed was all wrong, and while the glimpses I saw were the most vivid I've ever seen, they amount to little.

"We have to go back," I say.

"Absolutely not."

I find the energy to stare up at Dom. He wobbles, my eyes finding it hard to focus. He looks at me with concern, and I hate it. I can't let myself be this weak. It just proves Yiayia was right to hide whatever she hid, because here I am discovering an entirely new dimension of our power and ending up collapsed in a puddle of sweat.

I wish Yiayia was here. I'm supposed to be saving her, but all I want is for her to rescue me from this life I was never supposed to live. Everything is going wrong. The more I look, the more I see, the more I ruin.

Tears sting the edges of my eyes, and for a moment Dom is just a blur. Still, I catch his hand just as it reaches for my cheek. I'm stronger than this. He was right before, when he said that maybe the thing I've hidden all along could be the key to revealing the truth. And maybe if we do that, no one has to die as a result of my curse. It never occurred to me that I could use the Sight to save anyone. If I'm the only one who can do it, then I have to do it. If I'm the only one who can be a witness, I don't have the right to turn away. Even if I'm scared. It's just like Dr. Wei said. I've got to be brave enough to look my fears in the eye.

God, I'm scared. And yeah, Yiayia is a million miles away, but I'm not alone.

I let Dom wipe the tears from my cheek.

"I need to tell you something," I say, doing my best to stop the shaking in my voice. "About what's in the mirrors. There's . . . a presence. I saw it in the elevator, and I think I've glimpsed it before. I didn't understand what it was until just now, but I think it's part—"

In a flash, Dom's hand is over my mouth. He's gentle but firm. *Don't say more.*

"Can you walk?"

I nod, and he releases me so that he can help me up. We head outside and join a pack of people heading for the High Line, this elevated park that snakes between the buildings on the ruins of an old freight rail. Dom puts us on a bench hidden by some tall grasses.

"Start with what you saw just now," he says.

I tell him about the fragments of Ellery's life—her in the wash of white, her inspecting her reflection as it swam across the mirrored faces of her sculptures. And her staring at the droplets of blood. I repeat as much as I can remember of that voice, the one that seemed to narrate Ellery's life as it happened, almost like it was compelling her narrative's direction.

"And in the elevator at Uhler's?" Dom presses.

This I'm less sure of, but I try anyway.

"In the elevator, the mirrors faced each other and formed an infinity mirror. My . . . Sight interacted with that in a weird way. I saw this thing in the distance. It was trying to get closer. It was . . . breaking through the barriers. It . . ."

I huff. Even in my memory, the thing darts and evades, jumps and scampers before I can catch a detail, a color, or even a shape.

"It has eyes," I say. "But they're our eyes."

That sounds right. But it also makes no sense.

I look at Dom, expecting confusion or, if I'm lucky, an eye roll. But he just stares up into the city. He looks lost in contemplation, like he understands what I'm saying.

"Why didn't you tell me before?"

I shake my head. "My yiayia has told me stories about curses for as long as I can remember. She said that if I looked into mirrors, something might look back, and if I saw it then it could never be unseen. I think that's what happened in the elevator. And I guess I didn't want you to see it, too."

Tell him, I think. *Tell him about the strands that trail from him, like the ones that had Ellery bound.* But then I think, *No, I can't*. It's the way Dom

150

stared at the drop, the way he shied away from the train. It's like he can already hear the voice that whispered Ellery toward her death, toward a suicide I'm sure she did not want to commit. If the void is already calling to Dom, I cannot tell him to listen closely. I can only try my best to keep him safe and show him that when the void calls, you do not answer.

"You said your family was cursed with the Sight," Dom says finally. "By who? Or what?"

I shake my head. "It doesn't feel gifted. Not a blessing or a curse. It feels like an exchange. The Sight for something else. It's that last part, the *else*, that I think about all the time. For years after the fire, I thought using the Sight attracted the attention of . . ." I trail off. "It sounds silly."

"Go on," Dom urges.

"Doom," I say. "Like, a conscious thing, you know? That kept score. Like anytime I would use the Sight to see into the past, the price was something in my present. So I stopped looking backward, but I also never looked ahead. Never finished school. Never made goals. It all felt pointless, until I got help. Not from Yiayia—she won't talk about any of it—but a therapist. He urged me to face my fears and prove to myself that nothing bad would happen. He wanted me to break the pattern myself."

"And what happened?"

I take a shaking breath. "I looked, at the party. Something looked back. I thought all your theories about death and Uhler were just delusions, but what if Uhler was talking to that thing in the elevator? What if he wasn't on the phone at all?"

Dom has his sketchbook open to a drawing of a thorny plant cluttered with berries. He writes in sharp cursive: *Doom, Mirror Monster, Hungry, Uhler, Death, Ellery.*

I take the pencil from him and trace a line between *Doom* and *Mirror Monster* and *Uhler*.

"And you think whatever you saw, or *didn't* see, in Ellery's vision is that thing from the elevator at Uhler's?"

I nod. I thought its thoughts, so it must think. And I felt a hunger in its words as it compelled Ellery Pike toward her doom, so it must eat. And I saw through its eyes, so it must have eyes. But all I can recall about the monster from the elevator is that it had *too many eyes*.

I make a decision, right there on the High Line.

"I want to do it again," I say. "I want to know what happened."

Now Dom *does* roll his eyes. "Athan, you don't need to play hero. We can figure out another—"

"No." I grab Dom's hand, maybe to convince him I've made up my mind, maybe to convince myself. "If this is connected to the doom, or that thing, or *whatever* my grandmother never wanted me to find, then it's probably connected to why Uhler took her away. So I need to do it. Again. I know how to do it right this time."

Dom glances back the way we came. Though the entrance was in the food hall, the building hiding the theater could be any one of the modern warehouses spread around us.

"We can't go back in there," he says.

"We'll go back tonight."

"It'll be locked up," Dom says. "This isn't like the D&D Building. I don't have access."

I've regained some of myself during this exchange; I give my best, most devilish grin and say, "But I might."

For once, Dom has tons to say, but I shush him as I take the lead. We walk along the High Line as I tap out a few texts.

"Is this what I'm like?" Dom asks, trying to see what I'm typing.

"You're worse."

"Just tell me what the plan is."

"Show some patience and see for yourself."

My phone pings with a response. A second later, I've got coordinates for us to head to. A few blocks south, parked on a side street, is a large white box truck. We approach it from behind, looking into its open back, where a few guys sit with their legs hanging over the bumper, eating out of plastic to-go containers.

"Yo!" I shout, throwing a hand up into a big wave.

Dom nearly faints, I think. He's aghast as he looks from me to the men, who are squinting at us as we approach.

"Yo!" I yell again.

And then they yell back, slapping the side of the truck in a thunderous greeting.

"Well, well, well," says a short, wide woman with arms so thick it's hard to imagine her bending them. She wraps me in a hug that feels like home.

"If it isn't the Little Prince himself," she says, clapping me on the shoulder. Then she looks at my too-tight outfit. "Your yiayia's been keeping you fed, I see. How's she doing? Still lovely as ever, I hope?"

"Actually," I say as I exchange fist bumps with the rest of the Forum Fine Arts crew, "that's why I texted. The Bakirtzis family has finally learned how to ask for help."

Before you became one of them, you always wondered if the men (and woman) who worked as handlers were real people.

It was a common enough thought for you back then, child that you were. Sometimes you wondered if people really went home at the end of the day, or if they simply drew backward into the long shadows of dusk, waved goodbye, and vanished. That seemed easy to do. Your parents had done it, after all. Just withdrew from your life in a smoky puff, melting out of the world like they were never there at all.

What did the barber do without your father's hair to cut? What did the deli make without your mom ordering a breakfast sandwich? Did the world know what was missing, or was the emptiness you felt only yours now?

When the world went on without your parents, it minimized their memory in a way that offended your childlike sense of reality. It felt so wrong, you decided it was the world and all its people who weren't real.

Ironically, it was Bernie and the boys who proved you wrong. Even after the fire, they visited you and your yiayia. They rushed into your life and brought their own lives with them. You met their kids. (They had kids!) You visited their homes. (They had homes!) Gradually, you slipped out of the ruins of your own world and into theirs. And even though you could feel the pity that permeated all of it, you felt loved.

When you were finally old enough to join the truck, you didn't even need to ask. They were already there, waiting in the cargo area, a hand extended to the not-so-little-anymore Athan.

Our Prince, they called you.

Call you, still.

You haven't seen Bernie and her crew in a while, though. The shop's operation has outgrown the once-familial bond. Bernie is always on some job too important to fuck up, which means too important to bring the Prince along. *Not that you'd fit between us in the cab anymore*, she would joke, *and you're too precious to throw in the cargo area.* You didn't have a chance to feel left out; these past months, you've barely been at the shop, too busy keeping an eye on Yiayia. And no one has been by to visit in even longer.

But the love is still there.

It's a shame you'll have to exploit it now.

But that's the art world, baby. That's what Uhler would say, you think, as you hug the handlers one by one.

CHAPTER FIFTEEN

The mood at the back of the truck immediately sobers when I mention that Yiayia needs help. Most of these guys (and Bernie) know her, or of her. Some of them have known her for as long as they've known New York City.

Actually, Bernie has known her longer than me, technically. She's been part of Forum Fine Arts since my grandfather managed it. With Uhler in charge, she basically took over handling the handlers, but she still takes on shifts when there's something really important we're moving. I don't see her that much anymore—I'm too green to come along and too big to lug, she's said a million times—but now I'm starting to get the bigger picture of what Forum's been moving.

I explain as little as I can, hyperaware of Dom vibrating at my back.

"Yiayia is okay. She just had a fall. She's safe now."

"What can we do? You need food? A place to crash? Anything. You name it."

I glance from Bernie to the guys. Some new faces I don't know as well. Bernie notices right away. She loops an arm around my shoulders and pulls me to the front of the truck, so we can talk in private.

"You in trouble?" she asks, voice low.

"No. What? Why?"

She shrugs. "A hunch. You never ask for help. Your yiayia, too. Stubborn as fuck. You know we had to just show up to help move you into that place up in Harlem? She was too proud to say yes. But if we hadn't come through, there was no backup plan. And she didn't say *no*, which is the Greek *yes*. Now imagine my surprise getting a text from

Athanasios 'Little Prince' Bakirtzis asking for a favor. Imagine. So. I'm asking: You in trouble?"

I didn't know that Yiayia had never asked for help, that the handlers just gave it. That throws me. And Bernie probably has a few more secrets, I realize. But how much can I share about my predicament before she figures out something is really, *really* wrong, and tries to stop me? Even though I haven't seen her in months, she's the closest thing I've got to an aunt. She's coached me on everything from basketball to picking up girls. And when I told her I liked boys, too, she sat me down with her brother, also gay, to learn what went where. I was way too young, and her brother knew it. He said, *Ignore Bernie, there's no rush.*

Help, always offered. But now that I have something to ask for, I'm not sure I know how. I can't be too direct about it or she'll be implicated. It pains me, but I've got to play Bernie like I do everyone else.

"I checked your schedule and, every night this week, you've had a final stop at an address in Meatpacking. That's the Sub Rosa Gallery, right?"

I expect shock, but Bernie's got one hell of a poker face. "You know about Sub Rosa?"

"I've been." I flash the card Bruno gave me, and Bernie's eyes grow just a fraction, letting me know she *is* shocked. And impressed. "I was there just today."

"Uhler brought you? *There?*" she asks.

I smile. "And I need to get back in tonight. It's important."

I have no idea what Bernie will suspect I'm up to, so I quickly throw out a defense against an accusation she hasn't even made, to focus her suspicions. "I'm not stealing anything. It's more of . . . a personal matter."

Bernie studies me. Do I say more? Or have I said just enough? Then her eyes flick over my shoulder and she breaks into a grin. Footsteps scrape to a halt, and I whip around to find Dom approaching.

"I see," Bernie says, grin widening. "This the lucky guy? A prince for a prince? Got a little date night planned?"

Oh no. Dom must realize the misunderstanding, too, because his eyes widen to full capacity. Which is *wide*.

"It's not . . . we're not . . ."

"Yes!" I almost shout. This is it. This is our story. Bernie's eyes saw it before we did, but it's perfect. I pull Dom into our conversation.

"And they say the younger generation doesn't know how to do romance. Ha!" Bernie thrusts a hand at Dom, who takes it and—to my horror—shakes it so limply I can practically feel Bernie's lesbianism strain a muscle.

"Nice to meet you. I'm . . ." Dom looks to me, but I'm basically melting on the inside.

"Kenny Garfield," Dom says dourly.

Bernie squares her shoulders, playing at chivalry. "Nice to meet you, Kenny. Fancy seeing you out for a little . . . nocturnal rendezvous. Glad I could be of service, but what are your intentions with the Little Prince?"

There's desperation all over Dom—his shoulders shoot up to his ears as he tries to piece together what I must have told this small, burly woman. I want to set this all straight, but Bernie is so happy, so proud, so self-satisfied at figuring us out. I can't afford to derail that. Plus, it's amusing as hell.

But then Dom makes his best guess.

"Sex?"

Bernie freezes. I freeze. Dom, mistaking the pause as a cue to clarify, says, "Butt stuff—"

"A date," I cut in. "*Just* a date. Kenny likes art. I handle art. I wanted to give him a behind-the-scenes look at some stuff showing at Sub Rosa. We'll be careful, I promise. You know how good I am, right, Bernie?"

"Right. Very gentle hands," she says.

We all wince.

Bernie, for all her aunt-vibes, has completely abandoned any effort of playing it cool. She's terrified, I think, just trying to get through this awkward moment. She's running damage control now, saying, "Sub Rosa is our last stop. Got a few others before it. Could probably use a few extra . . ." A big pause. ". . . hands. Can't promise more than a pop-in, but hopefully you can make it quick."

Bernie is in shambles now, each new word deepening the grave we're all standing in. I decide to acknowledge none of this.

"Thanks, Bern. I knew I could count on you," I say. It sounds stiff.

She grumbles a thank-you, waving us back to the guys doing their best to eavesdrop from the back of the truck.

"Oh, and Kenny," she calls before we've turned the corner. "The whole 'Little Prince' thing . . . that's just our name for him. Don't let him use it in bed or anything. You gotta come up with your own."

It's dark out, but the horrible thing about New York City is that it's never dark enough. We can all see the blood rush to Dom's face.

"Yes, ma'am." He salutes.

Bernie salutes back, a silent understanding shared between them.

Bernie feels off to me after that. Nervous, almost, but I can tell she's trying not to show it. And she wasn't kidding about putting us to work. She makes us throw on a few spare shirts she keeps in the truck that read FORUM FINE ARTS & FRAMING. They smell like the damp cardboard box she pulls them out of, but I'm immediately more comfortable in working clothes. Dom seems unsure—probably about all this—but I give him an approving thumbs-up after he pulls the T-shirt over his long-sleeved black turtleneck. He leaves his bandanna on, defiantly.

Dom never does look sure, but that might just be because of the sudden shift into my home turf. I know these guys. I know how to roll with their punches and punch back as they swap stories about the crazy art they've moved, and the crazy clients they've moved it for. When it's time to get to the job, I fit into their process without a problem, forgetting about Dom for minutes at a time as we unload a massive wrapped canvas from the truck and carry it around the back of the building to a freight entrance. Unlike the pretentious elevator that required a special sequence, the service one simply goes down. We enter a brick-walled maze of corridors, and then suddenly I'm back on the Sub Rosa stage, facing a dimly lit emptiness devoid of another soul.

I make sure never to look at the display of Ellery Pike's sculptures. I notice Dom is diligent about avoiding them, too. He makes himself useful, helping two of the men find several pieces on their list. Then they have to analyze the art before packing it, to note even minor damages from being displayed. Otherwise they'll get blamed for it later. Dom, eagle-eyed as he is, wows the crew by finding several minuscule issues using just his cell phone flashlight.

"A natural," Bernie says, squinting at the canvas where Dom has pointed out a hair trapped beneath the paint. It's no more than an eyelash, but he saw it.

The rest of the work only takes an hour with the extra hands we provide. The men seem grateful for us—and in a rush. After this, they've still got to return to the frame shop, drop off whatever pieces are due to be framed, and only then do they get to go home.

Dom and I linger in the gallery as they head back up to the truck. The second the others are gone, we rush over to the Pike display.

"You sure this'll work?" he whispers to me.

I shrug. "Do we have another choice if it doesn't?"

"Yes. We try a different lead. I have tons of them."

"You said it yourself. Uhler's got plans for Friday. *This* Friday. You think we can really track down *another* entire collection of murder-witnessing mirrors by then?"

Dom glares at Ellery's mirrors. He's curious, I know he is, and it's a testament to how worried about me he must be that he still shakes his head and says, "You don't need to do this, Athan."

I shrug off his concern. "What I felt before when I looked at these mirrors . . . it was so much more intense than my other visions. We're onto something. Just let me try again."

"Try what again?"

We spin around. Bernie is right behind us. For such a muscular person, she moves with a ballerina's grace. Based on her face, she's heard enough of what we've said to know something is off.

"Nothing," Dom says. I almost wince. Too quick, Dom.

"You're not on a date, are you?"

"We are." Dom grabs my hand and holds it up, like *Look! Proof!*

I actually do wince, this time.

Bernie sucks on her teeth, nodding like this confirms some long-held suspicion. The chummy Aunt Bernie act drops away. She turns to make sure it's just us in here, then serves Dom with a steely glare.

"I've seen you at Orion, haven't I? You're one of Uhler's."

Dom's hand goes icy in mine. He looks at me again and I'm surprised to find his confidence has returned. He doesn't have to pretend anymore.

"You know of him?"

Bernie's brow crinkles. "Know of *my boss*?" She softens a smidge, maybe because she realizes we barely know what we're doing.

"Look," she says, checking again that we're alone. "Athan, your parents were good people. All these years I've checked up on you and your yiayia, I've been trying to pay them back for everything they did for me. When I had nothing, I had them. You know what I mean? They were good, godly people. But that doesn't mean I agreed with everything they did."

Here it is again. This feeling of being in the dark, facing down something huge and silent. A waiting crypt with the door cracked.

"What did they do?" I ask.

Bernie just shakes her head sadly. "That's a question for your yiayia, God bless her. A family's secrets can only be shared between blood. It's not my place."

A sound in the back room makes Bernie jump. She waits until she's sure no one is coming, then turns back to me.

"I only know rumors," she whispers. "About your parents, about Uhler and the Patrons. But in my work, you learn not to ask. You hear too much, you become a liability. You see too much, you vanish. I can't do that to my family again. I've done my time. I've got my own to worry about now. Still . . ." She puts a calloused hand on my shoulder. For the first time I notice just how much taller I've gotten. Bernie has to reach up to act like she's holding me down.

"Still," she repeats, nodding. "You're like a son to me, too, Athan. If I can help you with . . . whatever it is you're doing, I will. But if it comes down to it, I've got to pick me and mine. Okay?"

I swallow. "Okay."

Bernie steps back, like she's relinquishing the space to us. She seems to understand more about what we're doing here than we do. I'm caught between wanting to follow her out of here, to beg for more information, and needing to stay and take the chance she's giving us.

Dom, cool as ever, finally interjects. "We aren't stealing anything. We promise. We just need time to take a closer look. We're trying—"

Bernie puts up a hand, closing it slowly so that one finger remains up and against her lips. A signal for silence, but one that feels fearful. She won't hear a word more if she can help it.

"You have until sunrise. I'll be back with the truck by then. When I call, you get your asses ready. I'll open the freight door, back in, and you'll climb aboard. The only cameras are outside the building. Do not let them see you."

Bernie turns and stalks toward the back door, but I catch her before she exits. When she looks at me now, there's *blatant* fear there. It's like all those months I was gone suddenly crowd between us, and she doesn't even recognize me.

She hugs me before I can say thank you.

"Do what you gotta do," she whispers, just for me to hear. "But then you get away from Uhler. You get out of all this, before it's too late."

"Okay," I whisper back.

When we pull apart, the fear is still in Bernie's eyes, but now I understand that it's not for herself. It's for me. She's scared for me, and the beginning of that fear traces back to the mention of Uhler. Even now, she keeps glancing at Dom, who has turned his back to give us some privacy.

"Whoever he is, *actually* is, I mean," Bernie says. "He's not worth it. None of this is. I told your dad that, too, about the jobs with Orion. He didn't listen, but you can. Promise me this is it. Tonight, and then no more."

I want to grab on to Bernie and make her stay here until I know everything.

"I promise," I say.

Then she's gone a second later, and the door latches loudly in the empty gallery.

Then it's just us. Me, Dom, and whatever is left of Ellery Pike.

"I'm ready."

I'm not, but whatever.

Ellery's ruined rug lies on the stage between the sarcophagus and the crashed car. It helps us approximate the dimensions of her living room, and we use boxes from the back to simulate her furniture. Dom references his files on Ellery to place each mirror piece where they would have been in her home, because something tells me their position to one another matters.

The stage is lit from the front, so that's how we orient the makeshift room. If I close my eyes, it's like looking up through Ellery's massive windows, at the sun.

"I'm here," Dom says, but he can't hold my hand this time. He kneels at the rug's edge, in the darkness. Alone, I step onto the stain. From above, it looks like my own shadow.

I take a deep breath, open my eyes, and bring my gaze down into the reflections surrounding me, willing their mirror-smooth faces to open up. And it works. They do. And

You are Ellery Pike.

You stare into me in a thousand ways.

You are, of course, staring at yourself, but it's me you're looking through.

You are lying on the couch in your apartment, staring up at the ceiling. You're very still, but inside you're picking at this strange anxiety that's stuck out of your subconscious, like a hand punching up through the placid surface of a lake. A hand, but nothing more, stubborn and offensively incongruent with the background. And it's waving.

It reminds you of your mother, but you're not sure why. Hands often do bring the woman to mind. It's because you never saw hers. She had them (oh, did she have them), but they felt practically mythical since she always hid them away in those gloves.

Germs.

That was her explanation for the gloves. Brief. Disgusted.

It was with those same gloved hands that she caressed your face, tucked you in at night, held your firstborn. The world disgusted her, and you were part of the world.

You get up and get to cleaning. Grimly. Dutifully. It's the way you honor the late Mrs. Pike. And that hand sticking up from the water? The one that waved at you? It waves you on, like *go, go on, my dear.*

You go, go on, humming to yourself as you fetch the buckets, the rags, the chemicals. Even though you'll need to roll up the carpets to really scrub, you like to take everything out first and set it up, like a little temple to her. The entire process will take you hours into the night, but you weren't sleeping anyway. You were just lying there, thinking of Dane Boucher again. Poor Dane. You haven't articulated this to yourself yet, but you blame yourself for what happened to them. Or you will, once you realize Uhler's part in all of it. The Patrons, you are constantly discovering, have a part in everything around you, a design so sublime you barely see it behind everything else. Like a perfect wallpaper in a lived-in room.

You clean until you're heady with the fumes. That's usually how you know to stop, because just assuring yourself things are clean enough won't do. It didn't do for Mom, certainly. It takes a migraine to get your cramping hands to put down the scrubbing brush and strip off the rubber gloves. And, for a time, you feel better.

That week, you head to the D&D Building. You stop in to see some friends, endure morose gossip about Dane, and of course have your usual bout with Uhler. Still, you meet him at the mural at his request, standing beneath the gaze of a painted bee until the door opens, leading you to his latest horrific obsession. You scrub it all off you at the end of the day with a shower so hot it makes you itch. And itch. And itch. You can't sleep that night, either, so you get up and vacuum.

You know to vacuum at night. In the day, with the light, the vacuum kicks up a nauseating amount of debris. You can't see it without hearing your mom remind you that the biggest contributor to dust in a home isn't dirt from the outside.

It's . . .

It's skin, Ellery, she would say with a morbid, joyful smile. *Skin! It sloughs off us, into the air, and makes dust. Horrible, isn't it?*

Mother's solution was to scrub very, very hard. On the few times you did see her hands, they were bright pink. Like fresh little piglets.

The night you get up to vacuum somehow turns into the morning you wake up standing in your living room, the vacuum screaming as you push its mouth over a mess of shattered glass. The noise is what snaps you out of it. You're horrified—one of your own pieces, smashed by your own clumsiness as you . . . what? Daydreamed? Sleepwalked?

You rush to pick up the pieces, starting with the biggest shards. You recoil, because one has sliced your knuckle. As you suck on your bloodied finger, you gingerly pick up the shard again. Your face is smeared across it, and you look like a mess. Tired, still in your nightshirt. Ridiculous.

You stick out your tongue, a habit when you catch yourself being even remotely concerned with vanity.

But your reflection stays still and serious. Then it smiles.

But *you* haven't smiled. *Aren't* smiling right now.

You drop the shard and it bursts into fragments, too small to reflect much. Still, you kick off your slipper and grind the rest of the mess into dust.

Dust, you think, laughing at yourself. *At least this time, it's not skin.*

You are Ellery Pike. You've got a good sense of humor about these things. You have to, when you're an artist. You tell a few of the other Patrons at the next dinner party, and they scold you about seven years of bad luck and all that other bullshit you can't afford to believe in. Not when you've broken more mirrors than probably anyone else on the planet Earth. *Risks of working in the medium*, you say, shrugging it off.

But you watch for me, after that, in all the mirrors you pass.

You watch me as much as I watch you, but of course you do. You are an artist. Your entire body of work is a study in yourself. To you, I look like you. We have the same face. You blink, I blink. You move, I move. Sometimes a little after, if you're quick, but you can't seem to replicate that moment when your reflection smiled while you didn't.

There was a time when you tried constantly to surprise me, moving oddly, making faces in the reflections on cars and windows to see if I'd slip, but I only did that once.

Just once was enough, though.

Funny how all you needed was some tiny, terrible proof, and it's enough to make everything else just come apart.

Time passes. Your guilt around Dane grows. At one of the dinner parties, another Patron reminds you that you introduced Dane to Uhler, and you leave before that night's demonstration. The small bursts of cleaning continue, but they're becoming more frequent. You need it more, whatever it provides. The payoff is never enough, and the fumes somehow dull in your nose. And you notice something odd: spots. They appear at the edges of your vision, standing out against the warm white of your house, but when you turn it's just a dimple of shadow skittering across the mirrored face of one of your pieces. Not really there, just a trick of the light.

You polish them, like you can buff out the shadows in the reflections. You turn on all the lights, too, because now it's night. You work until early morning, but every time you stop you see one of those spots. They're spooky, like cockroaches, always darting and scampering. You can practically hear them! But they always know you're about to look, and they get away. Every time.

You consider breaking every single mirror, just to prove a point, but the mess it would create . . . The dust it would release. No. You'll have to be more innovative than simply destructive.

The Patrons call on you—Uhler calls on you—and you do not answer. Your assistant comes to check on you, worriedly knocking on your door, but you hold your breath until he goes away.

You stand in your home, and you wonder how it came to feel like such a prison. You've touched every surface, crafted every angle. What a horror, you think, to understand that all your toiling has built you a cage that you can't even see. Better to let no one else in. Better to let nothing else out.

In the morning, you think, *I will have enough light to burn all the spots away.* You assure yourself of this as you slump to the carpet. The couch is off-limits now, and you don't want to risk opening the bedroom door just in case more spots get in.

The sun rises, waking you. The first thing you see when you open your eyes is a floating coil of thread. It's not more than a fiber off one of your knitted blankets, but the moment you see it, you see everything else, too. The sun, sideways from the window, lights up the air with a thousand glowing filaments. They're all over you, they're sucking into your nose and mouth. You spit them out, disgusted. You run to the windows and pull the curtains closed, but it's too late. You've seen every spot you missed, grime in every corner of your house, and in the heaving darkness you think you can hear it spreading.

You can't let people see this. Can't let people know the filth you live within. And then a horrible thing happens. You get a call. It's Uhler, letting you know he's so proud you've had a change of heart.

What?

You can hear his smile through the phone. *The Patrons will be so pleased*, he says in that condescending fuck-you tone. *Dane was a loss, and they weren't eager to let you go, too. Sending out that invite was the perfect way to renew your fealty.*

You don't know what invite he means. After a confused back-and-forth, he texts you a photo of a handwritten invitation. From you to him. For a dinner party tomorrow night.

Right here, in your home.

You hang up on him. You have several missed calls and messages. Other Patrons, responding to the invitation with glee or respectful declination. Someone offers to bring wine, but wants to make sure you're still not allowing reds in your home. Someone is asking about allergies, because they want to bring dessert. Several people ask if there will be a demonstration, which is the expectation, and a few even ask outright if Uhler will be there to reveal his latest findings.

You stare at the photo Uhler sent you. The address on the invitation is yours. The stationery is yours. But the handwriting. *The handwriting.*

It's your mother's.

You have to get back to work. You don't think this, but I do, so you do, and it's done. You get back to scrubbing, fluffing, brushing, shining, buffing, mopping, sweeping. Swearing all the while. So much swearing, until you stop mid-*fuck* because swearing is a kind of contamination, too, isn't it? What if the guests enter and can hear some residue of the filth pouring out of your mouth?

That would be a disaster, you think as you scrape at the grout with a toothbrush. Mother would hate that, you think. If she could see you now, would she be embarrassed? Or proud that you're once again hosting the Patrons for one of their little parties?

The brush snaps.

Your knuckle slices over the grout. That old wound splits open.

You stare at the droplet of red. Droplets, actually. One sits round and perfect on the tile. The other has already soaked into the grout.

You'll never get that out.

The party vanishes from your mind because you'll never get that out.

You could die trying, but you'll never, ever get that out.

And you feel . . .

What do you feel, Ellery?

You feel . . . light. Relief. The monumental dread that bent you over your own knees so that you were crushed to the floor, scrubbing and sweating and swearing, is gone. Gone! You are suddenly yourself again. Not the person desperately cleaning and seeing spots where there are no spots, and not the person who is trying to catch mirrors misbehaving. You're Ellery Pike all over again.

You walk to the center of the room, not caring that you're dripping blood into the carpet. It's somehow morning again, and in the sun everything feels fresh and clean. So *impossibly* clean. So *mocking* in its cleanliness that, without much thought, you drive your hand into the nearest sculpture.

Comically, your hand punches right through it, the hole slices the skin of your arm on the way out, and a sheath of blood flows down your hand, into the webs between your fingers.

You mash your palms together. Gleefully, like you used to do when your mother stood over you at the sink, making sure you scrubbed every crease in your skin. She'd make you hold your hands up for inspection, like a person praying to something bigger than them. You hold your hands up now, to the light, and laugh.

You're wearing your mother's gloves.

You laugh! I laugh. We laugh.

You rush to the windows. No, the space between them, just blank white except for a subtle pattern in the paper that's caught your eye. It's a warm white paper gifted by Uhler months ago, as a makeup gift after you told him you wanted nothing to do with him, his Patrons, or his special projects. None of it, after Dane died. But you accepted the paper because you wanted to be kind and, if you're honest, its texture intrigued you from the moment he surprised you with it.

It intrigues you now, though that's too polite a word for what the paper does. It demands you, all at once.

It's because the light has caught it just right and revealed a texture in the design, like little bits of grit caught between the wall and the paper. The effect is subtle, but undeniable: tiny pocks, like open pores, like skin, all up the wall. Another you would be horrified—all those spots, all that skin, all that dust—but this version is fascinated.

Your mother's voice comes to you in a litany of warnings. Don't touch. Don't move. Don't make a mess. Don't leave a mark.

But you're an artist. Leaving a mark is what you do.

You press your bloody hand into the wall, delighted at the shiver that sweeps across it. You caress the paper in a large red arc, and wonder at how something could feel both soft and hard, firm but supple.

You should stop. You know that. The rules.

You hated the rules.

Your mother's life was dominated by rules and look what happened to her. A lifetime of fastidious upkeep in an eternal war with dust. But in the end, dust was all that was left of her. No marks, no mess. Not even her gloves. Just dust.

You don't want to end up like your mother, do you?

No, you don't, I whisper.

No, I don't, you agree.

You reach for a shard of mirror. You're going to need more blood.

CHAPTER SIXTEEN

I am Athan.

Athan.

Athan.

Athanasios.

I lie with my head in Dom's lap, at the center of the many mirrors, their surfaces still flickering like TV static. Not that I look at them. I have my hands out before me, and I turn them over again and again, afraid that if I even blink I'll see those bloody gloves dripping down my wrists.

Dom pets my hair back and away from the sweat trickling off my forehead. His touch is so gentle, and I'm embarrassed by how badly I need it right now. I'm damp all over. It was like witnessing Ellery Pike's death wasn't just an act of observation but one of participation, like I was actually there, around her and within her, pushing her toward the end.

Not me, I remind myself.

I am Athan.

Whatever pushed Ellery was something—or someone—with a distinct will. That spidery mass that I saw breaking through the infinity mirror, that speaks my name in a voice made of edges. It nested in her reflections, and used that strange, breathing wallpaper to land its final blow. I was only watching. Even so, I'm sick with guilt, like it was me in all those mirrors, poking and picking at the threads of Ellery's mind until it was wound so tight that unraveling felt like ecstasy.

Dom and I both jump when a new sound breaks the quiet. It's my phone. I must have forgotten to turn it back off after I contacted Bernie. Years of muscle memory overcome my shock and, without thinking about it, I roll over and pick up the call.

"Athan, dear, it's Linda. Are you home?"

"N-no," I stutter. "What's wrong?"

Has Yiayia come home? Is she there now while I'm once again somewhere else?

"I'm looking for my bird lamps," Linda says, and through the phone I hear the crash of objects being pushed aside. She was already downstairs in the apartment before she called to ask if I was, too.

"The bookcase," I say automatically. "And the other is plugged in . . . in Yiayia's . . . in the bedroom."

"I'll need to unplug it, of course," Linda says. "I found someone who wants to buy them. And a few other things, but I'll need your help with the rest. They're on their way. Are you going to be home soon?"

"What?"

"Are you," Linda repeats, "going to be home soon?"

"I . . . no. I'm staying with a friend tonight."

"Athan, dear, I've let you use these things as a courtesy, but it was always under the assumption that I may need to get them later. I can't do that with all this stuff in the way."

I'm sitting up now. "I'm sorry, but what do you need to get to?"

"The mattress, but it's under all these sheets."

"You mean Yiayia's bed? You're taking Yiayia's bed?"

"Are you there?" Linda's volume goes up. "Can you hear me? Yes, I just said I sold it. It's mine. Where are you?"

Dom waves for my attention. He makes a motion to hang up, and I catch on. We can't trust anyone.

"I'm . . . on vacation," I tell Linda. "Out of town. Sorry. Just leave the sheets on the floor."

I hang up on Linda. The brief call seems to have snapped me out of my daze. Or it's Dom, half-crouched, like he was ready to snatch the phone right out of my hand if I didn't hang up. He's watching me with eyes wide and luminous, like a cat.

"What happened?" he asks.

He doesn't mean the call.

I start at the beginning, and I talk until Ellery's end.

Dom handles it better than me. Of course he does. He didn't have to see it. Still, he and Ellery actually knew each other. I expect shock or maybe even tears, but he absorbs the story with a steady, unyielding focus. Like it isn't revealing anything new, just confirming what he already suspected.

"That thing in the mirror," he says at the end. "It was the same thing that chased you in the elevator, right? That you think Uhler spoke to?"

"I don't know. I think so, but what's up with the wallpaper, then?"

Dom flips open his sketchbook to a picture of a butterfly. "In nature, some creatures have evolved elaborate designs to hide or to hunt. What if the paper is how this thing hunts? Like a spider's web, right?" Dom looks at me and I shrug, because I don't know shit about animals other than cockroaches, rats, and pigeons. He goes on with, "I don't understand the mirror part of this, though."

"I might," I say. "Yiayia talked about mirrors like they were portals sometimes, connecting time and space in weird ways. They couldn't be trusted, but not because they didn't show the world as it was. It's because they showed too much. Maybe this thing exists around us, but in its own dimension, and mirrors just allow us to see each other?"

Dom shrugs. "You're the expert on mirrors here. I'm just . . ." He looks into his hands, never finishing the thought. He starts a new one instead. "Maybe it's not a thing, so much as it is a force? It sounds like it was driving her insane? Maybe that's how it eats?"

I nod. "Yeah, it definitely felt like a force, by the end. It surrounded her. Like on the outside *and* the inside. I don't know if she saw it this way, but it seemed like everything around her served a specific purpose in this, like . . . design." I close my eyes, seeing the bloody grout once again.

"A deadly design," I say.

"Like a pattern?" Dom asks.

I nod.

Patterns make me think of Dr. Wei telling me for the hundredth time that *our brains look for patterns to organize the chaos of the world. Sometimes, we see designs that aren't really there, yet the longer we look, the clearer they become. It's like those particles in quantum physics, the ones that aren't real until they're observed. The act of looking, of seeing, can take random coincidence into compelling composition. And we prefer it that way. It's easier to see what we believe than to believe what we see, which is that usually there is no order to anything. No order at all.*

Dr. Wei is wrong. Ellery's demise was not one of coincidence or chaos; there was order and intention designed to compel her toward her death. Something wove that web she was struggling in, until she was too exhausted to extract herself, and at the moment she was most fragile, it pounced.

Dom stands, helping me up. We're quiet, both lost in thought as we set the display back up and replace the things we moved. In the back we find dustcloths to wipe down the shiny sculptures. I don't fear them now that I know their secret. I resent them.

Behind the stage, in the farthest corner of the theater, we find a trove of packing materials that'll have to do for bedding. We set up a mattress of cardboard layered with the moving blankets. When we finally kill the lights, we're surprised to find a warm, golden glow falls into the small space from a high-up window that faces the ever-lit streets. Dom doodles in his sketchbook. I lie on my back, looking up and out into the night.

"You know, I think I get it." I angle myself toward Dom. "When Ellery finally gave in, she wasn't sad or upset. She was . . . relieved. She finally felt peace."

"That's grim," Dom says flatly.

"That's what I'm getting at," I say, sitting up on an elbow. "That thing toyed with her. Tricked her. It told her that anything was better than the constant torture of living, but it was also the thing torturing her. It made her feel like it was her decision to give up, but it wasn't. If it hadn't trapped her like that, who knows what she would have decided?"

"I think I know," Dom says, still not looking up.

"Same," I say. I listen to the scratch of his pencil for a few minutes, wondering what he's drawing. Not me, I think. He hasn't looked up once.

"But I get it," I try again. I have something I need to get out, but I'm not sure how to say it. I just feel a strange connection to Ellery now, like there's a morbid familiarity between us.

"What?"

"Just." I sit all the way up. "Okay. So, you know how I survived that fire?"

Dom nods.

"There's more to the story."

I take a deep breath. This feels right, talking about this.

"It was my birthday," I say. "I remember because my parents and Yiayia were all there, and they sang to me, and before I blew out the candles, Yiayia left. Just walked away. Back then she was still lucid, so it was weird but not, like, alarming. I was upset, though, because I wanted her to see me blow them out, and she missed it. So after the cake was cut, I put a candle back into Yiayia's piece, and I lit it, and I went to go find her."

Dom closes his sketchbook and finally looks at me, but now I'm the one staring off into the distance. Each word feels like a step forward into a darkness that could drop me at any moment.

"I think I went to her room, because I remember looking out her window and seeing her in the street below. She was waving at me. I remember she had her hand mirror with her, and she was using the light to catch my eye."

I turn the memory around in my mind. I touch it so rarely, the shape feels strange. I notice new things.

"Actually, I think that's how I knew to go to the window. I saw a light flashing on the ceiling, and it was her outside. She was sending a signal, I think."

"Why?"

"I don't know. But I ran outside to get her. It was cold and she didn't have a coat on. She didn't even have shoes on. And that's when the fire started. I remember people running and yelling. I remember asking where my parents were, and when I realized they were inside, Yiayia held my hand and refused to let me run back in.

"And it all felt so . . . slow. I thought that fires were fast and full of action, but it all felt like it happened slowly. It was mostly people standing around, looking up. Like there were a million moments when I could have run upstairs to find my parents. But we just watched the door as the firefighters brought people out—whole families—and my parents were never there. They never got out."

I stop here. I don't remember why I started telling Dom all this. He knew about the fire already. But Dom seems to pick up the thread I dropped.

"You think you started it," he says. "With that lit birthday candle?"

I don't say yes and I don't say no. I don't say anything for a little while.

"You were a kid," Dom offers.

"I still knew I shouldn't have a candle," I snap. "And placing it on a windowsill next to those drapes was stupid. Even for a kid."

"So you blame yourself?"

"I blame . . ."

I trail off. Because it's not that I spent all these years blaming myself, exactly. I *was* a kid, and they never managed to pinpoint exactly where the fire started. It could have been anything. Still, even those facts never seemed to matter, because I knew without a doubt that I had triggered the events that led to Yiayia leaving, me following, and my parents getting left behind.

Actions have consequences. I have always believed that. And for some actions, no matter how seemingly innocent, the consequences rage out of control, just like that fire did.

"I blamed the universe," I say. "Everyone did. They said it was just bad luck. But that felt worse to me. It shouldn't be possible for luck to line up in such a bad way, so that innocent mistakes add up to so much pain. And if luck works like that, it meant anything else I did could result in the same thing. Even small, harmless actions."

This, I think. This is it. It's the dread that loomed over me for years, telling me that one wrong move could spell disaster. That same dread inhabited Ellery, whispering to her until finally she snapped, and the wrong move was made. But in the snap there was no anguish. Just relief, and that blinding ecstasy that told her never to go back.

"I don't believe in luck," Dom says. "I think we make our own luck. There's nothing paying attention, waiting for us to make a mistake. It's just random. There's nothing watching."

"What about God?"

Dom gives a guilty frown. I can't help but pick at this playfully.

"Really? No God? Wow, harsh, Dom. What about heaven?"

Dom shakes his head.

"Now, *that* is grim," I say, lying back down. Dom lies by my side. I have my hands clasped behind my head. He could easily fit under my bicep, but he puts a narrow gap between us.

"What about you?" he asks. "Any gods up there in a supposed heaven?"

I'm surprised when I don't answer *yes* right away. Yiayia would be horrified. But I've never been asked like this, so I take my time to see what I'll say.

"I'm not sure about a big man with a beard calling the shots," I say. "But I do think there's a heaven."

"Pearly gates and harps? Fat little cherubs gossiping in the clouds?"

"Nah." I wave away Dom's mocking. "Not like that. Maybe some people are into that shit, but it would be hell for me. I bet it's different for everyone."

"What's it for you?"

I stare up at the orange spotlight. I could say anything right now. A beach, all sand and sunshine, or a circus full of laughter and games. I don't think Dom is really asking for the truth; this is just some late-night banter. I could just say I don't know, and pull him toward me, and we could fall asleep.

But I know.

"Heaven is like this dream I have, sometimes," I say. "I'm walking up a staircase in an apartment building. Maybe mine, maybe someone else's. I'm not sure. But as I walk up, I can hear people in the apartments. TVs and radios and singing, stuff like that. And then I get to this one door, the one I'm looking for, and behind it there's a party.

I hear laughing and talking, and I don't understand any of it, but it's loud. And happy, and it fills up the stairwell. And then I reach for the handle, but . . ."

When I stall, Dom tries to fill in. "You wake up?"

"No, not that."

"It's locked?"

"It's not," I say, finding my way toward the dream's end. "The door is never locked. But I don't open it. I just stand there, listening. Just enjoying knowing they're all in there, safe and happy and ready to welcome me inside. I know they would be happy to see me. They're waiting for me, all the people in the apartment. And I can't wait to see them. I'm so, so excited."

And I can hear them, in the dream. My mom's chattering laugh, like a tiny silver hammer. My dad's singsong shouting. Even Yiayia, telling a story or clapping to the music. I hear life and joy, and I can't bring myself to open the door and let it all out.

"That's heaven," I say to Dom. "It's me, in the hallway, savoring that moment. Forever."

"But you don't go in?"

"I don't go in."

"Why not?"

Because you'd ruin it.

I squeeze my eyes shut. I put my hands over them, so it's just me and the cool dark of my palms. I don't know when the tears start, but a few find their way down my temples, tickling my ears. I rub at them, trying to get that little voice to go away. I rub harder and harder and—

"Hey, hey."

Dom's hands are warm. They curl around mine, so that I have something to hold. I need that. I hold on to that. To him. He lets me, like he did last night. He makes it so that I'm not ashamed, lying in the back of this dark gallery, talking about doors and birthday candles and heaven.

"Maybe that's why you understand Ellery," Dom whispers, once I've stopped crying. "If I thought there was something beautiful waiting for me after I died, maybe the end wouldn't seem so bad. Maybe it would even seem better than . . ."

"Than what?"

"Fighting."

I put a hand over Dom's head, stroking his hair. "I've learned the hard way that it's worth the fight. No matter what waits for us, I never want to get there before I'm ready."

"That's true. It's rude to be late to a party, but it's just as bad to be early."

"Exactly," I say.

Dom lets me play with his hair for a few more minutes. Then he's asleep.

I drift after, never quite catching up.

You dream of the door, which you knew you would. It's half of why you told the story. But it's the first thing you dream of, and it's lost in a wash of vignettes that ramble over you throughout the night. Random scenes from your life, brief glimpses into the others' lives. Flickering faces.

But the last thing you dream before a phone call wakes you up is a long corridor. The door is back, all the way at the end this time. You walk toward it but each step swings with a terrible momentum, downing you, so that you must crawl to make any progress. You focus on the door, and at the small thing right in front of it, which is a slice of cake on a little paper plate. The candle sticks up out of it, unlit, thank God, but the second you notice that, it sparks to life.

No, you call out. Your voice is muffled, like it doesn't make it more than a few inches from your face before bouncing back.

No!

The door opens right before you get to it. Just a crack. Just enough space for a hand to reach out, pick up the plate, and bring the birthday cake inside.

Smoke drifts under the door. The alarms begin to ring. They scream, telling you to get up, get up, *wake* up.

CHAPTER SEVENTEEN

Bernie's truck vibrates in the frigid predawn air. The back is open and we climb in among the large secured canvases and boxes that make up the day's delivery. Just part of the cargo.

We drive for a while. I try to make sense of the turns but after almost an hour I have no idea where we are. Finally we pull to a stop, Bernie kills the engine, and the door unlatches. It rolls up and I'm looking at the back lot of the frame shop.

"Breakfast" is all she says before walking off. We follow wordlessly. She leads us inside to a large studio with big tables everywhere. By now the sun is up and light streams into the high windows, making everything glow. At the back there's a small kitchenette with signs prohibiting eating outside the designated area for fear that something will get on a priceless painting.

Bernie sits us down, unpacking a bag of bagels. I'm grateful for the food and I try to show it, but Bernie is almost stony as she fires up an old coffee maker. What does she think we did? If she's so sure we're up to no good, why is she helping us? She pours herself and Dom mugs of steaming coffee, and then we sit in silence until the sound of crunching and chewing drives me over the edge.

"What did my parents do?" I blurt.

"Told you already," Bernie says without a pause, like she knew I'd ask. "You talk to your yiayia about that."

"Well, I can't do that, because—"

I cut myself off, but something tells me Bernie knows already, because she doesn't even look surprised.

"Checked around last night," she says. "She was discharged from Mount Sinai yesterday, in the care of Uhler. Did you know that?"

It's just like Dom said. Uhler is holding on to her, to get to me. I sink my head into my hands, staring down at the crumbs on the table. Visions of Ellery keep flashing across my mind. How is it possible that we've come so far but we're still no closer to saving Yiayia? How have we discovered so much to know so little?

"We're not working for Uhler," Dom says. It's the first thing he's said all morning. I look up. He and Bernie are locked in a staring contest.

"I know you think I'm bad news for Athan, but we're not helping Uhler. We're going to stop him."

Bernie backs away from the small island. She hits the back counter, toppling her mug of coffee. It splashes over the counter but she doesn't even react. What Dom is saying has her terrified.

"It doesn't matter," she grinds out. "I'm not getting more involved with the Patrons than I already am."

The Patrons. I had forgotten about the moments in Ellery's vision where her mind flitted to Uhler and those mysterious people and their mysterious dinner parties, always with disdain and rebellion.

"But who are they?" I ask.

"No, no." Bernie waves off the questions. "I never would have helped you if I knew you were acting *against* them, dammit. These people, Athan—they are powerful and dangerous. They're not . . . they don't play by the rules of the world. They break them. They break people. You can't go up against Uhler. You just need to pray he doesn't come after you, or you're fucked. And so am I."

"It's too late," Dom says. "He wants Athan for something. That's why he took Yiayia. But if you could just tell us—"

"No."

Bernie snatches a rag and starts mopping up the spilled coffee. She's furious. Scared. Not the loud, jovial lady I've known all my life. It makes me scared, too. I start to imagine the terrible things that could happen to Bernie because of us. I was wrong to involve her. I've basically brought my fire right up to her doorstep and demanded she take it inside.

"I'm sorry," she says. "I really am sorry. I know you haven't had it easy, Athan. Lots of people who should be there for you aren't. I hope you know it's not your fault. I wanted to make it up to you, but . . . I've got a family now. A little girl. I hope you can forgive me."

And Bernie leaves. She drops the coffee-soaked rag, grabs up her keys, and heads to the door we came in from. Half out, she stops, and without turning says, "You remember the studio upstairs? The one we use for storage sometimes?"

"Yeah," I say.

"It's being rented out to a lighting supplier right now, but they're not doing showings anymore. It's empty. You remember the lock on it?"

"Just for show," I say.

"Just for show," she says. Then she places her keys on a wall-mounted hook. I know she's supposed to close the plastic door locking up the keys, but she doesn't. Instead, she pauses with her hand on the door, then slips out from the frame shop, leaving the keys open.

That's no accident. I'm at the keys in a flash, pocketing the set for one of the smaller vehicles, a cargo van. Voices from outside make me pause at the door and I see Bernie waving at another van that's just pulled up. She stands between us and the frame shop, buying us time.

I run back to Dom, who's already sweeping up our crumbs and dumping them in the trash. There's not much we can do about the coffee so we quickly rinse out Dom's mug, put it on the drying rack, and leave the mess behind. Then we duck into the back halls of the shop. I take Dom's hand so he doesn't fall in the dark as I race us toward the freight elevator. It's already waiting for us, and I pull down the doors. It lurches upward, slow as hell, and we break onto the third floor.

It's brighter up here because of skylights. The floor of scarred linoleum is swept clean, but pallets lean against the walls and there's a smell of mildew and dust. We find the studio door and, sure enough, it gives way with a little hello from my shoulder.

We walk into a wide room ablaze in rainbow, the sunrise filtering through graffiti sprayed over an entire wall of floor-to-ceiling windows. Like Bernie said, the space is half showroom, half storage. Pendant lights hang from rigs, unlit and looking like abstract icicles. On the other side, it's all boxes, crates, and more boxes. My eyes dart to the walls, but they're bare. Thank fucking God.

Behind the boxes, in the back corner, we find some lawn chairs, a folding table, and even a mattress. This makes sense; back when my folks owned the frame shop, they used to let some of the guys crash here after long jobs. It was rumored that Bernie even lived here for a few months. Seeing the mattress, I realize what Bernie has given us: shelter. I think she even put out the sheets and towels for us to use.

There's a bathroom, too, basically just a tiny tiled room of sickly yellow, with a drain in the middle. Someone's left behind a sliver of soap and some generic shampoo. Bernie, maybe, or just the last person to squat here.

Still. This is more space than I've ever had.

"You want first shower?" I ask.

Dom is looking at the room with poorly concealed horror. I follow his eyes to a small grove of floor lamps. Grouped together and unlit, they look a little bashful, like we've caught them gossiping about us.

"You good?" I ask Dom.

"No," he says, backing away. "I mean, I'm good. But no, I don't want first shower. I'll let you test out the water."

"Suit yourself," I say, stripping off my shirt.

The water stinks at first. After a few minutes the rust seems to run out and a minute later steam dampens the walls of the small bathroom. I get busy with the leftover soap, trying not to think about how long any of this has been here.

I think about Bernie. She's not normally like this. I feel like I've met a brand-new person who stole away the woman who helped raise me, but gave me something else in return: a piece of my parents. From the little she said, I'm forming a theory: All this is bigger than just Uhler, Ellery Pike, and a few sheets of wallpaper. Now I've heard the Patrons mentioned in both the past and the present, and it seems like Uhler and Ellery belonged in that group. Maybe my parents did, too.

Something Bernie said keeps turning over in my mind, though. *I've got a family now*, as if getting involved with the Patrons would threaten that. I wonder how, and like a whiff of smoke, the answer brushes over me.

A fire, maybe.

On the steamed glass of the mirror, I trace the vague shape of a ginkgo leaf. It's bad. Dom could do a better job, I bet.

Fires don't just start. Something sparks them. What Bernie has told me has lit embers in my memories of my parents. I wish I knew enough about them to say there was no way they'd involve themselves with the Patrons, but they brought Uhler into our lives. Maybe they brought the Patrons in, too? And if betraying the Patrons comes at the cost of one's family, and my parents are dead, who does that punish? Who's left? Me, I guess. But also Yiayia.

"Where are you, Yiayia?" I whisper. "Who are we?"

I stare at my blotchy face in the steamed-up mirror, like the blur of me might reveal the answer. Like this, I can't really rewind anything, so the mirror is safe. I lean into it, helping myself to a long stare-off with my silhouette.

Behind me, something shifts. I freeze, watching as massive fingers uncurl from the ceiling, and a hand the size of a car rushes at my back.

I spin, arms raised, dropping my towel. No gigantic fist grabs me. I just hear a yelp—not from me—and crack an eye open to see Dom standing in the bathroom doorway with his hands over his face. Clothes lie at his feet.

"I'm sorry!" he says. "I knocked and the door just opened, and I had all this stuff in my hands!"

My fear evaporates. I clap my hands over my crotch, but clearly Dom has seen it all. We stand this way for a bit, him covering his eyes, me covering very little but trying anyhow.

"It's okay," I say. "We showered together yesterday morning, didn't we?"

"It's different," Dom states, turning his back.

He's right. It is different.

"I found clothes," he says, kicking at the garments on the floor. He's found painter's jumpsuits for us, and more shirts sporting the framing company logo. I grab them up and pull them on while Dom remains focused on the windows of the loft.

"They fit," I say, stepping out of the bathroom.

"Great," Dom says, flustered. He brushes by me, into the bathroom, and the door slams shut. I hear the water start a second later.

I laugh, but not loudly enough that he could hear me. It's funny that in the dark, Dom is so ready to draw me toward him, but in the day he can hardly look me in the eye without blushing. I like it—not his discomfort, but the contrast. The other guys I've met all seem to know what they're doing, even when they're doing it poorly. Dom feels just as unsure as I do, and that alone makes me feel safe around him.

Plus, he's very cute when he blushes.

But what was that in the mirror, behind me?

My fear trickles down my back, and at the same time my eyes land on the table, where Dom's left his sketchbook. It's open. He never leaves it open. He must have really been distracted with getting that door closed between us. I would normally be amused, but the trickle of fear has grown into a steady stream.

All over the pages of Dom's book are sketches. Graceful, purposeful lines of graphite. They weave into incomprehensible shapes that make a bit more sense as I spin the book around to face me. Still-life studies. Doodles. Notes that I can't even hope to read. Toward the end there are the sketches of me.

I pause on these. They are . . . startling. The sketches aren't more than a few lines each, racing over one another, looping into eyes and nostrils and lips, but there I am in each of them, smiling or scowling or with my head turned away just slightly, an invisible sun lighting up my face. What unsettles me is not that they are photo-perfect portraits—it's that they're the opposite. Messy and abstract and smudged, not realistic at all.

But at the same time, I feel unveiled. This is not what I look like to myself, but it's how Dom sees me. In them I'm not anything so simple as beautiful. I'm dynamic.

Now I'm blushing. I flip away from myself, feeling vain and vulnerable all at once. The next pages are ripped out, and I notice a few more areas of the book that have been destroyed.

We're all our toughest critics, I guess.

Then I turn to the book's final drawing, and gasp.

It spans two pages, so much charcoal gouged into the paper that the bright loft seems to darken as the pages yawn. At first I can't make out anything in the scribbled mess, but then I see fingers stretched wide. A hand reaching up out of the pages. But it's not a hand, because the fingers aren't fingers. They're jointed legs, furred and delicate, ending in hooked points. And they don't merge into a palm. It's a scribbled void, like Dom's hand couldn't decide how to shape it. But still, if I look at the drawing at an angle, I can see the figure-eight body that Dom tried to draw again and again and again.

A spider. The drawing is the underside of a spider.

I start to shiver. It's like Dom has dipped into my head and found a memory I myself have forgotten. This shape, this thing—it's what crawled through the infinity of mirrors to try to get to us. It's the scuttling shape at the edge of my visions that never lets itself be seen. Somehow Dom has done what I cannot: captured the impression of something beyond comprehension, just based off the few details I was able to give him.

But is it just that? I glance at the closed door, making sure the water is still running. The first time I saw Dom—really *saw* him—was a reflection in the chrome of an espresso machine. It was a warped reflection streaked in neon, and I was a tired, frantic mess as I made my escape from the penthouse massacre. But I saw those threads that come and go.

Perhaps Dom knows this thing better than I do. The perspective of the drawing is telling. It's not the clinical, head-on sketch I would have assumed. It's the point of view of prey watching its death descend on silver strings.

Something crawls over my ear, fast. Spiderlike. I slap at it, but it's just a drop of water from my wet hair. But the motion wakes me up and I blink up at Dom, who's materialized in front of me. He's dripping wet, the clothes almost soaked on his body, like he threw them on without drying off. And he's jerking the sketchbook away from me. He jerks me along with it, and I stumble toward him.

"Let go," Dom says through gritted teeth. I do, because I've been clutching it this whole time without realizing it. I let go, and Dom flies backward, the sketchbook splashing open on the floor. The sheaf of papers comes undone somewhere in the arc, and they rain down on us.

"Again?" Dom growls. "What's your *deal*, Athan?"

"I'm sorry," I blurt, racing around the table to help him up. "I'm sorry, I just saw the book open and wanted to look at your drawings and I saw—"

"Stop, just leave it alone—" Dom is saying, racing to pick everything up before I can see more. "I should have kept it with me. It's not your fault—"

"No, listen," I say, catching his hands. "I saw it. Your drawing. Of that thing."

Dom doesn't pretend to not know what I mean. "It's just a sketch."

I blink. I'm right, then. "So you've seen it, too?"

Dom realizes what he's revealed, and he slides away from me like he's about to make a run for the door. The blushing boy is gone. He's back to his serious, guarded self.

"No," he says finally. "I've never seen it. But when you described it, it was like I could suddenly see something that was there all along. I don't know how to describe it, but I've . . . felt it around me for years. Like it's always hanging over me, watching."

I nod. This is how Ellery felt before it killed her. I want to rush to Dom and hug him, tell him we'll find a way to escape it. But then he does something that chills me to the bone. He smiles.

"Don't be sad, Athan," he says. "Now that I know it's real, I think I know how I can hurt it back."

My shivers return. It's like I'm talking with the Dom who was dead set on murdering Uhler, except the vengeful edge is gone. Now he sounds gleeful and his eyes are wide and wild, almost near tears. It's my turn to step back.

"How?" I ask.

Dom shakes his head. The joy goes out behind his stare.

"Just tell me your plan," I groan.

"It won't work if I tell you."

I'm getting angry now. I've told Dom so much—about the fire, about my cursed Sight—and he still won't trust me. "Fine," I snap. "Then the next move is mine."

I expect Dom to take the bait and push back, but he just nods. And now I'm stuck with following through on my bluff. Shoot. He seems to know, and just sits down at the table, drying his hair with a blank stare.

My thoughts scramble and I end up back at Ellery Pike. "In the vision, I saw way more than just Ellery's house. It was like I was watching through her mind's eye. I saw glimpses of her life. She kept thinking about . . . dinner parties."

"Dinner parties?"

"Like, spooky dinner parties," I say defensively. "Like the Patrons are into old-school séance shit, maybe."

"Is that what you saw or what you suspect?"

Damn, this is hard. Maybe Dom doesn't tell me his plans because I'd ask just as many questions. I start over.

"There was something else in Ellery's vision. I didn't get a good look at it, though. But she was thinking about meeting with Uhler at the D&D Building, and then there was a mural with a door in it."

"Like at a museum?"

I slump into the other chair, shaking my head. That's not right. I try to picture it, but Ellery's mind was being eaten away. It's like trying to reverse engineer a recipe from crumbs.

"It was just a spray-painted mural on a wall somewhere. There was a service door. But that's all I got."

With an edge of sarcasm, Dom says, "The city is full of street art and random doors. I'm sorry, Athan, but—"

Then it hits me! I stand up so quickly that Dom topples backward, off his chair. I rush to get him upright, and soon we're racing down the back stairs of the frame shop.

Our next stop has been waiting for me for a long, long time.

You drive.

You know right where to go.

When you were younger, you spent hours at the bus stop, next to Yiayia, never getting on the bus. You stared across the street at a mural of flowers and bees sprayed over a wall. And in that wall was a door. You'd never have noticed it unless you were bored out of your mind, which you were.

As you park the van around the block, you realize your yiayia was never waiting for a bus. She was watching for something else. Seeing the mural now, you're sure it's the same one Ellery vanished into for her meetings with Uhler. You are so close. But how do you get in?

You and Dom barely discuss it, because not two minutes after you arrive, a little light above the door blinks on, and the sound of locks sliding apart vibrates the wall. It's trash day (it's always trash day in New York City) and you manage to duck behind a stinking pile of black bags just as the door opens. Who else could it be but the only person who could serve as living proof that you're not where you should be?

Uhler strides through the door, phone to his ear, issuing orders.

People say New York is so big you could live an entire life without seeing a familiar face. People are wrong. The second the city knows what you're running from, it rearranges to make sure you run into it face-first. By coincidence, perhaps? Or by a composition so strange and elegant as to be undeniably compelling?

You and Dom go for it. You dash along the wall and reach the door just before it clicks shut. There's no time to wonder if this is a bad idea, which it probably is. You slip inside and the door locks behind you.

CHAPTER EIGHTEEN

Dom races behind me, trying to get me to slow down, but I'm running.

That was Uhler. *Uhler.* Which means Yiayia is here, too.

We're in a winding hallway that feels like it's made from the leftover space between buildings that didn't quite fit together. This is confirmed when we pass under a skylight that shows up into the back sides of the surrounding apartment windows. Pipes line the walls, gurgling and hissing. At one point I think we must pass under the street, because I hear traffic above and trains below. Then we reach a spiral staircase and Dom manages to squeeze in front of me.

"Wait, just wait!" he pants. "What if it's another trap?"

I glance around and the fact that we're traveling through some eternal, backroom corridor made of spare parts of other people's basements finally penetrates. I hadn't considered traps.

Dom slumps onto the stairs. "It's probably not. I just wanted you to slow down and think. If there was a trap, we'd have triggered it by now."

I shush Dom because I hear music. Piano, like Uhler likes to play in his apartment. Dom must recognize it, too. It gets louder as we climb the spiral staircase. At times the climb unwinds, shooting us in sharp sideways angles, like we're traveling around other rooms. But then we reach the top. There's a hatch door that's already open, flooding the final steps with sunlight. We pause, our eyes adjusting to the light.

"She's here," I whisper to Dom.

"So go," he whispers back, but my hands stay fastened on the railing. What Yiayia will I find? The quiet, praying woman? The frantic, paranoid lunatic? Or some new version formed from all I've learned the past couple days? A witch communing with an otherworldly creature? A Patron?

Dom squeezes by me and takes the final steps, vanishing into the bright space above. I wince, as if he's been vaporized, but then his head of curls pops back into view. "It's safe."

The room is wide, with a low ceiling, almost like it exists between floors. The windows confirm this; they rise from the floor, stop midway up the wall, then start again just below the ceiling. Display shelves form a spindly maze throughout the room, though most are empty. There's a sense of things being recently moved; stamps of clean, dark floor stand out among layers of dust and sun bleach. Something massive and heavy clearly used to hang on a section of the back wall, but now there are only empty braces and a scarred floor where it was dragged away. How did they get something so big out of here? My question is answered by the rattle of a freight elevator passing by on its way between floors.

"Over here!" Dom calls. I race to him, but halt when I see what he's found.

There's an unmade bed pushed into one of the corners. Facedown, on the floor, is Yiayia's mirror.

Oh no. Seeing the mirror without Yiayia holding it makes my stomach flip, like finding a bloody tooth. I lunge for it but then reel back when I catch sight of its broken glass. Cracks web through it, cutting me into a dozen horrified faces. I let out a frustrated cry and nearly hurl the thing at the wall.

"Is that her mirror? You can rewind it, right?" Dom tries to console me, but he doesn't know the rules. I leave him by the bed and rush through the strange space one more time, but she's not here. She's not *here*. I end up slumped on the bed, head in my hands, while Dom does his best to calm me down.

"Once a mirror breaks, I can't see into its past," I eventually mutter. "I can see up until the point it broke, but nothing before."

"Maybe it broke a while ago," Dom offers.

He has a point. There's no harm in trying. I flip the mirror over on the bed and take a steadying breath, then lean over it. The cracked glass jitters for a moment, but eventually the shards begin to rewind. I have to fight to keep them in sync, and instantly a headache sprouts behind my eyes.

I see black. The floor. Then a tumble of colors as the mirror falls. I wasn't expecting to see a fall; it means the mirror *did* break prior to being left on the floor. And then I see her. Yiayia, face cut through with cracks, staring into the mirror with mournful eyes.

"She's alive," I whisper. Dom's hand tightens on my shoulder. "She was here! Just now!" The vision skips and jumps, falling out of sync. I push all the shards back to the moment they broke, lining them up, then let the vision play forward.

This is just glass! A trinket! Uhler shouts. His hand smacks the mirror face. *Where is the true mirror?*

He tosses it onto the bed. It shows me the underside of his chin. Veins bulge in his neck.

If you don't cooperate, it'll be your grandson who pays the price this time. Do you understand me, Evangeline? You're running out of family to sacrifice for your mission.

I suck in a breath. That's Yiayia's name. Which means—

I hear Yiayia's laugh, a sound I haven't heard in so long that I instantly want to restart the vision, just to hear it again. Then I hear her familiar accent wrapped around strained words.

You don't have my Athanasios.

A vein in Uhler's neck jumps. *We can find anyone in this city.*

You are trying. You are failing, Yiayia says. *You no have Athanasios. You don't have all the shards. You have a broken mirror and an old woman. I will not help you. The Patrons—they will kill us both, and you will never open the Eye of—*

The rings of Uhler's hand flash as he strikes Yiayia. I jolt, like I can feel the sting on my own cheek. Dom's grip reminds me I'm watching from the future. My headache throbs and tears shake out of the corners of my unblinking eyes.

Do not make the lethal mistake of underestimating me. Uhler uses a handkerchief to clean something off his palm. Spit, or blood. Then he's talking to someone behind him. *We're moving her. Is the frame already loaded? Good. Take all your supplies. We're not coming back here.* He pulls out his phone and makes a call. *Do you have a pen?* he says to whoever picks up. *Good. I have a message for Magda. The wording is specific. Tell her: The installation is complete at her downtown property, and it's time to take a look. Stefan Uhler will meet her there shortly for tea, to see how she likes it. He has much to share in preparation for this Friday's gala. Those exact words. Repeat them back to me.* He listens. *Oh, and add that I would love to say hello to the children. Good.*

He hangs up and there's a flurry of motion as men in black turtlenecks reach over the mirror, pulling Yiayia out of bed. That's when it falls facedown, everything going dark. But I can still hear Yiayia struggling as they drag her away.

Put her with the cargo, Uhler says, somewhere in the distance now. *I'm going out the back.*

And that's it. I let the vision go and my headache cracks open, releasing a dull pain into the rest of me.

"We were so close," I tell Dom. "She was *just here.*" He rubs my knee as we sit on the bed and I get my emotions under control. I tell him the rest of what I saw. When I get to Uhler's phone call, Dom nearly jumps off the bed.

"I know that apartment," he says. "How did I not put this together sooner?" He slings his bag onto the bed, rummaging around until he comes out with a sheet of wallpaper swatches. His finger smacks onto one in particular. Gold, with a snaking design.

"Magda Côté is a philanthropist who just renovated a luxury space downtown with Orion House. Very standard job, but the paper"—he taps the swatch—"didn't have a standard SKU number in the system." I have no idea what this means so Dom explains, "A number associated with a product. It means the paper isn't for sale. It's custom. Like the paper Uhler gifted Ellery."

"The paper you think killed her," I correct.

"*Know.* There's tons of fake jobs in Uhler's files, but I never knew what to look for to figure out who might be a victim. But now we have a name. Magda." Dom opens his phone to a series of photos of a computer screen showing a spreadsheet. While he looks, he talks. "Ellery was exposed to the paper for weeks before she gave in. The people at the party were only exposed for hours. The exposure window is getting shorter and shorter. Which means—"

"Magda could still be alive!" I blurt.

"Magda is probably already dead," Dom says at the same time.

"Come on!" I shove his wallpaper swatches back in his bag and pull him toward the freight elevator. Then I stop, rush back to the bed, and grab the mirror. It's warm from the vision, almost like Yiayia was just holding it. She was here.

And she's alive.

The elevator opens and we hop in, turning to face down the strange room one last time. The bed hovers in a beam of dusty midday light. Dom grabs my hand.

"We'll find her," he assures me.

"But we're going to save Magda first," I say. The doors shut and down we go.

You pop out in the loading dock of a Whole Foods. Go figure. Outside, you're on a completely different block than where you started. You look up at the building and try to count the floors, but it's impossible to detect the secret space within.

You drive the van while Dom navigates. He never says where you're going, just giving you one turn at a time, and you realize it's not on purpose. It's just the way he exists in time. Perpetually pinned to the present, like how you're forever falling into the past.

Traffic catches you, holding your van in gridlock, crushing your hope into a compact sense of being too late. Your anxious eyes jump across the buildings pressing the traffic together. You wonder what's behind every service door, down every ramp. The city must be full of negative spaces, and you imagine your yiayia being dragged through all of them.

And now she doesn't even have her mirror. Just a trinket, after all. A thing of comfort and not the occult. You hold it in your lap every time the van's brakes hurl you forward. It's already broken, so now it's a trinket to you, too. A thing of comfort. It might be the last time you hear that laugh.

CHAPTER NINETEEN

The destination ends up being deep in the Financial District. Dom is surprised when the doorman just waves us in, but I'm not.

Before we left the van, I found a discarded sheet of carbon paper tossed onto the dash, spread it onto a clipboard, and tucked a pen behind my ear. In the back of the van we found a large box, the sort we usually used to pack up midsize art. Very sturdy, not like normal cardboard, and heavy even when empty.

I instructed Dom to look like he was struggling, which, to be honest, was pointless because even the empty box made him buckle. The result: The doorman rushes to get us inside, probably worried we'd tip at the wrong time and shatter the huge lobby windows. The only check we have to pass is when the doorman looks at my clipboard and asks, "Côté?" I nod, and then he pushes the elevator button for us.

"One of you will need to take the stairs. The other elevator is out," the doorman says, returning to his post. "Apartment 615. Sixth floor. Better run."

I help Dom get the box into the elevator, then jog to the stairs. As I climb, I can hear the faint sounds of other people's lives from the apartments. It feels familiar, like my dream, but the building is all wrong. The stairs are tiled in ugly black-and-white hexagons, barely scuffed after the second floor. And there's a smell of old onions caught in the carpeting of the third. The fourth is quiet, and a child has drawn on the wall with markers—a flower growing out of another flower. The fifth is when I hear the music, which gets loud as I break out onto the sixth.

It's coming from the unit at the end of the hall: unit 615, like the doorman said. Along the bottom of the wall, leading up to the door, I see more signs of a child. There's another cartoonish flower, and on the doormat lies an abandoned marker.

There's a kid in there, I realize.

I backtrack down the halls to the elevator and Dom, and we ditch the empty box near the stairwell. The music swells as we knock on the door, and then it cuts off. The door opens.

Before we can back up, a lady—I think it's a lady, I just see long blonde hair wrapped over a gasping face—lunges. She gets both our arms and pulls us inside, into sudden light and sound. Music. Laughter. A screech and a thunk, like a body hitting the floor.

"Welcome!"

The lady sweeps her hair from her face and she's smiling at us, eyes wide and alert. She's wearing a ruffled dress that bells around her as she gives a spin in the entryway, like she's presenting it to us. I back up, but Dom is already pressed to the door behind me.

The lady laughs at our concerned expressions. It's not a maniacal laugh, but a self-aware one, I think. There's a shade of apology to the way she slows her spin, pinning the dress to her thighs.

"You've come just in time! The girls are having a tea," she says. Just matter-of-factly.

I glance at Dom. He's looking past the woman, into the apartment, and he seems more confused than I am. His eyes widen as a new sound enters the moment—rapid, tiny footsteps. Then a little girl, wearing an identical dress, wraps around the woman's legs.

"Princes," she says when she sees us. A statement.

The woman ushers the girl back inside, indicating we should follow. We do, at a distance, entering a wide, circular living room. The most remarkable thing about the room is the height—it goes up three stories at least, with interior balconies hemmed in by white spindly railings. The second most remarkable thing is the sculpture at the room's center. It's simple: just three spires of stone reaching up a dozen feet from a fused base. It's lit directly from above by a skylight at the top of the room, concentrating all the natural light into a beam that causes the rest of the room to vanish into shadow.

"Sorry about the mess," the woman says, throwing a hand toward a table tucked into an alcove. There's a tray, a teapot, and teacups. When I check, I see that the tea has evaporated from the cups. The mess has been here for a while. Magda keeps apologizing. "I just got the call from downstairs. I didn't realize Orion was sending more help over or I wouldn't have let the little ones set up shop. I hope it's not an issue? My husband, Evan, has been dealing with you guys and usually he lets me know about these things, but it must have slipped his mind. Can't blame him; it's been so hectic with the move. I'm sure a lot has slipped through the cracks. Do you want something to drink? Tea maybe? I can brew a fresh pot, and there's always the fake tea the kids are drinking."

She winks. There's something so reasonable about her. The situation's strangeness begins to make a bit more sense. The little girl skips across a floor strewn in toys and costumes. The music is coming from a TV showing animated characters. Fairies fly across the screen trailing sparkles, and glowing yellow lyrics instruct the viewer to twirl, curtsy, twirl, curtsy.

"We're fine," I say quickly, hoping my long pause hasn't tipped the mom off to the fact that we actually have no business being here.

"Suit yourself. Sorry about the mess, again. Are we in your way?"

What does she think we're here to do? I scramble to think of something we can fake.

"We're just taking measurements," I say.

The lady nods knowingly, waving us toward a series of propped-up paintings on one wall. There are ladders, too, and painter's tarps. It looks like lots of work happens here each day.

"These here. The rounded walls have been an issue, so we never got to putting anything up. I'll admit, I've grown used to the clean look. The paper is strange, though, isn't it?"

We all look at the wallpaper. It's nothing as subtle as Ellery Pike's paper. It's just a simple striped pattern in creme and gold, but the stripes ripple. Upon closer inspection, I realize they're snakes.

"Quite strange," the woman says, then she sweeps back toward where her daughter plays.

Dom and I drift to the leaning paintings. I lower my voice so I can talk beneath the music.

"She seems fine," I say.

"I'm not sure," Dom hedges. "But the paper."

"Orion?" I ask.

Dom nods. Up on the second floor I see a pair of small hands grasping the banister, but they vanish a second later. I think Dom catches it, too.

"She said *kids* before," Dom whispers. "We should check on anyone in the house."

We walk the circumference of the room, to where the stairs sweep up to a second floor. The mom barely notices, waving us on as she and the girl twirl to the music.

The second floor is carpeted, muffling our steps as we enter a hallway of closed doors. One is ajar, but when we get to it, it slams shut.

Dom and I exchange a look, and then I gently knock.

"Anyone in there?" I whisper.

"No," someone whispers back. The small voice of a child.

Dom reaches to open the door but I catch his hand. Did he not hear the kid? We can't just barge in.

"Oh, okay," I whisper, sounding super sad. "That's a bummer, cuz we were hoping there was a princess hiding up here."

I sigh, long and loud. I give Dom a look like, *Well?*

Dom's eyes go wide, but after a pause he adds, "Yeah, that's too bad. No princesses here. Just . . . goblins?"

Goblins? I mouth. *Really?*

Dom winces. "Not that you're a goblin, whoever you are. I'm sure you're a princess, except you're not here, which is why I said there are goblins . . ."

I shake my head, aghast. How is he so bad at this? How come I can barely get a word out of him for hours, and now he won't shut up?

"I mean . . . not that goblins can't be princesses," Dom adds quickly. "I'm sure there's a goblin princess *somewhere.*"

The door swings open and a small, serious-faced little boy confronts us.

"I'm not a princess," he says. "And I'm not a goblin, *either.*"

"We're sorry," I say quickly as I crouch to the kid's level. "We just wanted to check on you and make sure you're okay."

The little boy regards us with open skepticism, no trace of his mother's easy trust to be found.

"Did she send you?"

"Your mom? No, no," I say, sensing it would be a mistake to lie here.

"Okay," the boy says. "You can come in."

He leads us into a mostly empty room that was maybe once a spare bedroom, or an office. Stacked boxes force us to meander through a small maze to reach the window, where he's set up a bunch of art supplies. I recognize the markers right away, along with the flowers that cover the printer paper strewn across the floor.

"You drew these?" I ask, and when he nods, I join him on the floor like I need a much closer look at such genius. "These are great! You know, Dom here is an artist, too. He can draw all sorts of stuff."

The boy peers at Dom, showing real interest for the first time, but Dom is looking around with a guarded expression. I reach for Dom's sketchbook and, surprisingly, he hands it over. I open it to pages full of wending lines that lock together and repeat, making an organic, water-like design. Then we flip to a drawing of a fern leaf. Then a tiger. The boy's face lights up.

"Do you like drawing?" I ask as the boy flips through Dom's sketchbook. I make sure he never reaches the back pages.

"Yeah."

"Do you like to draw with your sister?"

After a pause the boy decides, "I used to."

"Oh no, that sounds sad. Do you want to tell us what happened?"

No answer. I try again. "How about your mom? Does your mom draw with you?"

The boy is absorbed in Dom's drawings. His tone is full of childlike wonder, but his words feel hollow and ancient.

"That's not my mom. Not anymore. The walls are really hungry. Can you hear them, too? They're chewing on Mama right now. Then it will be your turn, I guess."

You stare at the boy while the boy stares at the drawings. *What?* you ask, but get no answer, because the mother appears in the doorway and with a shout she informs you: *It's almost time!*

She leads you back down the stairs. Dom wants your attention—you can tell by the way he tries to catch your eye—but the mother is chattering on and on about plans to redecorate, then plans to move. Contradictions. She seems confused until she bumps into the sculpture in the center of the room. She stares up at it and shakes her head. *This thing* will *be the death of me, I swear,* she says. *Evan's taste, though.* She shrugs.

You don't blame her for hating that thing. It reminds you of the makeshift sculpture in the penthouse, but before you can tell Dom, a scream from above cuts through the music. Then something blots out the skylight. A body plunges through the tower, but in a blink it's gone, only a puff of air rushing over you.

An illusion, you're sure. Some trick. But within the most insidious illusions there always hides a kernel of the truth, some grit around which the tides of desperation and heartbreak might form a pearl.

The body you saw falling was too small. A child. And that's what convinces you the little boy is in trouble.

You run for the stairs but they're gone. Vanished, into the papered walls. You feel around the room and Dom races after you, a silent shadow, but you're trapped. All the while, the mom stands at the base of the sculpture, frantic as she stares up into the brightness, like she can catch whatever might drop from above before it smashes against the floor.

Athan?

It's the little boy from before. You see him clearly, reaching to you through the railing of the second floor. Behind him you glimpse the wallpaper, but as the light of the tower shifts, so, too, does the pattern. The snakes on the wallpaper begin to glide over one another. Something horrible is about to happen, and you need to get that boy down from there.

You grab one of the ladders and heave it to the second floor, starting up before it's even stable. The boy cries for you to hurry. You hear the terrible, sticky-stretch of paper being peeled from the wall. Something is trying to break through it! Jaws, or hands, or faces; you try not to look as you climb to the screaming child.

Hurry, Athan!

You get to the boy but he can't fit through the railing's balusters. He reaches for you through the spindles of wood, just like the things in the paper reach through the pattern. You climb higher, reaching the ladder's top, wondering what will happen if you break the balusters and pull the boy through the breach.

Then the music, which was blaring this entire time, stops. The wallpaper settles, all the dancing fading around you. The railing fades, too, slithering apart like the snakes on the paper.

The little boy smiles, and he says, *Got you.*

CHAPTER TWENTY

What?

I snap out of it but it's too late. I know it's too late the moment the music stops and I blink away the illusion slithering over my eyes.

I'm breathing heavily. The ladder rocks precariously under me and I reach for something to grab on to, but the railing and the balusters are gone. I'm not facing the second floor anymore. There's just a dusty ledge, with the boy perched upon it.

I look up into blinding light. I'm a few feet from the skylight.

I look down.

Three floors below, the spires of the sculpture glare up at me. I teeter over the drop on the top rungs of my ladder, which is barely balancing on the third-story railing. The slightest movement—even the shaking in my limbs—creates a deadly wobble. I steady myself just in time to halt my fall and drag my eyes back up to face the boy, who's tucked himself into the smallest of crawl spaces just under the skylight's glass.

He smiles so wide that I wonder if he's even real. Then he braces his feet on the top rung of the ladder, crushing my knuckles. He gives it a little push, as if to experiment.

I grab the ledge he's sitting on. Layers of dust make it slippery. There's nothing to hold on to but him.

"Don't . . ." I whisper.

A scream rings out in the air behind me. I make the mistake of turning. I see a cloud falling. A frothy white dress whipped around a body, reaching out for anything to catch it as it plunges down from the skylight. The mother. A ladder, just like mine, falls with her, bouncing violently as it catches on the railings and wedges itself to a screeching stop before it can hit the ground.

The mother isn't as lucky. I close my eyes a split second after seeing her abdomen explode upward as the stone sculpture impales her through the back. Eyes closed, I hear the gurgle of blood pouring through her wrecked body, down into her still-gasping throat.

She was on a ladder just like mine, drawn up into this trap, maybe also by the need to save these children. And sure enough, across the drop, Magda's daughter sits in a pose identical to the son, legs dangling in the open air as she smiles.

My ladder lurches again as the boy gives a little push.

"Please," I say, ready to beg. But he's just waiting for me to look at him before he gives one final shove, and I'm tilting back.

Move, I scream at my muscles. There's a brief moment where I catch my balance, the ladder going straight up beneath me, and I think I can maneuver it back against the wall. Then the railing it balances upon lets out a crack. Just a brittle cry for warning, and the ladder plunges down with me still on it.

I glimpse the end rushing up at me, my own shadow expanding to catch me. Magda's splayed body looks like an angel as I whip around. I don't feel like I'm falling. I feel like I'm being swallowed in the throat of some massive beast.

Then I jolt to a stop. Lightning shoots through my arm. Somehow, I've halted just inches from the tip of the spire. I'm still clinging to my ladder, except now I dangle from it, my arm twisted into the rungs. I swing precariously, trying to make sense of what saved me. It's the other ladder, which pinned itself across the drop. My ladder intersects it, but with a screech they slowly begin to slide apart.

"Ring around the rosie . . ."

The voice comes from below, and it's full of blood. Magda stares up at me. Her eyes are tearful and bright. She reaches up to me—past me—to the sky. I hear the laughter of children.

"A pocket full of posies . . ." she gurgles.

I try to get my arm out from where it's caught, but I don't have the strength to lift myself up. The ladders jolt and my toe kicks the spire.

"Ashes! Ashes! We all fall . . ."

The interlocking ladders give another screech and slide apart.

And I do fall.

I catch the spire right before it drives through me. Both hands, wrapped around it, but the point still nestles into the soft flesh where my body violently folds over the sculpture. It's slick with gore and my hands slip, causing the tip to dig into me, just above my belly button. I slip again and the sharp pain widens into an agonizing pressure. I have to tip myself off before it's too late, but it's impossibly slippery. I can't get the leverage I need to pull myself free. Every time I move, I fall farther down. Slowly, I'm being skewered.

Shadows below me are the only warning I get as I hear the little boy and girl toss themselves from their ledges. They fall slowly, like ghosts, melting in the brightness moments before they pass me. I feel them go by, like gravity pulling on my legs, my arms. I scream as they drag me down the spire. I feel my skin break, and drops of blood splatter my fumbling hands.

"Brace yourself!"

Dom. He flashes out of the shadows, ramming his shoulder into the base of the sculpture, and it begins to tip.

"Hurry!" I scream.

Dom screams back as he puts everything into toppling the spire. But he's too late. It's not going to work. I'm going to be impaled, like Magda. Like Dane. I took every step of the climb that is going to end my life.

My hands finally give out, putting my full weight on the spire. At the same time the spire finally topples sideways. Magda is crushed, but her body cushions the fall, and somehow when I hit the floor, I land softly. On a couch. Among a mess of fuzzy decorative pillows.

Dom is all over me in seconds.

"Please no, please no, not you," he's crying as he wrenches up my shirt. I hiss in pain at his touch, but together we realize I'm okay. Despite the ache still seizing in my guts, the cut is shallow. I wait to die, but when I don't, I let out a surprised laugh, which makes the ache worse. I smile anyway. Dom releases a grateful sob. Then his hands clap over my eyes.

"Don't look at the paper. Keep your eyes closed. Can you stand?"

I stumble upright, clinging to him. Each step feels like a blessing. I can hear a muffled creaking, like teeth grinding together. The silence that's caved in over us is settling, but only for now. I'm waiting for the music to begin again. Hoping it will, because maybe then the mother will get back up. Dance a little longer.

"Athan, focus," Dom snaps, and I realize I've opened my eyes and am looking at the walls. I cover my face with my hands, while Dom pushes us toward the door.

"But the kids," I protest.

"Don't worry about them," Dom says.

"They're safe?"

"They're safe. Just go."

I stumble over the hearth and land on the thin carpet of the hallway. And then I have my body back. I'm on my knees, new bruises throbbing where the ladder caught my arm, but I don't think it's broken. The pain centers me. I feel the illusions drain from my skull.

We hobble toward the stairs. Where are the kids? I stop us, but before I can ask there's a ding and the elevator doors open. No one is inside— but the far wall is mirrored. In it I see . . .

I see . . .

I close my eyes and let Dom lead me to the stairs. He makes me strip off the shirt and hold it against my wound until the bleeding slows.

"Wait here," he orders me. He leaves and comes back with rags from the back of the van. Fresh coveralls, too. We clean me up the best we can and I change clothes. Then, when I'm ready, we head through the lobby. The doorman from before gives us a friendly wave.

"All set?"

"All set," Dom says, smiling. I can barely speak. It's all on him to handle any departing small talk.

"Nice place, right?" the doorman asks.

"Super nice," Dom says flatly.

"I'm not surprised they're moving, though." The doorman leans closer, speaking in a hoarse whisper. "Back to the Southwest, I heard, where the wife grew up. The city isn't for everyone. It can get hard to be away from family, especially after, well, you know . . ."

Dom shakes his head. The doorman smiles, like he's eager to finally talk to someone about this.

"I heard . . ." The doorman breaks off to smile at a lady in jogging clothes who sweeps into the building.

"I've been working here a long time, seen a few families buy and sell that unit. Seen kids grow from little to big. Never any problems, just the usual stuff. Rich people problems, you know? All the luck in the world. But then *they* moved in. Nice little family. Always traveling. But one time they came back without the kids. We were told not to say anything to them. At all. Let them grieve in private. But I heard the children had a bad fall. Both of them. Some freak accident somewhere. And now they're downsizing. Can't say I blame them. All that space up there? Must be painful. Rich as fuck, but no amount of money can replace what they lost."

The doorman sighs, mistaking our silence for tribute, and we leave. I'm still a little dizzy as we walk, so Dom stays right by my side, even helping me into the van. We sit in the cab, the motor running, and I tell Dom where the first aid kit is. While he presses gauze to my wound, I break the silence.

"There weren't any kids, were there?"

Dom looks unsure if he should tell me the truth, like I might freak out if I know. But I already know. I knew it the moment I looked into the mirrors of the elevators and saw them standing next to me, eyes blank yet imploring, little hands reaching up to hold on to my sleeves. But they were only in the reflection. Only ghosts in the mirror. Still, I felt their grip on me, like they wanted to pull me up and away, maybe to drop me again.

"You couldn't see them, could you?" I ask.

Dom wraps the bandages all around my waist. He shakes his head no.

"I didn't realize you were seeing anything until we went upstairs," he says. "You were talking to the air, it looked like."

"The woman was real, though, wasn't she?"

Dom nods.

"So she's dead."

Dom nods again. He's done bandaging me up. I ease back into my seat and breathe through the pain.

"Tell me what actually happened."

Dom explains a version of what I saw. We entered the apartment and the mother was there, dancing, talking about tea and children, but no little girl sat by the TV. The TV was on, the dolls were scattered on the floor. Dom waited for a child to show themselves. We went upstairs, but the doors were locked. One *did* finally open, though Dom couldn't see how. At first he thought I was talking to a kid hiding somewhere in the room, but he never actually heard the child speak himself. And when we entered he only saw the child's drawings. But no child. He watched me talk to thin air. He urged us to leave, but then the mother found us.

This is where our memories completely diverge. While I recall running up the stairs, Dom recounts a bizarre sequence in which the mother and I worked together to bring the ladders up to the top of the tower. He tried to get us to stop—me to stop—but it became clear he needed help. He was about to run to get the doorman, but that's when the mother fell. I was next, and he only barely managed to topple the sculpture, which is the moment our memories reconverge. He hugs his shoulder, like it hurt.

"That was hard-core," I tell him, with a smirk I only half feel. "Never thought I'd see you ruin a piece of art like that."

"It was bad art," Dom huffs.

"Thank you," I say. I take his hand, because I need to hold something. It's like as he talks, the memory fills in for me, and I can see both versions of the last hour. Mine and his. It's not a matter of picking which one was real. Real and unreal have very little to do with truth, I'm understanding.

Suddenly Ellery Pike's decision makes sense. What she saw—how she felt—wasn't obvious on the outside to anyone. But then something merged her interior and exterior, drew them into a strange focus that only she could see. I glimpsed it briefly, watching through her mirrored sculptures, but just now I experienced it for myself, together with the mother and her dizzying tower.

Something unlocked her mind, dragged out the horrors hidden inside, and reflected them back upon us with savage, inescapable beauty. Something toyed with her as it devoured her, and it nearly got me, too. Like the people who died in the penthouse party, I could have run but I couldn't have escaped.

Once your interior becomes your exterior, there's nowhere left to hide.

"We should go," Dom says, squeezing my hand.

"What about the mother?" I ask.

"If Uhler planned this, which I very much suspect he did, his men will be along shortly to clean up. And we can't be here."

"What if the police find out first?"

"Maybe they will," Dom says. He peers through the dirty windshield of the van, like he can see that version of the future. "If they do, we're going to jail. I think this counts as a homicide. You helped, I watched, and someone died."

I feel sick. What Dom says makes sense, yet it doesn't. How can this be happening? Whose life have I stumbled into? The fleeting security I felt this morning has curdled into something slimy that drags down through me, and I nearly give in to the urge to heave it all up.

Someone died.

Someone *died*.

I put the van into reverse. I back out, swinging us onto the road. Dom rocks in his seat, holding on to the handles, telling me to slow down, asking me where we're going. But then he sees for himself. A police station emerges from the busy New York chaos, obvious by the fleet of cruisers parked out front like soldiers lined up and waiting for orders. I nearly clip one as I double-park. Dom catches my hand before I can heave open the door.

"No," he says. More like orders.

I pull, expecting him to let go, but instead I heave him across the center console. Half in my lap, he repeats, "No."

"We have to tell the police." I'm surprised at how small I sound.

"No, Athan, we can't. Not yet. The police are already after you for the party. And now we're both suspects. There's evidence of us sneaking around all over the city. We have to get to Uhler, and we have to stop him ourselves. I know that scares you. It scares me, too. It's not playing by the rules—it's breaking them—but we're past the point of no return. We either catch Uhler, or we get caught ourselves and he gets away with everything."

"The police will catch him."

"Will they?" Dom cocks his chin. He's so close that I can see the dark wells of his pupils focus. He's looking into me, just as I'm looking into him.

A knock at the window makes us jump apart. Outside, a woman in a police uniform steps back from the van, arms crossing in obvious annoyance. I pop on a surprised expression, like I had *no* idea I was blocking in the cruisers. Thankfully, she doesn't appear to recognize me. She motions for us to move on.

I go to open the door.

"Listen," Dom whispers. "Listen to me, Athan. It's all up to us. The police can't see what you can see. They don't know what I know. Even if we helped them, their goal would be to grab Uhler, and where does that leave Yiayia? It has to be us. We can't trust anyone else."

I pause, hand on the latch.

"Let's go, fellas," the police officer intones outside.

I glance at her in the side mirror, and I think I catch a flash of silver in the air. But I can't be sure. I'm not sure about anything anymore.

"Sorry!" I shout back. I put us into drive, and ease away from the cruisers. Dom is right. We can't trust anyone when the web being woven around us is invisible until it's too late.

I give the officer a final wave, and we speed off.

Distrust comes freely to a broken heart. Sometimes, it even crawls out of the breach, mucking up the edges and making it hard to put the pieces back together.

At a stoplight, you angle the rearview mirror so that you can see Dom. You try to be subtle about it, but it doesn't matter because he's lost in thought. His eyes look up into the windows of the skyscrapers you drive past. His face is stern, like always, but soft, too. Tired. Hurt, maybe?

Harmed. That feels like the right word. He has been harmed by what you just endured, too, in a way that makes you want to hug him. Because now you understand the mask he wears, and you're starting to understand the fear that it hides.

What else has he seen? How long has he hidden with all this? What's it like to hide with such horrible things as your only company?

A car beeps and you lurch through a green light. The sharp pain in your abdomen reminds you that you are fragile, too. Dom shifts out of his own daydream. He notices you glancing at him, and his expression turns self-conscious. This sparks something in you—your instinct to protect and provide. To be the brightness that burns away the dark.

You check your cross streets and do some mental mapping, turning the van down the next avenue, gliding up the edge of Central Park. When you're close to your new destination, you announce: *It's time for lunch.*

Dom blinks at you.

Well, you say, *can't catch a serial killer on an empty stomach, right?*

And he smiles. And it's the most reassuring thing you've ever seen.

CHAPTER TWENTY-ONE

I know a spot. The best Vietnamese sandwich shop on the Upper West Side, and a favorite of the guys at the frame shop. I make Dom look up the menu so that we can call in an order and be in and out, just in case another Forum crew is making deliveries in the UWS. Then I squeeze the van into a spot near a wrecked hydrant, grab Dom, and lead him into Central Park. I don't know why, but I'm determined to do lunch like normal people.

Maybe I do know why.

Nothing is normal. Nothing will be normal ever again. I can feel normal pulling away from me, like waves on the beach, except it'll never wash back over me. It'll just pull farther and farther back, like when a tsunami drags away all the water, letting you know that what comes next is certain ruin.

I feel ruin building, far off. I feel it rolling closer, a rising dark wall pouring forward. I know there's no running from that. Running admits you're being chased. Staying still and having a Vietnamese sandwich on a park bench, though? That admits nothing. Denial, safe and delicious.

Dom is less convinced. He picks at his sandwich while I tell him about the ginkgo trees, all aflame above us. I talk about the time I roller-skated around the park with a skate so loose it fell apart on the very hill we're looking over. I talk about anything but what just happened.

Dom is silent. I run out of things to say, and the moment I stop talking he jumps up, like it's his cue. He digs into his pocket and pulls forth, of all things, a spoon.

"I forgot," he explains, which isn't an explanation at all. He thrusts it at me.

"Forgot what?"

"I'm sorry." He sits down again. He shines the spoon on his knee. "I grabbed this in the apartment. Something reflective, for you to rewind. I know it's not much, but can you do it?"

I've never rewound a spoon, but I also avoid looking at myself in them. Knives, too. I just know not to, so I guess Dom's hunch is right. I can try.

"What do I look for? It has to be specific or else it's just gonna be a lot of soup."

"Try looking for Uhler."

Oh, duh. I take the spoon, eager to impress Dom but not eager to find out where this thing has been. When I look into it, my upside-down face gazes back in the shining bowl. I lock eyes with myself, and the other me shifts to incredulity, then vanishes as the reflection slips backward.

Teeth, tongue, wet chomps. I'm slid between lips, plunged into bowls, tapped against teacups. I'm left in drawers for days and days until the light above rips open and a hand grabs me, and then it's back to teeth and tongue and—

Uhler. I try to picture him. *Show me Uhler.*

I'm looking up at a familiar skylight. I almost look away. But then a shadow swings around the curved reflection, and I recognize Uhler's slicked-back hair. I hold on to that moment, pulling my focus into the seconds on either side of it. Slowly the sounds wobble through the reflection, warping badly in the bowl of the spoon. I catch the conversation in swoops.

I'm sorry, Stefan, but it's been decided.

I think that's a woman's voice. It's hard to tell. The sounds are never right, and they're worse through a spoon. Surprise, surprise.

You're not sorry, someone responds—Uhler, I think. *You're barely containing your glee, Maggie. If you were actually my friend, you would spare me the pretense of humility and just gloat.*

The spoon must be balanced on a cup of steaming tea, because fog washes over the bent vision of Uhler and this Maggie talking. I'm looking up at their throats, so expressions are hard to read, but the voices are rich with disdain.

Our friendship ended after whatever you did to Ellery. Perhaps the glee you sense is justice, the woman says. *You and your experiments have thrived in the ambiguity of our bylaws for years, but I can assure you that once I'm named president, there will be an immediate motion to expropriate your little . . . projects.*

The spoon is lifted and I catch a glimpse of blonde hair. The mother. Magda. Maggie. Then the reflection is plunged into coffee. When I surface, the conversation has jumped.

There are forces bigger than the Patrons, Uhler says in warning.

You don't think I know that? Maggie laughs. *My family and the Pikes have kept the Patrons operating for years, and do you know how? Because of a precise understanding of power. We rule those below, and do not question those above.*

I'm not talking about people, Maggie. I'm talking about forces. And if we could only tap into—

Enough, Maggie cuts in.

The Bakirtzis family guards real power, Maggie, not the parlor tricks of our little dinner parties. If the Patrons would permit me to utilize just a few of the artifacts in the collection to extract what I need from the old woman, or even the boy—

Maggie slaps a hand on the table, and the spoon clatters. Everything jumps as she plucks it up and, as best as I can guess, thrusts it at Uhler.

You are not as strong as you think, she growls. *And the forces you are contending with will eat you alive. We collect. We conceal. We do not make quix-otic bids for power. And we don't hurt . . .*

I can't see her, but I hear Maggie's voice crack. Fire flashes in her throat.

We don't hurt children.

The spoon is dropped to the floor. It peers up at the skylight, and along the edge of the vision I make out the walls. They are simple gray, just paint on them, no paper. This scene I watch happened well before Uhler papered the walls of Magda's home in poison. Maybe, I think, I am watching the inspiration for his revenge.

You've made up your mind, then, Uhler says.

I have.

And you plan to oust me after you're named at the gala this November, I presume?

I do.

And you expect me to simply go in peace?

Maggie bends to pick up the spoon, setting it back on the table. I can once again see her and Uhler at the edges of the reflective bowl.

No, I expect more from the Patrons' dark star, Maggie says in acidic sar-casm. *Not only will you go in peace, but you will return to being a sniveling, sycophantic underling barking at the heels of high society, begging for scraps. You will fulfill the orders we give you. You will furnish our homes as we see fit. You will design us the beautiful spaces required for our business and entertainment. And you will ask no questions about it. That is the price of the Patrons' not killing you. It's what I can do for you now, as your friend. Are we clear?*

Uhler stands and exits, but I hear him faintly from wherever he's gone.

Crystal, he says, and then a door closes.

The conversation ends. But there must be more. If they were once friends, they must have met many times. This spoon was their witness once; why not again? I push backward, digging through bowls of ice cream and steaming polenta and tea turned cloudy with cream. I sense for any trace of Uhler. Any glimpse. The edge of my vision glows white, burning inward until the past begins to bubble and pop.

"Athan! Stop!"

I'm jostled so hard I drop the spoon. I blink out of the vision and it takes a few seconds for the color to return to the world. Dom is on the ground, flapping his hands at the strangest thing: a little fire in the grass. And my hand throbs with a slight burn, like I placed it on the hood of a car in the summer for a second too long.

I look for the spoon and realize *it's* the flaming thing in the grass. Actually, the grass is on fire. The spoon sits white-hot in a charred little crater. Molten.

I blink.

"Give me your water," Dom demands, and I do. He douses the molten spoon and then jumps back as steam spits up at us. He hits it again and finally it's over, and we're both staring at a wet blob of metal in a little burned bed.

Dom picks himself up, dusts himself off, and sits on the bench. Dignity personified once again.

"It melted," he says.

"I didn't know that happened," I say. "I've never rewound that far."

"And it wasn't a true mirror," Dom offers.

I guess not, though I don't see why this matters.

"So?" he asks.

"So," I say. I explain the strange conversation. Before I'm even done, Dom has his sketchbook out, and it's back to the pages of notes on victims. He checks something on his phone and, with a victorious smile, shows me.

It's the mother from the apartment, but a nice photo. She's in a turtleneck, hair in a bun, looking expensive and professional in a portrait on the website Dom has found.

"Magda Côté," he says. "I knew there was something familiar about her."

"You've seen her before?"

Dom is scanning his notes, checking for something. He turns to a new page in his book that's just a drawing of a dragonfly and starts scribbling more notes. I try to peek but it's illegible. Thankfully, he starts talking.

"Magda is a previous vice chair on the board of the Smithsonian. Very, very connected. She was supposed to host the gala where Uhler is presenting his new designs this Friday, at the Vantage Observatory downtown."

Dom shuffles through his papers and extracts a card of stiff, expensive paper, embossed with gold filagree. An invitation like the one I saw in Ellery's vision. I point this out to Dom.

"I stole this from Dane's room," Dom confesses. The way he clutches it, I realize he maybe admired Dane like he did Ellery. "Dane was like a sibling to me. They lived with Uhler for a while, too, when they first moved to the city. We were close."

Dom passes his thumb over Dane's name.

"Dane. Ellery. Magda. Uhler. They're all connected in the art world. And these other victims." Dom jabs at his notes. "They're powerful people, too, all official or unofficial clients of Orion House. What if they were part of the same secret society?"

"So you think they're the Patrons?"

Dom nods.

"Patrons of what, though?"

Dom ponders this. "There are stories about occultists in the art world who sought to contact other dimensions through the sublime nature of art. Mediums would channel aliens and paint landscapes from other worlds. Séances, and stuff like that. Maybe the Patrons are like that? It would explain why they're so interested in you and your yiayia. Your power is like scrying, except instead of the future, you can see the past. I bet that's valuable for people who collect ancient occult artifacts."

It's hard for me to imagine Yiayia at a séance, but not impossible. I love her to death, but there was always something a bit eerie about the way she babbled into her hand mirror. That reminds me of something else.

"Hey, speaking of ancient occult artifacts, does the term O-654-A mean anything to you?"

Dom cocks his head, and I explain how I saw it on the notes Uhler was taking on Yiayia. Somewhere in my dirty clothes, there's a crushed-up pink Post-it note with that scrawled upon it.

"The *O* is for object," Dom says. "That's like a code that would be given to something at an auction. Maybe it refers to your yiayia's hand mirror?"

"I don't think so," I say. "In the conversation I saw between Yiayia and Uhler, he was mad that the hand mirror was just a regular trinket. If it was important, he wouldn't have left it behind. Yiayia seems to be the important part. The 'object' must be something else." I close my eyes and drum my fingertips on my forehead, trying to remember details from the vision. "Right before Uhler hit Yiayia, she told him he would never open something. The Eye of something. They both seemed to know about it."

"She never mentioned anything about it to you?"

I laugh. "Are you kidding? She's a senile Greek grandmother. She's *constantly* spouting warnings against evil eyes. Maybe there was some truth in there, but it's impossible to sort out what was real and not real from all the things she rambles about. If only . . ."

If only she talked to me more, instead of that mirror. If only Uhler hadn't broken it. Maybe I could have made some sense of all her prayers.

"Do you think she's a Patron, too?" Dom asks.

I'm silent. I feel like I've swallowed gravel. I don't want to think of her that way. I focus on what we know.

"Uhler and Ellery and Magda are all in a secret society. After Dane was killed, Ellery wanted out. So Uhler killed her, too. He's after something, and it has to do with my yiayia and that thing in the mirror. Magda accused him of hurting people, of conducting experiments, and she was going to kick him out. But then he killed her, too." I sit up, a new avenue opening up in the mystery. "Do you think his experiments are with the wallpapers?"

Dom is about to answer but I cut him off. "Actually, before we get to sleuthing, you need to eat something. You haven't even touched your sandwich."

Dom grumbles, but he snatches up his abandoned lunch and takes a bite. A small one. Too small. I cross my arms and, with an eye roll, he takes a second, huge bite. Good, that shuts him up so I can start us off.

"We know that both Ellery and Magda knew Uhler personally. Same with the people at the penthouse party, presumably, since Uhler was my connection there. We know Ellery and Magda both suffered hallucinations that caused them to harm themselves. Same for the people at the party. Maybe."

I think of the way that girl knocked on the walls, searching for the door, never finding it. And how she died under a stampede of people looking for a way out of a room with three exits.

"Definitely," I amend.

Dom swallows. I make him drink some water. He chugs half the bottle resentfully, then wipes his chin. Also resentfully.

"Each incident involves wallpaper Uhler has designed and

225

manufactured himself," he says, "outside the product lines produced by Orion House."

"But now we know the paper isn't just the mark of a killer—it's the killer itself," I state academically. "But *how* does it work? Is it exposure? Is the paper laced with a hallucinogen?"

"Like drugs?" Dom offers incredulously.

I huff. "I guess not." On account of my Sight, I avoid anything that might mess with my head. But from what I've gathered watching others, drugs don't just wear off when you leave the room. I grope around for another word, and come up holding the bristling fear that seems to grow on all my memories of this cursed wallpaper. "It felt . . . evil. That's the only way I can put it. But that's not enough of an explanation."

Dom sighs. A little sadly, I think. Then he pulls something up on his phone. "I've looked into all the more reasonable explanations. Trust me. This is from the early days of my investigation." It's a web page with the title "Death by Wallpaper." Dom summarizes as he scrolls. "It says that in the Victorian era, people in nice homes began to fall ill from no clear cause, because there were so *many* possible causes. Eventually, they figured out a pattern. It was the walls. The wallpaper, specifically, which used colors made with arsenic. Arsenic is a common yet lethal poison that accumulated in the bodies of the victims over time. It was popularized in a certain shade of green, but was commonly found in many colors."

"I didn't succumb to arsenic poisoning," I say. "I was attacked by *mirage children* tormenting a grieving mother. This is so much more dangerous than a lethal pop of green."

"I know," Dom interjects. But does he? I feel a flash of anger toward him, so sharp it scares me. Suddenly, I hear how I sound—superstitious, ranting about an implacable doom. I sound like Yiayia.

I close my eyes and groan. "Sorry, I didn't mean to snap at you."

"I know," Dom repeats, quieter. "The arsenic was just an example. I have tons of hypotheticals. I guess I just hoped one would turn out to be true, but the more we learn, the less my research makes sense."

"Yeah, because like I said, it's *evil*, Dom. Devil shit."

Bitterly, I think about how Dom's approach is so intellectual because he hasn't faced this thing. He doesn't understand it, so he still hopes it can be conquered. That's not why I'm bitter, though. My anger is aimed at myself. In Dom, I see a reflection of the way I used to think just a few days ago. I realize I haven't invoked Dr. Wei or his advice in a while. Not since I started to get some perspective on Yiayia's superstitions. Now all that work's been undone.

I let out another groan, longer. More comedic, hoping it lightens the awkwardness of my outburst.

"My therapist is gonna kill me," I mutter. I glance up, and Dom's suppressing a grin at my anguish.

"You just melted a spoon with your eyes," he says. "And you saw a giant spider crawl out of infinity. An hour ago, ghost children tried to turn you into shish kebab."

I laugh, but then double over as pain webs out of my still-tender stomach. I play up the drama of breathing through the pain until I get what I want: an eye roll from my artsy Wednesday Addams.

"Ah, yes," I say, recovering. "Melted spoons. Giant spiders. The antics of haunted little ghost children. What's your point?"

"You'll have plenty of material to make it up to your therapist with. If we survive this."

Damn, does Dom know how to set the mood to spooky. I glance at the mangled spoon at our feet. It's still steaming a little bit. My hand prickles where I held the too-hot metal. I smell smoke, and I'm not sure if it's real. I hold my breath until I can be sure it's gone.

"I was so close to believing this curse wasn't real," I say. "That I had made it all up. But it's real, isn't it? I really almost died. I don't know how to fight something like that."

"I can fight it," Dom says. "It didn't affect me, remember?"

For the first time, I realize this is true. Both at the penthouse party and at Magda's place, Dom was somehow untouched by whatever drove everyone else to hurt themselves.

He nods at my expression. "I've never seen whatever drives the exposed victims mad. Maybe I'm immune. Maybe that's how we beat this thing. Let me be our eyes for once."

Dom puts out his hand, but I don't want to take it. I don't want him looking at something so unsafe. It reminds me of the call of the void, the seduction of self-destruction. I'm not confident Dom is as immune as he thinks. At the same time, I know there's no stopping him. The safest he'll be is by my side, so I take his hand and ask, "What's next?"

"We figure out how the wallpaper works. There are a few other installations we can check out—"

"No," I say firmly. "Too dangerous."

Dom grimaces in exasperation. "Then what?"

I realize it as I say it. "There's one place, one *obvious* place, we haven't looked yet." It's not a secret gallery or a person's house. Dom senses the renewed determination in me and tugs at my arm as I pull us toward the edge of the park. He has to jog to keep up.

"We've been doing this all wrong," I say. "We're looking at the paper when it's in people's homes. It's too late by then. We've got to find it before it gets there."

Dom looks over my shoulder at the cargo van, unsure. I cue up another hint for him.

"Orion House charges such a high premium for Uhler's custom

work for two reasons, right? He says them all the time to potential clients. What are they?"

Dom thinks for a second, then quotes: "No custom design is used in more than one home. Each is as personal as a portrait."

"And?"

Dom's eyes widen. "And all the paper is printed domestically."

"Where?" I press.

We say it at the same time.

Red Hook, Brooklyn.

You decide to go at night.

Safer, right? Less likely to get caught, right?

But this means you've got to find a way to kill the rest of the day and some of the night. Neither of you wants to just sit in the van, and you can't go back to the frame shop until you know it's safe.

So you go to IKEA.

It makes a bizarre kind of sense. The vast parking lot is full of moving vans rented by people hoping to fill up their tiny apartments with just a day's worth of errands. Your van doesn't stand out. And the store is massive, with the busyness of a touristy museum but none of the tense silence. Best of all, there are plenty of places to hide. Entire rooms that open up, one after the other, like dollhouses melded into chains of empty interiors.

And there are mirrors all over, so that you can keep an eye out for any of those spectral strands. How clever of you, Little Prince.

You sit among the many dads, discarded by their families to play on their phones, in a room that is all sofas and chairs. It's loud enough that you don't need to whisper to talk. You ask Dom something that's been on your mind.

Why wallpaper?

A strange question, but an obvious one.

Well, Dom says, *it's the art we surround ourselves with.*

The best design can disarm us. It's a truth you have learned in all the homes you've entered, a truth you've seen in all the beautiful interiors that you knew would never be yours. It's the reason why a place you have never been, that flew together under the hands of another person who knows nothing about you, can feel kind, or comfortable, or like a home.

But why not paintings, or pictures, or something else? Why does it have to be the wallpaper?

Because, Dom says, *all other art is escapable.*

CHAPTER TWENTY-TWO

The best part of the IKEA plan is, of course, the Swedish meatballs. We get them as the sun sets outside, sitting so that we face the line of people slowly churning through the cashiers. I start guessing as to what sort of houses people live in based on what they're buying.

"That lamp is for the solarium.

"That's a bookcase but it's going to be used to shelve dinosaur figurines.

"That huge box is a bed frame. A canopy bed frame. For a kidnapped princess."

Eventually I get Dom to join in. His speculations are decidedly grimmer.

"Those are pantry organizers for a cannibal. The snap lid keeps the eyeballs fresh.

"That wicker hamper is actually going to be the home for a singular, gigantic bee.

"That lamp will be used to light the crawl space in the attic, because the spiders need to be able to read."

At the mention of spiders, we get quiet and the game ends. The onslaught of shoppers becomes a trickle as the hour grows late, and we get ready to go. We grab a few more orders of meatballs for dinner and eat them in the van while we figure out our plan.

The Orion House print shop is close, also in Red Hook. The frame shop isn't far, either. Many businesses use the area's warehouses for storage or production. As we drive toward it, we pass a million other vans that look just like ours, backed up to freight entrances or sitting in lots, asleep and waiting for their drivers come sunrise.

Dom navigates. He's been here before. He seems to think getting inside the factory won't be that hard, but we're still too early to try. We end up parking the van in an alley a few blocks away, between an abandoned lot and a warehouse that vibrates with music from within. A door bursts open and lets out a pair of stumbling guys who fumble in their jackets for cigarettes, then hang on to each other as they steal kisses between plumes of smoke. A few more people join them, and they drift in and out of the club like fireflies. The way they wobble, we guess that they're drunk. This must be a nightclub.

"Hey," Dom says as we watch them. "You said you thought your family was cursed. And you got it from your yiayia, right?"

"Yeah."

Dom never takes his eyes off the drunk people. "Well, if Yiayia has the same skill, maybe that's why she loved that mirror so much. She looked into it so much that even if it rewound, it was always her face looking back, always getting younger."

"I mean, I guess," I say. "She never struck me as being that vain, though."

"I don't think vanity is always a bad thing," Dom says. "Sometimes I think what makes people feel invisible isn't that no one can see them, it's that everyone prefers to see someone else. And because that's the version people prefer, you're stuck wondering if that's the real you, even if you don't like how it feels. So maybe vanity can be good? Seeing yourself—your actual self—is like proving you exist even if there's no one around to reflect you."

"That's deep," I murmur.

"I think about confidence a lot." Dom says this like he's admitting something he doesn't want to. "Where it comes from. Who gets to have it. Why."

"Okay, so where's it come from?"

"I'm not sure. But I *think* it comes from knowing what you are, and what you aren't. And if you know that—if you can see that—no one gets to tell you different."

"I like that," I say. "I was always told vanity was a bad thing. Like, being prideful was the worst thing in the world."

Dom shrugs. "It is one of the seven deadly sins, I guess, but it feels like a trap."

"Yeah," I say. I wish I had more to say. I feel a little dumb next to Dom and all his brooding, big thoughts. For all the conversations I've had with fascinating people, I've never felt like I could say something back and be listened to. I know Dom will listen to me, but that makes me nervous to say anything at all.

"And sometimes pride is all someone has," he says. "When the world takes everything away, and all someone's got is their pride, it seems cruel to tell them they can't even have that. People need to feel seen."

I look at Dom, his profile carved in the buttery light. I want to kiss him. The urge is so strong that I nearly lean in, but I know it would shock him. It would shock me, too. It takes so much focus not to kiss him that I can't come up with a smart response. Then he feels me staring, and he glances at me, barely even turning.

"What do you see?" he asks me.

This question takes me by surprise. On instinct, I reach for any number of charming responses, but they flutter away from me like butterflies.

"I see someone . . . smart. And insightful. And intense. But you're also . . . shy and—"

"Shy?" Dom laughs. I feel myself blushing.

"Compared to me," I say quickly. "It's not a bad thing to be shy."

Dom shuts me up with a look. "Just because I don't run at

everything doesn't mean I'm running away. I'm just picky about what gets me to rush."

I'm a little lost again.

"I have an idea," he whispers, leaning into me.

"An idea?"

"Yeah," he whispers. "An idea."

Then he jumps out of the van and marches toward the door. The smokers barely notice him. I'm amused at his boldness. I wait for the moment when he turns around to see if I'm following him and realizes I'm not going to fall for this, but then he just walks into the nightclub.

I stare at the door, waiting for him to pop back out with a bewildered expression.

He doesn't.

"Dom?" I ask the silent van cab.

I will myself to wait another minute in this game of chicken, but I don't even last twenty seconds before I'm running after him.

The crowd is thick. You have to fight through it. Even the air drags against you, all the club's mayhem a living obstacle that suddenly turns fluid when you stop resisting and start dancing.

You move to the beat because it's the kind of beat that's so loud it moves you itself. You slip through the dancing crowd with ease as it opens, closes, breathes, contracts; you find him at the center of the organism you've both become a part of. His monarch bandanna marks him.

Dom looks lost, but when he finds you in the crowd, he finds his rhythm. You're pressed into him by the wall of sweating bodies around you, so close that your breaths are indistinguishable from the damp dance-floor air.

You ask him, *Why are you running?*

It's too loud to hear his soft voice, but you think you can read his lips.

So that you'll look for me.

That can't be right, can it? You lean down so he can shout into your ear, and you're surprised when he says instead, *You don't know me as well as you think.*

The look in his eyes is playful when he backs away, not scolding like the words. So it's an invitation. You gesture at him as he sinks backward among the dancers, like saying *show me*, just to see what he does.

In the thrust and bang and sink and rock of the club, you wouldn't think someone like Dom would appear at home, but you'd be wrong. He does, proving he's right. You don't know who you've got before you after all, so it's worth looking for him a little longer.

Someone nearby falls and the crowd raises them back up. The ripple forces you two together. You're ready to simply catch Dom, make sure he stays upright, but he twists in your arms, holds your hands at your sides, and kisses you.

Kisses you.

It takes you a second to kiss back, and by the time you think to, he flits away. He kisses like he exists; in brief, dark flashes of genius. He knows it, too, a devilish grin on his lips as he turns, letting you hold his waist to yours. You hold on tight, afraid he's going to run, but then you follow his gaze toward a vast mirror angled to reflect the crowd.

Dom goes still in your arms, but you tell him it's okay by keeping him swaying. In the mirror you make sure to keep your eyes off yourself, and on him. He sees you looking. He watches you back. The only two people slow dancing at a rave.

You lower your lips and, tentatively, kiss the nape of his neck, still watching Dom in the reflection. It surprises you when you hear his voice, because you'd forgotten he's not the distant boy watching you back from the mirror, but the one encircled in your arms.

What do you see? he asks you again.

You keep your eyes on him as you rock. *I see you.*

He smiles, watching you back.

I see you, too.

CHAPTER TWENTY-THREE

By the time we wrench ourselves out of the living dance floor, we're both a mess of sweat, smoke, and spilled alcohol. We're laughing, though, and our hands can't seem to untangle from our progressively more complicated grips.

It turns out, I'm the shy one. Dom leads, pulling me around the back of the van, pressing me up against it, getting all the way up on his tippy-toes to keep kissing me.

I haven't let myself wonder about what we're doing yet, because it's the only uncomplicated thing to happen these past few days. I just kiss him back until he suddenly pulls away. I open my eyes, already smiling, but a shadow stands between us now. There's a shout; Dom, saying, "No, please—"

There's a whoosh. At least I think there's a whoosh, like something rushing through the air, but I never figure out what it is. Something cracks against my skull just as I reach for Dom and I'm lost in strobe lights, falling to the ground, falling under the bottoms of boots that stomp down on me. I am screaming for him to *run, run away*.

I am screaming.

I am crying.

I black out.

Your usual dreams have trouble reaching you all the way down there.

Down, down, down, in the throbbing blankness you float within.

You're not dead. You know this, because if you were dead, you would be facing a familiar door. But there's no door. There's no anything. Maybe Dom was right, and this is what death is really like, you think dimly; neither heaven nor hell, but a dimensionless purgatory. No light and no darkness. Dull oblivion, forever.

But if that's true, then you're not dead after all. Because this isn't the end you know you deserve. And you realize that somewhere in the last few days you've gone from being someone who would have accepted nothing in the end, to someone who expects at least a chance at salvation.

CHAPTER TWENTY-FOUR

Something tiny and fast crawls across my throat, and I cough, suddenly awake again. I go to slap the insect away but my hands don't budge.

I'm bound to a chair. A gag fills my mouth. My neck is sore from the way I'm slumped.

I feel the tiny, fast thing again, on my nose.

I whip my head away and see a moth frantically rising up into the warm darkness of the room I'm in. The room smells small. Dank, like something sticky spilled and never got cleaned from the carpets. The lamps are dim and hang down into the air just above me. Even though there are tons of bulbs, the room is almost completely lightless.

No, I realize. There's just the one bulb. All the others hanging down are reflections. The room I'm trapped in is completely lined in upright mirrors, all angled toward me at the center.

I'm scared. The kind of fear that carves at the inside of your chest with icy claws. I strain against my bindings and the chair creaks. I strain harder and feel the chair flex—it's not sturdy. Can I break it? I arch my neck to see more. It's wooden, and upholstered, and fancy. The kind of chair that's meant to be placed around a banquet table in a Federal mansion.

Whoever attacked us works for Uhler. I know it. They tracked us using the van, maybe, and chased us—

Dom!

The chair screams as I pull against its arms. Where is he? I try to yell but it's muffled by the gag.

I have to relax. Think. I'm alive, and that must mean something, right? Uhler wants me alive. Or maybe this is when I die. Maybe this is another one of his little experiments.

Do I rewind the mirrors to find out more?

No. I keep my eyes away from them and look past their circle, trying to find signs of a door. My eyes adjust to the darkness and instead I find that the room is wallpapered in a rich crimson pattern that throbs like I'm trapped in the chamber of a beating heart. My own heart throbs with it. I squeeze my eyes shut, knowing even a glance can disorient.

I have no other choice. I have to look into the mirrors and see how they got me in here if I want to get out. I know it's a setup. But if I'm quick, maybe that thing won't find me.

Or maybe it's already here, waiting.

I look.

The mirrors hum with a hunger for you to see what they've seen.

You watch time reverse. You stare at yourself passed out. The moth jumps from your throat, to your ear, then back up toward the light. You sit for so long without moving, it's like viewing your own corpse, and then those men are suddenly standing around you, binding you to the chair. When it comes time for the reflection to show them bringing you into the room, you search for how they entered, but the angle isn't right. You switch to another mirror, then another. You begin to panic as time rewinds all around you, out of sync, so that you are suddenly surrounded by reflections of you, deathly still in the chair, that moth spiraling over you like a slow-motion halo.

In one of the versions of the past, some night earlier than tonight, Uhler taps against a mirror, like he's waking something up within it.

Shut it down for the day, he says. *We'll try again tomorrow.*

You see what this room held before. A sticky, furry thing, collapsed in the center, blood pooled around it. It un-dies in the reverse flow of the mirror, its blood sucking back into it and propping it up in an eerie swoop.

It's a goat. And it's screaming, and screaming, and screaming, because there is something circling it in the mirrors, and like all animals meant to be prey, it understands that it is about to die.

You understand this, too. You scramble to get the mirrors under control, and for a moment you do get them to snap back to the present, but you already know it's too late. Something has been called here. Like a giant fist, it uncurls behind you, not in the room and not in the reflections, but in the reflections of the reflections. It's closer than it's ever been, scampering across the glass with a famished urgency. It finally finds the upright mirror right in front of

242

you, and you see two immense, furred appendages draw back and *slam* into the reflection, webbing it with cracks.

Your skull is made of glass. You feel the cracks burrow through the bones of your face. Beneath your skin, you soften.

Slam.

SLAM.

You feel yourself caving inward. You can't breathe as your nose is pressed into the back of your skull. The glass is about to give way. Will the creature crawl into the room, or will it finally crawl into you?

You're about to find out.

The creature backs up, then brings its full force down on the ruined barrier. The mirrors—all of them—shatter. You are sure you're about to die. Your mind flings out of your body, flees toward the far-off fantasy of being home on your couch. With Yiayia. Her humming. Her prayers, even. The tap of her fingers soothing your aching eyes. If you die here, which you're about to, who will save her?

You squeeze your eyes shut just in time to cut off the vision of something unimaginable crawling from the breach. This seems to make whatever it is flinch backward—the fact that you stopped looking has hurt it.

Your inattention repels it.

It's furious.

I'm furious.

CHAPTER TWENTY-FIVE

Eyes closed, I breathe.

My face still throbs with the crushing force of that thing, but I think I'm okay. I won't look to confirm.

I rock on the chair until it tips, and I fall into the bed of broken glass. I can still hear that thing thudding around me, the mirrors vibrating with its weight as it runs across them from the other side of the—its—dimension. But it's fading. I don't know why, but I start to sing, like Yiayia used to sing to me. If I stop looking at it, it seems to feel some sort of pain, and I think maybe that goes for drowning out the sounds of its approach, too. The less I perceive, the less there is. So I sing:

Κοιμήσου, αγγελούδι μου, παιδί μου, νάνι νάνι,
να μεγαλώσεις γρήγορα σαν τ' αψηλό πλατάνι,
να γίνεις άντρας στο κορμί και στο μυαλό
για να 'σαι πάντα μες στο δρόμο τον καλό.

It's all I remember from an old Greek lullaby, and I sing-shout it right into the sticky carpet, filling my ears with my own voice until the thuds fade. I keep it up as I twist to get onto my back. The chair cracked in the fall, and the rope around my legs is loose. I kick off a shoe and gradually get one foot free, then use my knee to prop up a wedge of glass so that it's pinned against the ropes binding my wrists. I sing as I saw through the rope, and my voice is hoarse by the time I'm done. It goes quicker after that as I get one arm free, then the other, and finally cut through the ropes around my chest.

My hands sting with invisible cuts. The rope is pink with blood from where the shards nicked my fingers. I jam my shoe back on and, careful to keep my eyes unfocused among all the glass on the floor, pick my way out of the circle of mirrors. I don't look at the walls, either, only touch them as I slouch around the perimeter of the room. I feel for a door or some seam in the paper, but instead find an unlit passage that was totally hidden by the wallpaper's pattern when I first looked around. I rush through it, bumping into every corner as it wraps around the room. The image in my mind of where I just was is at the center of a gigantic spiral. A spider's web, rendered in hallways.

Finally I feel fresh air, and a moment later I exit into a vast, unlit warehouse with a bare concrete floor. Moonlight paints the emptiness in blues and silver. It's still night, which means I wasn't in there that long. I want to call out to Dom, but the space is so big and so quiet, I know better than to reveal that I've escaped.

I turn to see *what* I've escaped. I back away from a structure built in the warehouse's center. It's wide, low, and otherwise featureless. No windows, no doors except for the black frame I walked out of. From it breathes the odor of old blood and tarnished metal.

I hug the perimeter of the warehouse walls, eventually discovering a large sliding door, but before I can try opening it, I register the band of light beneath. I remember the bathroom the night of the party and pause, waiting to see if the light reveals someone waiting on the other side. Sure enough, I see a shadow pass. I hurry the other way, keeping my footsteps light. I round the low structure again, looking for another exit. I only find a metal staircase that leads up to—I see for the first time—a walled loft overlooking everything in the large room.

Behind me, I hear a clang echo from the sliding door. I don't wait a second longer. I climb up the stairs, push inside the loft, and close the door.

From up here, I can see directly down into the hallways of the low structure, like I'm a mouse looking down at the maze it escaped. The room I was trapped in has a ceiling, but it's clear from above, like a two-way mirror or something. I back away from the windows as the sliding door starts to open. My only option is to hide somewhere in this room.

Heart still pounding in my throat, I look at my options. The loft is a wide, low-ceilinged room. And it's not completely dark. Long tables cross the space and on them are small lit-up displays, like dollhouses. One catches my eyes. It's a miniature replica of the room I just escaped. It has the single hanging bulb, the circle of upright mirrors, and in the center there's a small plastic goat. It's been conspicuously knocked over into a small puddle of red paint.

All the displays are miniature rooms, I realize. The next one is taller than the rest, three miniature stories stacked in a hollow vertical drop, narrowing to a lens at the top. Recognition flickers through me. I draw closer. There are people in this one. Little toy people. They're glued to little toy ladders, and the ladders are attached to the walls at the very top of the tower, balanced like they could tip back at any moment, casting the people down onto the spiky wreath of toothpicks at the bottom.

I know I need to hide. Someone will check up here as soon as they figure out I'm gone. But now I'm looking at all the models. I find Ellery Pike's living room next, because of the bright LED lights used to make it glow warm white. A doll lies on the floor, hands painted red. The display's walls are covered in the strange wallpaper, too. As I look at the room, I notice it's dusty, like it hasn't been touched in a while. Spider-webs lace from the corners over the doll. It's too elegant to be natural.

It's Ellery's death, but minified. Dom was right. Uhler must have built each of these in the act of planning each death.

I'm powerlessly curious now. I see rooms I don't recognize, but I'm looking for one in particular. I search for a flash of gold against brooding gray, or the familiar shape of a ginkgo leaf, and I find it at the very front, in a model that looks freshly constructed. I expect to see my childhood bedroom, but this room—a den with a shabby couch and heavy curtains—is totally alien to me despite the familiar wallpaper. I get the eerie feeling it's a room I've yet to find.

Below the loft, footsteps rattle the staircase.

I rush past the miniatures, to a series of broad workbenches at the back of the space. There's a drafting table propped up and I think I can maybe squeeze behind it, but once again my curiosity makes me pause.

The drafting table is at the center of a wall plastered in pinned-up papers: wallpaper samples, test prints, and pages of notes. But there are also sketches that echo the wallpaper's designs. Sketches done in a whimsical graphite. On the drafting table, beneath a dim spotlight, I find another one. A transparent sheet of plastic covers it, like someone was tracing it, and all over the plastic are numbers and formulas, like a person was measuring every angle and curve.

I peel the plastic trace away. The drawing is of two birds, caught in a swirl of feathers, like they're about to collide. But the way they're drawn, I can practically feel the pressurized air trapped between their spread wings, can hear the sky rip apart as they swerve from each other at the last minute, leaving a gasp of emptiness and nothing else.

I've never seen this drawing, but I know the sureness in these lines, as legible as a signature. All the sketches pulse with the same artistic fingerprint, and when I step back, I understand that Uhler has been using them as inspiration for the wallpapers drafted all around me.

The door to the loft clicks closed; someone is already in here with me. It's too late, I wasted my chance to hide, but my fear has drained away. I recognize the cautious footsteps. The presence joining me in this room has come to feel like home these last few days of running.

"This is your art," I whisper. "*You* designed the papers."

There's only silence.

"I know it's you," I say to the boy at my back, waiting for the plunge of a knife or the cock of a gun. Some confirmation of the betrayal. "I know it's you, Dom."

I want so badly to be wrong. I want it to be anyone else behind me.

All I get is a drawn-out pause, and then Dom says, "I'm sorry, Athan."

Run, little Athanasios. Run all the way home.

CHAPTER TWENTY-SIX

I turn to face him.

A voice within me is telling me to run, but I can't look away from Dom, half-veiled in my shadow. He has his sketchbook with him, of course, but he hides it behind his back. As if I don't know exactly what's happening here.

"You designed the wallpapers," I say.

"No, it's not what you think," Dom says quickly.

"Then what is it, Dom?"

He doesn't answer, so I answer for him. "Uhler creates patterns for the papers, but they're based off *your* drawings, aren't they? It's not the paper that hurts people, but your drawings. That's why you're so sure of the cause, isn't it?"

"I didn't know," Dom says meekly.

"Bullshit, Dom. That's bullshit."

Dom turns away like I've hit him. It makes me flinch, too.

"I recognized my work," he says. "Orion House paper is everywhere, but it's only the paper with my designs that hurts people. That's why I started all this. That's why it's up to me to stop Uhler. Up to us—"

"Us?" The word booms out of me. "What *us*? How is there any *us*, if you don't even trust me enough to tell me the truth?"

Dom's jaw clenches and unclenches. His eyes stay on me, with a guarded expression glazing over them. Something occurs to me.

"Where are Uhler's men?" I ask.

Dom seems to get smaller, like he's shying away from this, too.

"I handled them," he whispers.

"How?"

No answer.

"You still don't trust me, do you?" I ask.

Dom doesn't deny it.

"Well, right back at you," I say, brushing past him. At the door he calls out to me to wait, but I'm already racing down the stairs. At the bottom I hear him shout: "Wait!"

I halt. His voice is swallowed by the large space, leaving his desperation to echo around us.

"I would never do anything to hurt you," he says. "Not on purpose. I never wanted to hurt anybody. All I wanted was a chance to fix this, but I couldn't find a way until you came along. Please, Athan, don't leave me. I am so close to doing something good for once."

I want to turn and look at him, but I know what I'll see. All his pain, risen to the surface, begging for someone to notice and do something about it. If I look, I won't leave, and I need to leave.

"Wait!" he calls again as I run for the door. "Where are you going?"

"Away from you," I yell back. The sliding door is cracked open and past it is a series of blank industrial hallways. One door is labeled PRINT SHOP. DO NOT CLOSE–DOOR LOCKS AUTOMATICALLY. Inside I hear the sounds of men arguing, and I don't have to wonder about what torments them. This must be how Dom handled Uhler's goons. I leave them there and follow the exit signs to a staircase that ends with a door marked DO NOT OPEN. ALARM WILL SOUND.

I let out a shout of frustration and kick it open.

Alarms blare at my back as I finally start to run.

I make it back to Harlem just as dawn breaks, when the streets are at their emptiest. I've come home this late, or early, before, and it always feels like being in a video game. Too bright to be this empty, and the rare person walking by seems anonymous and unreal.

I scope our street for any sign of Uhler or the police and see nothing, but I don't go for the front door. Instead I drift into the corner store at the end of the block, forever thankful that it's open 24/7. I walk to the back, where a draft reveals a door that's always ajar. Behind the corner store there's a gap between the buildings that's usually full of bagged trash, and a wall sticky with drainpipe drip. I hoist myself up, then walk along the edge of the garden units until I reach mine. I drop into our small back courtyard, which Yiayia always said would be a beautiful garden. In the gray light, the plastic flower beds just look lifeless. She planted seeds when we first moved in, I think, but anything that tried to grow was watered to death in all the seasons after.

I have to wrench the back door open—it gets so stuck in the winter that it might as well be locked, but in November it's still just sticky—and the rattle echoes in the narrow alley. I rush inside before Linda can peek out her back windows. Now I'm in Yiayia's bedroom, listening for the telltale sounds of Linda's radio, or creaking floorboards. I hear nothing.

I relax until I see the mess.

Yiayia's bed is just a bed frame now, and her sheets are strewn across the floor. Only now do I remember Linda's call. She just took the mattress away, even though she knows Yiayia has nowhere else to sleep.

I rush into problem-solving mode, wondering if we can afford a new one or if I'll have to trawl the streets for the kind people put on the curb wrapped in plastic. Then I realize something: For all my searching, for all I've discovered, for all I've endured, Yiayia isn't coming home today. I'm out of places to look. I'm out of friends to call. I have nothing and no one, and even here—our home—is being devoured by forces I can't control.

I walk into the kitchen-living-dining-room where I sleep. The cabinets hang open; Linda has been here a few times. I sink onto the couch, head in my hands. I want to cry. I want any relief from the dread that's been building in me all this time, that boiled over when I saw all of Dom's designs pinned up above Uhler's drafting table. But I can't cry. I'm too tired, or too broken. I just end up staring into the kitchen, waiting for the devouring force to find me and pick me apart, too.

My eyes land on Yiayia's big pasta pot on the stove.

I always feel bad when I see it. I haven't used it in months—Yiayia hasn't used it in longer. And I rarely cook anything grand enough to require it. Looking at it now, I realize that I resent it. A pot like this makes food for big families. When we first moved into this tiny apartment, it cooked the homecoming feast shared between Yiayia, me, and all the handlers who showed up to make sure we were taken care of. Before that, it oversaw every meal in my childhood apartment, like a fifth face between me, my mom and dad, and Yiayia. It's watched me grow up. It's seen everything, from my beginning to this end.

Wait.

I rise to my feet slowly, like it might spook and run away.

This pot has seen my whole life. It's always lived on the stove wherever we stayed, too big to put away in the tiny New York City cabinets.

In the darkness I hover my hands over the lid, stopping short of touching it on instinct, just in case it's still hot. But of course it's freezing.

My reflection stretches around its body like an embrace as I pick it up. I'm down on the couch a moment later, the pot on the table in front of me. How much can this show me about my past? About my family? Something tells me it's seen far more than I'm ready for. So do I look?

Remembering the melted spoon, I grab the fire extinguisher we keep near the garbage, blow off the dust, and hook my finger into the metal ring marked IN CASE OF EMERGENCY, PULL.

I take a deep breath. What do I want to see?

I want to see my family. I want to see our house. But within me there is a need more urgent than the longing to go home. I want to know where I come from, the disaster that forged the life I have today. The fire that ended everything; that started everything else.

Until I met Dom, I thought the fire wasn't just bad luck, but evil luck. Maybe it really was random, but adults always try to make sense of senseless things. They told me *everything happens for a reason*, and I heard *that reason is you*. But everything I've learned—everything I've survived—has tested the limits of what reason can explain.

So what is the nature of what hunts me? A man or a monster? An evil curse or simple bad luck? An insidious design or a stray birthday candle? If I'm too specific in what I'm looking for, all I'll be shown is something that confirms it. Instead, I reach through all the fear and pain I've held inside me these last few days, these last few years, and I make a simple request.

Show me the truth.

You fall backward through time.

You flip through years of dark kitchens and cupboards and storage boxes. The edge of the vision is already starting to whiten, the heat of all the light that's ever touched the metal compounding to summon forth these images.

Careful, you hear Dom whisper, but he's so far away now. Years in your future.

You are back in your childhood home.

And it's all on fire.

You rush through this, not ready to see the end just yet. You stumble further backward, out of the smoke and fire, into a rush of suds guided over the pot by a calloused hand wearing many golden rings.

Your mother.

She looks down at you—at the pot—in the sink, humming to herself. She places it on the stove, perfectly positioned to peer out into the apartment. You face a room bathed in mellow winter sunset. The same room that is about to burn. It stretches around you in the warped panorama of the pot's reflection.

Your mother dries her hands on a towel and then leans against the counter, somewhat blocking your view of the kitchen table. Two men sit there talking, mugs of steaming coffee between them.

You recognize Uhler by his voice. The other man is completely unfamiliar until you realize it's your dad. You have only heard his voice in dreams. Your mother's, too. Hearing them now, you realize how much time eats away at what used to love us. They talk and you have to force yourself to listen to their words, not just the sounds of them being alive.

They're arguing.

You didn't have to come all the way down from the Upper West Side, Dad is saying. *We told you at the shop. We're not interested in your offer.*

There's a smile to Uhler's voice. *But you've already accepted it, Theo. Do you know how much of your business is from Patrons, like myself? Do you think you could maintain any of this without our help?*

Your mother moves to stand at your dad's shoulder. She brings the towel with her, you note, and wraps it around her hand like a boxer.

Please, we're just a family business, she says. *We aren't who you think we are. We have nothing to offer . . . people like you.*

Uhler considers this. It's hard to make out the subtle expressions flickering across his face in the stretched perspective of the vision, but you can tell he's reached the end of his patience. He pulls a sheaf of papers from his bag and spreads it on the table. Your parents can't help but lean in to look.

In the thirteenth century, Uhler says, *an artifact was recorded in the prehistoric city of Akrotiri, on Thera. It was called the Evil Eye. Alternatively: the Eye of God. What's strange is there are hardly any records of it, but there are records of the records. Citations, you could say, pointing to myths and legends of the Eye's power. But all actual recordings of the thing have been destroyed sometime in the last five hundred years. My archaeology colleagues tell me this is odd, but they have pieced some clues together. For instance, we know the Eye had great power and was coveted by kings, queens, emperors, and conquerors. We don't know why. There are rumors it was destroyed, but there are just as many that it can be reconstructed if one should hunt down all the pieces. All eighty-eight of them. Isn't that strange? And then, in the sixteenth century, the Eye and all its pieces vanish. Likely lost during the Theran eruption.*

By now your parents have leaned back from the papers on the table, as though they reek.

Thera is the ancient name for Santorini, Uhler provides. *Melia, your family is from Santorini, yes? Yiayia talks about it fondly.*

Your mother plays the part of nonchalance so well. She shrugs. *I'm from Jersey.*

But Yiayia, she immigrated as a young woman, right?

You can ask her yourself. She'll be home in a few minutes, though I doubt you'll be staying that long.

Uhler smiles graciously. *Then I'd better get to the point. I know she's hiding the Eye. I even know where. It would be the easiest thing to steal it, but I also know better than to tamper with things I don't understand. So I'm here to make a deal.*

Your mother drops her act, too. *You can get fucked, Uhler. People like you are the exact reason we—*

Mel. Your father cuts her off.

Uhler smiles. *So you do have it.*

The three adults turn at a sound. You hear a door open, then slam. A little boy runs into the room and hugs your mother's leg. She gathers him up into her arms like she means to take him out of the room, but he sees the guest.

Uhler!

Uhler stands, smiling ear to ear. *Why, is that the world-renowned artist Athanasios! What an honor!*

You are looking at yourself. Your own reflection, deep in the past, at a time when you trusted anyone your parents trusted. Seeing it now, you realize they never trusted Uhler. They just didn't want you to feel the fear they felt.

I hear someone has a birthday today, Uhler says ponderously.

Little you squirms out of your mother's grip, dashing into the hall and pulling forth a woman carrying a box in her arms. Yiayia, younger, eyes bright. She takes in the scene and sees the papers on the table before Uhler can clean them up. There's only the slightest hint in her posture that she realizes something is wrong. She gives Uhler a false smile. Little you notices none of the tension. You want to do your birthday cake *now*, while your friend Uhler is here.

Uhler is very busy, your father says, but Uhler waves away the protest and accepts the invitation to stay. Your parents get out the plates and the candles, concealing the tension in their movements. Yiayia stays with you at the table, her shoulder turned to Uhler. The room dims as the curtains are pulled shut against the setting sun. The lights are doused, and then the cake is brought to the table, aflame with a crown of six candles.

Everyone sings to you. You remember this. You don't remember Uhler in the background, or the way "Happy Birthday" sounds so eerie. You do remember the part where Yiayia leaves the apartment, but as a kid you missed the reason why: a nod from your mother.

Little you blows out the candles. Your mom brings the cake back to the counter to cut. Uhler asks you questions about your day and you answer through bites of frosting.

Athan, sweetie, your dad says. *Looks like Yiayia forgot her slice. Go bring it to her? I'm sure she would share some with you.*

She didn't see me blow the candles, you say. You're miserable suddenly. *She didn't see me wish.*

Your dad grabs up the matches. *Go show her, I bet she would love to help you make a wish. Let her light the candle, though, okay?*

Okay.

Promise?

Promise.

Little you marches off with the plate and the pack of matches.

Your parents turn back to Uhler, who is just sitting there enjoying his slice of cake, contentedness oozing off him.

Leave, your dad says. *You don't know what you're seeking. This is not some collectible artifact for one of your rooms.*

What is it, then? he asks.

A curse.

You mom says that. She faces away from the table, grabbing the counter, looking down into the remaining wedge of cake. No one is looking, but in the hallway you can see a door open and close, a little shadow slipping out of the apartment.

A family's curse, Uhler says. *From Yiayia, to Melia, to who? Little Athanasios, I imagine? That's a shame. He's a sensitive child, hardly cut out for curses.*

Your mother spins to face the table.

Uhler carries on. *You know, we could help him. The Patrons have taken an interest in . . . young talent. Children, like Athan, who show early signs of a certain sensitivity. Tell me, has he started avoiding his reflection yet?*

Stay away from my family. Your mother's voice is both ice and fire. Her hand reaches behind her to wrap around the knife, still covered in frosting.

Uhler sees this. He smiles wider. *Or what?*

Your mother shows the knife. Your father stands between Uhler and the hallway. For the first time Uhler looks sorry.

Don't be crude, he chides.

Athan, your dad calls. *Get your coat on, buddy. We're going for a walk.*

No answer.

Athan? your dad calls again. *Athan, are you with Yiayia?*

No answer.

Your dad vanishes into the hall, his footsteps shaking the apartment. Uhler's eyes flicker to your mother. She holds the knife out, but she's tremoring.

Your dad calls your name over and over as he checks the bedrooms, and then he's back in the kitchen doorway.

He's gone.

With Yiayia? your mom asks. Demands.

The conversation with Uhler is forgotten as this new peril comes up. But Uhler hasn't forgotten anything. He springs up from the table, slamming into your mother. She nicks him in the cheek with the knife before he throws her down, her head cracking against the counter. Your dad lunges over the table just as Uhler reaches for something to fight with. His hand stretches toward the pot. Then everything swings—the entire apartment, all of reality itself, as you are lifted off the stove into a deadly arc.

No, you think.

The vision spins with sickening momentum as the pot is brought down in a crushing blow—once, twice, three times. You crash to the floor on your side, your vision coated in red. You are staring across the floor at your father's inert body, his head a ruin. You are watching your mother crawl away. Uhler stalks after her with the cake knife in hand. They exit your line of sight, and you hear her last scream. Before the knife takes her life, you think she was about to yell your name.

Athan!

Nothing moves for a long time, and then Uhler steps back into sight. He drags the bodies to the table, sitting them up in the chairs like a family sharing a meal. The pot is picked up and righted on the stovetop. Uhler uses a towel to wipe the blood from his face and wash his hands. The way he moves—precise and calm— tells you he has done this before.

Once clean, Uhler surveys the scene. He sits back in his chair, picking up the last bite of cake left on his fork, thinking. His eyes land on your father's plate, untouched, the snuffed candle still standing proudly atop it.

He smiles.

Uhler drags the plate away from your dad's corpse. He reaches into his pocket and produces a lighter, flicking until the candle catches. He looks around, eventually focusing on the still-drawn curtains.

Tacky, he scolds. Then he brings the plate with the birthday cake to the window and sets it down on the sill. The curtain begins to smoke.

Uhler moves quickly now, but without any panic. He gathers up his things, sparing only a moment to peer through the smoke filling the room, to give your parents one last pitying look. Then he turns, hopping over the blood in the hall, and whistling a song as he leaves.

Happy birthday, to you.

CHAPTER TWENTY-SEVEN

Everything goes white.

Even the smoke.

White.

My consciousness whips out of the glowing metal and I'm thrown back against the couch. Back home, forward in time. But the smoke follows me. White fills the air, hissing and spitting, as though the fire is trying to claw its way into the present.

"I got it!" someone yells, and there's the *whoosh* of the fire extinguisher as it douses the column of flame I was staring into. The smell of burning chemicals mixes with the smell of burning plastic. Everything is lost in a cloud and all I can do is listen for some sense of what's happening. I hear coughing, and then a familiar voice lets out a single, sardonic *fuck*.

"Dom?"

Like a ghost, Dom materializes from the cloud. He stands above me, tossing the spent extinguisher onto the couch.

"Hey," he says. He holds out Yiayia's hand mirror. I didn't even realize I had lost it.

"Hey," I say, taking it. I'm too stunned to say more.

"Are you okay?" he asks.

"I think so."

"What were you doing?"

"Rewinding a pasta pot," I say. The words hardly make any more sense outside my head than they did inside it.

"That's what it looked like," Dom says. Then, again, he asks, "You okay?"

Tears are streaking down my cheeks. When I wipe at them, my fingers come away coated in white powder. I'm a ghost, too, just like Dom. I don't know how to answer his question. I can't make sense of Dom here, either. I know I'm supposed to be mad at him, but in light of what I just saw, I feel an immense relief at the incongruity of his presence.

All I can think to say is, "Welcome to my house."

"It's nice."

"It's not, but thanks."

His jaw clenches.

"How did you find me?" I ask.

"I knew you had nowhere else to go, so I thought you would go home. I'm glad I got here in time. This place was about to—" Dom cuts himself off.

I stare at the angry, charred ring on the coffee table where the pot still sits, smoking. We're both looking at it as it goes from red-hot to a tarnished silver. Unlike the spoon, the pot didn't melt. That's craftsmanship, Yiayia would say.

"It worked," I whisper. "I saw . . . I saw them. I saw it happen."

My voice breaks. I break, too. Somewhere inside me the memory of what I just saw is already burning me up. My parents loved me. *Loved me.* They gave everything to protect our family, and it didn't even matter. It wasn't enough. He killed them in seconds. Their lives were smashed out of them and he hardly broke a sweat. Like it was nothing.

"He killed them," I whisper. "Uhler killed my parents. And he caused the fire. He's the one behind all this. He—"

I sink to my knees, right on the kitchen tile, and stare into my hands. For years, it was these hands I blamed for taking everything away. These hands that had to hold that guilt as it grew heavier and heavier and *heavier.* I read once that love has a weight, and that we become strong holding it up. So does guilt. Guilt made me strong, but I didn't have to become this way. I didn't have to turn into whatever you become after a lifetime of guilt has changed you. It was never my burden. But I didn't know.

I didn't know.

"It was always Uhler," I whisper to Dom, who has knelt beside me. Tentatively he gives me his hand, and I take it. It helps me find my voice.

"I saw him come to my house the day of my birthday. He wanted something called the Eye of God. Some sort of ancient artifact. He thought . . . he *knew* my family had it. And . . ." I swallow. The powder on my lips is bitter. "They wouldn't give it up, so he . . ." Another blistering wave rolls through me, and I squeeze every muscle in my body just to keep from falling apart. Dom squeezes back until it passes.

"I think Yiayia was hiding it, but he has it now."

"So O-654-A is the Eye," Dom whispers to himself. "If he's had it all along, what has he been looking for?"

"Pieces," I say. "It's in pieces, I think. He thought Yiayia's mirror was one of them, but I guess he was wrong. If he finds them all, he can open it. He wants to at the gala."

"What does it do?"

I shake my head. I can't pull my thoughts together enough to think about the future. The past is still burning inside me, in a place I can't even hope to extinguish. But Dom is my anchor to the present. He needs me here, in the right now.

"I don't know, but it's bad," I say. "There's a reason it was broken and hidden. My parents died protecting this secret. And me."

Hearing myself, I put something together.

"He needs me," I say, sitting back on my heels. "Or Yiayia. Someone with the Sight has to open the Eye. So that must mean it's . . ." My eyes fix on the still-steaming pot on the table, glassy and black and swallowing the weak light around it. "It's a mirror, and something hides inside it."

Dom takes a quick breath.

"I think I know what," he says. "It's time I told you everything."

"Really?" I ask. "You? Giving me the whole picture? You sure you're okay?"

Dom rolls his eyes and it's the most beautiful thing I've ever seen.

"Get up," he says, standing. "If I'm gonna tell you my tragic life story, I at least want to do it in fresh clothes. Can we clean up first?"

"You're stalling," I point out.

"And we're both very sticky. Your point?"

I give him a quick kiss on the head, then cough as more powder catches in my throat. Dom laughs all the way to the tiny bathroom.

The living room is a mess, and Yiayia's bed is gone. We duck out the back to walk through the streets of Harlem while we talk. I put Dom in one of my old puffer coats. It's huge on him, going down to his knees so that he looks like a giant, grumpy bell. He scowls when I make him do a spin, but it makes me happy to keep him warm.

For the first time since I met Dom at the party, he's eager to talk. He doesn't seem to know how, though. His composure cracks and re-forms, cracks and re-forms. He's like Yiayia's mirror: broken pieces locked together, the integrity of his smooth facade webbing into sudden, sharp edges. We left Yiayia's mirror at the house, along with Dom's bandanna hung up in the kitchen to dry. Dom's hands keep drawing my eye to his bare throat, and without Yiayia's mirror to hold, the urge to touch him sparkles in my fingertips. I give him space, though—you cannot pick at someone else's broken pieces, you'll get all cut up—and I shove my hands deep in my pockets.

"I don't know where to start," he says.

"Start at the beginning."

Dom hugs himself against November's chilly air. To show him I mean it, I banish all traces of amusement from my face.

"When I was little, I liked to draw," he starts. "I liked painting and watercolors, too. Anything visual. My parents were supportive. They sent me to classes and got me tutors, made me show off for their friends. That included Uhler. We would always see him when we visited the city for holidays, and he liked to take us on tours of his showrooms. His warehouses, too."

He pauses, turning over the next thought in his mind.

"The storage space between floors? I think I've been there before. I remember the graffiti mural, and the way the windows were split in half. I remember Uhler bringing me there one time and telling me to stay put while the adults did something. I had my art supplies, so I didn't care. But I remember thinking it was weird how they left me alone. And . . . I remember feeling like something was in the room with me."

"Like a presence?" I ask.

"Kind of. It was like being watched, but the room was empty. Or I guess it wasn't empty—there was stuff everywhere at the time—but when I looked around, no *people* were with me. But I did find something else. This huge copper frame mounted on the back wall. I remember being fascinated by it, and thinking it was a million years old, and wondering about the painting that used to be inside it. But now I think I know what it was."

"Not a painting," I say. "A mirror."

"*The* mirror," Dom confirms. "But it was totally ruined. There were only a few shards stuck in the frame, just at the edges. I remember being scared. I banged on the door for someone to come get me, but no one did. Eventually, I fell asleep under it. I dreamt about a spider crawling from the frame and into my ear. I woke up screaming. I could hear it in my head. My parents and Uhler were there, standing over me, watching. Uhler was taking notes.

"Then . . . it was over. They took me to get ice cream, and my family left New York City, and we went home to LA. But I tried to stop doing art after that."

"Why?"

Dom shrugs. "Because it felt . . . wrong. Whenever I picked up a pencil, I felt something bad happening in me, like something was slowly coming awake. And then . . ."

Dom swallows. I know he hasn't told many people this story, because it sounds like it doesn't want to come out of him.

"If I stopped drawing for even a day, I would fall into these trances and end up drawing for hours. You're probably thinking I drew, like, ghosts and shit, like in the movies. But my work was beautiful. It just wasn't . . . only mine. It felt like something was using me to create, like I was the pencil in someone else's hands. I tried to tell my parents, but all they saw in my work was beauty. *Such* beauty."

When Dom says *beauty*, it's not with pride.

"I remember painting a picture of a butterfly." Dom squints, like he can still see it. "A monarch butterfly, specifically. With a brand-new set of gouache paints. It came out gorgeous. My parents were amazed. My mom wanted to hang it up, but my dad wanted to try and sell it. I remember my parents fighting a lot, but this one got bad. They screamed at each other, right in front of me, arguing about this stupid painting. But it wasn't really the painting they were arguing about—it was just the thing that got them going that time. I basically watched their marriage end right in front of me. My mom said my father only cared about money, and that he didn't even love us. My dad said she was a bitch. A *cancerous bitch*. It went on for so long, they didn't even notice me leaving. And a few months later, they were getting a divorce."

Dom pauses. We've stopped in front of a deli. In the fluorescent light he looks exhausted, like saying all this is draining the life from him. I want to tell him to stop, but I don't think he wants to, or can. Sharing like this hurts, but it helps, too. Then he surprises me by reaching out a hand. I take it, surprised again when there's no cut to his touch, no bite. He's not like Yiayia's mirror at all. I squeeze his fingers.

"I'm okay," he sniffs.

We keep walking.

"By then it was a relief. I thought maybe they would be happy again. But then, when they finally sat me down to talk about it, it was only because they wanted me to decide who got the butterfly painting. They had their lawyers present and everything. Isn't that insane? Saying it now . . . it sounds so, so wild, but I was only a kid. I didn't understand how wrong it all was. I just knew that everyone was angry, and it was my fault. I destroyed the painting that night. It ruined everything. *I* ruined everything. I thought ripping it up could put everything back together, but I was wrong. The divorce happened, and my mom won custody, but she hardly seemed like my mom anymore. She would look at me like I was a stranger, like she couldn't figure out how I fit into this new life of hers. My dad never forgave me, either. He didn't even fight for visitation."

Dom's hand is at his throat again, feeling for the bandanna that isn't there. I wonder what it means—why he always wears it. I wonder about the colors. Orange, black, and white, in the stained-glass spray of a monarch butterfly's wings. I'd thought it was some type of ironic flourish, a bit of cheeky rebellion against the chic facade of his black clothing.

I start to realize how wrong I was.

"I'm sorry," I say, but it sounds stupid. Probably because I don't even know what I'm apologizing for. Not yet.

"After that, I noticed that the art I made had . . . an effect on people. Specific art on specific people. I could never predict when it would happen, but I'd draw and someone would see it, and . . . something would just unravel within them. Like one time I painted a still life of some blood oranges for a class, and the teacher marveled at it for days. She hung it up, and she would stare at it while we worked, and then one day, in the middle of class, she . . . ate it."

"Ate it?"

"Yeah, she walked right up to it, let out this terrible groan, like she didn't want to do it, and then she just . . . bit into the canvas. It was one of the wooden-framed ones. Even when her mouth started bleeding, she wouldn't stop. We had to call for help. When they rushed us out of the classroom, I stepped on a tooth."

Of all the unsettling details, it's the idea of the teacher groaning that makes me feel nauseous. Like she knew better but couldn't help it, and it was just easier to give in.

"Another time," Dom says, "I was asked to paint a mural on the side of the school. I thought if I did something simple, no one would get hurt, so I just made up some nonsense design. Just black and white circles, like a topographic map. Abstract bullshit. But still, it had a hunger. Birds kept flying into it. Hundreds of them, until all the white was stained pink. And then people started getting pulled into it. Someone on the track team broke their nose, and a mom rammed her stroller right into it. And then . . . and then—"

Dom halts. "Someone died," he chokes out. "A car swerved off the road and totaled itself against the mural, killing the driver. She was thirty. She was on her way to her friend's wedding. Someone else painted over the mural after that. As a memorial. Thank God."

"That's horrible," I say. "But . . . why? How could art—anyone's art— do that?"

"You said it yourself, Athan. It's evil. 'Devil shit,' is how you put it. And I agree."

The look of sadness on Dom's face is so deep, I feel myself falling into it. I take a breath. In this moment I know I will do anything—I will never stop trying—to prove Dom wrong. "Dom, I didn't mean . . . *You* aren't—"

"Maybe I am." He snatches himself away.

I keep reaching. "Dom, I'm sorry, I shouldn't have said that. I don't think you're evil—"

"Well, *I* do!"

We are both quiet, the sounds of the city filling the tense space between us. I search for the words that will undo this, but I also know that words aren't enough. I'm afraid that if I push back too hard, he'll close back up. I choke down my protests. Just for now, just until he's said what he needs to say. Dom hugs himself, but not tenderly; he is the vision of a person who has learned how to hold themselves together. He goes on. "For a long time, I thought there was something fundamentally disturbed about the way I saw the world, and my art showed that. When people looked at it, it triggered something in them. But I could never see it. The spell never worked on me. All the people around me kept getting hurt, but not me."

"Like how you couldn't see the kids at Magda's apartment," I offer.

Dom nods.

"I tried to stop, but . . . it controls me. *It.* The beauty, or the demon, or whatever it is inside me—it takes over. I tried so hard, never letting myself sleep, or wrapping my hands in duct tape. I even . . . broke my fingers once. I used our dining room table. Tipped it right over onto my hands, but it didn't matter. That's what cost my mom custody, though. The school thought she was hurting me. I denied it, but do you want to know something fucked up? She didn't. She saw her way out and gave me up, even though I begged her to tell the truth. The courts ruled her unfit, and with my dad out of the picture, Uhler came forward to claim me."

Dom pushes his hair off his face. He's trembling when he does it. I place a tentative hand on his back, not rubbing. Just holding him steady as we keep walking.

"I eventually figured out if I kept drawing every single day, I'd stop blacking out. That sketchbook I carry? I have dozens of them stacked up in my room at Uhler's house. I had no idea he was stealing from them until recently, when I recognized a design of mine in one of the Orion House custom wallpapers. As soon as I did, I glued all my sketchbooks shut. It was too late, though. He had plenty to work with already."

I finally look up as something cold kisses the back of my neck. It's starting to snow. The flakes cross the milky headlights of passing cars like swarming static. It reminds me of the shifting patterns in Magda's apartment.

"The penthouse party, Ellery's white room, Magda's fall," Dom says, also looking up. "All because of the demon that makes me draw. Do you know what it's like to have to create, never knowing who your art might hurt?"

"No," I say, a steely firmness in my voice. "You didn't put those people in danger. Uhler did. It was Uhler who created the wallpapers and designed those deathtraps. The miniature rooms we saw prove it."

"Those weren't designs," Dom says. "They were re-creations. Studies. Experiments, like that red room you escaped. He's trying to unlock something using my designs. Trying to . . . talk to that thing, I think. Bait it or feed it. I don't know why. Maybe he wants it as his own diabolical muse."

"Power," I say. "Whatever my parents were protecting, they thought it was too dangerous for normal people to know about. But he has it now. He's just missing a final piece of the Eye of God."

We stand in uncomfortable silence. The more we discover, the less we can do about it.

"You know what . . . ?" Dom says. Flakes catch in his eyelashes and don't melt, like he's ice-cold. "Now that I think about it, it was Uhler who sent me the gouache paints. The ones I used to make the butterfly. And isn't it fitting? A butterfly, like the butterfly effect? A bug flaps its wings and, somewhere else in the world, a hurricane destroys everything. Most people never see the connections between what they create and what they ruin until it's too late. But I do."

He reaches for the bandanna again, and something in my head clicks. I've misunderstood Dom entirely, but now I see him as he sees himself. We're the reverse of each other. All my color, all my shine, is meant to lure people close enough that they can't see all of me, like moths made dizzy by an artificial light they've mistaken for the moon. Dom shines differently. Not a desperate blaze, like me, but a modest slash of color, right at the throat. A subtle but efficient warning to all: *Stay back. No closer, for your own good.*

And maybe the bandanna is a reminder to himself, too. Dom told me once that monarchs are poisonous. Now he's told me that his parents fought more for a butterfly than they did for him. When he looks at his reflection, what does he think? *You are a ruinous thing. You will only bring harm to the eye that beholds your beauty.*

"No," I whisper. I won't let him do this to himself anymore. "No, Dom, you can't think like that. It's not you."

He looks at me, but he can't hold my gaze. "I know you think your family is cursed, Athan. I used to think I was cursed, too, but the truth is worse. I *am* the curse."

"Absolutely not," I counter. "You're not a curse. You have to trust me."

Dom is looking down. "How do you know?"

What can I say? What can I do to convince him otherwise? What matters? I tilt his chin up, just to get his eyes back on me. He gives me a defiant look. Dom is always ready to argue, even if it's against himself. But deep in his gaze, past the defiance, is a vulnerability I remember from our dance at the rave. I have to bring that version of him back into focus.

"Well, for starters, I can't kiss a curse," I say, and the joke catches him off guard. He lets out a breath of steam. "But I sure can kiss you."

Dom lifts a challenging eyebrow. "Oh yeah?"

I lean in, but it's a fake-out. I kiss him on the cheek, then pause. "So far so good," I whisper. The snowflakes melt in the growing heat between us. I kiss away the crystals in his eyelashes next, stamping out his protests as I work down his jaw. When I finally pull away, his eyes stay closed, his mouth slightly open. Waiting for a kiss. Waiting for me to prove my point.

I'm about to, but I briefly have that sense of heaven, the craving for an eternity spent facing something amazing, like a room full of love, like a kiss in winter's first snow, and I want time to stop and hold me here forever in this anticipation. But I'm too young to think about forever, and Dom needs to know he's worth finding out what happens next. So I kiss him. The boy, the butterfly. I press my lips to his and let time rush over us.

Someone honks a horn and cheers, and we break apart, laughing into the steam of our breaths.

"Could a curse do that?" I ask Dom. I have to adjust myself in my pants, and when the gesture makes Dom blush, I point and ask again: "Could a curse do *that*?"

Dom grabs my arm and pulls me along. I kiss the top of his head. "Points for showmanship, but I'm not sure how to document this in my folder of evidence."

We turn the corner of my block. I can see a faint brightening of the sky. The sun is about to rise. "We aren't cursed," I say. "And we aren't curses. And if you consider that kiss as evidence, just wait for me to make my case when we get home. I gotta warn you, though. The couch is a tight squeeze for two."

"It's a sofa," Dom corrects me, but with one eyebrow raised so there's a devious leer to it.

I don't get to respond, because just then I notice the lights are on inside my apartment—lights I definitely left off.

Linda.

Fucking Linda. She probably heard the ruckus and decided to investigate. Just as I remember the wreckage my vision left behind, I hear her scream right through the apartment walls. I rush inside and find her mid-rant even before I've announced myself. She flaps her hands at the burned table, the white powder, the general chaos all around.

"Are you trying to kill me?" she shrieks. "I could have suffocated! My smoke alarm has been going crazy. I'm calling the police!"

We manage to calm Linda down, to explain to her that the fire is out, and that nothing but the table got burned, and no one needs to be calling any police. Still, she's quick to point out that it's *her* table. I promise her I'll pay for it, and she tearily accepts, then stands there expectantly. I realize she means *right now*. I give Dom an embarrassed look as I start to dig through the cabinets for the tin where I keep extra cash. The way Linda throws on a smug look when I reach for the cabinet, I can tell she knows about the hiding spot.

I count out a hundred dollars, and Linda frowns.

"The table is walnut," she says. "Solid wood. Furniture appreciates, you know."

Dom steps in, plucking the money from her waiting hand, and says, "Nice try, but solid wood doesn't bubble."

We all look at the table and he's right, the top of it is a blistered nova. "It's laminate on particle board," he says, "and you're a greedy asshole."

Linda purses her lips, snatches back the money, and huffs up the stairs. I'm about to burst out laughing when Dom stops me with a raised hand. He's looking at the couch.

"Athan, where's your yiayia's mirror?"

A perfect silhouette of the mirror sits on the white dust of the couch, where I must have dropped it before. It was there when we left for our walk, but now it's gone.

We both look up at the ceiling, hearing Linda creaking through her apartment. Something in me snaps and suddenly I'm marching up the back stairwell. Dom follows, whispering, "Why would she take it?"

"Because she's a thief," I snap.

"Athan, are you *sure* that mirror isn't something powerful?"

I give him an incredulous look on the landing. "Even if it is, *Linda* definitely isn't. She's always talking about being so in touch with the supernatural, but trust me, there's not a spirit within a hundred miles that would communicate with her. She's just a greedy asshole, like you said. I want my mirror back."

I push open the door and find that Linda's apartment is dark. Way too dark for early morning. The kitchen windows are heavily shaded, but the crack in the curtain falls over a countertop cluttered with dishes. A sink full of pots. I feel the ghostly touch of fruit flies floating near my eyelashes.

"Linda?" I call again.

"Yes, dear. In here, dear."

That creeps me out. There's no trace of anger in her voice, though it's been only a minute.

From vague memories of the apartment's layout, I think she's in her living room at the front of the house. We push open a pair of French doors. Somehow the living room is even darker, and I'm only able to make out the shapes of a lumpy couch, a chaise, and some chairs pushed against the far wall. Linda is sitting in one of them. I see the hand mirror flash in her lap.

"Give it back," I say.

"Give what back, dear? You know, you and your yiayia have a very strange way of showing gratitude. Very strange. Someday you'll be as old as me and you'll understand how naive you are, making all these demands on someone who has opened their home to you."

Dom grabs my hand. I twist out of his grip but he catches me, pulling hard.

"Athan," he says.

I turn to him, seeing too late the shadow creeping along the wall where we entered. It's not that huge, spidering monster. It's the form of a little old lady with messy hair, raising something over her head. I can't see what it is. I just hear a metallic *thunk* and Dom drops to the ground.

"Dom? Dom!" I curl over him, shielding him from another hit, but it never comes. I search the shadows for Linda, but I can't make anything out. How did she get behind us? She was just on the couch. Or sofa. Or whatever! Now I see her shape everywhere in the clutter that covers the bookshelves, the old furniture, the—

The curtains swing apart, ripping open the darkness with a sudden, butchering light.

"Don't look," Dom groans beneath me.

But it's too late. I'm in the real-life version of the miniature den I saw in Uhler's workshop. The entire room is aflame with a pattern of autumnal gold. Ginkgo tree leaves—they swish in a cool wind, falling in frantic twirls, landing in my eyes.

You are Athan Bakirtzis.

You sit on a swing, in a park, head drooped so low your chin nearly rests on your chest. Your feet drag a scar into the ground beneath the swing, revealing the frozen earth beneath the layers of rotting, golden leaves.

Such a sadness wells up inside you. Such a heaviness lines your muscles and bones. It makes it easy to stay so still, and you start to think you'd have no problem being one of the gargoyles that overlook the eves of the church you walk by every day to get to the park. Dad calls them grotesques.

If you're sitting so still, why are you drifting back and forth? What other force moves you, against your will?

You have long wondered about the mechanics of this world. How things work, how they fit together. Why they work for some people and not others. Why some people get to fit. It's the kind of contemplation that becomes precious to a person who is convinced they don't belong here, yet badly wants to. So it becomes important to figure out why the world works, and how.

You've known the answer since you were very, very little. Our world is an artful illusion—of light, color, and sound. It feels spontaneous when you're in it, but it isn't. Beneath it all, or above it all, there's something both significant and unknowable. A design. A sequence that can be maneuvered within, but never escaped.

That's the force that moves you, you think as you swing back and forth against your will. That's the force that moves *through* you. It takes what it wants, but with your hands, so you're the one left holding all the pain.

It's enough to make you want to give up.

You straighten, surprised at yourself. For a moment, that felt real—the idea of giving up. You have that kind of intrusive thought all the time, but just now—that was different. You shake your head, raising your hands to tap, tap, tap your forehead. You want to see Yiayia. Ask her things again and see if she answers. So you get up from the swing and kick a new path through the mounds of ginkgo leaves.

The park is big but empty, probably because it's freezing. The golden leaves of the aspen and ginkgo trees are so bright, they appear printed into the blank white of the November sky. It has a strange flatness, like if you picked up a rock and threw it, it'd catch in the middle distance, twist the world like a fish in a net before bouncing back at you.

You pick up a rock.

Before you throw it, there's a crash behind you. You spin around, rock raised, but nothing is there. Just a storm of leaves kicked up, like a great and invisible hand plunged down and punched the earth.

You're aware that something is wrong but not sure what. Your heart feels tight, like you're forgetting something important. You think and think, but what could it be? Or who?

Something creaks in the trees above you, and you look up in time to see it—a sprawling net of lines printed in a throbbing negative against the white sky and yellow foliage. It pulls together into a bulky core that seems to see you back, then it moves quickly upward, climbing like a spider, right into the sky, using the sun to hide.

You open your mouth to scream, but instead you find words: *It's you.*

The thing—more a phantom than anything physical—speaks back in an echo. uoy s'tI.

You back away as quickly as you can from the thing in the trees. The golden ground ripples. The wind is playing with you, coiling the leaves into patterns in the bright air. Time slows, and the leaves slow, too. They hang there, pressed into peculiar planes around you, like walls.

You close your eyes, wander a few feet forward, and sure enough your hand comes to rest on smooth flatness. You knock, and it *is* a wall.

Hello? you call out. Your voice bounces back, like you're in a small room. Then comes the echo of the thing following you:

¿ollɘH

You can hear it crawling across the sky, picking at the ground with its long legs. It's looking for you, but with your eyes closed you've suddenly become invisible to it. Like peekaboo with your own reflection.

You feel forward and while your mind moves through the park, your body moves through a room. You bump into the soft arm of a couch, then the corner of a low table. Your foot catches on something and you fall, hands meeting a carpet. You feel for what it is and then jump back when it grabs you.

Please. Athan, help me!

It's a voice you know.

Linda? Your landlady. What is she doing here? You open your eyes and she's suddenly next to you on the ground, in the park. She looks terrified, snapping her neck this way and that. You can hear that thing in the trees still, but you know better than to look. You focus on Linda. She's clutching something to her chest. You reach for it but she pulls away, hissing at you.

It's mine!

She has your yiayia's mirror. It's not hers. Even if she thinks that, even if she believes it, it's not true. You try to be gentle with her as you pry apart her wrinkled hands and pull the mirror free. She screams bloody murder the entire time.

With a yank you get the mirror free, feeling a moment of joy at having it back before you see what Linda has done. Smears of blood clot in the cracks where she tried to pry the pieces apart.

You—

But she's not next to you anymore. Her mewling just cuts off. A new sound rises, and it rises from the broken mirror.

Why did you fight to retrieve this thing? Why do you even want it? Why not put it down and move on? A broken mirror is a metaphor for all that's wrong with you, Athanasios. The past has held your focus long enough, hasn't it? Let the lens crack; look forward.

Look up. At me.

But instead of looking up, you raise a fist and finish what Linda started. You smash the mirror, your bones versus its brittle skin. A hiss of pain opens into a gush of blood, but you smash and keep smashing, until the jingle of glass sobers you. Shards lie on the golden ground, rosy with blood, but they look different. *Clear.* Not reflective at all.

You stare at the ruined mirror.

Your eyes widen.

Where the glass has chipped away is a shiny blackness. You pick off the rest as delicately as you can to reveal what has always been below: a sheet of flawless obsidian. The mirror's true face.

And in the face of the mirror, where you should be, there is another person looking back.

There you are, says your yiayia. *Finally, you've found me.*

CHAPTER TWENTY-EIGHT

The black mirror shines.

Or it does the opposite of shine. It doesn't reflect light out; it pulls it inward, contracting the air around it like I'm holding not a mirror but a snag in the fabric of space.

I stare at my yiayia's face.

She wears a sad smile.

I recognize the sensation of my Sight focusing on the reflection, causing it to back away from me through time. But unlike the other mirrors I've rewound, this one only ever shows my yiayia's face. The rooms shift wildly around her, the lighting flashing through days and nights and weeks, but it's always her same face, and she is always speaking.

"There you are, Athanasios."

I catch the phrase again and again as the reflection plunges backward. I'm so shocked to see her, to *hear her talk to me*, that the oddness of this—that I can understand her—doesn't register right away. The words are garbled and strange leaving her lips. It's because, I realize, she's speaking backward.

Has been speaking backward, into her hand mirror. For years.

"I don't know where I begin or end anymore," Yiayia is saying in that garbled monotone, like she's recited this a thousand times. "But maybe I don't need to know. It wouldn't change my fate. All patterns find their symmetry. Everyone—every life—must meet the mirror eventually."

"What?" I whisper. "What are you saying?"

"And so *you* must close it, Athanasios. You must close the Eye for good." There's no indication she can hear me. It's just the next sentence in her recitation. And she keeps going.

"There you are, Athanasios," she begins again. "Finally, you've found me. Which means the opening has begun. I have fought this fate my entire life, tried everything to avoid it for you, but it will not work. I see that now. I was a foolish woman."

I can't help it; I touch the black glass. It's freezing. A moment after I touch it, Yiayia does the same, like I've seen her do a million times.

"There is something you must know," she says. "The Sight in our blood goes forward and backward, Athanasios. The future is as visible as the past, but not every eye is willing to see it. And the second we do see the future, it likes to change."

"But I can only see backward," I say.

"You can only see backward because that's all you can imagine," she says, an edge of reprimand in her voice. "Grief is love for a past that is over, a present that has changed, and a future that will never arrive. I'm afraid your heart was wounded too young. It yearns to collect the pieces of the past because it cannot face the present. And for a heart like that, what use is the future? You cannot see forward because you cannot look forward."

I know she's right. The inertia of grief is great, like pushing against a mountain. Especially now that I've seen it all for myself. How it happened, and why. The pointlessness of my parents' deaths, a pointlessness that has spread into everything else.

"He killed them, Yiayia," I say. My voice cracks.

"I know. I knew then."

I wipe at my tears, blood stinging my eyes. I fight to keep them open and on Yiayia's stoic expression. Now she sits in her bedroom, the headboard behind her. She looks weak, the light from the lamp carving hollows into her neck and eye sockets.

"Our curse is not a simple one. To see what was and what will be costs us perspective on what matters, which is what's now. The riddle of telling someone their future is this, Athanasios: A future foretold is a future destroyed. For you, in the rarest glimpses the mirrors allow me, I have seen such wonderful things, and I have watched you destroy them all. I see our curse spreading through the world. I risked telling you nothing, to save you. To save everyone. But . . ."

The bored recitation of Yiayia's speech cuts off, a small flare of emotion breaking through her voice. Her eyes focus, like she can really see into mine. She sits up so that the light is at her back, spreading a halo through her messy white hair.

"In the future I see now, there is hope. For you. For all of us. I do not dare look away. I guard you the only way I know how. I speak to you in a language only you can understand, and only in the precise moment you need to understand it. This is my prayer, not to God, but to you. To your future. The Eye will open, and you must be the one to close it."

"How?" I scream at the black glass. "Tell me *how!*"

"I wish I could have been there for you in the way you wanted," Yiayia answers. "I wish I could take this burden from you, my dear Athanasios, but I am fading. I don't know where I begin or end anymore. But maybe I don't need to know. It wouldn't change my fate. All patterns find their symmetry. Everyone—every life—must meet the mirror eventually. And so *you* must close it, Athanasios. You must close the Eye for good."

She's said this before. I realize the message is repeating. Without skipping a beat, she resumes with: "There you are, Athanasios. Finally, you've found me."

Her message repeats in that lurching backtalk, leaving me with a swarm of questions buzzing in my head. I want to shout them into her face, but it wouldn't matter. She can't hear me, can't respond. All that awaits me in this dark mirror is the same answer, again and again.

I speak to you in a language only you can understand, and only in the precise moment you need to understand it. But I don't understand it. Even as it replays, I only feel my dread deepening. So what if I have grief? What right does she have to tell me that my pain has cost me my future? How is it my fault, what hurt me as a child?

The past is the past. It can't be changed. I raise the mirror over my head to throw it, wishing I'd never pried its false face off, but I stop.

I'm still standing in the park, the ginkgo leaves still falling in their perpetual patterns. But they fall upward now, in fluid spires of gold, yellow, and orange. They rustle and crack. Soft and pretty, but with a threat that takes me a moment to place.

Fire.

The autumn leaves collage into tongues of fire, reaching all the way up into the blank white sky, creating patterns that repeat. My eyes hurt, looking so long. There's something I'm not seeing. A pattern—

All patterns find their symmetry.

I unfocus my eyes and look into the middle distance. It makes it easier to detect the moment the dancing leaves repeat, and gradually I make out a seam in the air, like two walls meeting at a corner. I close my eyes and approach it, arms outstretched, until my bloody fingers curl against a flat surface. I use the hand mirror's metal handle to slice into the seam, carving open a flap of air and revealing—I finally have to look—a blank wall.

The entire scene falters.

Ahead of me in the distance, something bristles. I know what. It's the beast from the infinity mirrors, hiding in the sky. I can't help but look, desperate to finally see it. What I see hurts to look at—but it hurts more to look away.

It's translucent, its body bending the light into rainbow edges. It pulls itself through the air on long insect legs. It moves so quickly I nearly turn and run. But it's too late to run. It's already crawled down into the park; it's scuttling over the playground. A mass of unblinking eyes shimmer like bubbles as it stampedes forward. It moves with fury and hunger. It's so close now that I can see my reflection in it. I'm terrified, arms raised, bloody fingers still digging into the seam I just found.

Right before it reaches me, I pull, peeling a great strip of wallpaper out of the air.

Whatever my hunter is, it can scream.

I keep pulling, keep peeling. I clear a small section and then back up against it. The wall shakes behind me as the thing flexes from within the paper, but it can't find me anymore. I'm safe, huddled against the peeled wall. And with my eyes closed, it loses me entirely. The room stops shaking. The crackling fire fades.

I breathe in deep breaths while I wait for it to return, but it doesn't.

"Dom?" I call.

Nothing.

I keep my eyes closed as I crawl over the floor, bumping into furniture and downing what sounds like framed photos. Near the wall, huddled in the curtains, my hands squish over Linda's blubbering face. I draw the curtains closed until darkness cloaks the room, then manage to get back to the French doors. Then, because I'm a good person, I double back and drag the little old lady out with me, bumping into absolutely everything along the way.

In the hall, I slump to the floor, breathing hard. I open my eyes. Linda is covered in blood, but it's all mine. My hands are cut up from the mirror. I barely think about that as I right the landlady.

"Linda. Are you there? Linda, snap out of it."

Linda's eyes fly open. They focus on me and a look of childlike surprise opens on her face.

"Oh, Athan, hello, dear."

"Where is he?"

"Where is who?"

"Dom. The boy I was with. What did you do to him?"

Linda pinches her lips together. She gives me an annoyed look as she stands herself up. She's seemingly fine, until she looks at her hands. Bloody handprints cover her wrists.

I lose her to hysterics. Of course. I let her run about her apartment screaming as I walk down her hall, looking for something to rewind. Near the doorway, I find what I'm looking for: a narrow mirror. But not just any mirror. The very one Yiayia forbade me from taking into the house when we moved in. The one from my old bedroom, with the sea glass frame. I've spent years looking into windows, wondering which neighbor picked it off our stoop and stole away all my childhood memories. It was Linda, of course, all along.

I have to laugh. It's my own damn fault for not suspecting her first.

"Get to it," I tell the mirror, and it snaps to attention, tumbling backward in time. It doesn't show much, just a sliver of the entryway lit by the outside. The sun rises and sets, confirming I've been stuck in the paper's hypnosis for almost a day. Then figures blur by. I pause, go forward, freeze.

One of Uhler's doormen walks backward, dragging along a body by the armpits. Dom, face slack. The man wears dark sunglasses and a too-nice watch. His partner is holding Dom's legs. They carry Dom off into the night.

"No," I whisper, gripping the mirror's frame.

"Athan, are you still there, dear? Say, is this blood yours? It's on the wall. You know, that won't come off that easily. I'm going to paint it. I have the paint, it's downstairs in the closet. Oh, actually, someone moved it. So that'll cost a little bit, I'm sure—"

"Shut *UP*."

Linda looks at me from the hall, stunned. Offended. For emphasis, I take my bloody hand and smack the hallway wall. The mirror pops off and slides to the floor, but I catch it before it shatters. In a way, I now understand why Yiayia never allowed it in the house. If I could have watched my parents tuck me in every night, would I have ever looked away? My grief and guilt would have trapped me. Forever. But now I know the truth about their deaths. As horrific as it was to face, it will be worth it if I manage to survive what comes next. And if I survive, I deserve to move forward with a version of the past worth cherishing. That is why I break Yiayia's rules and hug the sea glass mirror to my chest.

"I'm taking this," I say. I brush past Linda to the back staircase. Before I descend, I stop and correct myself. "I'm taking this *back*."

I slam the door behind me.

You escaped.

    I don't really want to talk about it.

    No matter. I'll see you again shortly.

    It's time. The Eye is about to open.

CHAPTER TWENTY-NINE

I stare up at the Vantage Observatory, clutching the invitation for the gala in my hands. Most New Yorkers I know avoid these places. They're traps for tourists who want to see the city from a safe distance. It's fitting that this is where Uhler and his Patrons choose to meet, far above the hustle and bustle of the city, at the tip of a skyscraper.

From the base of the tower, it's just like any other huge downtown building. Being close to it renders it less remarkable, its tremendous height compressed into a stubby block punching up into the night. It glows from within, but the light is cold. It feels like the bioluminescence of some deep-sea creature, floating in the dark abyss of the night sky. The thought turns the world upside down. I have to turn my eyes back to the ground to keep from losing my balance.

I stare at the entrance like it's the mouth and I'm the morsel. For strength, I hug Dom's sketchbook to my chest. His bandanna is knotted around my neck.

Just go, I urge myself. *Just walk in.*

Guards in suits stand by the doors. Occasionally a well-dressed couple will roll up in a nice car, get out, and walk in, but they vanish into the building's passageways before I can see what happens next.

Just go, Athan.

What if this is Uhler's plan, getting me here? What if it's a trap? If is, it doesn't matter. Uhler has Dom now, and Yiayia. I've lost another person while I was distracted. I've failed someone, once again.

I turn my back on the building and pull Yiayia's mirror from my coat. It's just the same message over and over. *You must close the Eye for good.* Even from all the way down here, I know that *thing* is at the top of this tower. It makes a grim kind of sense: Uhler has spent years manufacturing this moment, placing each piece just right so that when disaster struck, it did so in a perfect, beautiful cascade, trapping me into this moment. Yiayia had the power of foresight and she still saw no way to stop him. She could only find a way to urge me forward, at the very moment I might run.

Right now, I guess.

I'm no more inspired by her words than I was without them. But now, knowing what happened with my family, I feel something more powerful than inspiration. I feel spite.

Even if this curse gets me in the end, I'm not going to let Uhler set his little trap without at least reaching in and knocking everything around. A bit of cosmic pettiness as I go.

I march up to the doors, keeping behind a couple dressed in suits. Another pair follows me, dressed more casually. Still stylish, though. I hope my shabby blazer looks artsy. I try to hide the bandages on my hands from where the mirror shards cut me.

We follow signs through a lobby. Other people waiting glance at us—at me—but I keep my eyes up and my stride confident. The observatory entrance is up ahead. I'm almost inside when a man steps in my path. He wears a suit and a name tag identifying him as observatory staff.

"Private party," he says. I watch the other guests drift inside without any questions.

What do I do?

What would Dom do? He was so much better at this than me. He walked through the world like it was nothing more than a set on a stage, and he was the lead. This was his world, so how do I get into it?

The answer is obvious, I realize. *Act rich.*

I look the man right in the face and do my best eye roll. I take out the sketchbook and make the guard watch me sift through papers and wallpaper samples until I find the invitation, and I thrust it at him.

"Oh, I see . . ." the man says, plucking up the invitation. I know from watching Dom that this moment is pivotal. You press harder, until the other person just wants it to be over.

"What's that say?" I ask, in a bored tone.

"It's an invitation—"

"No," I snap. "That. The note, right there."

I feel terrible being this rude, but I have to pull this off to get inside. The man clenches his jaw. He looks where I'm pointing and finds the handwritten note.

"*We would be honored to have you,*" the man reads.

"And who wrote that note?"

The man reads the signature, and his eyes widen just a bit more.

"Stefan Uhler," I say, a little too loud. Other guests glance our way. They look at me with sudden intensity, wondering who I am.

The guard shifts uncomfortably. "Sorry, I just thought—"

"That's right. You *thought*. But now you know. Okay?"

"Okay," he grumbles. "My apologies."

I snap back the invitation and walk through the double doors. My heart bounds around my chest. I'm in a dark hallway now, meandering toward the elevators with a few other guests. People whisper. Music whooshes over us from invisible speakers. I keep my eyes forward, willing the curious glances to slide away.

The elevators open and I stifle a yelp. The entire interior is mirrored. All of it, except for a glowing white floor. I stare at my feet as the elevator shoots upward. The guests titter with excitement when their ears pop from the altitude. In less than a minute we slow, the doors open, and we're ushered out.

We enter a glowing blue passage. The sounds of a party echo toward us. I hear voices and music and haughty laughter. I keep my head down as I follow the crowd past a coat check, into the observatory's main area.

Immediately, I see why Uhler has chosen this place for his unveiling. The room is infinite. The elevator should have been a warning, because the observatory is lined with wall-to-wall mirrors. The floors and ceilings, too. Even the pillars are mirrors. Everywhere I look, I see myself spinning in a thousand crowds. I plummet skyward in a hundred versions of the room and float downward in a hundred more. I squeeze my eyes shut but people keep jostling me, so I stumble sideways, bumping into a wall of glass. A window. I peek, and I'm looking down at New York City.

Finally, a view I can trust. I focus on that until I feel the eyes of all the other Athans in all the mirrors drift away.

I have to be careful here, or else I'll trigger every reflection. And that thing that lurks in the mirrors will come. Beauty, Dom called it. Not the concept, but the demon.

"Champagne?"

A server is talking to my back. Making sure to keep my eyes off the reflections, I turn. My jaw drops.

"You!" we both say at the same time.

It's the boy from the café. The one who made me coffee the morning I escaped the penthouse crime scene. He recognizes me with a look of satisfaction.

"What are the chances?" he says.

I'm stunned. What *are* the chances?

"Sam," he reminds me. "We met a few days ago."

"I know, I remember," I rush to say. "I'm just surprised. I didn't . . . think I'd know anyone here."

Sam shrugs. "I told you I catered, didn't I? Right before you tried to ghost me."

I look down, but the floor is a mirror, so I wince.

"Don't worry," Sam adds with humor. "God works in mysterious ways, I guess. And everything happens for a reason, right?"

"Yeah. I guess so. I'm sorry about that. I figured I'd never see you again."

"Maybe it's a sign," he offers. He holds out the tray and I pick up the champagne. It sparkles like liquid starlight in the faceted glass. I raise it, like for a toast, but looking through the glass, I pause. The champagne is enough to disrupt my Sight, and for the first time I'm able to see into the room's center.

Entire staged rooms have been set up, each with two perpendicular walls, so that the observatory floor looks like a dissected dollhouse. The staged rooms are complete with furniture, and of course the walls are patterned in designs that show butterflies, birds, and bees. All sorts of organic patterns that swim through the facets of my glass. I take in what Uhler has created.

"Crazy, isn't it?" Sam says, watching me. "I hear that guy over there is a huge deal in the design world. My coworkers say he knows everyone, and that's why this party is so secretive. We had to sign NDAs and everything just to show up for work."

"What guy?" I ask.

Sam scans the crowd and then gestures at a knot of people. I squint, afraid of seeing too much. I don't find Uhler in the knot, but I do find someone else looking back at me.

Dom. Hands clasped in front of him, staring at me with a look that only I could read as fear. To everyone else, he looks bored. His cuts have been cleaned up, and he's wearing a finely tailored jacket over a black mock neck. Something sparkling on his shoulder, a hand wearing many rings. I follow it to Uhler, standing beside Dom, holding him there like a dog.

Uhler turns toward me, but right before he sees me, Dom springs to life, cracking some sort of joke and pulling the focus onto himself.

"Whoa! Careful!"

A sudden chill slips down my front. I jump back, correcting my tilted champagne glass before the rest spills on me.

"Hey, don't even worry about it," Sam says, dropping a napkin onto the mess I've made and pushing it around with his shoe. He blocks me from view, grabbing more napkins to dab at my shirt. I shiver, his fingers passing through the soaked fabric to graze my stomach.

Sam catches the shiver. A curiosity clarifies in his eyes. "We've got extra shirts for the caterers in the back. Nothing fancy, but we can get you out of this."

I nod. An idea is forming.

"We've got stronger stuff in the back, anyway," the older boy offers slyly. He takes my hand, leading me away from the mirrors, the crowd, and Dom.

The older boy knows all the secret doors to the observatory. He leads you into passages that lead to stairs that lead to a maze of dark back halls. Briefly you glimpse the other waitstaff setting up what looks like a boardroom, and he ushers you past, saying that not even he's allowed in there. It all feels like a self-aware secret, up here. It all feels like Sub Rosa.

The kitchen is bright and hectic. The boy brings you through the mayhem of chefs and servers loading up trays of pretty little bites. Barely anyone looks at you. The boy has a destination in mind: a storage room lined in shelves of plates, with crates of glasses stacked nearly to the ceiling. There's a box shoved against the wall and he digs through it, pulling out fists of black fabric.

Large, I'm guessing? He winks at you.

You don't know what to do next. If you take off your shirt, he'll take that as a confirmation that you're both here for the same reasons. He sees the preoccupied look in your eyes and mistakes it for the thrill of lust. You're nervous. He likes it.

You strip off your soaked shirt. The boy hungrily stares at your shoulders, your chest, but hunger turns to confusion as his eyes find the grungy bandages Dom wrapped around your abdomen. He links these to the bandages around your hands. A question opens on his face, and you have to think quick.

It's safer if you don't ask, you say with a grin so slick you hope his horniness slides him right past critical thinking.

After a moment, he grins back. *I like a little danger.* He wags a new shirt at you. Black, like his uniform.

Nothing fancy, I know, he says sympathetically. But you don't need fancy right now. You need invisibility.

Thanks, I'll bring it back, you say, grabbing for it, but he pulls it away.

You play dumb.

I should get back, you say, trying to be polite about this.

So should I, he says, voice lowering. You shake your head no, and he pouts. *Come on, don't you believe in fate?*

You grab at the shirt and catch it this time, but the boy doesn't let go. You pull, he moves closer. Then his lips are on your jaw. He yanks Dom's bandanna to the side to kiss your throat. His palm skims over your bruised stomach, fingers aimed down. They crawl, spiderlike, under your waistband.

Please, you whisper. *Stop*.

He just hears *please*.

Your eyes career sideways, searching for something—anything—to pull his focus off you. Someone will come in, right? But no one does, and his kisses are marching toward your mouth. You tilt your head, giving him your ear, and he drags his tongue behind it with a murmur.

You pin your eyes to the stack of plates on the shelf beside you. The shelf is metal. Steel. You see yourself minified in the beams. It'll have to do. You lock into the Sight. You watch you and Sam break apart, your shirt sliding back over your shoulders. You both rush out backward as the vision speeds up.

Faster, you whisper. Sam takes this as a command and unzips your pants.

In the reflection, waitstaff flicker in and out of storage, loading up their arms with plates. You glimpse other things, too. A woman hiding to watch something on her phone. A man crying. Two friends joking. A hundred little lives flickering in your vision, like sunlight caught on the facets of a diamond.

More, you whisper, bracing yourself against this boy's cold touch.

The shelf creaks. A burning smell wafts through the cramped space. You don't let your focus slip, not for a second. You pull more and more light into the cascade of visions, and all of a sudden the world sags. Then there's a terrific crash as plates smash to the floor.

The boy jumps off you and gawks at the strings of molten steel dripping off the shelves, which creak forward like they're about to topple. You catch it where the metal isn't hot.

Here, hold it here, you tell the boy. He takes over. You let go, pushing the sloping stacks of plates upright again. Then it's settled, but it needs someone to hold it.

Go get help, the boy whispers.

You pull on the black caterer's shirt. Then you untie the apron around the boy's waist and take that, too, slipping Yiayia's mirror into its pocket.

Everything happens for a reason, you tell him before you head back to the party.

CHAPTER THIRTY

I'm invisible now. People see the uniform and stop seeing my face. As I pass through the kitchen, someone hands me a tray of oysters. They glisten in the low light of the back halls. When I think no one is looking, I pull sideways, retracing my steps toward the meeting room I saw getting set up. If the Patrons are using the gala to meet, I have a hunch it's not going to be in anything less than a fancy boardroom at the top of the world.

Sure enough, the doors are now closed. Damn. I weigh my options. Get back to the party and try to grab Dom and run, or carve my way into Uhler's plans and do what I do best: burn them to the ground.

The boardroom doors pop open before I can make up my mind.

"There you are," a man in a tuxedo hisses. He hurries me inside. "I told the kitchen to send the shellfish first. Imbeciles."

The man hustles me around the perimeter of a meeting already in session. A dozen people sit around a circular table. I see Uhler in his dark sunglasses, but before I can see more, the man in the tuxedo grabs my face, turning me away.

"Where is your mask?" tuxedo guy asks.

"I . . . uh . . ."

With the most displeasure I have ever seen in a person touching me, the man grabs something off a banquet credenza and fastens it to my face. I feel cold leather straps pulled tight, and metal snaps tug my hair. When it's on, I can't see more than a few feet in front of me.

"Go," the tuxedoed man spits. "Go!"

I nearly stumble as he pushes me toward the table. My vision is narrowed, and I have to swing my head if I want to see anything at all. It's easier to just keep my eyes down, but I can't help but gawk at the other servers floating around the room, all of us wearing the blinders I saw in Sub Rosa. A few of the Patrons glance at me, but it's only because of what I'm carrying. They put up lazy hands, and I waste no time lowering my tray so they can select a morsel. They slurp the oysters noisily as they talk.

"Magda's death is sure to reach the press," says a tiny white man with a voice like a cartoon frog. "There's no sense in obfuscation. Let them write a puff piece about her. I'll have my contact at the *Times* send it over for review before publishing. Same as we did with Ellery."

A woman with skin that matches her long ochre gown leans forward. "That's too many cover-ups this year. How confident are you that your contact won't start to dig into any possible associations?"

"Fair," the frog man says. "After this, I'll arrange an accident and develop a fresh contact. Happy?"

"Out with the old," the woman practically purrs. "In with the new."

"Speaking of," the man says. "We have one final order of business to attend to before we get back to the evening our dear Stefan has so lovingly arranged for our guests. We must name an interim president until we can restart our election process."

Here, Uhler speaks up for the first time.

"Thank you, Rufus, but perhaps we'll be back to the revelry sooner than expected. I've checked the bylaws. In the event that both the president and vice president are indisposed, it appears that the duty now falls to me, the secretary."

The room settles into an uneasy quiet, except for the servers, who continue their busywork. I try to do the same while paying attention.

"Stefan," the woman in the ochre gown says sympathetically. "Come now, be realistic."

Uhler's voice pitches up, like she's wounded him. "Our rules state—"

"Enough." An older Black man claps his hands. "I can't stand this nonsense. Will someone just tell him?"

No one speaks.

"Fine," the man who clapped says. "Stefan, we'd planned on letting you have your little show first, but we've already voted on it. Your time as a Patron has come to an end. Magda was the only reason you were here in the first place, but even she felt you'd lost your way these last few months. It has been a pleasure evaluating you, but it's over. I'm sorry."

"Evaluating me?" Uhler presses his hands to the table but catches himself before he can stand up. "I have loyally served the Patrons for *twelve years*. I've built an infrastructure for our operations out of the cavities of this rotting city, and I've done it *beautifully*."

I expect silence, not laughter, but the room rings with mockery as the people around the table fight to compose themselves. The woman in the ochre dress barely manages to stifle her giggles.

"Stefan, darling. There are those around this table who have served for decades. There are names here that have given *generations* to our cause. No one would deny you've impressed us, but . . . twelve years? Ascending can't be crushed into such a tedious measurement as time, and it certainly isn't a matter of *beauty*. If anything, this shows us how deeply you've misunderstood our mission. And now we've decided your best use to us is perhaps in a more . . . limited capacity."

"I am not to be underestimated."

"We have estimated you adequately," she snaps, all the humor gone from her voice. "Do you really think your eviction was decided in haste? No, Stefan. We've watched your ambition curdle into distraction. Chasing myths? Your obsession with the Bakirtzis family? That daffy old woman has occupied too much of your time, with hardly anything to show for it. And what happened to your little project cultivating the child sensitives? Magda discouraged it for her own reasons, but at least *that* was interesting. Yet every one of your subjects has ended in failure. Dane Boucher is dead; your godson Dominik is a morose shut-in; and that Bakirtzis boy is the worst of all of them. He spends his days whining in therapy, showing not one iota of his grandmother's scrying aptitude."

Uhler snaps his head sideways, toward another Patron at the table.

"You didn't," he growls.

"I'm sorry, Stefan," says a familiar voice.

Seated to Uhler's left is Dr. Wei.

My heart hammers against my chest. It's like the world is crashing down around me. As if I'd notice. As if I could see anything past these claustrophobic blinders. I want to rip them off, but it wouldn't matter. The true blinders are the ones Dr. Wei gave me. His mantras, the truisms, his academic scolding against the delusion that the world was conspiring against me . . . when all along it was. *He* was. And his blinders worked wonderfully, because only now am I glimpsing the true scope of what has hidden in my periphery all along.

I want to lunge across the table. I want to run. But I just stand there, a tray of ice and oysters trembling in my clenched fists.

Wei, like everything else Uhler gave me, had an ulterior purpose. He was just another illusion.

My therapist folds his hands, like he always does at our sessions when he's ready to make a point.

"Athan is a regular, if badly damaged, young man," he says. "In all our time together, he hasn't even hinted at possessing the Sight, and I gave him plenty of opportunities. He can't do what his grandmother can. It's honestly unclear to me if his grandmother even has the scrying gift herself. That is my professional opinion."

Uhler turns his attention back to the rest of the room. He is speechless. The man with the frog voice stands up. He's as tall standing as he was sitting.

"We will ask this only once, Stefan. In light of our revelations, is there anything else you would like to share with us of your own volition? It will make all the difference in your new life to come as a civilian."

Uhler says nothing.

"Very well. Bring her in."

The doors open. Two men in turtlenecks push through and between them struggles a figure with a bag over their head. They're thrown onto the floor and the bag is ripped off.

Bernie blinks up at the Patrons. Her nose is bloody, and one of her eyes is swollen shut.

"What is *that*?" someone asks.

Uhler shoots out of his chair. "Not a word, Bernice." Bernie sees him and her eyes dim, like this confirms her worst fear. She's shaking all over.

"Avery, do you have your supplies for a demonstration?" the frog man asks of a middle-aged woman in a fluffy feathered top the color of cotton candy.

"Of course."

She reaches into a large purse in her lap and pulls out a small wrapped canvas, as big as a book. It shines in the light. I shudder when I realize what's stretched over the wood isn't fabric, but skin. She looks around for a moment, then points at me.

"You, you're strong. Come here. Hold this. Do not drop it."

I angle my head down, hoping the cumbersome blinders block my face, and obey. The skin is . . . warm. I swear I feel goose bumps spread over it as I hold it up. It's stretched so tight I can see the light through it. The woman maneuvers me until I'm standing right where she wants me, and then from her bag she pulls out a paintbrush. She nicks Bernie's neck with the sharpened end, collects the blood in her palm, and saturates her brush, all with a clinical efficiency, all as if Bernie isn't whimpering before her.

The room watches, intrigued and excited.

"Here we go!" the painter woman says giddily.

It's a performance. Her eyelids flutter as she sways into a trance, and upon the canvas she drags one long, deliberate line that gradually curves into the shape of a face. Bernie goes rigid. The painter never lifts her brush. She doesn't even look at the canvas. She first paints a grimace—Bernie's mouth—and from Bernie comes a muffled scream. In a blink, the skin of Bernie's lips has fused together. The painter smiles dreamily and her brush carves out the ovals of Bernie's eyes. Bernie's screams blow out of her nose between panicked breaths as her eyelids shut, dissolving into smooth flesh. The painter starts on her nose, taking her time, making the blood on the brush last as long as possible as she steals Bernie's face feature by feature.

I look at Uhler. He is staring at the bandages on my hands, which hold the cursed canvas, and then his eyes flick up to my face. I look away, but not quick enough.

"Come now, Stefan, be a good sport about this. She'll die," someone whispers at Uhler.

"And so will all she knows. I have many secrets; I couldn't be sure which ones she might give up. This was an idiotic threat."

He saw me. He's threatening me with her life. Bernie's nose vanishes. The trapped air in her body inflates a veiny layer of skin over her face, like a bullfrog's. Her screams lessen and lessen as the air grows stale in her lungs.

"Stop!" I throw the canvas down, snatch the brush from the painter, and rush to Bernie so I can slice open her mouth, but when I turn her over she's already gulping air. Her face is back. The men in turtlenecks heave me off her and slam me against the wall. The paintbrush clatters to the floor.

"Ah, finally!" I hear Uhler shout over the commotion in the room. "Marvelous timing, Athan." He chuckles. He is suddenly in a wonderful mood. This, even more than the horror I just witnessed, sends a spike of fear through me.

"I had no delusions about the Patrons going along quietly with my bid for power," he continues, "though I'm grateful to hear how you all really feel. In my line of work, one must always be open to feedback. I'll keep what you've said in mind. But now, with the arrival of the Little Prince, it's time to begin tonight's festivities in earnest. Ladies, gentlemen, if you'll join me in the observatory, the demonstration is about to begin."

The Patrons could have run after the scene in the boardroom. The doors have not yet been locked. But they file out after Uhler in a grumbling clot, led to their doom by a combination of their own morbid curiosity and a nearly pathological numbness to the idea that anyone they deem beneath them could make good on a threat. Standing in the audience now, they exchange smug, pitying looks, ready to laugh the second Uhler's little demonstration fails. They think their stolen baubles will protect them. Each has spent their fortune pilfering the corners of both the seen and unseen worlds, accumulating fragments of power they believe add up to godliness, or at least an inviolability that borders on divine. Meanwhile, in his twelve years as a Patron, Uhler's never shown them a single thing worth collecting.

This Friday night at the observatory, he will. A few minutes before everyone dies, Stefan Uhler prepares to take the stage and speak about his future.

CHAPTER THIRTY-ONE

Every time I struggle, the grip on my arms gets tighter, to the point that I'm sure my elbow will soon snap the wrong way. I keep my eyes down, thankful for the blinders as I stand in the crowd of people surrounded by Uhler's lavish, fake rooms. We're back on the main floor of the observatory. Everyone is waiting for the big show, all eyes aimed up at a raised stage wrapped in a column of impenetrable black curtains.

I only trust what I can hear. The sounds of the crowd . . . they begin to sour. It's like a stink wafting from a sewer, except it gets worse and worse. At first I just hear snippets of conversations.

These wallpapers. So whimsical! So bold.

I've never liked the chinoiseries but I can't take my eyes off that butterfly.

The depth. It's stunning. Like I could walk right into it.

Is it a projection? Do you see it moving?

My eyeballs itch.

And then a women screams, right behind me. A glass shatters, shards skating over the floor. People give her room, crunching over the glass and ice from her drink. I can't help but look at her.

She might as well be a mirror herself. Her horror is the best reflection of whatever she's seeing. She's rigid, head to toe, arms out in front of her, hands splayed like she's pushing against the air. She screams again. Then she claps her hands over her face and begins to claw. Another woman rushes to her, stopping her in time to save her eyes, but the blood gets everywhere.

People murmur. Someone calls for a doctor, but their plea is cut off by another scream. Another flute of champagne is dropped. This time it's a man. He bats at the air like he's boxing a swarm of bees. He trips on the edge of the false room, landing on a glass coffee table. It shatters, but he never stops fighting. Three people have to step in the glass to pull him out.

I expect panic, but the murmuring never rises above a vague acknowledgment of what's going on. I glance at the faces around me. They don't look scared. They look captivated.

The lights dim. The room and the thousands of reflections darken, and I'm finally able to make out the hairline fissures in the air, those silvery threads I keep seeing on people who have fallen under Beauty's control. They bundle around the necks and wrists and torsos of the crowd, stringing back into the wallpapers. I unfocus my eyes, afraid even just a peek will cause those threads to weave through me, too.

All at once the crowd moves, drifting toward the stage. Occasionally a person will begin to shiver and shout, and then fall to the side. People have stopped helping one another. They step over the fallen, like zombies. The few lucid left dig backward through the crowd, but the exits of the observatory all swing shut, and they're dragged back toward the displays by a crowd that suddenly feels more like one massive entity.

"Fuck," I whisper.

A clinking sound cuts through the murmuring and Uhler steps onto the stage, tapping his glass with a ringed finger. He has on his dark sunglasses, but they do little to hide the glee on his face.

"Welcome, welcome," he calls. "It's an honor to have so many of you join tonight's festivities. I can't remember the last time there were so many Patrons in one room! But before we celebrate, I must deliver some unfortunate news. As some are already aware, our beloved Magda has decided to step down from her role as president."

This gets a reaction from the captivated crowd, but it's dampened, no doubt by the hypnosis. Uhler smiles, pleased as can be. He raises his glass at his staged rooms all around the floor.

"Captivating, aren't they? These new designs are the latest in a private line I have been developing. The initial tests proved difficult to stabilize, but with the right help, I've produced the compelling work you see before you today. You know, Magda never really supported this project, but she also never recognized true genius. I will be a different sort of leader for the Patrons."

On *true genius*, Uhler motions offstage. Then Dom stumbles up. Uhler claps him on the shoulder.

"All houses are sustained by fresh young talent. I introduce you to Dominik Rupasinghe, my godson and protégé, and the artist behind many of my most . . . arresting motifs."

Dom shrugs off Uhler's grip. The man laughs it off, like *aren't teens so funny?* He clasps his champagne glass with both hands and rocks on his feet. The pause would be awkward if the crowd was waiting for more. But they're not waiting. They're shivering and bucking and laughing. The murmuring has risen to an incoherent simmer. I think it has something to do with Dom appearing before them. Suddenly the air in the observatory is full of a frantic, barely restrained devotion.

"You feel it, don't you?" Uhler intones. "It's in your heads now, isn't it? Too much for one mind to bear for too long—that's what I've found. Like the legends of old, some things are too beautiful for mortals to behold. No matter. It will all be over soon, my friends."

Uhler turns, grabs the thick fabric of the backdrop, and tears it down, unveiling a massive copper frame that holds . . .

A mirror.

The mirror.

Despite the size, it's simpler than I imagined. Just a tarnished frame in the shape of a sideways oval, like an eye. The surface is wet and black. Obsidian, or some sort of volcanic glass. It's buffed to a high shine, reflecting the upturned faces of the crowd. But all across the surface are cracks. The mirror is webbed in them.

Uhler places his hand on the broken mirror lovingly.

"For centuries, the Eye of God was lost to us. Not lost, *hidden*. But I have done what none of you dared to do. I have restored the Eye and recovered its pieces. All but one. Athan, if you please."

I didn't see it before, but sure enough there is a small fragment of the mirror missing, just left of the middle. It's no bigger than Uhler's palm. About the size of Yiayia's mirror.

I immediately realize what I've done. I brought it here. I brought it right to Uhler. I'm dragged forward, then thrown onto the stage at his feet. A boot crushes my head into the stage as Uhler pulls the mirror from my apron.

"Be careful with him," Uhler chides. "He looks big, but he's just a child." The boot is removed and I'm pulled upright. The second my feet are under me, I lunge forward and pin Uhler to the black glass. It tilts precariously, and Uhler goes still, unwilling to struggle. If the mirror fell on us, we would both be crushed.

"Careful, Little Prince," he coos.

I'm so close I can see the small scar on his cheek, put there by my mother before he killed her. I can smell the expensive serums he uses on his skin, and the smoky oil he uses in his hair. Everything about him is perfectly arranged and beautifully balanced, betraying none of the wild hunger he harbors. Except his eyes. His glasses dip down his nose as I squeeze his throat, and I can see right into his head.

There is no love for me in there. All I see looking back is amusement, like the way the Patrons looked at *him*. The same condescending pity.

"I wouldn't do that if I were you," Uhler whispers. He glances over my shoulder.

"Athanasios."

My full name, said by that voice. I release Uhler and turn. A guard stands behind a wheelchair holding a bundle of colorful fabric. A withered face peers out from the bundle.

"Yiayia?" I whisper.

I rush to her but stop, because the man has a knife in his hand, and it's poised right at Yiayia's neck.

"We were waiting for you," Uhler says, his voice a bit unsure as he tenderly probes his throat. "Your yiayia has been worried *sick* these past few days."

"Let her go!" I shout at Uhler. He ignores me, picking up the hand mirror from the stage. A crack runs down its center now. He clucks his tongue, reprimanding me. Then he gingerly pries one piece loose, then the other. He holds them toward the larger mirror.

The lights in the observatory fade. Or rather, something drags the light into the mirror with a force I can feel behind my eyes. It tugs so hard I'm afraid if I keep looking, my eyes will be pulled from my skull. But then the shards in Uhler's hands cut through the air like they're magnetized, slotting into the Eye with a hiss.

And it's complete.

Uhler turns to Yiayia.

"Open it. Rewind it. Whatever you call it."

Yiayia glares at him.

Uhler sighs. He motions to one of the guards and they hand him a gun. He cocks it and levels it at . . . me?

"Beg her to open it, or I kill you," Uhler instructs me.

I open my mouth but Yiayia just closes her eyes, squeezing out tears. She's refusing. She's not going to do it.

"Fine," Uhler says, exasperated. The gun goes off.

I fall to the floor, but the ringing in my ears must mean my head is still attached to my body. Uhler steps over me, to Yiayia, and admires a new, blooming red flowing from her shoulder. Through her screams, Uhler claps a hand onto the gunshot wound and gives a sharp squeeze. It's the worst sound I have ever heard. It's pain—true pain—tearing out of the throat of an elderly woman. Not Linda's exaggerated wail, but something raw. Something real.

"Now, then," Uhler calls over her. "I only need one of you alive. Athan, I know how you love to show off. Well, it's your time to shine." Uhler stops squeezing and Yiayia's scream cuts off. He puts all his menace into his words. "Open. The. Eye."

"I can't!" I cry back. Wei told the Patrons I'm powerless. I kept the secret of the Sight from *everyone* until Dom. There's no way Uhler could know I have the ability for sure.

But his sly smile tells me I'm wrong.

"Why does everyone underestimate me?" Uhler sneers. "You *can* command mirrors. You've done it many times before. I know it. Dr. Wei was too dismissive, Athan—about you *and* about your yiayia's warnings. What you see in a mirror does see you back. *We* have been watching you all along."

Uhler tightens his grip and Yiayia's screams rise so high her voice breaks. His thumb vanishes into her bloody clothes and her eyes roll with agony.

"I'll do it!" I shout.

Uhler smiles as he digs his thumb deeper beneath my grandmother's flesh. "Then do it."

"Athan, don't," Dom pleads.

I stand myself upright.

I turn, and I face myself in the Eye of God.

For a moment there is only you, standing in the abyss of the black mirror.

And then you shatter.

You view the world in pieces. All the shards flicker through their own individual lives before Uhler reunites them. It's like staring into a kaleidoscope of faces. You focus on Yiayia's pieces, her chanting and prayers and warnings flowing backward as the wrinkles melt from her face. Her eyes clear of their cataracts. Her hair blackens. She is getting younger, like you saw her in the vision of the sauce pot's reflection.

You see other faces, too. Each shard seems to have had its own guardian. They look like Yiayia in some ways—the Roman nose, the swarthy hair. They look like you, too. Maybe they are family, maybe lost relatives. They chant like Yiayia chanted. Their words press something back, something down. But occasionally you catch a glimpse of violence in a shard. A bloody hand reaches up, or a blur of motion, as someone is ambushed from behind.

You think: *These are the other shards of the Eye, the ones Uhler spent years collecting. He had them all this time—all except Yiayia's. For years it was only her chanting. Her pressing back, suppressing whatever lurks behind the Eye.*

You want to look away.

You can't find the strength.

Though the mirror stays black, you sense something moving within it. Something sees you back. Its gaze intensifies as the chorus of chanting rewinds. It compels you to look further, deeper, and you can't help but oblige.

The visions flow quickly now, layering over one another. A wave of heat breathes from the mirror. Hot, smoky, metallic. The cracks between the pieces begin to glow.

Now you view a candlelit room. All the shards show it at the same time; this is when they were last together, which means it's when the mirror was first broken. The room is a temple, you think, for up the walls crawl mosaics of gods and heroes. A group of people in robes sing in unison. Triumphantly. They separate the shards and wrap them each in cloth. Then, like the mirror, the group breaks apart, each piece and person vanishing into the night.

What was before that, though?

You don't want to look, but it's important to me that you see.

See me. How I got here.

The cracks in the mirror glow brighter, the harsh edges going soft, then molten. They begin to heal. Soon, the face will be smooth again.

Before the breaking, before the temple, back when the mirror was whole, there were other rooms—great rooms in palaces, tiny sanctuaries, and merchant tents full of sweet smoke and incense. You watch through the mirror as cities burn. You see rulers slaughtered by assassins. They look to you one final time, wondering how you could have been both the blessing that brought them to power, and the curse that betrayed them.

You view the mirror's hundred lives, and the hundred empires it consumed. In each, it chose its pawns. Sometimes it gave them power over crafts—like drawing, or painting, or design. Sometimes it gave them power over people—those silvery threads that cut through the light to hook into the tender seams of the mind. But the goal was always the same—pry the minds open and crawl inside. Nest, and feast, and grow strong enough to make a home in this reality.

You vaguely understand how it works. You are nothing until you become something, and it's in the act of being seen that most things evolve from nothingness to somethingness.

So I made myself beautiful.

I *became* beauty to each of my meals.

Beauty is in the eye of the beholder, it's true. And so it's also true that beauty must then be beheld. So I make them see me. Make them look so that I might grow solid with their perception.

I do not care that it drives them mad.

The mirror is almost whole now. Bubbles belch ancient, volcanic air into the observatory. The stage is catching on fire.

But you keep your eyes on me.

We are at my beginning now. A hissing, fiery birth, when the world was a molten hell. When the stars were new. When the substrate of reality itself hadn't woven shut yet. That's when I slipped into this world. Just a bit of me, no more than a notion, snuck through the portal you've just healed. Opened.

You back away from the Eye, the fumes knocking the strength from you. Your face is raw from the heat. Finally the tears are enough to muddy your Sight, and the visions stop. You close your eyes, but it doesn't matter. The mirror cools rapidly, taking on a faultless, glassy finish. The Eye is whole again. Whatever prowls within it, you feel the prickling sensation of its focus crawling over you. You've felt it watching you all your life. But it's different now. There are no cracks to hold it back.

You are not surprised that no alarm sounds.

You are not surprised at all.

The most simple, fundamental magic of mirrors is not that they reflect. It's that they are seams of symmetry. One world ends upon the mirror, but another begins behind it.

Yours is the one that's ending.

Mine is about to begin.

CHAPTER THIRTY-TWO

A hand slaps my face and I'm myself again.

Dom drags me backward, just as burning curtains fall onto the stage. I search for Yiayia and find the wheelchair on its side nearby, but she's gone. A dark stain mars the back of the seat. I twist in Dom's grip, screaming for her. The mirror looms over us, black and beautiful and so perfect it's like looking through a window into an identical room. The glass is fluid, like an eye welling with tears. It's bright with fire.

I turn away. The crowd is crawling alongside us, people stumbling over one another to escape from the flames. Those silvery threads still drift through the air, but now they're drawn back toward the Eye, extending from its round edges. Like eyelashes. The people fight their own bodies trying to get free, but the traction is beyond resisting.

I cling to Dom as he pulls me.

"She's here!" he's shouting in my ear.

Yiayia is curled behind one of the display rooms, hands pressed to her shoulder. Relief washes through me when I see her eyes open, alert. She reaches for me and I hug her, taking care not to move her.

"Athanasios," she sobs. "I'm sorry, I'm—"

A screech cuts the smoky air. The rig holding up the curtains finally crashes down. Embers scatter everywhere, out into the thousands of reflections that make up the observatory. I stare down at the floor, and I can see the creature scrambling its way up through the infinite reflections.

I hold on to Yiayia, like my body can shield her.

"What do we do?" I beg.

"It must be closed," she slurs. "For good."

She pushes me off to raise her hands up toward the Eye, and begins to sing. I recognize the song from the hand mirror's vision. It's the desperate chanting to entrap the beast within and seal it away. But it's just Yiayia's voice, not the thousands it took to keep the thing slumbering all this time. And I realize that it's been only her these past few years, as each of the shards was stolen and their keepers killed by Uhler. Only Yiayia and her chanting holding this creature at bay.

Uhler walks through the fire, gazing dreamily up at the mirror. He climbs the smoldering wreckage of the stage to stand before it. From where we huddle, I can see both him and his reflection.

"It's you," he says. Reverence fills his voice. It looks like he's talking to himself, but I know better. "It's you!" He hovers his palm over the rippling black surface. "How do I get you out? Tell me. How do I make you mine?"

The lips of his reflection move soundlessly, but Uhler nods to himself. Then he backs away and holds his arms out like he's greeting an audience. Whatever he sees, it makes him go rigid. There's a moment when he looks like he's going to run. But he holds his ground, staring at himself. I search the Eye and see nothing, but in every other mirror lining the room there's a shape bending the fiery light. It's so close I can hear its nimble feet tinkling against the glass between our worlds as it searches for the weak spot.

Beauty must be beheld, it told me.

"It needs a host," I realize out loud, just as Uhler begins to scream.

Dom wraps my arm and pulls, but I can't leave Yiayia here. She tries to rise, her singing losing its melody. The song tears out of her in desperation.

"Athan, you need to take her and *run!*" Dom yells.

I can't do that. All these people transfixed in the fire—I can't leave them behind. They'll burn if I don't save them.

Uhler's screams strangle off, and I finally see the thing in the Eye. It's like looking down into the ocean and making out the shape of a gaping mouth just before it rushes up at you. Or turning at a crosswalk and catching sight of the barreling bus. It's the legs of a spider spread open to pounce. It's all those things at once, and it closes around Uhler's reflection. Crashes into him like the bus. Eats him like the mouth.

His reflection is chewed apart in a blink. On our side of the mirror, the real Uhler waves a hand, dreamlike. But there's nothing there to wave back. His reflection is gone.

Uhler turns his back on the Eye. He is smiling. Pleasure and pain roll from his tongue as a strange force makes its home in his limbs. His hands go to his face. For a moment, I think he's going to claw at his eyes like that woman, but he just gives an ecstatic sob.

When he lowers his hands, his face has changed. His eyes are wide, an inky black bleeding out from the irises. Something flickers under his skin, inside his cheeks and above his brows. Fluttering slits appear, each lined in delicate lashes.

And they open.

All over Uhler's face, eyes open. Six of them framed in perfect symmetry around his human two. They are uniformly glassy and black, and they look upon the world around him like it's brand-new.

"Behold me," he demands. He raises his hands and, like marionettes, the guests hiding at the walls of the observatory lurch forward. They crawl, hands pawing over the still-burning shrapnel.

"Behold me!" Uhler repeats. "For I have become the Beholder!"

Uhler turns toward me now. He lifts an arm and I cry out as my own arm shoots up. Threads of silver flash between us, and he pulls on them to drag me closer. Soon they catch my other hand, too.

"I won't hurt you," Uhler coos. "I won't hurt you, Little Prince. You did what your family could not. You were my key. You will stay by my side forever. But first, a test of loyalty."

He spins an index finger and I spin, too, as though hung on a string. I'm facing Yiayia now. The threads won't touch her, but they pluck curiously as she tries to keep her song going.

"To fight through your failure—I admit I admire your resolve," Uhler mocks Yiayia. "It must be where your daughter got her stubbornness. And Athan. A fine quality, but I've spent an eternity listening to this song. This *fucking* song."

My hands lift of their own accord. They form claws, pulling me forward until they wrap around Yiayia's throat.

"Squeeze," the Uhler-thing demands.

I squeeze.

I scream. I try to stop, to unclench my hands, but I can't. I just keep squeezing, feeling the spine deep beneath Yiayia's thin flesh. I choke the song out of my grandmother's throat.

With a cry, I manage to lock my fingers to one another, diverting the pressure into my own hands for a moment. Yiayia gasps a precious breath.

"Admirable," Uhler says, "But it's not about muscle, Athanasios. I couldn't make you do this if you didn't want to. And you do want to, don't you? I can feel it. I feed upon that lovely, wicked want. You yearn to be free of her. Of all people. If you are alone, you can't hurt anyone else. This just proves it, does it not? Everyone you love, everyone you touch, suffers. And you know why. A curse can be a person. A curse can even be a child."

Yiayia manages another sobbed verse, her prayer momentarily whisking away the threads that have gathered at my wrists. But Uhler draws up behind me. His hands crawl over mine, and together we squeeze.

Yiayia stops breathing. She jerks as the life leaves her body. Still, she finds the strength to lift her old hands and place them, shaking, on my eyes. She does not want me to watch this death, too.

"Let her go," Uhler whispers in my ear. "Let her suffering end. Let—"

Uhler lurches off me. The threads wink out. All over the observatory, they vanish, leaving pulsing, neon negatives in the darkness. I can feel my arms again. I use them to catch Yiayia before she falls. I feel her tender neck and find her pulse. She is silent, but she's alive.

I cradle her in my arms and stand. It's like she weighs nothing at all. I rush her to a pillar, away from the fire, and watch as Uhler stands up and yanks a splinter of wood from his side. Dom stands over him, another makeshift stake raised.

"Get out," Dom demands.

Uhler laughs. He lifts his shirt to inspect the wound. It doesn't bleed. Instead, those little hairs trickle from the ragged flesh. They knit together into furry seams, then spring open. More eyes peer out from his side.

"Get out," Dom repeats. "Now."

"Dominik, that's no way to treat your godfather—"

"I'm not talking to him, asshole," Dom snaps. "I'm talking to *it*."

Uhler looks offended. "We are the same now. I've merged myself with a force you can barely comprehend. I am the Beholder. It's my destiny—"

"It only picked you," Dom shouts, "to get to me!"

For a split second Uhler looks uneasy, but then his haughty expression re-forms and he starts to say something. Dom isn't taking his shit today, though. He cuts him off instantly.

"I'm right, aren't I? It's me you want, isn't it?" Dom tosses down his weapon. He opens his arms, like he's waiting for a hug. "It's me you called to, and it's me you worked through. You just used this man's vanity to get your fucking Eye back together, but if you had your choice between hosts, it's me you want, isn't it? Well, I'm giving you the choice."

I'm not sure that I see it right, but I swear Uhler blinks his two human eyes in disbelief. All the others stay open. They watch Dom, while Uhler's human eyes narrow.

"Quiet!" he shouts, but Dom isn't talking. "I said, *quiet*."

Dom stiffens, like he hears it, too.

I want to pull him away, but Yiayia clings to me. I can't leave her.

The momentary look of fear melts from Uhler, and he begins to laugh. "As if a weak little boy like you could better serve as a vessel for—"

Uhler abruptly stops talking and pitches over, onto his knees. Bumps roll under the back of his sweat-soaked shirt. He shivers, snapping his head to glare at Dom.

"I said, *be quiet!*"

Dom's face closes into an expression of determination.

"I'm ready," he says.

Uhler scrambles backward. I can hear him muttering a low *no, no, no, no, no.* He's clawing at his shirt, ripping it off to grab at his skin. All over his arms and back, those small black eyes flutter open. Some are bigger than others. Some are so big I can see them rolling in their sockets. They lock onto Dom.

Dom closes his eyes, like he can't watch. But I can't look away.

"You're mine!" Uhler pleads, but another voice—the voice I have come to know as the thing that whispers from the depth of the mirror—speaks, too. It echoes Uhler—*you're mine*—but it's talking to Dom.

Uhler screams, turning from Dom like he's the sun burning into all those eyes. But the eyes must want to burn. They cluster together like a bubbling infection, spreading until Uhler is covered in them. They jiggle with his sobs as he begs for them to close. But they just keep multiplying, keep jostling for space, crowding tighter and tighter and ripping the clothes off his body.

And then, all at once, they merge. All the eyes, all at once, and Uhler is gone. It's like watching a water balloon pop in slow motion. One second there's a rippling cocoon of black, and then it bursts over the floor in a hissing wave of molten glass. The glass cools quickly, though, and all that's left of Uhler is a black mirror in the vague shape of a man.

The glass cools *too* quickly, almost before I get to Dom. He looks upon his own reflection in this new, human-shaped mirror. And that thing in the glass—the yawning jaws rushing up from the deep, the screaming bus, the spider's embrace—is nearly at the surface. And Dom's reflection turns, like it can hear the thing approaching.

I reach him a split second sooner, tackling him backward. Dom starts to say something, but that's when the floor behind us explodes.

YOU.

The voice fills my head. I turn but my eyes can't make sense of what they see. The mirror Uhler's body left behind has distended outward, and long, furry legs *reach* up through it, stabbing into our reality.

It's not real. It can't be. It can't exist without a vessel.

Yet here it is, both tangible and intangible, visible and invisible, forcing itself into our world with pure determination. Its legs scissor through the air, fanning around the breach. It pulls forth a body that—

All I see are eyes, and the outline of a bulb-like body where the legs join, but it's rendered in the rainbow edge of mirror light. It hardens in my perception, solidifying the more I look at it.

"Don't look!" I shout, grabbing Dom's hand. We have to get it away from these people. From Yiayia. There are stairs ahead of us leading up to a balcony—to the observation deck. We run toward them, around the flaming debris. There's a moment of silence when I think it won't follow, and I make the mistake of glancing backward.

It's enough. The beautiful monster lunges into my mind, taunting me in a thousand intrusive whispers.

You run from me.

Me.

Not the illusion, and not the dream. Not the feeble host I ate right through.

But me. The real me. You run, screaming.

And I'm *very* offended, Athanasios.

This body is unwieldy. The laws of your dimension are bothersome, always forcing things into shapes and forms and bodies. Disgusting limits pulling my beauty into the horrifically physical, when I much prefer to work through the medium of another's flesh.

But to have a body, even a temporary form such as this, has its advantages.

Namely, violence.

You hear that. *Violence.* By the time the sun rises, you will be a mist of red rained upon the people of this city.

You stumble at the thought, but shove it away, knowing it's not yours. You know better than to pay attention to this voice, but how can you ignore me now? You've opened yourself up to me, pressed your ear to the wall and strained to listen to every word as I whispered to people in other rooms, feeding them beauty, promising them relief, leading them away from this world and all its obligatory ugliness.

The boy pulls you around up to the observation deck. Glancing back down the stairs at the ruined party, you see my massive, translucent shape climbing up the glass. The partygoers trail after like balloons on those silver threads. They're slow and clumsy, clogging the stairs, breaking one another's bones in their rush to follow.

You realize you're trapped. You feel the futility, finally. What can you do, cornered all the way up here in the sky? There's no fire escape.

You could always jump, I whisper.

No, you shout. But what's left, if not an end on your own terms?

You and the boy spin and spin, looking for anything that could help. In the darkness, with only the lights of the city shining up from below, I'm harder to see. It's as though my skin eats the light. The chase slows to a crawl as you attempt to run without looking where you're going. You keep seeing flickers of me in the mirrors around you. Then one rushes at you and you jerk in the opposite direction. But you've made a mistake—fleeing from a mere reflection.

You run right into me.

It's not like fighting something physical. It's like all the will to move just evaporates from your blood. You go still. You can't even blink. We are inches apart, your eyes against mine. And I have so, *so* many more than you. The more you look at them, the more they come into focus. They're silvery, like balls of mercury, and gradually your own reflection forms inside them. Dozens of you, staring.

What do you want to see?

What do you expect to see?

At the end, you expect to see a door, so that's what I show you.

You forget the smoldering observatory and the thing wrapping its legs around you. You are now walking up a flight of stairs to a hallway, to a door that sings.

It sings "Happy Birthday"! You hear it now. You know it sounds wrong—the syllables stretch so long, and voices never meld together. They are the voices of people far away in some vast empty space, maybe one full of smoke and mirrors, like the observatory—

I refocus you on the door. Who cares what the singing sounds like? What matters, dearest Athan, is that they're singing for you. *Happy birthday. Happy birthday!* Again and again, they cycle through the song, and they'll cycle on forever until you open it up.

It's this moment you've dreamt of so many times, yes? Never the moment after, when you enter, but this suspended juncture. You're ready now for what lies beyond. For the rest of it, or the end of it. So you put your hand around the doorknob, twist, and the door opens.

Just an inch.

You stop yourself.

Why are you stopping?

The knob is hot in your hand, and through the sliver of the open door a familiar light flickers. Smoke drifts from the room. But the people inside don't feel the heat, see the light, smell the smoke. They haven't yet begun to burn. They just keep singing.

They're waiting for you. What are you waiting for?

You want to be together again, don't you? Don't you? *Don't you?*

Yet you let go of the knob.

I know something is wrong, you think.

Unknow it. Open the door. Don't you want to be reunited with your family, finally? Yiayia won't live much longer. This is where she'll be next. In heaven, with everyone else. Waiting for you.

You flinch. *Yiayia is still alive?* you wonder, and: *Wasn't I with someone else, too? A boy with butterfly wings wrapped around his neck, who pulled me back from the void's call once before?*

You step away from the door, leaving it ajar, and watch the smoke pour out.

Then, because you have obsessed over fire safety for the last twelve years, you grab the blazing knob one last time and shut the door for good. It burns, but it's what keeps the fire in, and everyone else safe.

You step backward, out of the illusion.

Somehow, your eyes focus. You reach sideways, and because I was so consumed by your pain, my every eye failed to see the boy sneaking toward you. I only notice him now as he hands you something, which you raise in triumph. Moonlight catches on polished copper. Your grandmother's ruined hand mirror.

And you stab me with it.

You.

Wretched, lucid you, bursting me like a bubble as you let your beautiful dream go.

CHAPTER THIRTY-THREE

I know something about Beauty now.

It hides in mirrors, designs, and dreams, unreachable sanctuaries that force you to look but stop you from seeing—really seeing—what dwells within. But when all those defenses fall away, and it's just you and the beast, it's easy to see Beauty for what it is: a desperate, vulnerable thing.

This is what I think about as I watch my door close, sealing off the smoke forever. As the real world rebuilds in my senses. It was the Patrons I heard, not my family. I knew the moment they started that terrible singing that it wasn't my family.

The Bakirtzis family knows how to sing.

Whatever this is, it isn't a song. It's love disfigured through manipulation, pouring out of the many mouths under the beast's control. It sounds terrible. I want it to end. So I stab, and stab, and stab, until I feel the pinch of the beast's jaws release my legs, and it scuttles backward.

That's what gives me my next idea. I learned the hard way that you can't run away from something coming at you from behind. And in this observatory, the spider crawls at me from every direction. The whole room is its web. But we're not fighting a spider. We're fighting a freaking dimensional force that has half-manifested in reality, desperate for a host of eyes to make it real. Otherwise, it's just a thing in a mirror with really strange taste in wallpaper.

And lucky for everyone, I know a thing or two about manipulating mirrors.

There's a flash as the spider launches toward me. Instead of running, I find it in the closest reflection, and I *push back*.

The mirror reacts instantly, zipping backward, sweeping the spider away with it. It tries again, another angle and another mirror, and I catch it again. Each time I see that luminous cluster of legs dart at me, I push the reflections to rewind.

"Dom?!" I shout, keeping my eyes on the mirrors.

"I'm here!"

I stretch out my arm again, and he takes my hand.

I catch Beauty another time on the stairs. Another time coming up through the floor. It gets closer each time. I can't keep up with the assault. My eyes water, spinning in their sockets as I try to keep everything rewinding at once.

Just hold on, I urge myself. We're close. Just grab Yiayia, get the doors open, and get to the elevator.

I don't worry about how the elevator is a box of mirrors all its own and my energy is draining quickly. I just keep the reflections rewinding. But in return, I'm flooded with their collective visions. I lose track of Dom, but he helps me gather Yiayia into my arms. Somehow, we make it to the exit. With Uhler's men now swept into the mob, the doors just open. Then we're at the elevators, rushing inside, and Dom is pushing the button for the lobby. He's hugging me, and he's saying he's sorry, and goodbye, and please forgive him, and I can hear him crying but I can't see anything with the past of every mirror flashing in my mind.

The doors shut. The descent flips my stomach and I nearly fall to the side. But I'm holding Yiayia up, so I need to stay standing. I remember the floor is safe to look at and focus there. I see my feet. I see Yiayia's feet. But that's it.

"Dom?"

The elevator is empty except for me and Yiayia. Not even Beauty charges toward us from the infinity.

Because they're both still upstairs.

We hit the lobby and the doors open, and I'm facing a wall of firefighters. They're expecting me, or at least expecting people fleeing from the smoke alarms going off upstairs. I rush to give them Yiayia, pausing long enough to point out where she's been hurt. Then I'm back in the still-open elevator.

They order me to wait, but I slam the button and the door closes.

My heart plummets in my chest as I shoot back up to the observatory. What the fuck is he thinking? I search the mirrors for Beauty, begging the beast to show itself, but it's nowhere to be found.

"Don't do it," I whisper. Over and over.

"Don't do it. Don't do it. *Please, Dom.*"

The elevator slows. Opens. I rush out. The alarms needle back into my ears and the air chokes me. I run through the burning fake rooms, reaching the stage just as Dom turns away from the Eye of God.

"I'm sorry, Athan," he says to me.

I look at him.

He looks at me.

His eyes, once so stern, fill with emotion just as the pupils spill forth, coating his vision in obsidian.

You look upon me.

You search me like I'm one of your mirrors; like if you look hard enough, I'll rewind, and you'll come with me into our past. I wonder what you hope to find there. The moment when I, Dominik, made this choice? The moment when you, Athanasios, could have said something to convince me otherwise? The wasted opportunity to save me?

You could search forever, but you'll never find it. I told you once that I knew I could hurt this monster, but if I told you how, it wouldn't work. I couldn't tell you because the very first thing I ever knew about you when I looked into your eyes was this: You want to be good.

You are good. It didn't matter that I was a stranger; you would have done anything to stop me. And when you failed, you would have felt the loss like a new weight on your back.

You don't own this choice of mine. The blame isn't yours for the taking. But thanks to you, I've learned something in these last few days, Athan. I don't own this choice, either. It's not a choice at all. It's just the only thing that was left to do.

Beauty hides within me now. It was never going to accept another home. We would have spent our lives turning up pockets of pain where it laid its eggs in the minds of innocent people. We would have spent our lives hiding away shards of mirrors, fending off collectors and human curiosity and the lust for power. Yiayia would die, her songs dying with her, and the Eye's influence would grow too powerful to resist. It would find a way to open, and Beauty would crawl out again and again, as many times as it needed to get under my skin.

Well, it's here now, at home within me.

Trapped.

You understand, don't you? I can see that you do, staring up at me. The surprise on your face turns to anguish as you finally notice the silver threads trailing from my fingertips. They parade the many hypnotized guests toward the back of the Eye of God, where they can press their hands against the still-warm frame. I make them push.

Dom. You say my name and within it I hear a huge emptiness. I wonder, if we had more time, could we have filled it with love?

The Eye of God creaks behind me.

Dom, what are you doing?

I feel Beauty's eyes opening in my skin. It's not painful, not at all. My merger with the demon wasn't violent like Uhler's. I allow just a quartet of small black eyes to flutter open above my brow, and two more at the crest of my cheek-bones. As small as fingertips. Much more restrained than Uhler. Much more my style, to be honest.

The Eye of God looms over me, tipping forward. Its surface still ripples with the uncanny consistency of the open portal. I pull the strands tighter, and the Patrons heave against it.

Dom. Dom!

I begin to cry. Just from my human eyes. By now I feel the beast growing conscious within me. Once it discovers what I intend to do, it will try to stop me, so I don't think about it. I stay focused on you.

Athan, I say. I hope your name rings in your ear with the love I feel. *It's the only way.*

You run to me, but I catch you with a net of my silvery strands. You fight so hard, I have to lift you off the ground, just a few inches.

Within me, Beauty shudders at the pleasure of you caught in our web. The sick hunger is a reminder of why this must be done, and why it must be done this way. I tighten your bindings until you stop struggling and look at me. Really *look*.

Thank you, I tell you. I wish I could tell you the rest. That even though I always knew it had to end this way—this demon locked inside me, and me locked away from the world—you taught me something.

I'm good, too.

I never knew that, Athan. Never even considered it. All my life I've hurt people, and even though it was only ever accidents, I thought a part of me meant it. Together we discovered this wasn't true, that this wasn't a part of me. It was something else, lodged in me so deep and for so long that I'd mistaken it for myself.

I can't undo the hurt I caused, just like I can't allow Beauty's connection to live on. I can't change a single thing about this ending. But because of you, I understand that this isn't some noble sacrifice. It's a tragedy.

I should have been allowed to be good. So allow me this, at least. And know that even if you couldn't save my life, you did save my soul.

The Eye of God finally tilts forward, off its stand. It wobbles, finding a precarious balance, like it could tip one way or another. I hold it there, just a second more.

Thank you, I say, just for you.

For what? you choke.

You saw me. And through you, I saw myself.

You swallow. You can't speak, so you nod. Your body goes limp with resignation.

See you later, Windsy, I say with a nod.

The massive mirror finally tips forward.

You barely stop yourself from screaming as it swallows me, because you don't want it to be the last thing I hear.

Then the only sound is glass shattering.

CHAPTER THIRTY-FOUR

I know Dom's dead the instant I hear the Eye of God smash into the floor.

I hang in the sudden stillness, and a moment later the threads flicker away. I drop.

I know Dom is dead, but I run to the ruins of the massive mirror anyway. The Patrons and other partygoers stare at me, blinking like they've just woken up. I cry for their help as I try to lift the massive copper slab, but they just watch.

Beams from flashlights cut through the smoke as the firefighters run in. I cry for their help, too. I'm sobbing and inarticulate, but they understand. They grab the sides of the copper slab and we lift all at once. Finally, it moves, but slowly. I swear I'm the only one even trying, but I find the strength in me to raise it up and drag it to the side, off the mess of volcanic glass below.

No.

There's no body.

There's not even any blood.

I grab the obsidian, the newly shattered edges peeling away the skin of my hands. I'm screaming.

Screaming.

Screaming.

And then I'm dragged away.

I sit with Yiayia in the hospital, staring into the flat white of the walls while I listen to the beeps of her heart. The nurses who come in are kind. They even offer to clean out the cuts in my hands, and they rewrap the gash on my abs. I let them douse my flayed skin in stinging liquid, surprised I can feel anything at all.

They keep Yiayia for a few days, urging me to let her rest. I sit in the hospital atrium, waiting for the police to finally come for me now that I've finally stopped running, but they never do. At one point I swear I see a Patron cross the lobby, a woman in head-to-toe black wearing huge sunglasses and carrying a spray of cut flowers, but she's gone in a blink. I find the flowers in a vase in Yiayia's room, but there's no note, not even a *get well soon* card. I shove them deep in the trash labeled BIOHAZARDOUS WASTE.

In time, I regain enough nerve to see what became of the Patrons and their party. There's one news story about someone setting off the fire alarms at the Vantage Observatory, then two, then six, and then suddenly there's none. I have the screenshots, though. In them are images captured by people in the surrounding buildings that show a strange blaze of light crawling across the observatory glass. If you look at them long enough, you can almost make out the legs.

I don't need to wonder why the news stories and posts vanish. I don't need to wonder why the police suddenly leave me alone, or why no one seems to miss the people who died in the penthouse.

Some alarms will never sound. Or somewhere an alarm has sounded, only to be silenced by a velvet fist.

We take a cab home, but Yiayia makes us stop at the market. After days of hospital food, she's convinced I'm dying from malnourishment and is out for justice. I marvel at how alert she is as she picks out produce with her good arm. I carry the bags, and for the first time in years, she is the one leading *me* on our walk.

When we get home, a familiar box truck is parked outside our building. Yiayia and I halt. Forum Fine Arts & Framing is scrawled across the back. Yiayia reaches for me, as if she really thinks we could run, but then the back door slides up and reveals Bernie and a crew of familiar faces.

"We heard the queen was in need of a new bed," Bernie announces, hands on her hips.

Yiayia is maybe too alert now. She glares from them to me. "You asked them for help?" she whispers in Greek, and ice freezes in my veins.

"Yiayia, you don't have a bed, and our home is a mess. They insisted."

Yiayia's glare does not soften. She raises her chin, just like a queen, and I swear everything with hips in a three-mile radius must feel the instinct to bow.

"You will stay for dinner," she announces in English. "All of you." And that's that.

Bernie bounds out of the van and gathers me into a hug so tight my bones realign. She's gentler with Yiayia, offering just the customary cheek kisses and taking care not to touch Yiayia's arm in its sling. The other handlers do the same. A crushing hug for me, a *kiss kiss* for Yiayia.

Then it's time to work.

We do our best to convince Yiayia to relax, but it's like telling the tides to time out. She oversees the cleaning of the fire extinguisher mess, and when I tell her in Greek how the coffee table got scorched, she screams with laughter. Tears in her eyes, she corrals Bernie into helping her prepare dinner. I work with the other guys to set up the new bed frame, box spring, and mattress. The works—though I doubt Yiayia will be spending much time in bed. After years lost in her mirror, she seems determined to take care of us.

"Go, go, clean yourself up," she urges me. I'm pushed toward the bathroom. Inside, the sudden quiet feels strange. I turn the hot water on and keep my back to the mirror until the mist covers it in steam. Then I consider my blurry reflection. Tentatively, I press my hand to the glass, swiping just enough moisture away to see my eyes.

They look back, unblinking, going nowhere. They are red-rimmed and sunken into my face. Tired. Heartbroken.

But they don't rewind away from me. They hold my stare. Experimentally, I urge the reflection to flow forward. After a moment, the mirror shudders and my reflection vanishes. The mirror flickers through unremarkable hours of darkness until suddenly it's me again, staring back.

The tears have gone. My eyes are clear. They're close to the mirror, as my reflection applies eyeliner.

I jump away. I don't own eyeliner. That's me, but in the future.

I hurry into the shower, hoping it will hide the sound of me crying. When I get out, Yiayia has put out clothes on her newly made bed. I change, then decide I need to test out the bed. Just to be sure it's safe, you know? Sometime later, I'm awoken with a gentle shake.

"Athanasios," Yiayia whispers. "We made your favorite."

I sit up. Yiayia sits beside me. Her hands are soft on my face as she clears away a mess of tears.

"It was a bad dream," she tells me, maybe knowing something about what it's like to have a head full of picture-perfect visions of the past.

"I know," I say. I sniff, and register the aroma of baked cheese and nutmeg.

"Pastitsio?" I guess.

"It is still your favorite?" Yiayia asks, guilt and hope in her voice. It's like she's asking: *Are you still the grandson I knew?* But it's also like she's asking: *Is there still time for me to be your grandmother?*

"Absolutely." And I smile.

The living room has been transformed during my nap. All the

chairs that cluttered our apartment have finally been put to use around the coffee table, which is covered in a way-too-big tablecloth. Someone made a run to the corner store and grabbed beers, and when I try to take one, Yiayia scolds me. We make her sit at the head of the "table," and cheer her homecoming. I notice someone has found the sea glass mirror, and now it hangs on the wall over my sofa. Yiayia catches me looking at it, and she gives me a sad but reassuring smile. *In time*, it seems to say. Then she makes us take one another's hands for a prayer. Before she gets two words out, though, we're interrupted by a creak on the stairs.

"Oh, hello, I thought I heard a party," says Linda, leaning down over the railing.

"We're having dinner," I answer, unsure of how much Linda recalls from her run-in with Uhler's paper. She looks annoyed, but there's no other sign that she's come to take any sort of revenge.

"A bit late for dinner, don't you think?" Linda asks. "Anyway, I wasn't sure if anyone was home, and then I smelled . . ." She waves at the air, like we're sitting in a cloud. She looks at us expectantly, as if surprised we haven't rushed to apologize. No one moves. Finally she clears her throat and says, "Athan, dear, could you help me with something upstairs? I require your strength."

Yiayia gives me a wary look, but I put her at ease with a nod and follow Linda upstairs. Her apartment has been cleaned up, too, except for a great stretch of wallpaper that was torn away from the walls of her sitting room. I stare at the pattern, but it doesn't move, doesn't deepen. It's just regular paper now that no malevolent force works through it.

"We need to talk," Linda says. I think she's going to bring up the fact that she tried to kill me, but instead she slides a shoebox across the table and waits for me to open it. Inside are the shards of Yiayia's hand mirror, the part she broke to reveal its true face.

"I found these in my living room, near the window," she says. She nods at the ruined wallpaper.

"I didn't want to alarm your yiayia," Linda says in a hushed voice. "I know how superstitious the Greeks are. I don't want to set her off. But I have reason to believe . . ."

She leans forward, eyes wide and compelling. I get ready to run.

She finishes: ". . . that this building is being haunted."

My mouth drops open. She rambles on before I can even ask, *What?*

"I've been having the strangest spells of sleepwalking. At first, I thought it was just the new rejuvenating tea I was drinking. It's meant to clear your chakra, and you're always bound to feel unbalanced when you're being put back *into* balance. But then one day I woke up in this room, just standing here, and the walls had been changed."

She points at the paper.

"I did not do this. *They* did."

"Who?" I whisper.

Linda purses her lips, and now she looks smug. "There are forces in this world beyond human comprehension. I know you think it's nonsense, my teas and cards and oils, but the spirits are always among us, Athan. Probably drawn here by my spiritual practice. This proves it."

She eyes the swath of blank wall.

"I discovered the paper torn down, and my hands were cut up, as though I had touched an energy too powerful for human flesh. And I had a vision, Athan. Of *you*."

Now she eyes the shoebox with the shattered glass.

"You were in my hallway, and you stole my mirror. And guess what. When I awoke, the mirror was gone! And this glass was on the floor. *Broken* glass."

"I was on vacation," I say quickly, thanking every lucky star she hasn't yet spotted the sea glass mirror in our apartment downstairs.

"I know that," Linda snaps. "No one was around to help me with the bed, for heaven's sake. What I'm saying is that at first I thought the spirits were here for me, but I now suspect they're here for *you*. Athan, I don't mean to alarm you, but I believe you have been cursed."

I choke on my breath, covering my sudden laugh as a cough of disbelief. Linda nods grimly.

"I'm afraid so. But don't worry. I know people who can help. I myself have been known to commune with the great beyond. I rarely share this, but I'm a medium, you know. An *empath*, too. I can feel so many things. I can help you. Wait. Where are you—sit *down*. I am trying to save your life."

I pause in my exit, at the doorway.

"I don't believe in that shit," I say.

Linda is not happy to hear this. As I walk down her hallway, to the back stairs, she rises to a shout.

"You broke the mirror! That's seven years of bad luck! Seven years! I do not claim this negative energy! I will not allow this energy to live in my house!"

I call back, "Then it's a good thing we rent!"

I start back down the stairs but stop myself at the landing. Dinner has gone on without me below, and I don't want to ruin it by bringing in my bad mood. I smooth out my temper. I breathe in the smells of Yiayia's long-lost cooking. I listen to the sounds of laughter, of conversation, of bottles being clinked together in impromptu toasts, of people starting stories they've told a hundred times before.

It's all there, waiting for me to take those final steps.

"Athanasios?" Yiayia calls. "Your food will get cold!"

I trot the rest of the way down the stairs. Linda's an idiot. I'm not cursed.

I'm home.

EPILOGUE

A few months later, when you're ready, you finally acquire the eyeliner.

You put it on in the bathroom mirror, marveling at how you couldn't have done this before. Look at yourself, for this long, without retreating into the past. Your face is a wondrous thing, you discover.

Then, because you're already wearing makeup, you decide to get dressed. You add on his bandanna, knotting it just right. And because you're all dressed up, you decide you should have someplace to go.

You only know one place you're sure you can get in by yourself.

You take the train down to Brooklyn, gazing at yourself in the reflection of the subway windows as it darts through the dark pockets between stations. You rewind the reflection, aimlessly searching the faces of anonymous New Yorkers. A few times you catch a flash of something—those wide, dark eyes, or a sketchbook clutched to a chest—but of course it's never him.

Because he's gone, you think.

The train plunges downtown and you try to stop thinking about him. You'll cry, and then you will have put on the eye makeup for nothing.

The club is so much bigger than you remember it, maybe because the last time you were here, you had someone to focus on. Now, alone, your eyes dart over everyone. Lots of people look back, intrigued by your lonesomeness, wondering who you're here with and why you ditched them. Wondering how old you are, because you look old enough to have gotten in but too young to know what to do about it.

A man asks to buy you a drink and when you shrug, he does it anyway. He is tall and lanky and has a mustache that smells a bit like smoke when he tries to kiss you. You duck away and hide in the dancing crowd. You try to dance, too, because that's the only way you can move in this world, but it's hard to find your rhythm.

Then, before you're ready, you're in the exact spot where you danced with him, facing the exact same mirror spanning the dance floor. You stare up into it and the urge to rewind to that moment is so, so strong. That's what you came here to do, isn't it? Of all the mirrors in all the world, this is the only one that got to see you two together and happy.

You rewind it with ease, the flash of light at its edges hardly visible among the lasers whisking the steamy air.

You bring the reflection back to that night that you danced with him, but it's only you standing there. His reflection, like him, is gone.

Now you mess up your eyeliner with a few tears. You finally turn away from the past. You know that if you look into it for much longer, you're never going to want to look at anything else. So you let the mirror wobble forward through time, colliding with the reflection of the cruel present.

This present is not what you wanted, but at least it's real. And if you can't accept that, then you'll never be able to accept whatever's next. So you accept it, and it helps. Slowly, you find your rhythm. You close your eyes because—what's the saying again? Dance like no one is watching?

You dance and dance, alone and anonymous. You push off two people who slide up to you and try to pull you into their drunken orbit. You cry, forgetting about the makeup, and it scares off any more would-be pursuers. That's the beauty of New York; it's the only place that a public breakdown makes you suddenly invisible. People think you want them to look, and so they don't, and you vanish.

But you do want to be seen, desperately.

It's then that you open your eyes, because you feel yourself being watched. Your instincts tell you to avert your gaze from the walls, to scan for threads of starlight. You back yourself against the mirror, splaying your palms against the cool glass.

There's a knock from the other side, and the phantom sensation of something fluttering against your ear. You can barely believe it. You whip around.

You see him.

See me.

You blink, but I don't vanish. You reach out a hand and in the reflection I take it.

Chills sweep over your damp skin. If you focus on what you're seeing, it's almost like I'm beside you. You keep your gaze on me, not even trying to hide your wonder as you look me over, asking with your eyes: *Are you really there? Is that really you?*

It depends.

What am I to you now? A boy? A demon? A curse? I look the same, except for the beads of black along my brow, new eyes that blink when I blink. But you proved to me with a kiss that whatever makes me up, it's not all curses. There's good there, too. There's integrity, and pain, and hope, and all sorts of colors I get to use to design the new me.

To prove that it's really me, I roll my eyes. All of them. And you finally smile.

We dance slowly, the mirror between us. On one side it's you, alive yet alone. On the other it's us, intangible yet together.

It's not enough, yet it has to be.

It's a miracle, as delicate as a rainbow's edge. A lie of light, gone in a blink, so you'd better not look away.

We both seem to understand this, so we don't waste a moment marveling at the pain or the beauty of this final impossibility. We dance like we don't think it's final at all. You could ask the mirror what comes next, and I could show you, but we both know better. Some futures are too fragile to be foretold.

We hold one another to the present, twirling upon our rainbow's edge.

The future will never see us coming.

ACKNOWLEDGMENTS

You are Ryan La Sala.

You are sitting down to write these acknowledgments on a breezy April afternoon, when the branches of the ginkgo trees in Central Park are only just starting to feather with green as life grows back into the city.

And you're wondering: Who on earth would want to be acknowledged as instrumental in the writing of a book about psychic claustrophobia, intrusive thoughts, and one really, *really* eccentric demon-spider? Seems a bit mean, don't you think? Who would want that?

And then you think, *Oh, I know who: all the weird people of my world who aren't scared off by my imagination, who love and understand me, and who even allow me out of my house once in a while (and occasionally even into theirs! Ha ha! Suckers!).* And then you think, *Hmmm, the gimmick of writing this in second person is probably going to get tedious, so you confusingly switch mid-passage, and suddenly*

I am Ryan La Sala, and I would like to say thank you to:

Zack Clark, my editor for first *The Honeys*, and now *Beholder*, for his uncanny ability to take a horrific vision in my head and guide it out of my fingertips, so all of you readers can have the nightmares you paid for. Thank you, Zack, for your tremendous faith in my work, and for being a stellar editor and advocate for the strangest books I could have written during our time together.

Peter Knapp, my agent, who swooped in just as this book was getting underway, and who has been a true champion of all my ambitions. To the entire Park & Fine team, too, but specifically to Jerome Murphy for insightful feedback alongside Peter, which gave this book many of the finishing touches that took it from a haunted house to a haunted home.

David Levithan, your friendship, mentorship, and inspiration has made a world of difference to me. When I said demon wallpaper, you said *okay cool*, and I respect that!

Speaking of, there are many people at this book's publisher, Scholastic, who deserve thanks. Maeve Norton, who we all get to blame for the gorgeous, unsettling, and perfect design of this book (and the incredible artwork is by Mishko, who I think understands exactly what goes on in the wallpapers). Getting this book out to readers is a magnificent and complex feat in itself, and for that I thank: Brooke Shearouse, Emily Heddelson, Janell

Harris, Rachel Feld, Melanie Wann, Carlee Maurier, Caroline Noll, Savannah D'Amico, Elizabeth Whiting, Roz Hilden, Jody Stigliano, and Nikki Mutch. As of this writing, books like this are being challenged in many states, and I have such admiration for all of you for standing with authors like me, characters like Athan and Dom, and readers who depend on depictions—horrific and joyful and everything in between—to see themselves through to brighter, more colorful futures. You're all amazing.

To my family, for always warming the walls of any gathering with laughter, cheer, spirited discussion, and art. Always art, through photos, drawings, story-telling, and occasionally a family-wide game of Fax Machine. I have to give my mom a particular shout-out for our shared love of interior design. Mom, I know you'll deny it, but you are a genius at making any space feel personal and special. And Dad, thanks for letting me draw all over X-ray boards for years—I swear none of the doodles were deadly! At least not knowingly!

To my many writer friends, who are really just like my other close friends except in need of more therapy, thank you! To my darlings of the WAPera, Phil and Claribel, for daily meditations not just about writing, but also being a writer while suffering from being so staggeringly hot. How do we manage? To my gay group chat for the exact same thing, except more upsetting memes. To John Fram for listening to me talk for literal hours without taking a single breath, and Victoria Lee, who is always a willing, dark mirror for me to converse with. I also want to thank Arvin Ahmadi for bringing me to several parties I had no business attending, which inspired parts of this book. Not saying which parties and which parts! Will Shields, not a word out of you! Pogo-stick promise!!!!

Andrew, you get a special thanks. I wrote this book in a single deeply chaotic month, and you were there for all of it. (Except when I had covid, but even then you texted me every day.) While others among the acknowledgments got to cavort through expensive parties with me, you assisted in the real work of this book: pretending to be rich and sneaking into million-dollar penthouse showings, and exploring the D&D Building with me, which I only found out was considered trespassing afterward, I swear. Thank you for the daily encouragement, and for being bafflingly game for any- and everything.

That goes for my friends, too. The ones who don't write books yet seem to write mine alongside me as I jot down lines from our dialogue and priceless moments from our real-life adventures that I think deserve to live forever in my fictions. I admire you all so much. Please, please, please keep inviting me along so I can continue harvesting our friendships for material!

Speaking of *the material*. A thank-you to Cindy Greene, a talented designer of many things, including wallpaper. I can't wait to put up some Absolem Fawn paper in my future home! And to George and Thalia Mesologites, who helped confirm the Greek lullaby I wanted to include. I love you both! To Evan Todd, who very graciously allowed me, a total stranger, into his home based simply on the request I put on Instagram, which was something to the effect of: "Does anyone have a beautiful apartment that I can pretend to die within?"

To my cousin (and childhood hero!) Douglas Einar Olsen, who I attribute quite a bit of *Beholder*'s inspiration to, from Athan's job as an art handler (albeit a pretty inaccurate one) to the lifelong suspicion that strange, uncanny art might be found behind the most innocuous of doors.

And finally, to my readers. My glorious, gorgeous readers!! I am sitting here (by now it is night) overcome with wonder that we're four books in and we've traveled from dreamt drag shows to cosplay contests to honey-scented summer camps, to here! A book that was thrilling to write but difficult to share, that opens rooms in myself I rarely invite anyone into. I thought I'd be scared, but I'm just happy you're all here with me. I'm so excited I get to light up the darkest corners of my mind with your company.

Thank you for looking for me.

Thank you for finding me.

Thank you for seeing me.

I hope you know that all art reflects, so this book is a type of mirror, too. If you feel unseen, I see you, and if you feel lost, I'm looking. Whatever darkness you feel this book might reflect back at you, please know my hope in writing it was to give people like us a means to see the unseeable things that terrorize us from within. If you're fighting, I hope you know that you are not fighting alone. You'll be found, so stick it out just a little longer. And if at any point the fight feels like it might be too much, ask for help. Just like I spend my life creating books to help people explore the dark and difficult corners of their lives, there are those who have dedicated themselves to the remarkable work of keeping the living alive long enough for things to get better. Trust them; call them. The national Suicide & Crisis Lifeline's number is 988.

Love always,

Ryan

April 25, 2023

ABOUT THE AUTHOR

Ryan La Sala writes about surreal things happening to queer people. He is the author of *The Honeys, Reverie,* and *Be Dazzled.* He lives in New York City, allegedly. For legal reasons, all of the trespassing in this book was completely concocted, and not at all researched in person. When not writing, Ryan likes to throw parties in fancy penthouses with strange decor and even stranger wallpaper. Visit him, if you dare, at ryanlasala.com.